"THE MOST ENJOYABLE FICTION OF THE
SEASON!"   —*The New York Times*

"EROTIC AND EXOTIC . . . A MASTER OF LITERARY
MAGIC . . . A NOVELIST OF THE SENSES . . . A
MARVEL!"   —*The Charlotte Observer*

"AN EXCITING WRITER IN FULL COMMAND OF
HIS ART, who dares to take the beauty of modern
living, turn it inside out . . ."   —*Philadelphia Bulletin*

"A MARVELOUS BOOK, BRILLIANT, DISTURBING,
MANY-LAYERED, AND INTENSELY PROVOCATIVE
. . . like a deep, swift-flowing stream of thought and
feeling which Fowles explores and plays like a patient,
skillful angler."   —*National Review*

JOHN FOWLES, born in Essex, England, in 1926, was educated at Bedford School and at Oxford University. Following
his studies in French at Oxford, Mr. Fowles taught in France
and other places abroad before becoming a full-time writer.
His first novel, *The Collector* (1963), was an immediate bestseller. The *Magus* (1966), followed by the acclaimed bestseller
The French Lieutenant's Woman (1969), confirmed Fowles's stature
as an internationally recognized writer of major importance.
His next novel, *Daniel Martin* (1977), was also a bestseller and
has been hailed as a masterpiece by critics. His most recent
novels are *Mantissa* (1982) and *A Maggot* (1986). His collection
of aphorisms, *The Aristos: A Self-Portrait in Ideas* (1970), demonstrated the author's versatility in a literary form quite different from the novel. Mr. Fowles has also contributed verse
to *Antaeus*, an international review published abroad, as well
as literary criticism and translations which have appeared in
a number of other publications. Mr. Fowles lives in Lyme
Regis, Dorset.

Books by John Fowles

THE ARISTOS
THE COLLECTOR
THE FRENCH LIEUTENANT'S WOMAN
THE MAGUS
THE EBONY TOWER

John Fowles

The Ebony Tower

A PLUME BOOK

PLUME
Published by the Penguin Group
Penguin Books USA Inc., 375 Hudson Street, New York, New York 10014, U.S.A.
Penguin Books Ltd, 27 Wrights Lane, London W8 5TZ, England
Penguin Books Australia Ltd, Ringwood, Victoria, Australia
Penguin Books Canada Ltd, 10 Alcorn Avenue, Toronto, Ontario, Canada M4V 3B2
Penguin Books (N.Z.) Ltd, 182-190 Wairau Road, Auckland 10, New Zealand

Penguin Books Ltd, Registered Offices:
Harmondsworth, Middlesex, England

Published by Plume, an imprint of New American Library, a division of
Penguin Books USA Inc. Published in arrangement with Little, Brown and Company, Inc.

This book previously appeared in a Signet edition.

First Plume Printing, December, 1991
10 9 8 7 6 5 4 3 2 1

 REGISTERED TRADEMARK—MARCA REGISTRADA

Original hardcover design by Barbara Bell Pitnof
Printed in the United States of America

LIBRARY OF CONGRESS CATALOGING-IN-PUBLICATION DATA
Fowles, John. 1926-
   The ebony tower / John Fowles.
      p.   cm.
   ISBN 0-452-26710-2
   I. Title.
   [PR6056.O85E2   1991]
   823'.914—dc20   91-23507
                                            CIP

PUBLISHER'S NOTE
This is a work of fiction. Names, characters, places, and incidents either are the
product of the author's imagination or are used fictiously, and any resemblance to
actual persons, living or dead, events, or locales is entirely coincidental.

Contents

The Ebony Tower

✠══■══■══■══■══■══■══■══■══■══■══✠

. . . Et par forez longues et lees
Par leus estranges et sauvages
Et passa mainz felons passages
Et maint peril et maint destroit
Tant qu'il vint au santier tot droit . . .
— CHRÉTIEN DE TROYES, *Yvain*

D AVID ARRIVED at Coëtminais the afternoon after the one he had landed at Cherbourg and driven down to Avranches, where he had spent the intervening Tuesday night. That had allowed an enjoyable meander over the remaining distance; a distant view of the spectacular spired dream of Mont-Saint-Michel, strolls around Saint-Malo and Dinan, then south in the splendid early September weather and through the new countryside. He took at once to the quiet landscapes, orcharded and harvested, precise and pollarded, self-concentrated, exhaling a spent fertility. Twice he stopped and noted down particularly pleasing conjunctions of tone and depth — parallel stripes of watercolor with penciled notes of amplification in his neat hand. Though there was some indication of the formal origin in these verbal notes — that a stripe of color was associated with a field, a sunlit wall, a distant hill — he drew nothing. He also wrote down the date, the time of day and the weather, before he drove on.

He felt a little guilty to be enjoying himself so much, to be here so unexpectedly alone, without Beth, and after he had made such a fuss; but the day, the sense of discovery, and of course the object of the whole exercise looming formidably and yet agreeably just ahead, everything conspired to give a pleasant illusion of bachelor freedom. Then the final few miles through the forest of Paimpont, one of the last large remnants of the old wooded Brittany, were deliciously right: green and shaded minor roads, with occasional sunshot vistas down the narrow rides cut through the endless trees. Things about the old man's most recent and celebrated period fell into place at once. No amount of reading and intelligent deduction could supplant the direct experience. Well before he arrived, David knew he had not wasted his journey.

He turned off down an even smaller forest road, a deserted *voie communale;* and a mile or so along that he came on the promised sign. *Manoir de Coëtminais. Chemin privé.* There was a white gate, which he had to open and shut. Half a mile on again through the forest he found his way barred, just before the trees gave way to sunlight and a grassy orchard, by yet another gate. There was a signboard nailed to the top bar. Its words made him smile inwardly, since beneath the heading *Chien méchant* they were in English: *Strictly no visitors except by prior arrangement.* But as if to confirm that the sign was not to be taken lightly, he found the gate padlocked on the inner side. It must have been forgotten that he was arriving that afternoon. He felt momentarily discomfited; as long as the old devil hadn't forgotten his coming completely. He stood in the deep shade, staring at the sunlight beyond. He couldn't have forgotten; David had sent a brief note of reminder and grateful anticipation only the previous week. Somewhere close in the trees behind him a bird gave a curious trisyllabic call, like a badly played tin flute. He glanced around, but could not see it. It wasn't English; and in some obscure way this reminded David that he was. Guard-dog or not, one couldn't . . . he went back to his car, switched off, locked the doors, then returned to the gate and climbed over.

He walked along the drive through the orchard, whose aged trees were clustered with codlings and red cider-apples. There was no sign of a dog, no barking. The *manoir*, islanded and sundrenched in its clearing among the sea of huge oaks and beeches, was not quite what he had expected, perhaps because he spoke very little French — hardly knew the country outside

Paris — and had translated the word visually as well as verbally in terms of an English manor house. In fact it had more the appearance of a once substantial farm; nothing very aristocratic about the façade of pale ochre plaster broadly latticed by reddish beams and counterpointed by dark brown shutters. To the east there was a little wing at right angles, apparently of more recent date. But the ensemble had charm; old and compact, a warm face of character, a good solid feel. He had simply anticipated something grander.

There was a graveled courtyard opposite the southward of the house. Geraniums by the foot of the wall, two old climbing roses, a scatter of white doves on the roof; all the shutters were in use, the place asleep. But the main door, with a heraldic stone shield above, its details effaced by time, and placed eccentrically toward the west end of the house, was lodged open. David walked cautiously across the gravel to it. There was no knocker, no sign of a bell; nor, mercifully, of the threatened dog. He saw a stone-flagged hall, an oak table beside an ancient wooden staircase with worn and warped medieval-looking banisters that led upward. Beyond, on the far side of the house, another open door framed a sunlit garden. He hesitated, aware that he had arrived sooner than suggested; then tapped on the massive main door with his knuckles. A few seconds later, realizing the futility of the weak sound, he stepped over the threshold. To his right stretched a long gallery-like living room. Ancient partitions must have been knocked down, but some of the major black uprights had been retained and stood out against the white walls with a skeletal bravura. The effect was faintly Tudor, much more English than the exterior. A very handsome piece of dense but airy space, antique carved-wood furniture, bowls of flowers, a group of armchairs and two sofas farther down; old pink and red carpets; and inevitably, the art . . . no surprise — except that one could walk in on it like this — since David knew there was a distinguished little collection besides the old man's own work. Famous names were already announced. Ensor, Marquet, that landscape at the end must be a "cool" Derain, and over the fireplace . . .

But he had to announce himself. He walked across the stone floor beside the staircase to the doorway on the far side of the room. A wide lawn stretched away, flower beds, banks of shrubs, some ornamental trees. It was protected from the north by a high wall, and David saw another line back there of lower buildings, hidden from the front of the house; barns and byres when the place was a farm. In midlawn there was a catalpa pruned into a huge green mushroom; in its shade sat, as if posed, conversing, a garden table and three wicker chairs. Beyond, in a close pool of heat, two naked girls lay side by side on the grass. The further, half hidden, was on her back, as if asleep. The nearer was on her stomach, chin propped on her hands, reading a book. She wore a wide-brimmed straw hat, its crown loosely sashed with some deep red material. Both bodies were very brown, uniformly brown, and apparently oblivious of the stranger in the shadowed doorway thirty yards away. He could not understand that they had not heard his car in the forest silence. But he really was earlier than the "teatime" he had proposed in his letter; or perhaps there had after all been a bell at the door, a servant who should have heard. For a brief few seconds he registered the warm tones of the two indolent female figures, the catalpa-shade green and the grass green, the intense carmine of the hat-sash, the pink wall beyond with its ancient espalier fruit trees. Then he turned and went back to the main door, feeling more amused than embarrassed. He thought of Beth again: how she would have adored this being plunged straight into the legend . . . the wicked old faun and his famous afternoons.

Where he had first intruded he saw at once what he had, in his curiosity, previously missed. A bronze handbell sat on the stone floor behind one of the doorjambs. He picked it up and rang — then wished he hadn't, the sharp schoolyard jangle assaulted the silent house, its sunlit peace. And nothing happened; no footsteps upstairs, no door opening at the far end of the long room he stood in. He waited on the threshold. Perhaps half a minute passed. Then one of the girls, he didn't know which, appeared in the garden door and came toward him. She now wore a plain white cotton *galabiya*; a slim girl of slightly less than medium height and in her early twenties; brown and gold hair and regular features; level-eyed, rather wide eyes, and barefooted. She was unmistakably English. She stopped some twenty feet away, by the bottom of the stairs.

"David Williams?"

He made an apologetic gesture. "You were expecting me?"

"Yes."

She did not offer to shake hands.

"Sorry to steal in like this. Your gate out there's locked."

She shook her head. "Just pull on it. The padlock. I'm sorry." She did not seem it; and at a loss. She said, "Henry's asleep."

"Then don't wake him, for God's sake." He smiled. "I'm a bit early. I thought it would be harder to find."

She surveyed him a moment: his asking to be welcomed.

"He's such a bastard if he doesn't get his siesta."

He grinned. "Look, I took his letter at its word — about putting me up? — but if . . ."

She glanced beyond him, through the door; then back at his face, with an indifferent little tilt of query.

"Your wife?"

He explained about Sandy's chicken pox, the last-minute crisis. "She's flying to Paris on Friday. If my daughter's over the worst. I'll pick her up there."

The level eyes appraised him again.

"Then I'll show you where you are?"

"If you're sure . . ."

"No problems."

She made a vague gesture for him to follow her, and turned

to the stairs; simple, white, bizarrely modest and handmaid-
enly after that first glimpse.

He said, "Marvelous room."

She touched the age-blackened handrail that mounted beside
them. "This is fifteenth century. They say." But she looked
neither at him nor the room; and asked nothing, as if he had
driven a mere five miles to get there.

At the top of the stairs she turned to the right down a corridor. A long rush mat ran down the center of it. She opened the
second door they came to and went a step in, holding the
handle, watching him, uncannily like the *patronne* at the hotel
where he had stayed the previous night. He almost expected to
hear a price.

"The bathroom's next door."

"Lovely. I'll just go and fetch my car."

"As you wish."

She closed the door. There was something preternaturally
grave about her, almost Victorian, despite the *galabiya*. He
smiled encouragingly as they went back down the corridor to
the stairs.

"And you're . . . ?"

"Henry calls me the Mouse."

At last a tiny dryness in her face; or a challenge, he wasn't
sure.

"You've known him long?"

"Since spring."

He tried to evoke some sympathy.

"I know he's not mad about this sort of thing."

She shrugged minutely.

"As long as you stand up to him. It's mostly bark."

She was trying to tell him something, very plainly; perhaps
just that if he *had* seen her in the garden, this was the real
distance she kept from visitors. She was apparently some kind
of equivalent of his hostess; and yet she behaved as if the

house had nothing very much to do with her. They came to the bottom of the stairs, and she turned toward the garden.

"Out here? Half an hour? I get him up at four."

He grinned again, that nurselike tone in her voice, so dismissive of all that the outside world might think of the man she called "Henry" and "him."

"Fine."

"Make *comme chez vous.* Right?"

She hesitated a moment, as if she knew she was being too cool and sibylline. There was even a faint hint of diffidence, a final poor shadow of a welcoming smile. Then she looked down and turned away and padded silently back toward the garden; as she went out through the door the *galabiya* momentarily lost its opacity against the sunlight beyond; a fleeting naked shadow. He remembered he had forgotten to ask about the dog; but presumably she would have thought of it; and tried to recall when he had been less warmly received into a strange house . . . as if he had taken too much, when he had taken nothing, for granted — and certainly not her presence. He had understood the old man had put all that behind him.

He walked back through the orchard to the gate. At least she hadn't misled him there. The hasp came away from the body of the padlock as soon as he pulled. He drove back and parked in the shade of a chestnut opposite the front of the house, got out his overnight bag and briefcase, then an informal jeans suit on a hanger. He glanced through the doorway out into the garden at the back as he went upstairs; but the two girls seemed to have disappeared. In the corridor above he stopped to look at two paintings he had noticed when she first showed him up and failed to put a name to . . . but now, of course, Maximilien Luce. Lucky old man, to have bought before art became a branch of greed, of shrewd investment. David forgot his cold reception.

His room was simply furnished, a double bed in some rather

clumsy rural attempt at an Empire style, a walnut wardrobe riddled with worm, a chair, an old chaise longue with tired green upholstery; a gilt mirror, stains on the mercury. The room smelled faintly musty, seldom used; furnished out of local auctions. The one incongruity was the signed Laurencin over the bed. David tried to lift it off its hook, to see the picture in a better light. But the frame was screwed to the wall. He smiled and shook his head; if only poor old Beth were there.

David had been warned by the London publishing house — by the senior member of it who had set the project up — of the reefs, far more formidable than locked gates, that surrounded any visit to Coëtminais. The touchiness, the names one must not mention, the coarse language, the baiting: no doubt had been left that this particular "great man" could also be the most frightful old bastard. He could also, it seemed, be quite charming — if he liked you. Naïve as a child in some ways, had said the publisher. Then, Don't argue with him about England and the English, just accept he's a lifelong exile and can't bear to be reminded of what he might have missed. Finally: he desperately wants us to do the book. David was not to let himself be duped into thinking the subject of it didn't care a fig for home opinion.

In many ways his journey was not strictly necessary. He had already drafted the introduction, he knew pretty well what he was going to say; there were the major catalogue essays, especially that for the 1969 Tate Retrospective . . . the British art establishment's belated olive branch; those for the two recent Paris shows, and the New York; Myra Levey's little monograph in the *Modern Masters* series, and the correspondence with Matthew Smith; a scatter of usable magazine interviews. A few biographical details remained to be cleared up, though even they could have been done by letter. There were of course any number of artistic queries one could have asked — or would have liked to; but the old man had never shown himself very helpful there, indeed rather more likely on past record to be hopelessly cryptic, maliciously misleading or just downright rude. So it was essentially the opportunity of meeting a man one had spent time on and whose work one did, with reservations, genuinely admire . . . the fun of it, to say one had met him. And after all, he was now indisputably major, one had to put him with the Bacons and Sutherlands. It could even be argued that he was the most interesting of that select band, though he would probably himself say that he was simply the least bloody English.

Born in 1896, a student at the Slade in the great days of the Steers-Tonks regime, a characteristically militant pacifist when cards had to be declared in 1916, in Paris (and spiritually out of England for good) by 1920, then ten years and more in the queasy — Russia itself having turned to socialist realism — no-man's-land between surrealism and communism, Henry Breasley had still another decade to wait before any sort of serious recognition at home — the revelation, during his five years of "exile from exile" in Wales during the Second World War, of the Spanish Civil War drawings. Like most artists, Breasley had been well ahead of the politicians. To the British the 1942 exhibition in London of his work from 1937–38 suddenly made sense; they too had learned what war was about, of the bitter folly of giving the benefit of the doubt to international fascism. The more intelligent knew that there was nothing very prescient about his record of the Spanish agony; indeed in spirit it went straight back to Goya. But its power and skill, the superbly incisive draftsmanship, were undeniable. The mark was made; so, if more in private, was the reputation of Breasley's "difficulty" as an individual. The legend of his black bile for everything English and conventionally middle-class — especially if it had anything to do with official views on art, or its public administration — was well established by the time he returned to Paris in 1946.

Then for another decade nothing very much happened to his

name in popular terms. But he had become collectible, and there was a growing band of influential admirers in both Paris and London, though like every other European painter he suffered from the rocketing ascendancy of New York as world arbiter of painting values. In England he never quite capitalized on the savage impact, the famous "black sarcasm" of the Spanish drawings; yet he showed a growing authority, a maturity in his work. Most of the great nudes and interiors came from this period; the long-buried humanist had begun to surface, though as always the public was more interested in the bohemian side of it — the stories of his drinking and his women, as transmitted in the spasmodic hounding he got from the yellower and more chauvinistic side of Fleet Street. But by the late 1950s this way of life had already become a quaintly historical thing. The rumors and realities of his unregenerate life-style, like his contempt for his homeland, became amusing . . . and even pleasingly authentic to the vulgar mind, with its propensity for confusing serious creation with colorful biography, for allowing van Gogh's ear to obscure any attempt to regard art as a supreme sanity instead of a chocolate-sucking melodrama. It must be confessed that Breasley himself did not noticeably refuse the role offered; if people wanted to be shocked, he generally obliged. But his closer friends knew that beneath the continuing occasional bouts of exhibitionism he had changed considerably.

In 1963 he bought the old *manoir* at Coëtminais and forsook his beloved Paris. A year later appeared his illustrations to Rabelais, his last fling as a pure draftsman, in a limited edition that has already become one of the most valuable books of its kind in this century; and in the same year he painted the first of the pictures in the last-period series that was to establish his international reputation beyond any doubt. Though he had always rejected the notion of a mystical interpretation — and enough of the old left-winger remained for any religious intention to be dismissed out of court — the great, both literally and metaphorically, canvases with their dominant greens and blues that began to flow out of his new studio had roots in a Henry Breasley the outer world had not hitherto guessed at. In a sense it was as if he had discovered who he really was much later than most artists of his basic technical ability and experience. If he did not quite become a recluse, he ceased to be a professional *enfant terrible*. He himself had once termed the paintings "dreams"; there was certainly a surrealist component from his twenties past, a fondness for anachronistic juxtapositions. Another time he had called them tapestries, and indeed the Aubusson *atelier* had done related work to his designs. There was a feeling — "an improbable marriage of Samuel Palmer and Chagall," as one critic had put it in reviewing the Tate Retrospective — of a fully absorbed eclecticism, something that had been evidenced all through his career, but not really come to terms with before Coëtminais; a hint of Nolan, though the subject matter was far less explicit, more mysterious and archetypal . . . "Celtic" had been a word frequently used, with the recurrence of the forest motif, the enigmatic figures and confrontations.

Breasley himself had partly confirmed this, when someone had had the successful temerity to ask him for a central source — and for once received a partly honest answer: Pisanello and Diaz de la Peña. The reference to Diaz and the Barbizon School was a self-sarcasm, needless to say. But pressed on Pisanello, Breasley had cited a painting in the National Gallery in London, *The Vision of St. Eustace;* and confessed it had haunted him all his life. If the reference at first sight seemed distinctly remote, it was soon pointed out that Pisanello and his early fifteenth-century patrons had been besotted by the Arthurian cycle.

What had brought young David Williams (born that same year of Breasley's first English success, 1942) to Coëtminais in the September of 1973 was precisely this last aspect of the old man's work. He had felt no special interest in Breasley before the Tate Retrospective, but he was forcibly struck then by certain correspondences with an art, or rather a style, the International Gothic, that had always interested the scholarly side of him. Two years later he had formulated the parallels he saw in an article. A complimentary copy had been sent to Breasley, but it was not acknowledged. A year passed, David had almost forgotten the whole thing, and certainly had not pursued any particular interest in the old man's work. The invitation from the publishers to write the biographical and critical introduction to *The Art of Henry Breasley* (with the added information that the offer was made with the painter's approval) had come very much out of the blue.

It was not quite a case of a young unknown visiting an old master. David Williams's parents were both architects, a still practicing husband-and-wife team of some renown. Their son had shown natural aptitude very young, an acute color sense, and he was born into the kind of environment where he received nothing but encouragement. In the course of time he went to art college, and settled finally for painting. He was a star student in his third year, already producing salable work. He was not only *rara avis* in that; unlike the majority of his fellow students, he was highly articulate as well. Brought up in a household where contemporary art and all its questions were followed and discussed constantly and coherently, he could both talk and write well. He had some real knowledge of art history, helped by many stays in his parents' converted farmhouse in Tuscany, as distinct from mere personal enthusiasms. He was aware of his luck in all this, and of the envy it might provoke in his socially and naturally less gifted peers. Always rather fond of being liked, he developed a manner carefully blended of honesty and tact. Perhaps the most remarkable thing about him as a student was that he was on the whole quite popular; just as he was to be popular later as a teacher and lecturer — and even not wholly detested by his victims as an art critic. At least he never panned for panning's sake. He very rarely indeed found nothing at all to praise in an artist or an exhibition.

At his own choice he had gone for a year to the Courtauld Institute after college. Then for two years he combined the teaching of painting and general appreciation lectures. His own work came under the influence of Op Art and Bridget Riley, and benefited from her star. He became one of the passable young substitutes those who could not afford Riley herself tended to buy. Then (this was in 1967) he had had an affair with one of his third-year students that had rapidly become the real thing. They married and bought, with parental help, a house in Blackheath. David decided to try his luck at living by his own painting alone. But the arrival of Alexandra, the first of his two small daughters, and various other things — one of which was a small crisis of doubt about his own work, now shifting away from the Riley influence — drove him to look for extra income. He did not want to return to studio teaching, but he went back to lecturing part-time. A chance meeting led to an invitation to do some reviewing; and a year later still that had become lucrative enough for him to drop the lecturing. That had been his life since.

His own work began to get enough reputation as it moved from beneath the Op Art umbrella to guarantee plenty of red stars at his exhibitions. Though he remained a fully abstract artist in the common sense of the adjective (a color painter, in the current jargon), he knew he was tending toward nature and away from the high artifice of his "Riley" phase. His paintings had a technical precision, a sound architectonic quality inherited from his parents' predilections, and a marked subtlety of tone. To put it crudely, they went well on walls that had to be lived with, which was one good reason (one he knew and accepted) that he sold; another was that he had always worked to a smaller scale than most nonfigurative painters. This again was probably something he acquired from his mother and father; he was dubious about transatlantic monumentality, painting direct for the vast rooms of museums of modern art. Nor was he the kind of person who was ashamed to think of his work in flats and homes, enjoyed privately, on his own chosen scale.

If he disliked pretention, he was not on the other hand devoid of ambition. He still earned more by his painting than his writing, and that meant a very great deal to him; as did what one might call the state of his status among his own generation of painters. He would have despised the notion of a race, yet he kept a sharp eye on rivals and the public mention they received. He was not unaware of this; in the public mention constituted by his own reviewing, he knew he erred on the generous side with those he feared most.

His marriage had been very successful, except for one brief bad period when Beth had rebelled against "constant motherhood" and flown the banner of Women's Liberation; but now she had two sets of illustrations for children's books to her credit, another commissioned and a fourth in prospect. David had always admired his parents' marriage. His own had begun to assume that same easy camaraderie and cooperation. When he was approached about the Breasley introduction, he took it as one more sign that things in general were shaping up well.

He came to Coëtminais with only one small fear: that Breasley had not realized that he was a painter — to be precise, what kind of painter he was — as well as a writer on art. According to the publisher, the old man had asked no questions there. He had seen the article and thought it "read well"; and shown himself much more concerned about the quality of the color reproduction in the proposed book. Breasley's view that full abstraction had been the wrong road was widely known, and on the face of it he could have no time for David's own work. But perhaps he had softened on that subject — though he had had coals of fire to spare, when he was in London in 1969, for Victor Pasmore's head; more probably, since he lived so far from the London art scene, he was genuinely unaware of the partial snake he had taken to his bosom. David hoped the matter could be avoided; and if it couldn't, then he would have to play it by ear — and try to show the old man that the world had moved on from such narrow-mindedness. His accepting the commission was proof of it. Breasley "worked" — and that he worked emotionally and stylistically in totally different, or distant, ways from one's own preferred line of descent (De Stijl, Ben Nicholson and the rest — including the arch-renegade Pasmore) in twentieth-century art was immaterial.

David was a young man who was above all tolerant, fair-minded and inquisitive.

He took advantage of the half hour or so before "Henry" was awakened to have a look at the art downstairs. Occasionally he glanced out of windows behind the house. The lawn remained empty, the silence of the house as when he had come. Inside the long room there was only one example of Breasley's own work, but plenty else to admire. The landscape was indeed a Derain, as David had guessed. Three very fine Permeke drawings. The Ensor and the Marquet. An early Bonnard. A characteristically febrile pencil sketch, unsigned, but unmistakably Dufy. Then a splendid Jawlensky (how on earth had he got his hands on that?), an Otto Dix signed proof nicely juxtaposed with a Nevinson drawing. Two Matthew Smiths, a Picabia, a little flower painting that must be an early Matisse, though it didn't look quite right . . . there were those, and they were outnumbered by the paintings and drawings David couldn't assign. If one accepted the absence of the more extreme movements, one had a room of early twentieth-century art many smaller museums would have cut throats to lay their hands on. Breasley had collected pre-war, of course, and he had apparently always had a private income of sorts. An only child, he must have inherited quite a substantial sum when his mother died in 1925. His father, one of those Victorian gentlemen who appear to have lived comfortably on doing nothing, had died in a hotel fire in 1907. According to Myra Levey, he too had dabbled with art collecting in a dilettante way.

Breasley had granted himself pride of place — and space — over the old stone fireplace in the center of the room. There hung the huge *Moon-hunt*, perhaps the best-known of the Coëtminais *oeuvre*, a painting David was going to discuss at some length and that he badly wanted to study at leisure again ... perhaps not least to confirm to himself that he wasn't over-rating his subject. He felt faintly relieved that the picture stood up well to renewed acquaintance — he hadn't seen it in the flesh since the Tate exhibition of four years previously — and even announced itself as better than memory and reproductions had rated it. As with so much of Breasley's work there was an obvious previous iconography — in this case, Uccello's *Night Hunt* and its spawn down through the centuries; which was in turn a challenged comparison, a deliberate risk ... just as the Spanish drawings had defied the great shadow of Goya by accepting its presence, even using and parodying it, so the memory of the Ashmolean Uccello somehow deepened and buttressed the painting before which David sat. It gave an essential tension, in fact: behind the mysteriousness and the ambiguity (no hounds, no horses, no prey ... nocturnal fig-ures among trees, but the title was needed), behind the mo-dernity of so many of the surface elements there stood both a homage and a kind of thumbed nose to a very old tradition. One couldn't be quite sure it was a masterpiece, there was a clotted quality in some passages, a distinctly brusque use of impasto on closer examination; something faintly too static in the whole, a lack of tonal relief (but that again was per-haps just the memory of the Uccello). Yet it remained safely considerable, had presence — could stand very nicely, thank you, up against anything else in British painting since the war. Perhaps its most real mystery, as with the whole series, was that it could have been done at all by a man of Breasley's age. The *Moon-hunt* had been painted in 1965, in his sixty-ninth year. And that was eight years ago now.

Then suddenly, as if to solve the enigma, the living painter himself appeared from the garden door and came down toward David.

"Williams, my dear fellow."

He advanced, hand outstretched, in pale blue trousers and a dark blue shirt, an unexpected flash of Oxford and Cambridge, a red silk square. He was white-haired, though the eyebrows were still faintly gray; the bulbous nose, the misleadingly fastidious mouth, the pouched gray-blue eyes in a hale face. He moved almost briskly, as if aware that he had been remiss in some way; smaller and trimmer than David had visualized from the photographs.

"It's a great honor to be here, sir."

"Nonsense. Nonsense." And David's elbow was chucked, the smile and the quiz under the eyebrows and white relic of a forelock both searching and dismissive. "You've been looked after?"

"Yes. Splendid."

"Don't be put off by the Mouse. She's slightly gaga." The old man stood with his hands on his hips, an impression of someone trying to seem young, alert, David's age. "Thinks she's Lizzie Siddal. Which makes me that ghastly little Italian fudger . . . damn' insulting, what?"

David laughed. "I did notice a certain . . ."

Breasley raised his eyes to the ceiling.

"My dear man. You've no idea. Still. Gels that age. Well, how about some tea? Yes? We're out in the garden."

David gestured back at the *Moon-hunt* as they moved toward the west end of the room. "It's marvelous to see that again. I just pray the printers can rise to it."

Breasley shrugged, as if he didn't care; or was proof to the too direct compliment. Then he darted another quizzing look at David.

"And you? You're quite the cat's pajamas, I hear."

"Hardly that."

"Read your piece. All those fellows I've never heard of. Good stuff."

"But wrong?"

Breasley put a hand on his arm.

"I'm not a scholar, dear boy. Ignorance of things you probably know as well as your mother's tit would astound you. Never mind. Put up with me, what?"

They went out into the garden. The girl nicknamed the Mouse, still barefooted and in her white Arab garb, came obliquely across the lawn from the far end of the house, carrying a tray of tea things. She took no notice of the two men.

"See what I mean," muttered Breasley. "Needs her bloody arse tanned."

David bit his lips. As they came to the table under the catalpa, he saw the second girl stand from a little bay of the lawn that was hidden by a bank of shrubs from the house. She must have been reading all the time; he saw the straw hat with the red sash on the grass behind her as she came toward them, book still in hand. If the Mouse was odd, this creature was preposterous. She was even smaller, very thin, a slightly pinched face under a mop of frizzed-out hair that had been reddened with henna. Her concession to modesty had been to pull on a singlet, a man's or a boy's by the look of it, dyed black. It reached just, but only just, below her loins. The eyelids had also been blackened. She had the look of a rag doll, a neurotic golliwog, a figure from the wilder end of the King's Road.

"This is Anne," said the Mouse.

"Alias the Freak," said Breasley.

Breasley sat, and waved to David to sit beside him. He hesitated, since there was a chair short, but the Freak sat rather gauchely on the grass beside her friend's place. A pair of red briefs became visible, or conspicuous, beneath the black singlet. The Mouse began to pour the tea.

"First visit to these parts, Williams?"

That allowed David to be polite; sincerely so, about his new-found enthusiasm for Brittany and its landscapes. The old man seemed to approve; he began to talk about the house, how he had found it, its history, why he had turned his back on Paris. He handsomely belied his rogue reputation; it was almost as if he were delighted to have another man to talk to. He sat turned away from the girls, completely ignoring them, and David had a growing sense that they resented his presence; whether it was because of the attention he distracted, the formality he introduced, or that they must have heard all the old man was telling him before, he wasn't sure. Breasley wandered off — again belying his reputation — to Welsh landscapes, his early childhood, before 1914. David knew his mother had been Welsh, of the wartime spell in Breconshire, but not that he retained memories and affections for the place; missed its hills.

The old fellow spoke in a quirky staccato manner, half assertive, half tentative; weirdly antiquated slang, a constant lacing of obscenity; not intellectually or feelingly at all, but much more like some eccentric retired (it occurred to David with secret amusement) admiral. They were so breathtakingly inappropriate, all the out-of-date British upper-class mannerisms in the mouth of a man who had spent his life comprehensively denying all those same upper classes stood for. A similar paradox was seen in the straight white hair, brushed across the forehead in a style that Breasley must have retained since his youth — and which Hitler had long put out of fashion with younger men. It gave him a boyishness; but the ruddy, incipiently choleric face and the pale eyes suggested something much older and more dangerous. He chose transparently to come on as much more of a genial old fool than he was; and must know he deceived no one.

However, if the two girls had not been so silent — the Freak had even shifted her back to rest against the front of the other girl's chair, reached for her book and begun reading again — David would have felt comparatively at ease. The Mouse sat in white elegance and listened, but as if her mind were somewhere else — in a Millais set-piece, perhaps. If David sought her eyes, she would discompose her rather pretty features into the faintest semblance of a formal confirmation that she was still there; which gave the clear impression that she wasn't. He grew curious to know what the truth was, beyond the obvious. He had not come prepared for this, having gathered from the publisher that the old man now lived alone — that is, with only an elderly French housekeeper. During that tea the relationship seemed more daughterly than anything else. There was only one showing of the lion's claws.

David had mentioned Pisanello, knowing it was safe ground — and the recently discovered frescoes at Mantua. Breasley had seen them in reproduction, seemed genuinely interested to hear a firsthand account of them and genuinely ignorant — David had not taken his warning very seriously — of the techniques involved. But David had hardly launched into the complexities of *arricciato, intonaco, sinopie* and the rest before Breasley interrupted.

"Freak dear gel, for God's sake stop reading that fucking book and listen."

She looked up, then put the paperback down and folded her arms.

"Sorry."

It was said to David, ignoring the old man — and with an unconcealed boredom: you're a drag, but if he insists.

"And if you use that word, for Christ's sake sound as if you mean it."

"Didn't realize we were included."

"Balls."

"I was listening, anyway."

She had a faint Cockney accent, tired and brutalized.

"Don't be so bloody insolent."

"I was."

[22]

"Balls."

She pulled a grimace, glanced back up at the Mouse. "Hen-*ree*."

David smiled. "What's the book?"

"Dear boy, keep out of this. If you don't mind." He leaned forward, pointing a finger at the girl. "Now no more. Learn something."

"Yes, Henry."

"My dear fellow, I'm so sorry. Do go on."

The little incident produced an unexpected reaction from the Mouse. She gave a surreptitious nod at David behind Breasley's back: whether to tell him that this was normal or to suggest he got on with it before a full-scale row developed was not clear. But as he did go on, he had the impression that she was listening with slightly more interest. She even asked a question, she evidently knew something about Pisanello. The old man must have talked about him.

Soon afterward Breasley stood up and invited David to come and see his "workroom" in the buildings behind the garden. The girls did not move. As he followed Breasley out through an arched gate in the wall, David looked back and saw the thin brown figure in her black singlet pick up her book again. The old man winked at him as they strolled over the gravel toward the line of buildings to their left.

"Always the same. Have the little bitches into your bed. Lose all sense of proportion."

"They're students?"

"The Mouse. God knows what the other thinks she is."

But he clearly did not want to talk about them; as if they were mere moths around his candle, a pair of high-class groupies. He began explaining the conversions and changes he had made, what the buildings once were. They went through a doorway into the main studio, a barn whose upper floor had been removed. A long table littered with sketches and paper by the wide modern window looking north over the graveled yard; a paints table, the familiar smells and paraphernalia; and dominating the space, at its far end, another of the Coëtminais series, about three quarters completed — a twelve-by-six-foot canvas on a specially carpentered stand, with a set of movable steps in front to reach the top of the painting. It was a forest setting again, but with a central clearing, much more peopled than usual, less of the subaqueous feeling, under a first-class blue, almost a black, that managed to suggest both night and day, both heat and storm, a looming threat over the human component. There was this time an immediate echo (because one had learned to look for them) of the Brueghel family; and even a faint self-echo, of the *Moon-hunt* in the main house. David smiled at the painter.

"Are any clues being offered?"

"*Kermesse?* Perhaps. Not sure yet." The old man stared at his picture. "She's playing coy. Waiting, don't you know."

"She seems very good indeed to me. Already."

"Why I have to have women around me. Sense of timing. Bleeding and all that. Learning when not to work. Nine parts of the game." He looked at David. "But you know all this. Painter yourself, what?"

David took an inward breath and skated hastily over the thin ice; explaining about Beth, her sharing his studio at home, he knew what Breasley meant. The old man opened his hands, as if in agreement; and seemed amiably not interested in pursuing the matter of David's own work. He turned and sat on a stool by the bench at the window, then reached for a still life, a pencil drawing of some wild flowers: teaselheads and thistles lying scattered on a table. They were drawn with an impressive, if rather lifeless, accuracy.

"The Mouse. Beginning of a hand, don't you think?"

"Nice line."

Breasley nodded down toward the huge canvas. "I let her help. The donkey-work."

David murmured, "On that scale . . ."

"Clever girl, Williams. Don't let her fool you. Shouldn't make fun of her." The old man stared down at the drawing. "Deserves better." Then, "Couldn't do without her, really."

"I'm sure she's learning a lot."

"Know what people say. Old rake and all that. Man my age."

David smiled. "Not anymore."

But Breasley seemed not to hear.

"Don't care a fart about that, never have. When you start using their minds."

And he began to talk about age, turned back toward the painting with David standing beside him, staring at it; how the imagination, the ability to conceive, didn't after all, as one had supposed in one's younger days, atrophy. What declined was the physical and psychological stamina — "like one's poor old John Thomas" — to execute. One had to have help there. He seemed ashamed to have to confess it.

"Roman Charity. Know that thing? Old geezer sucking milk from some young biddy's tit. Often think of that."

"I can't believe it's so one-way as you suggest." David pointed at the drawing of the flowers. "You should see the kind of art education most of the kids are getting at home now."

"You think?"

"I'm sure. Most of them can't even draw."

Breasley stroked his white hair; again he seemed almost touchingly boyish, lacking in confidence. And David felt himself being seduced by this shyer yet franker being behind the language and the outward manner; who apparently had decided to trust him.

"Ought to send her packing. Haven't the guts."

"Isn't that up to her?"

"She didn't say anything? When you came?"

"She gave a very good imitation of a guardian angel."

"Come home to roost."

It was said with a hint of sardonic gloom; and remained cryptic, for the old man stood up with a sudden return of energy and a brief touch, as if of apology, on David's arm.

"To hell with it. Come to grill me, what?"

David asked about the preliminary stages to the painting.

"Trial and error. Draw a lot. See."

He led David to the far end of the bench. The work-sketches were produced with the same odd mixture of timidity and assertiveness he had shown in talking about the girl — as if he both feared criticism and would suspect its absence.

This new painting, it seemed, had sprung from a very dim recollection of early childhood; of a visit to a fair, he was no longer sure where, he had been five or six, had been longing for the treat, had taken an intense pleasure in it, could still recall this overwhelming wanting — the memory seemed dense with desire — to experience each tent and stall, see everything, taste everything. And then a thunderstorm, which must have been apparent before to all the adults, but which for some reason came to him as a shock and a surprise, a dreadful disappointment. All the outward indications of the fair theme had progressively disappeared through the working sketches, much more elaborate and varied than David had expected, and were completely exorcised from the final *imago*. It was rather as if a clumsy literalness, a conceptual correlative of the way the old man spoke, had to be slowly exterminated by constant recomposition and refinement away from the verbal. But the story explained the strange inwardness, the lighted oblivion of the central scene of the painting. The metaphysical parallels, small planets of light in infinite nights and all the rest, had remained perhaps a fraction too obvious. It was all a shade too darkly Olympian; put in words, something of a pessimistic truism about the human condition. But the tone, the mood, the force of the statement carried conviction — and more than enough to overcome any personal prejudice David felt against overt literary content in painting.

The talk broadened out; David managed to lead the old fellow back further into his past, to his life in France in the twenties, his friendships with Braque and Matthew Smith. Breasley's veneration for the former was long on the record, but he apparently had to make sure that David knew it. The difference between Braque and Picasso, Matisse "and crew" was between a great man and great boys.

"They knew it. He knew it. Everyone but the bloody world in general knows it."

David did not argue. Picasso's name had been actually pronounced as "pick-arsehole." But in general the obscenities were reduced as they talked. The disingenuous mask of ignorance slipped, and the face of the old cosmopolitan that lay beneath began to show. David began to suspect he was dealing with a paper tiger; or certainly with one still living in a world before he himself was born. The occasional hint of aggression was based on such ludicrously old-fashioned notions of what shocked people, what red rags could infuriate them; to reverse the simile, it was rather like playing matador to a blind bull. Only the pompous fool could let himself be caught on such obvious horns.

They strolled back to the house just before six. Once again the two girls had disappeared. Breasley took him around the ground-floor room to look at the work there. There were anecdotes, some peremptory declarations of affection. One famous name got a black mark for being slick, "too damn' easy."

"Dozen-a-day man, don't you know. Bone lazy. That's what saved him. Fastidious my arse."

And there was more frankness, when David asked what he had looked for when he bought.

"Value for money, dear boy. Insurance. Never thought my own stuff would come to much. Now how about this fellow?"

They had stopped before the little flower painting David had tentatively ascribed to Matisse. David shook his head.

"Painted rubbish ever since."

It was hardly a clue, in present company. David smiled.

"I'm stumped."

"Miró. Done in 1915."

"Good God."

"Sad."

And he shook his head, as over the grave of someone who had died in the flower of his youth.

There were other small treasures David had failed to identify: a Sérusier, a remarkable Gauguinesque landscape by Filiger . . . but when they got to the far corner of the room, Breasley opened a door.

"Got a greater artist out here, Williams. You'll see. Dinner tonight."

The door led into a kitchen: a lantern-jawed gray-haired man sitting at a table and peeling vegetables, an elderly woman who turned from a modern cooking range and smiled. David was introduced: Jean-Pierre and Mathilde, who ran the house and garden. There was also a large Alsatian, which the man quietened as it stood. It was called Macmillan, to rhyme with Villon; because, Breasley explained with a sniff, it was an "old impostor." He spoke French for the first time, a strangely different voice, completely fluent and native-sounding to David's ears; but English was probably more the foreign language now. He gathered the dinner menu was being discussed. Breasley lifted potlids on the stove and sniffed, like some officer doing mess rounds. Then a pike was produced and examined, some story was being told by the man, apparently he had caught it that afternoon, the dog had been with him and tried to attack it when the fish was landed. Breasley bent and wagged a finger over the dog's head, he was to save his teeth for thieves; David was glad he had chanced to arrive when the animal was off the premises. He had the impression that this evening visit to the kitchen was something of a ritual. Its domesticity and familiarity, the tranquil French couple, made a reassuring contrast with the vaguely perverse note the presence of the two girls had introduced into his visit.

Back in the long room, Breasley told David to make himself at home. He had some letters to write. They would meet there again for an *apéritif* at half past seven.

"You're not too formal, I hope?"

"Freedom House, dear boy. Stark naked, if you like." He winked. "Gels won't mind."

David grinned. "Right."

The old man raised a hand and walked to the stairs. Halfway up he turned and spoke back down the room.

"World isn't all bare bubs, eh what?"

A discreet minute or two later David also went upstairs. He sat on the chaise longue, writing notes. It was a shame one couldn't quote the old boy direct; but those first two hours had proved very useful; and there must be more to come. After a while he went and lay on the bed, hands behind his head, staring up at the ceiling. It was very warm, airless, though he had opened the shutters. Strange, he had experienced a little tinge of personal disappointment, finally, with Breasley; a little too much posing and wicked old sham for the end product, too great a dissonance between the man and his art; and illogically there loitered, even though David had wanted to keep off the subject, a tiny hurtness that he had been asked nothing about his own work. It was absurd, of course; merely a reaction to so blatant a monomania; and not without an element of envy . . . this rather gorgeous old house, the studio setup, the collection, the faintly gamy ambiguity that permeated the place after predictable old Beth and the kids at home; the remoteness of it, the foreignness, the curious flashes of honesty, a patina . . . fecundity, his whole day through that countryside, so many ripening apples.

But he was being unfair to Beth, who after all had been more responsible than himself in the frantic last-hour discussions on Monday morning, when Sandy's chicken pox had moved from threatened to certain. Her mother was already there with them, ready to take over when they left, and perfectly able to cope . . . and willing to do so; she took David's side. It was just Beth's conscience, that old streak of obstinacy in her — and a little hangover of guilt, he suspected, from her brief mutiny against the tyranny of children soon after Louise was born. Even if there weren't complications, she insisted, she wouldn't be happy not knowing; and David must go, after all it was his work. Their intended week in the Ardèche, after Brittany, could still take place. They had finally agreed, when he set off for Southampton on the Monday evening, that unless there was a telegram at Coëtminais to the contrary on Thursday, she would be in Paris the next day. He had rushed out and booked the flight before he left; and brought flowers and a bottle of champagne home with the ticket. That had gained him a good mark from his mother-in-law. Beth had been drier. In his first frustration he had rather too obviously put his hatred of traveling alone, especially on this journey, above responsible parenthood. But her last words had been, "I'll forgive you in Paris."

A door by the top of the staircase, the one Breasley had gone into, opened briefly and he heard the sound of music, a radio or a record, it seemed like Vivaldi. Then silence again. He felt like a visitor; peripheral, not really wanted. His mind drifted back to the two girls. Of course one wasn't shocked that they went to bed with the old man; whatever one did with old men. Presumably they were well paid for their services, both literally and figuratively; they must know the kind of prices his work fetched now, let alone what the collection would be worth at auction. In some nagging way their presence irritated David. They must be after something, exploiting the old man's weaknesses. They were like a screen. He sensed a secret they did not want him to know.

He wished Beth were there. She was always less afraid of offending people, more immediate; and she could have got so much more out of the girls than he ever would.

He was glad he had finally decided to dress up a little — the jeans suit, a shirt and scarf — when he went downstairs. The Mouse was in a creamy high-necked blouse and a long russet skirt, laying the long wooden table at the far end of the room. There were lamps on, the first dusk outside. David saw the back of Breasley's white head in a sofa by the fireplace; and then, as he came down the room, the Freak's frizzed mop leaning against his shoulder. She was slumped back, her feet on a stool, reading aloud in French from some magazine. She wore a bare-shouldered black satin dress with a flounced bottom, a Spanish line about it. The hand of the old man's encircling arm had slipped beneath the fabric and lay on the girl's left breast. He did not move it away when he saw David, merely raised his free hand and pointed down the room toward the Mouse.

"Have a drink, dear boy."

He too had changed; a pale summer coat, a white shirt, a purple bow tie. The girl twisted her head and slipped David a look up, charcoal eyes, intense red mouth, a thin grimace, then began slowly translating what she had read into English. David smiled, hesitated an awkward moment, then went on to where the Mouse moved around the table. She looked coolly up from her work.

"What can I get you?"

"Whatever you're having."

"Noilly Prat?"

"Lovely."

She went to an old carved *armoire* beside the door through to the kitchen; glasses, an array of bottles, a bowl of ice.

"Lemon?"

"Please."

He took his glass, and watched her pour a similar one for herself; then some frizzy fruit drink; and finally a whisky . . . poured with care, dispensed, she even held the glass up and lined two fingers to check the level of the ration before topping it with an equal amount of soda. Her blouse, made of some loose-woven fabric the color of old lace that allowed minute interstices of bare flesh, was long-sleeved and tight-wristed, high-necked, Edwardian in style; rather prim and demure except, as he soon realized, that nothing was worn underneath it. He watched her face in profile as she served the drinks; its quiet composure. Her movements were deft, at home in this domestic role. David wondered why the old man had to make fun of her; taste and intelligence seemed after all much more plausible than silliness. Nor did there seem anything Pre-Raphaelite about her now; she was simply a rather attractive bit of seventies bird . . . and a good deal easier to relate to than the absurd sex doll on the sofa, who was reading French again. Now and then the old man would correct her pronunciation and she would repeat a word. The Mouse took the drinks down to them, then came back to where David waited. He passed her her glass, and was aware of a very straight pair of eyes; suspiciously as if she had half read his thoughts. Then she silently raised the glass to him and sipped. One hand went to hold an elbow. And at last she smiled.

"Did we behave ourselves?"

"Absolutely. Very helpful."

"Give him time."

He grinned. Definitely, he began to take to her. She had fine features, very regular and well-proportioned; a good mouth; and the very clear eyes, blue-gray eyes set more intense by her tanned complexion, had lost their afternoon abstraction. They were made up a little now, a faintly Slavonic oblongness about them accentuated; and they had a directness he liked. One of his theories began to crumble. It was hard to believe they were exploiting the old man in any mercenary way.

"He showed me one of your drawings. The teasels? I was impressed."

She looked down a moment at her glass; a very deliberate hesitation; then up into his eyes again.

"And I liked your exhibition at the Redfern last autumn."

He gave a not entirely mock start of surprise; another smile.

"I didn't realize."

"I even went twice."

He said, "Where were you?"

"Leeds. For my Dip AD. Then two terms at the RCA."

He looked duly impressed. "Well, good God, you mustn't . . ."

"I'm learning more here."

He looked down, it wasn't his business, but he managed to suggest that even so, postgraduate acceptance by the fiercely selective Royal College of Art was not something one jacked in lightly.

"It's all right. Henry knows he's lucky to have me."

She said it with another smile, but it was meant neither ironically nor vainly, and David revised his opinion of the girl a step further. She had given herself a reference; and she gained an immediate stature in his eyes, a seriousness. He had obviously got things badly wrong; been in some obscure way teased on his first arrival. He saw at once the very real studio help she must be giving the old man; and made a guess — the sexual services were provided by the other girl alone.

"The new painting's remarkable. I don't know how he keeps on pulling them out."

"Never thinking of anyone but himself. Mainly."

"And that's what you're learning?"

"Watching."

"He said he was very grateful to you."

"He's a child, really. He needs toys. Like affection. So he can try and smash it to bits."

"But yours has remained whole?"

She shrugged. "We have to play up to him a little. Pretend we're in awe of his wicked old reputation. The harem bit."

He smiled and looked down.

"I confess I was wondering what the reality was there."

"Our last visitor was told — within ten minutes of arrival — that we'd both been ravished three times the previous night. You mustn't look as if you doubt his word. In that area."

He laughed. "Right."

"He knows nobody believes him, but that's not the point."

"Understood."

She sipped her vermouth.

"And just to clear up any remaining illusions, Anne and I don't deny him the little bit of sex life that he can still manage."

Her eyes were on his. There was a defensiveness behind the frankness, some kind of warning. They both looked down; David momentarily at the line of the bare breasts beneath the blouse, then away. She seemed devoid of coquetry, of any trace of the flagrant sexiness of her friend. Her self-possession was so strong that it denied her good looks, that repeated undertone of nakedness, any significance; and yet it secretly drew attention to them.

She went on. "He's not verbal at all. As you must have realized. It's partly having lived abroad so long. But something much deeper. He has to see and to feel. Quite literally. The shadow of young girls in flower isn't enough."

"I begin to realize just how lucky he is."

"I'm only giving you the debit side."

"I realize that as well."

She glanced secretively to where the old man sat, then back

at David. "If he turns nasty, you mustn't get rattled. It's no good backing down, he hates that. Just stick to your guns. Keep cool." She smiled. "Sorry. If I'm sounding all-wise. But I do know him."

He swirled the lemon in the bottom of his glass. "I'm actually not quite sure why I'm allowed here. If he knows my work."

"That's why I'm warning you. He asked me, I had to tell him. In case he found out anyway."

"Oh Christ."

"Don't worry. He'll probably be satisfied with one or two mean digs. Which you needn't rise to."

He gave her a rueful look. "I suspect I'm being a bloody nuisance. For you."

"Because we looked bored this afternoon. Not very gracious?"

She was smiling, and he smiled back.

"Since you mention it."

"We're delighted you've come. But it wouldn't do to show that too obviously in front of Henry."

"As I now completely understand."

There was suddenly a grain of mischief in her eyes.

"Now you have to learn Anne. She's more difficult than me."

But they never got on to Anne. The door from the kitchen opened and the gray head of the French housekeeper looked into the room.

"*Je peux servir, mademoiselle?*"

"*Oui, Mathilde. Je viens vous aider.*"

She went into the kitchen. The other girl was on her feet, pulling Breasley to his. She was barebacked, the dress cut absurdly low. They came hand-in-hand down the room to where David waited. One had to grant her some kind of style. She had a little self-guying mince as she walked, something monkeyish, of repressed gaiety, provokingly artificial beside her white-haired companion's quiet walk. David doubted whether he would ever "learn" her.

Only one end of the long table was laid. Breasley stood at the head, the girl took the seat to his right. The old man gestured.

"Williams, dear boy."

He was to sit on the Freak's right. Mathilde and the Mouse appeared: a small soup tureen, a platter of *crudités*, another of variously pink rings of sausage, a butter dish. The soup was for Breasley. He remained standing, waiting with an old-fashioned courtesy to see the Mouse into her chair. When she sat, he bent over and lightly kissed the crown of her head. The two girls exchanged a neutral look. In spite of their seemingly disparate looks and intelligences there was evidently a closeness between them, a rapport that did not need words. The Mouse ladled soup into the dish before the old man. He tucked a large napkin between two buttons halfway down his shirtfront and spread it over his lap. The Freak silently insisted that David help himself first. The housekeeper went to a corner of the room and lighted an oil lamp, then brought it back and set it down in the empty space opposite David. On her way out to the kitchen she reached for a switch and the electric lights around them died. At the far end of the room a hidden lamp in the corridor upstairs remained on, silhouetting the handsome diagonal of the medieval staircase. A last pale phosphorescence in the evening light outside, over the trees; the faces bathed in the quiet lambency from the milky diffuser; the Mouse poured red wine from a bottle without a label for David, the old man and herself. The Freak, it seemed, did not drink; and hardly ate. She sat with the elbows of her bare brown arms on the table, picking up little bits of raw vegetable and nibbling at them, staring across at the Mouse with her dark eyes. She did not look at David. There was a little silence as they all set to; as if one waited for Breasley to declare conversation open. David was hungry, anyway, and feeling much more at home now that the girl opposite had cleared the air so completely. The lamplight made the scene like a Chardin, a Georges de la Tour; very peaceful. Then the Freak choked without warning. David flashed her a look — not food, it had been a stifled giggle.

The Mouse murmured, "Idiot."

"Sorry."

She made an absurd attempt, mouth pressed tight and down, leaning back, to control her nervousness; then abruptly clutched her white napkin to her face and twisted up away from her chair. She stood five or six feet away, her back to them. Breasley went on calmly eating his soup. The Mouse smiled across at David.

"Not you."

"Needs her bloody bum tanned," murmured Breasley.

Still the girl stood, long bare spine to them, fuzz of dark red shadow perched over the scarecrow neck. Then she moved farther away, toward the fireplace, into the darkness.

"Mouse is a fan of yours, Williams. She tell you that?"

"Yes, we've already established a mutual admiration society."

"Very pernickety creature, our Mouse."

David smiled.

"Footsteps of Pythagoras, that right?"

The old man stayed intent on his soup. David glanced for help at the girl opposite.

"Henry's asking if you paint abstracts."

Eyes on his laden spoon, the old man muttered quickly, "Obstructs."

"Well yes. I'm . . . afraid I do."

He knew it was a mistake even before the Mouse's quick glance. The old man smiled up.

"And why are we afraid, dear boy?"

David said lightly, "Just a figure of speech."

"Very brainy stuff, I hear. Much admired, Mouse says."

David murmured, " '*Als ich kann.*' "

Breasley looked up a second time. "Come again?"

But suddenly the Freak was behind her chair. She held three pink chrysanthemum heads, removed from a pot David had seen in the fireplace. She put one by his hand; one by the old man's and the third by the Mouse's. Then she sat down with her hands on her lap, like a self-punished child. Breasley reached out and patted her arm in avuncular fashion.

"You were saying, Williams?"

"As sound as I can make them." He went quickly on. "I'd rather hoped humbly in the footsteps of . . ." but he saw too late he was heading for another mistake.

"Of whom, dear boy?"

"Braque?"

It was a mistake. David held his breath.

"Mean that synthetic cubist nonsense?"

"It makes sense to me, sir."

The old man did not answer for a moment. He ate more soup.

"All spawn bastards when we're young." David smiled, and stopped his tongue. "Saw a lot of atrocities in Spain. Unspeakable things. Happens in war. Not just them. Our side as well." He took another mouthful of soup, then laid the spoon down and leaned back and surveyed David. "Battle's over, dear man. Doing it in cold blood, you with me? Don't go for that."

"As I've been warned, Mr. Breasley."

The old man suddenly relaxed a little; there was even a faint glint of amusement in his eyes.

"Long as you know, my boy."

David opened his hands: he knew. The Mouse spoke.

"Henry, do you want more soup?"

"Too much garlic."

"It's exactly the same as last night."

The old man grunted, then reached for the wine bottle. The

Freak raised her hands and ran her splayed fingers through her hair, as if she were afraid it might be lying flat; then turned a little to David, her arms still l igh.

"You like my tattoo?"

In the hollow of the shaven armpit was a dark blue daisy.

Through the rest of the meal David managed, in tacit alliance with the Mouse, to keep the conversation off art. The food itself helped; the *quenelles* of pike in a *beurre blanc* sauce that was a new gastronomic experience to him, the *pré salé* lamb. They talked French cooking and love of food, then about Brittany, the Breton character. This was Haute Bretagne, David learned, as opposed to the Basse, or Bretagne Bretonnante farther west, where the language was still spoken. *Coët-* meant wood, or forest: *-minais,* of the monks. The surrounding forest had once been abbatial land. Among themselves they dropped that part, one spoke simply of Coët. Most of the talk was between the Mouse and David, though she turned to Breasley from time to time for confirmation or for further details. The Freak said next to nothing. David sensed a difference of license accorded the two girls. The Mouse was allowed to be herself; the other was there slightly on tolerance. She too, it emerged at one point, had been an art student; but graphics, not fine arts. They had first met at Leeds. But she gave the impression that she did not take her qualifications very seriously; she was out of her class in present company.

The old man, having drawn his drop of blood, seemed satisfied, prepared to revert at least part of the way back to his predinner self. But if the Mouse was successful in maintaining an innocuous conversation, she was less so in keeping the wine from him. She drank very little herself, and David gave up trying to keep pace with his host. A second bottle had been produced from the *armoire.* By the time the meal was finished that was empty, too, and there was a glaze in Breasley's eyes.

He did not seem drunk, there was no fumbling after his glass; just that ocular symptom of possession by an old demon. His answers became increasingly brief; he hardly seemed to be listening anymore. The Mouse had complained that they never saw any films, and the talk had moved to that; what David had seen recently in London. Then the old man broke in abruptly.

"Another bottle, Mouse."

She looked at him, but he avoided her eyes.

"In our guest's honor."

Still she hesitated. The old man stared at his empty glass, then raised a hand and brought it down on the table. It was without force or anger, only a vague impatience. But she got up and went to the *armoire.* They were apparently at a point where giving way was better than remonstrating. Breasley leaned back in his chair, staring at David under the white quiff, almost benevolent, a kind of fixed smile. The Freak spoke to the table in front of her.

"Henry, can I get down?"

He remained staring at David. "Why?"

"I want to read my book."

"You're a fucking little ninny."

"Please."

"Bugger off then."

He had not looked at her. The Mouse came back with the third bottle, and the Freak looked nervously up at her, as if her permission was needed as well. There was a little nod, then David felt his thigh being briefly squeezed. The Freak's hand had reached along beneath the table, apparently to give him courage. She stood up and went down the room and up the stairs. Breasley pushed the bottle toward David. It was not a politeness, but a challenge.

"Not for me, thanks. I've had enough."

"Cognac? Calvados?"

"No thanks."

The old man poured himself another full glass of wine.

"This pot stuff?" He nodded sideways down the room. "That's the book she wants to read."

The Mouse said quietly, "She's given it up. You know that perfectly well."

He took a mouthful of the wine.

"Thought all you young whiz-kids indulged."

David said lightly, "Not personally."

"Interferes with the slide-rule stuff, does it?"

"I imagine. But I'm not a mathematician."

"What do you call it then?"

The Mouse waited, eyes down. Evidently she could not help him now, except as a silent witness. It was not worth pretending one did not know what that "it" meant. David met the old man's stare.

"Mr. Breasley, most of us feel abstraction has become a meaningless term. Since our conception of reality has changed so much this last fifty years."

The old man seemed to have to turn it over in his mind; then dismiss it.

"I call it betrayal. Greatest betrayal in the history of art."

The wine had gone to his cheeks and nose, and his eyes seemed almost opaque. He was less leaned than forced back against his armed chair, which he had shifted a little to face David. It also brought him a little closer to the girl beside him. David had talked too much to her during dinner, shown too much interest . . . he saw that now, and that the old man must have watched them talking before the meal. In some way he had to repossess her.

"Triumph of the bloody eunuch."

In that way.

"At least better than the triumph of the bloody dictator?"

"Balls. Spunk. Any spunk. Even Hitler's spunk. Or nothing."

Without looking at David, the Mouse said, "Henry feels

that full abstraction represents a flight from human and social responsibility." He thought for one moment she was taking Breasley's side; then realized she had now set up as interpreter.

"But if philosophy needs logic? If applied mathematics needs the pure form? Surely there's a case for fundamentals in art, too?"

"Cock. Not fundamentals. Fundaments." He nodded at the girl beside him. "Pair of tits and a cunt. All that goes with them. That's reality. Not your piddling little theorems and pansy colors. I know what you people are after, Williams."

Once again the Mouse interpreted, in an absolutely neutral voice. "You're afraid of the human body."

"Perhaps simply more interested in the mind than the genitals."

"God help your bloody wife then."

David said evenly, "I thought we were talking about painting."

"How many women you slept with, Williams?"

"That's not your business, Mr. Breasley."

It was disconcerting, the fixity of the stare in the pause before an answer could be framed; like fencing in slow motion.

"Castrate. That's your game. Destroy."

"There are worse destroyers around than nonrepresentational art."

"Cock."

"You'd better tell that to Hiroshima. Or to someone who's been napalmed."

The old man snorted. There was another silence.

"Science hasn't got a soul. Can't help itself. Rat in a maze."

He swallowed the last of his glass and gestured impatiently at the Mouse to refill it. David waited, though he was tempted to jump in and ask why he had been invited to Coëtminais in the first place. He felt rattled, in spite of being forewarned. It was the violently personal nature of the assault, the realization that any rational defense, or discussion, would simply add fuel to the flames.

"What you people . . ." the old man stared at the filled glass, jumped words. "Betrayed the fort. Sold out. Call yourself avant-garde. Experimental. My arse. High treason, that's all. Mess of scientific pottage. Sold the whole bloody shoot down the river."

"Abstract painting is no longer avant-garde. And isn't the best propaganda for humanism based on the freedom to create as you like?"

Again the pause.

"Wishwash."

David forced a smile. "Then one's back with socialist realism? State control?"

"What controls you then, Wilson?"

"Williams," said the Mouse.

"Don't give me that liberal cant. Had to live with the stench of it all my life. *Le fairplay.* Sheer yellowbelly." Suddenly he pointed a finger at David. "Too old for it, my lad. Seen too much. Too many people die for decency. Tolerance. Keeping their arses clean."

He finished his wine in one contemptuous gulp, then reached for the bottle again. Its neck rattled against the rim of the glass and he poured too long, some spilled over. The Mouse lifted the glass and poured off a little into her own; then quietly wiped the spilled liquid from the table in front of the old man. David said nothing. He felt cool again now; but embarrassed.

"Good wines, know what they do? Piss in them. Piss in the vat." He rather shakily got the glass to his mouth, then set it down. The pauses grew longer between each burst of speech. "Fit ten Englishmen into a Frenchman's little finger." Another hiatus. "Not oil. Pigment. All shit. If it's any good. *Merde.* Human excrement. *Excrementum.* That which grows out. That's your fundamental. Not your goddam prissy little bits

[43]

of abstract good taste." He paused again, as if he sought a way forward, and had finally to go back. "Wouldn't even wipe my arse with them."

There was a heavy silence. Somewhere outside an owl quavered. The girl sat, her chair pushed back a little from the table, her hands folded on her lap, eyes down, apparently prepared to wait for eternity for the old man's ramblings to finish. David wondered how often she had to suffer this monstrous bohemian travesty that the alcohol had released. All those ancient battles that had to be refought; when the matter was so totally, both *de facto* and *de jure*, decided, and long before David was born. All form was not natural; and color had a nonrepresentational function . . . you could no more argue any longer about that than about Einstein's famous equation. Fission had taken place. One could dispute application, but not principle. So David thought; and some of it must have appeared on his face. He had also drunk more than usual.

"Disappointing you, Williams? Think I'm pissed? *In vino* bollocks?"

David shook his head. "Just overstating your case."

More silence.

"You really a painter, Williams? Or just a gutless bloody word-twister?"

David did not answer. There was another silence. The old man drank more wine.

"Say something."

"Hatred and anger are not luxuries we can afford anymore. At any level."

"Then God help you."

David smiled faintly. "He's also a nonoption."

The Mouse reached forward and poured more wine.

"Know what turning the cheek meant when I was young? Fellow who turned his cheek?"

"No."

"Bumboy. You a bumboy, Wilson?"

[44]

This time the Mouse did not bother to correct him; or David, to answer.

"On your knees and trousers down. Solves all, does it?"

"No. But then nor does fear."

"Does which?"

"Being afraid of losing . . . what isn't in question."

The old man stared at him.

"What the hell's he talking about?"

The Mouse said quietly, "He means your work and your views of art aren't in any danger, Henry. There's room for everyone."

She did not look at David, but shifted a little, forward and away from the old man; put an elbow on the table, then her hand to her chin. A finger rose momentarily to her lips. David was not to answer back anymore. Outside, Macmillan suddenly began barking; wild paroxysms of suspicion. A voice, the housekeeper's husband's, shouted. Neither the old man nor the girl took any notice; to them it must have been a familiar night sound. To David it was intensely symbolic, fraught, echoing the tension inside the old man.

"That's the line now, is it?"

The girl looked across at David. There was a faint smile in her eyes.

"Henry thinks one shouldn't show toleration for things one believes are bad."

"Same old story. Sit on the bloody English fence. Vote for Adolf."

There was more silence, but then suddenly she spoke.

"Henry, you can't stop totalitarian ideas by totalitarian methods. That way you only help breed them."

Perhaps some dim realization percolated through that she was now taking David's side. The old man's eyes wandered away into the shadows at the end of the table. When she had last refilled his glass, she had put the bottle back to her left, out of his reach.

He said slowly, "Trying to tell you something."

It wasn't clear whether he meant, I didn't mean to insult you personally; or, I've forgotten what it was.

David murmured, "Yes, I realize."

The old man's stare came back to him. He had difficulty in focusing.

"What's your name?"

"Williams. David Williams."

The Mouse said, "Finish your wine."

But he ignored her.

"Not good with words. Never my line."

"I understand what you're saying."

"Don't hate, can't love. Can't love, can't paint."

"I understand."

"Bloody geometry. No good. Won't work. All tried it. Down the hole." His staring at David now had a desperate concentration, almost a clinging. He seemed to lose all train.

The Mouse prompted him. "Making is speaking."

"Can't write without words. Lines."

The girl stared down the room. She spoke very quietly.

"Art is a form of speech. Speech must be based on human needs, not abstract theories of grammar. Or anything but the spoken word. The real word."

"Other thing. Ideas. Can't care."

David nodded gravely.

The Mouse went on. "Ideas are inherently dangerous because they deny human facts. The only answer to fascism is the human fact."

"Machine. What's it, computer thing."

David said, "I do understand."

"*Tachiste. Fautrier.* Wols fellow. Like frightened bloody sheep. Drip, drip." He stopped, a silence. "Yank, what's his name?"

David and the girl said it together, and he missed it. The Mouse repeated the name.

"Jackson Bollock." Once again he stared off into the darkness. "Better the bloody bomb than Jackson Bollock."

They said nothing. David stared at the ancient surface of the table in front of him; blackened oak, scarred and rubbed, the patina of centuries' use; centuries of aged voices, ordering back some threatening, remorseless tide. As if time knew ebb.

Then the old man spoke, with a strange lucidity, as if he had only been pretending to be drunk, and now summarized with one final inconsequence.

"Ebony tower. That's what I call it."

David glanced across at the girl, but she did not meet his look. Foreclosing had apparently become more important than interpreting. It was very clear that Breasley was not really pretending; David watched his eyes, how they searched hazily for the glass, or several glasses, in front of him. He reached, a last effort to seem positive and sober. The Mouse caught his hand and gently set the stem of the glass between the fingers. The old man had difficulty in getting it to his mouth, then tried to down the wine in one brave swallow. It dribbled down his chin, then splashed on his white shirtfront. The Mouse leaned forward and dabbed with her serviette.

She said gently, "Bed now."

"One more."

"No." She took the half-empty bottle and put it beside her chair on the floor. "All gone."

The old man's eyes found David.

"Qu'est-ce qu'il fout ici?"

The girl stood and put a hand under his elbow to urge him up.

He said, "Bed."

"Yes Henry."

But still he sat, slightly bowed, a very old man in a stupor. The girl waited patiently. Her downward eyes met David's, a curious gravity, as if she were frightened she might see contempt in his for this role she had to play. He pointed at himself — could he help? She nodded, but raised a finger; not yet. A moment later she bent and kissed the old man on the temple.

"Come on. Try and stand."

And now, like an obedient but vaguely timid small boy, he pressed his hands on the table. He was unsteady as he came to his feet, and lurched forward against the table-edge. David went quickly to his other side. Suddenly he collapsed down again into the chair. This time they pulled him up. How drunk he really was did not become apparent until they started to walk him down the room toward the stairs. He was in a seeming coma, his eyes closed; only his legs, by some ancient instinct, or long practice, managed to go through the motions of shuffling forward. The Mouse pulled at the bow tie, then unbuttoned the top of the shirt. Somehow they got him up the stairs and into the large room at the west end of the house.

David saw a double and a single bed, the Freak standing off the latter. She still wore the black dress, but now with a white jumper over it. He had a glimpse of more paintings and drawings on the walls, a table by the window that faced out west with jars of crayons and drawing pencils.

"Oh Henry. You wicked old thing."

The Mouse spoke across the old man's bowed head to David.

"We can manage now."

"Are you sure?"

Breasley muttered, "Pee."

The two girls led him around the beds and to a door beyond. They got him in and all three disappeared. David stood undecided, at a loss; and then suddenly he registered the painting over the bed. It was a Braque, one he knew he had seen somewhere in reproduction. It must have been listed as "private collection," he had never associated it with Breasley. He thought wrily back: the jejune folly of throwing such a name, such a relationship, at the old man in his own self-defense. The Freak came out of the bathroom and closed the door behind her. The additional irony of it struck him . . . that painting, a certain six figures at any auction — and the gewgawish, unreliable-looking little creature who stood facing him across the room. There was the sound of vomiting.

"Is he like this every night?"

"Just sometimes." She had a thin smile. "It's not you. Just other people."

"I can't help undress him?"

She shook her head. "Don't worry. Really. We're used to it." He stood there in doubt. She said again, "Really."

He wanted to say that he admired them both for what they were doing; and found himself at an unusual loss for words.

"Well . . . say good night to . . . I don't actually know her real name."

"Di. Diana. Sleep well."

"And you."

She pressed her lips drily together and gave a little single nod. He left.

Back in his room, in pajamas, in bed, he lay propped on an elbow staring at a thriller he had brought. He felt he ought to stay at least potentially on hand for a while in case they did need further help; and though he felt tired, sleep was out of the question. He couldn't even read, the adrenalin had to calm down. It had been an extraordinary evening; and for the first time he was glad that Beth hadn't been there. She would have found it too much, flown off the handle probably; though the baiting had been so crude, so revealing of all the old man's weaknesses. Essentially one was dealing with a cantankerous child. And the Mouse, Diana, how staggeringly well she had handled him; quite a girl, quite a pair, there must be something better than was apparent in the other, a fidelity, a kind of courage. One took the Mouse's word now, the accuracy of her judgments; had needed her coolness; was curious to know if one had satisfied it. He recalled a certain amount of skeptical joking between Beth and himself: about the old man living up to his reputation, Beth's expecting to be groped at least twice or asking for her money back . . . that at least was taken care of. The stories to tell in private back home. He tried to settle to his thriller.

Perhaps twenty minutes had passed since he had left the girls to their tyrant. The house had fallen silent. But now he heard someone come out of Breasley's bedroom, then light footsteps, the creak of a floorboard outside his room. There was a hesitation, then a gentle tap on his door.

"Come in."

The Mouse's head appeared around the door.

"I saw your light on. It's all right. He's asleep."

"I didn't realize how far gone he was."

"We have to let him do it sometimes. You did very well."

"I'm jolly glad you warned me."

"He'll be all contrite tomorrow. Meek as a lamb." She smiled. "Breakfast around nine? But you know. Sleep as long as you like."

She drew back to go, but he stopped her. "What on earth did that last thing he said mean? The ebony tower?"

"Oh." She smiled. "Nothing. Just one of the bats in his belfry." She tilted her head. "What he thinks has taken the place of the ivory tower?"

"Abstraction?"

She shook her head. "Anything he doesn't like about modern art. That he thinks is obscure because the artist is scared to be clear . . . you know. Somewhere you dump everything you're too old to dig? You mustn't take it personally. He can only explain what he thinks by insulting people." She smiled again, her body still hidden by the door. "Okay?"

He smiled back, and nodded.

And she was gone, not back to the old man's room, but farther down the corridor. A door clicked quietly to. David would have liked to talk a little longer. The old teaching world — students you fancied, who fancied you a little, in some way the atmosphere of Coët reminded him of the days before Beth had entered his life; not that he had ever gone in much for having it off with students. He was a crypto-husband long before he married.

He read a little, then switched out the light and sank, in his usual way, almost immediately into sleep.

Once again the Mouse was proved right. Contrition was flagrant from the moment David appeared, punctually at nine, downstairs again. Breasley himself came in from the garden as David stood at the foot of the stairs uncertain of where breakfast took place. To one unversed in the recuperative powers of lifelong heavy drinkers, he seemed surprisingly spry, and newly dapper, in light trousers and a dark blue sports shirt.

"My *dear* man. So un*speak*ably sorry about last night. Gels tell me most ap*pall*ingly rude."

"Not at all. Honestly."

"Absolutely pissed. Very bad form."

David grinned. "Forgotten."

"Curse of my life, don't you know. Never learned when to stop."

"Please don't worry."

He took the abruptly extended hand.

"Very white of you, dear boy." The hand was retained, his eyes quizzed. "Say I must call you David. Surnames terribly square these days. That right?"

He used "square" as if it were some daring new piece of slang.

"Please do."

"Splendid. Well. I'm Henry then. Yes? Now come and have some breakfast. We pig it in the kitchen in the mornings."

On the way down the room, Breasley said, "Gels suggest a little *déjeuner sur l'herbe*. Good idea, what? Picnic?" There was sunshine outside, a faint haze over the trees. "Rather proud of my forest. Worth a dekko."

"I'd love to."

The two girls, it seemed, were already up and out — to Plélan, the nearest village, to shop for food . . . and incidentally, or so David guessed, to allow the old man time to prove his penitence. He was taken on a stroll around the domain after breakfast. Breasley revealed a pride in his garden, a little vanity over what must have been a comparatively recently acquired knowledge of names and cultivation methods. They came on Jean-Pierre hoeing in the vegetable garden behind the east end of the house; and as he listened to the old man and the housekeeper's husband discussing an ailing young tulip tree and what could be done for it, David had again that pleasing sense of a much more dominant key in Breasley's life than the previous night's "recessive" exhibition of spleen. He had very evidently learned to live in Coët and its seasons; and a little later, when they were out in the orchard beyond the vegetables, there was an old water pear already ripe, David was to taste one, they must be eaten straight from the tree, the old man began to say as much — to confess he was a fool to have spent so much of his life in a city; to have left himself so little time to enjoy this. Between bites at his pear David asked why it had taken so long to find that out. Breasley gave a little sniff of self-contempt, then poked at a windfall with the end of his walking stick.

"The bitch Paris, dear boy. Know that bit of rhyme? Earl of Rochester, isn't it? 'Where man may live in direst need, but ne'er lack land to set his seed.' Neat. Says it all."

David smiled. They strolled on.

"Should have married. Damn' sight less expensive."

"But you'd have missed a lot?"

Another sniff of self-reproach. "One's the same as fifty, what?"

He seemed unaware of the irony: that he still had not managed to make do with one; and as if on cue a small white Renault came down the private lane from the outer world. The Mouse was driving. She waved through the window to where they stood, but did not stop. David and Breasley turned back toward the house. The old man pointed his stick after the car.

"Envy you chaps. Weren't like that when I was young."

"I thought the girls of the twenties were rather dazzling."

The stick was raised in genially outraged contradiction.

"Absolute piffle, my dear man. No idea. Spent half your life getting their legs open. Other half wishing you hadn't. Either that. Catching the clap off some tart. Dog's life. Don't know how we stood it."

But David was unconvinced, and knew he was meant to be. The old man regretted nothing at heart; or only the impossible, another life. Somehow something of the former sexual bantam clung physically around his old frame; he could never have been particularly good-looking, but there must have been an attack, a devil about him, a standing challenge to the monogamous. One could imagine him countlessly rebuffed, and indifferent to it; enormously selfish, both in bed and out; impossible, so one believed in him. And now even those many who must have refused to believe had been confounded: he had come through to this, reputation, wealth, the girls, freedom to be exactly as he always had been, a halo around his selfishness, a world at his every whim, every other world shut out, remote behind the arboreal sea. To someone like David, always inclined to see his own life (like his painting) in terms of logical process, its future advances dependent on intelligent present choices, it seemed not quite fair. Of course one knew that the way to the peak was never by the book, that hazard and all the rest must play its part, just as action and aleatory painting formed an at least theoretically important sector in the modern art spectrum. But some such mountaineering image drifted through his mind. One had acquired the best equipment one could afford — and one looked up. There on the summit stood a smirking old satyr in carpet slippers, delightedly damning all common sense and calculation.

By eleven they were *en route*. The girls walked ahead with

baskets, down a long forest ride; and David walked behind with the old man, carrying a folding blue recliner on an aluminum frame — portable sofa for the senile, as Breasley disparagingly called it, but the Mouse had insisted on its being brought. He walked with a coat folded over his arm, a raffish old wide-brimmed panama on his head; engagingly seigneurial, pointing at shadows with his walking stick; lights, special perspective qualities of "his" forest. The visit had been allowed to return to its proper purpose. The silence, the rather strange lack of birds; how did one get silence into paint? The theater now, didn't David notice the quality of empty stage?

David was rather more noticing that all this could be used in his introduction. *Anyone who has had the good fortune to walk with the master,* no, *with Henry Breasley in his beloved forest of Paimpont, that still potent evocation* . . . the haze had gone, it was surprisingly warm, more like August than September, a peerless day; one couldn't actually write like that. But he was still basking — realizing his baptism of fire had been a blessing in disguise — in the old man's determined good graces. The importance, pervasive in the mood if tenuous in the actual symbolism, of Breton medieval literature in the Coëtminais series was generally accepted now, though David had not been able to trace much public clarification from Breasley himself on the real extent of the influence. He had read the subject up cursorily before coming, but now he played a little ignorant; and discovered Breasley to be rather more learned and lettered than his briskly laconic manner at first sound suggested. The old man explained in his offhand way the sudden twelfth and thirteenth century mania for romantic legends, the mystery of island Britain ("sort of Wild Northern, what, knights for cowboys") filtering all over Europe *via* its French namesake; the sudden preoccupation with love and adventure and the magical, the importance of the once endless forest — of which the actual one they were walking in, Paimpont now, but the Brocéliande of the *lais* of Chrétien de Troyes, was an example — as the matrix for all these goings-on; the breaking-out of the closed formal garden of other medieval art, the extraordinary yearning symbolized in these wandering horsemen and lost damsels and dragons and wizards, Tristan and Merlin and Lancelot . . .

"All damn' nonsense," said Breasley. "Just here and there, don't you know, David. What one needs. Suggestive. Stimulating, that's the word." Then he went off on Marie de France and *Eliduc*. "Damn' good tale. Read it several times. What's that old Swiss bamboozler's name. Jung, yes? His sort of stuff. Archetypal and all that."

Ahead, the two girls turned off on a diagonal and narrower ride, more shady. Breasley and David followed some forty yards behind. The old man waved his stick.

"Those two gels now. Two gels in *Eliduc*."

He began to tell its story. But consciously or unconsciously his distinctly shorthand manner of narration was more reminiscent of a Noel Coward farce than a noble medieval tale of crossed love, and once or twice David had to bite his lips. Nor did the actual figures of the two girls, the Freak in a red shirt, black dungarees and wellingtons, the Mouse in a dark green jersey (all bras were not burnt, David had noted) and pale trousers, help. More and more he realized the truth of what the latter had said: the old man's problem was an almost total inadequacy with words. If he didn't always cheapen, he certainly misrepresented everything he talked about. One had to keep remembering the way he could express himself in paint; and the gap was enormous. The art predicated a sensitive and complex man; and almost everything outward in him denied it. Though he would have loathed the comparison he was not unlike a certain kind of outdated Royal Academician — much more anxious to appear a stylish pillar of a dead society than to be anything that serious art was about. That was very probably one good reason for the continued exile: the old man must know his persona would never wash in the Britain of the

1970s. Only here could he still preserve it. Of course these were all things one could not put in the introduction, but David found them fascinating. Like the forest itself, the old man had his antique mysteries.

They came up to the two girls, who had stopped. It was a question of the point to leave the path and strike away through the trees to the forest pool that was the promised picnic place. There was a marker oak, a trunk with a dab of red paint. The Mouse thought they had missed it, but the old man made them go on; and rightly. In another hundred yards or so they arrived at the oak, and began to walk down a faint incline among the trees. The undergrowth became denser, they glimpsed the first water ahead; and a few minutes later they emerged on the grassy edge of the *étang*. It was much more a small lake than a pool, four hundred yards or more across at the point where they came to it and curving away on both sides. A dozen or so wild duck roosted in the middle. The forest stood all around its shores, not a house in sight; the water a delicate blue in the September sunlight, smooth as a mirror. The place had featured in two of the last-period paintings and David had a sense of familiarity, of *déjà vu*. It was very charming, miraculously unspoiled. They installed themselves in the thin shade of a solitary fir tree. The reclining chair was set for Breasley. He seemed grateful for it now, sat down at once and put his legs up; then made them adjust the back to a more upright position.

"Come on, you two. Off with your knickers and have your bathe."

The Freak slid a look at David, then away.

"We're shy."

"You'll swim, won't you, David? Keep 'em company?"

David looked for guidance from the Mouse, but she was bent over one of the baskets. He felt grossly unforewarned this time. Swimming had not been mentioned.

"Well . . . perhaps later?"

"You see," said the Freak.

"Not bleeding or anything, are you?"

"Oh Henry. For God's sake."

"Married man, m'dear. Seen pussy before."

The Mouse straightened and gave David a little glance, half apologetic, half wry.

"Costumes are considered unethical. Wearing them makes us even more impossible than usual."

But she lightened the taunt with a smile down at the old man.

David murmured, "Of course."

She looked at the Freak. "Let's go out on the spit, Anne. The bottom's harder there." She picked up a towel and began to walk away, but the Freak seemed now the more shy. She glanced resentfully at the two men.

"And easier for all the other dirty old birdwatchers."

The old man chuckled, and she put out her tongue at him. But then she too picked up a towel and followed her friend.

"Sit down, dear boy. Only codding you. Shy my arse."

David sat on the needled grass. He supposed that this had been sprung on him as a little demonstration of what they had to go through, though the previous night had seemed a conclusive enough witness to that. He felt teased, faintly conspired against: now it's our turn to shock you. The spit, a narrow little grass-topped promontory, ran out some sixty yards away. As the girls walked down it, the wild duck splashed off the middle of the lake and flew in a long curve up over the trees and away. The girls stopped near the end, and the Mouse began to peel off her jersey. When it was off she turned it outside out again, then dropped it and unhooked her bra. The Freak cast a little look back across the glassy water to where David and the old man sat, then kicked out of her wellingtons and slipped off one shoulder strap of her dungarees. The Mouse reached down her jeans and briefs together, separated them, put them beside the rest of her clothes. She walked to the water and waded straight in. The other girl let her dungarees fall, then pulled off her shirt. She was wearing nothing else. As she too walked down to the water, she turned sideways to face the two men in the distance and gave a ridiculous flaunting sidestep, a strip-dancer's routine, arms out. The old man gave another throaty little chuckle and tapped David's arm with the side of his stick. He sat enthroned, like a sultan, watching his two young slaves, the two naked figures, warm backs against the azure water, as they waded out toward the center of the lake. Apparently the bottom shelved slowly. But then the Mouse plunged forward and began to swim away; a crawl, neatly, rather well. The Freak was more cautious, wading deeper, keeping her precious frizzed hair above the water; when she finally fell cautiously forward she did a timid breaststroke.

"Pity you're married," said Breasley. "They need a good fuck."

By the time they were halfway through lunch, David felt a good deal more at his ease. It had all been rather stupid, his first embarrassment. If Beth had been there, for instance . . . they often swam like that on holidays themselves, even deliberately looked for deserted beaches, she would have joined the girls like a shot.

His recovery was partly due to the old man, who had started, once the two girls were swimming, talking again; or rather, at last, his ultimate proof of contrition, he asked David something about himself. The question of how and what he painted was avoided, but Breasley seemed interested to know how he had "come into the game," his life and background; about Beth and the children. He even came out with an invitation: bring your wife and kids one day, like to meet 'em, like little gels . . . and David was vain enough to feel pleased. What had happened after the dinner had been, rather in the medieval context they had discussed on the walk, a kind of ordeal. Very evidently he had passed the test; which left him wondering how much, besides the direct advice, he owed to the Mouse. She must have told the old man a few home truths when he woke up; and perhaps reminded him that his reputation was at least temporarily a little in David's hands.

Meanwhile the girls had come out of the water, dried themselves, and lay side by side in the sun on the spit. The ordeal had indeed been like a reef; and now David was through, after the buffeting, to the calm inner lagoon. Another echo, this time of Gauguin; brown breasts and the garden of Eden. Strange, how Coët and its way of life seemed to compose itself so naturally into such moments, into the faintly mythic and timeless. The uncontemporary. And then yet another such moment had come. The girls had stood. They must have come to some decision about modesty, or the cost of it before the old man's tongue, because they walked back as they were, carrying their clothes; without outward self-consciousness now, but with something of that studied and improbable indifference of people in a nudist colony.

"Hey, we're hungry," said the Freak.

The pubic was dyed the same red as her other hair. Naked, she looked even more waiflike. The girls began to unpack the baskets, kneeling in the sun, while David helped Breasley move nearer to the edge of the shade. Gauguin disappeared; and Manet took his place.

Soon, during the eating, the girls' bare bodies seemed natural. They seemed to still something in the old man as well. There were no more obscenities, but a kind of quiet pagan contentment. The lovely French bread, the little cartons of goodies the girls had brought back from Plélan . . . no wine, the old man drank Vichy water, the girls milk; a bottle of beer for David. The Freak sat cross-legged. Something about her, perhaps just the exotic hair and the darkness of her tan, was faintly negroid, aboriginal, androgynous. Psychologically she still repelled something in David, he couldn't quite say . . . but what began to seem very distinctly a kind of intelligent charity in the Mouse was shadowed in her by a fecklessness, a perversity. Though she made no cracks, one had the impression that the sexual implications of their behavior both excited and amused her. It might be "civilized" to the others; with her, and her not wholly concealed little air of knowingness, it was something else — not a moral inhibition, of course, but a hint that she knew David was getting something for nothing; which went with his feeling that he had yet to prove himself with her. She still vaguely resented his presence. What he had to learn about her, beyond a little ability to debunk, a trendily shallow narcissism, a life-style that patently hid a life-failure, he could not imagine. She seemed so much a mere parasite on the other girl's poise and honesty; her only apparent virtue, that she was tolerated.

And perhaps she repelled him also by physical contrast. The Mouse, despite her slightness, had a much more feminine figure, long-legged, attractively firm small breasts. She sat up on one arm opposite David, her legs curled away. He watched her body when she turned to pass something, when he knew the direction of his eyes would not be caught. They talked banally enough; and once again the ghost of infidelity stalked through David's mind — not any consideration of its actuality, but if he hadn't been married, if Beth . . . that is to say, if Beth didn't sometimes have certain faults, an occasional brisk lack of understanding of him, an overmundane practicality, which this attractively cool and honest young mistress of a situation would be too intelligent (for he saw in her something that he aimed at in his own painting, a detachment and at the same time a matter-of-factness) to show or at any rate to abuse. It wasn't that one didn't still find Beth desirable, that the idea of a spell together in France without the kids after Coët (hovering in it Beth's tacit reacceptance of motherhood, a third child, the son they both wanted) . . . just that one was tempted. One might, if one wasn't what one was; and if it were offered — that is, it was a safe impossibility and a very remote probability away.

The lights of the Mouse's skin were bronzed where the sun caught it, duller yet softer in the shadows. The nipples, the line of the armpits. A healed scar on one of her toes. The way her wheaty hair was drying, slightly tangled, careless; and a smallness, a Quattrocento delicacy, the clothes and long skirts she wore were misleading; contrasted with an animality, the nest of hair between her legs. She sat sideways, facing the lake, and peeled an apple; passed a quarter back to the old man, then offered another to David. It was antiseptic; and disturbing.

Henry had to have his siesta. The Freak stood and let down the back of the recliner. Then she knelt beside the old man and whispered something in his ear. He reached out a hand to her waist and ran it slowly up to the arm, then drew her forward; and she leaned over and touched his mouth with her own. He patted her bare bottom. Then he folded his hands across his stomach, while she arranged a purple handkerchief across his eyes. The fine mouth, the pink bulb of the nose. The girl stood and stared down at him for a moment, then grimaced back at the other two.

The Mouse smiled at David and murmured, "Free period. We'd better go out of hearing."

They stood. The two girls picked up their towels, and the Freak fished in one of the baskets and found her book. Then they walked back toward the spit, some thirty yards away, just out of earshot. The towels were spread, the girls both stretched out on their stomachs, feet toward the lake, chins propped on hands. David sat, then lay on an elbow, five or six feet away on the landward side. He had a brief and much more absurd recall of a painting: two little boys listening to an Elizabethan sailor. He could read the title of the Freak's book: *The Magus*. He guessed at astrology, she would be into all that nonsense. But now she suddenly grinned at him.

"Wish you hadn't come then?"

"Good lord no."

"Di told me. Last night. I'm sorry. I knew, I just couldn't face it."

He smiled. "I'd have asked to get down myself if I'd realized."

The Freak touched two fingers to her mouth and transferred the kiss to the Mouse's shoulder.

"Poor old Di. I always leave it to her."

Poor old Di smiled and looked down.

David said, "How long do you think you'll last out?"

The Freak made a dry little gesture at the Mouse: for her to answer. She shook her head.

"I don't think about the future."

"As an ex–art tutor . . ."

"I know."

The Freak pulled another of her faces at David.

"Common sense will get you nowhere."

The Mouse said, "It's not that."

"Just hard to leave?"

"Chance, I suppose. You know. It brought one here in the first place. And somehow it's got to take one away."

"How did it bring you here?"

She glanced at the Freak: some secret irony.

"Go on. Tell him."

"It's so stupid." She avoided David's eyes.

He murmured, "I'm all ears."

She reached a hand down from her chin and picked at the grass; the shadowed breasts; shrugged.

"Last summer. August. I was here, in France, with a friend. Another art student, a sculptor. He was on a Neolithic kick and we were hitching down to Carnac." She looked up at David. "The megalithic avenues? By pure chance we got a lift on the N24 out of Rennes from a schoolteacher at Ploërmel. Just down the road. We told him we were English art students and he told us about Henry. Of course we knew his name and everything. I even knew he lived somewhere in Brittany." She raised the bottom of one of her legs in the air. The hollowed back, the delicate brown cheeks. She shook her head. "It was just one of those absurd things. Let's be mad and knock on his door. So we camped at Paimpont. Turned up at Henry's about eleven the next morning. Pretending we hadn't seen the sign on the gate. Expecting the boot and nearly getting it. But we gushed like crazy. How much we loved his work. Inspiration to all our generation. All that. Suddenly he fell for it, we'd got a bloody nerve . . . you know. All this was at the door. So we got in and he showed us around a bit. The things in the long room. Most of the time we were trying not to laugh. That way he talks, he seemed such an old phony." She stretched her hands out on the grass, contemplated them. "Then the studio. I saw what he was doing. Perhaps you felt it yesterday. Bump. You're in a different world." She propped her chin again, and stared into the trees behind them. "You've spent three years getting all the right attitudes to painting. Knowing even less what you're doing at the end than you did at the beginning. Then you meet this ridiculous old ragbag of all the wrong attitudes. And he's there. All your own clever little triumphs and progresses are suddenly cut down to scale." She said quickly, "I'm sorry, I don't mean that you should have felt that. But I did."

"No, I know exactly what you mean."

She smiled. "Then you shouldn't. You're much, much better than that."

"I doubt it, but never mind."

"That's all really. Oh except at the end, Tom had gone away to fetch his camera, we'd left our rucksacks outside. Henry tells me I'm a very attractive 'gel,' he wishes he was younger. I laughed, said I wished I was older. And suddenly he took my hands. Kissed one. All rather corny. It happened so quickly. Tom came back, took some photos. Then Henry suddenly asked if we'd like to stay to lunch. But we felt it was just a nice gesture — one was meant to refuse. Silly. He never makes nice gestures. Without a reason. Perhaps I sensed that already, something in his eyes. And I knew Tom wanted to get on. Anyway, it sort of ruined everything. You know how it is, when you turn someone down because you don't think it matters and realize too late that it does." She glanced sideways down at the fir tree. "I suppose we left the impression that we'd been doing it just for jokes. That we weren't really interested in him. Which was true in a way. He was just a famous name. It was so stupid. Just celebrity hunting." She paused a moment. "It was strange. Even as we walked away, I felt bad. I wanted to go back."

She said nothing for a moment. The Freak had spread her elbows out on the ground and lay with her face couched and turned toward the Mouse.

"Two terms, nine months later, I'm not happy in London. It's all over with Tom. I feel I'm getting nowhere at the College. It's not their fault. Just the way I am." She picked at the grass again. "You meet someone famous, you start seeing their work in a different way. Noticing it. I kept remembering that day in August. How mean we'd been to what was basically just a poor old tongue-tied rather lonely man. Oh and . . . all sorts of other things. To do with my own work. One day I just sat down and wrote him a letter. About myself. Saying I wished we'd stayed to lunch. Not walked out like that. And if by any chance he needed domestic help. A paint mixer. Anything."

"He remembered who you were?"

"I sent him one of the photos Tom took. Henry and me standing together." She smiled to herself. "It was the sort of letter that starts sending shivers of embarrassment down your spine the moment you've posted it. I knew he wouldn't answer."

"But he did."

"A telegram. 'Can always use a pretty girl. When?' "

The Freak said, "Dear old him. Straight to the bloody point."

The Mouse pulled a face at David. "I came very innocently. Of course I knew about his past. His reputation. But I thought I could handle it. Keep a strictly granddaughterly sort of role. Or just walk out, if it got impossible." She looked down. "But Henry's got one rather extraordinary quality. A kind of magic. Apart from his painting. The way he can . . . dissolve things in you. Make them not seem to matter. Like this, I suppose. Learning not to be ashamed of one's body. And to be ashamed of one's conventions. He put it rather well once. He said exceptions don't prove rules, they're just exceptions to rules." She evidently felt herself at a loss for words. She smiled up. "We can't explain it to anyone. You have to be us to understand."

The Freak said, "Anyway, it's more like nursing."

There was a little silence. David said, "And how did you come here, Anne?"

The Mouse answered. "It began to get a bit much for me. No one to talk to. We shared a flat in Leeds. Kept in touch; I knew Anne wasn't very happy doing her ATD. So as soon as she finished that."

"I came for one week. Ha ha."

David grinned at the girl's couched face.

"At least more interesting than teaching?"

"And better paid."

"He can afford it."

The Mouse said, "I have to give it back to him. There's no arrangement. He just throws bundles of money at us. A hundred pounds. Two. If we go into Rennes with him, we hardly dare look at clothes. He always wants to buy them."

"He's sweet really," said the Freak. She turned on her back. The dark-ended boy's breasts, the tuft of reddened hair; she raised a knee and scratched just above it, then let it fall.

The Mouse said, "Working with him's very strange. He never loses patience with a painting. Even a drawing. You know, I'll hate what I've done sometimes. You rip it up? Henry'll throw things away. But always with a sort of regret. He gives work a kind of sacrosanct quality. Even when it's not going well. Everything he isn't with people." She paused, then shook her head. "And he hardly talks in the studio. Almost as if he's dumb, as if words would spoil everything."

The Freak spoke to the sky. "Well the way he uses them." She mimicked the old man's voice. " 'Are you bleeding or something?' I ask you." And she reached a hand skyward as if to push the memory away.

"He has to compensate."

The Freak clicked her tongue in agreement. "Oh I know. Poor old bastard. Must be terrible, really." She turned sideways, on an elbow, looked at the Mouse. "It's strange, isn't it, Di? He's still quite sexy, in his funny old way." She looked at David. "You know, when I first . . . you think of blokes your own age and all that. But he must have been sensational. When he was young . . . and oh Christ, you ought to hear his stories." She pulled another clown's face at David. "On the good old days. What was that thing the other night, Di?"

"Don't be silly. They're just fantasies."

"I bloody well hope so."

The Mouse said, "It's contact. Not sex. Memories. The human thing. What he was trying to say last night."

David detected a difference between the two girls. One wanted to play down the sexual side, the other to admit it. He had a sudden intuition that the Freak was using his presence to air a disagreement between them; and that in this context he was on her side.

"That housekeeper and her husband must have broad minds."

The Mouse looked down at the grass. "You mustn't tell anyone, but do you know how Jean-Pierre spent the late forties and fifties?" David shook his head. "In prison. For murder."

"Good grief."

"He killed his father. Some family quarrel about land. French peasants. Mathilde housekept for Henry when he came back to Paris in 1946. He knew all about Jean-Pierre. I've got all this from Mathilde, actually. Henry can do no wrong. He stood by them."

The Freak sniffed. "And more. With Mathilde."

The Mouse queried David. "That rather heavy model he used in some of the first postwar nudes?"

"My God. I never realized."

"Even Mathilde doesn't talk about that side of it. Just that 'Monsieur Henri' gave her faith to live. To wait, she says. She's also the one person Henry never but never loses his temper with. The other day he flew off the handle at dinner with Anne about something. Marched out into the kitchen. Five minutes later I go in. There he is. Eating with Mathilde at the table, listening to her read out a letter from her sister. Just like a vicar with his favorite parishioner." She had a small smile. "One could be jealous."

"Does he draw you two?"

"His hand's too shaky now. There are one or two of Anne. A lovely joke one. You know that famous Lautrec poster of Yvette Guilbert? A parody of that."

The Freak ran fingers up through her friz and toward the sky. "And he did it so *fast*. Can't have been thirty seconds. Minute at most, wasn't it, Di? Fantastic. Honestly."

She turned back on her stomach, chin on hands. Deep scarlet nails.

The Mouse eyed David again. "Has he discussed your article with you?"

"Only to claim he's never heard their names. Beyond Pisanello."

"Don't believe him. He's got an incredible memory for

paintings. I've kept some of the sketches he does. He's trying to tell you about some picture and you don't quite know which one he means — and then sometimes he'll draw them. Like Anne says. Like lightning. Almost total recall."

"That restores my morale a bit."

"He'd never have agreed to your doing the book if you hadn't been reasonably near the truth."

"I was beginning to wonder."

"He's always so much more aware of what he's doing than you think. Even at his most outrageous. I took him into Rennes one day, before Anne came, to see *Death in Venice*. I had some dotty idea the real Henry would rather like it. The visual part of it, anyway. He was good as gold for the first twenty minutes. Then that heavenly looking boy appears. Next time he's on the screen Henry says, Pretty gel, that — done many pictures, has she?"

David laughed; and her eyes were full of light, laughter. She was suddenly her age, not grave at all.

"Impossible, you can't imagine. He starts arguing about whether it's a girl or a boy. In a loud voice. In English, of course. Then we're on bumboys and modern decadence. The people around us start telling him to shut up. Then he's off with them in French. He didn't know there were so many queers in Rennes, and . . ." she put an imaginary pistol to her head. "There was nearly a riot. I had to drag him out before the *flics* were called in. All the way home he told me that what he calls the *k*inema began and ended with Douglas Fairbanks Senior and Mary Pickford. Totally obtuse. He hasn't seen ten films in the last twenty years. But he knows all about it. Like you last night. The more reasonable you are, the less he hears."

"But it's an act?"

"In a curious way, it's a sense of style. There's even something honest in it. You know, he's sort of saying I'm not going to be your age. I'm old, I am what I am, I don't want to understand."

The Freak said, "Like the way he talks. He keeps telling me I behave like a flapper. And you laugh, you say, *Henry*, flappers went out with lace-up corsets and camiknickers. For Gawd's sake. But it just makes him worse, doesn't it, Di?"

"But it's not as stupid as it sounds. He knows we've got to have something to laugh at. To hate in him, really."

"To forgive in him."

The Mouse opened her hands.

There was a little silence. The autumnal sun beat down. A butterfly, a Red Admiral, glided past and fluttered momentarily above the camber of the Mouse's back. David knew what had happened; a sudden nostalgia for the old art-college relationship. That need for frankness, chewing the fat; testing one's tutor for general humanity, seeing how far he was prepared to come off it; not just confessing, but using confession.

The Mouse spoke to the grass. "I hope all this isn't shocking you."

"I'm delighted you're both so intelligent about him."

"We sometimes wonder about that." She added, "Whether we aren't what he's nicknamed us."

He smiled. "You don't seem very timid to me."

"Except I ran out."

"But you said you were learning more."

"About life. But . . ."

"Not your work?"

"I'm trying to start from the beginning again. I don't know yet."

"That's not mouselike."

The Freak said, "Anyway, who cares. I'd rather fight old Henry than forty bloody kids."

The Mouse smiled, and the Freak pushed her shoulder.

"It's all right for you." She looked at David. "Honestly, I was a bloody mess. As a student. The drug thing. Not the

hard stuff. You know. Sleeping around. Di knows, I got involved with so many rotten bastards. Honestly." She pushed
the other girl's leg with a foot. "Didn't I, Di?" The Mouse
nodded. The Freak looked past David to where the old man
slept. "I mean at least with him it's not being just laid and
where's the next chick. Least he's grateful. I'll never forget
one bloke. He'd just . . . you know, big deal. You know what
he says?" David shook his head. " 'Why you so bloody
skinny?' " She hit her head. "I mean, honest to God, I think of
what I used to put up with. And poor old Henry with tears
in his eyes when he finally makes it." She looked down then,
as if she knew she had said too much, then suddenly grinned
up at David. "Make your fortune with *News of the World*."

"I think the rights are yours."

For a long moment she gave him a look: both questing and
quizzing. She had brown eyes, the most attractive things in
her small face. They also had a directness, a kind of gentle-
ness if you looked closely at them; and David realized that
he had in that forty minutes since lunch begun to learn her.
He guessed at an affectionateness beneath the flip language,
and an honesty — not the Mouse's kind of honesty, which
was an emancipated middle-class one based on a good mind
and proven talent, but something much more working-class,
something that had been got the hard way, by living the
"bloody mess." The friendship, the rapport became compre-
hensible; there was both an identity and a complementarity.
It must have been something to do with their nakedness, the
sun and water and low voices, the silent lostness of the lake
behind; but he felt drawn on into a closer and closer mesh
with these three unknown lives, as if he had known them
much longer, or the lives he did know had somehow mysteri-
ously faded and receded in the last twenty-four hours. Now
was acutely itself; yesterday and tomorrow became the myths.
There was a sense of privilege too; almost metaphysical, that
he had been born into an environment and an age that permit-

ted such swift process — and more banal, that career should grant such opportunities. One's friends, if they could see one now. He did then think of Beth.

He had looked down from the Freak's eyes, and there had been a little silence. And then the Mouse glanced around (but not quite casually enough, as if confession had got too near the bone) at the water and then at her friend.

"I'm going to swim again."

"Okay."

The Mouse turned and sat up, back to David. The Freak smiled at him.

"Be our guest."

He had foreseen this; and decided what to do. He glanced back at where the old man lay.

"If I shan't provoke anything."

She raised her eyebrows, Groucho Marx style; a little wriggle.

"Only us."

The Mouse reached out and smacked her bottom lightly. Then she stood and walked down toward the water. A silence, the Freak lay on, staring at the grass. Finally she spoke in a lower voice.

"Waste, isn't it?"

"She seems to know what she's doing."

She gave a dry little smile. "You're joking."

He watched the Mouse wading into the water; Diana, slim-backed and small-rumped; something underfoot, she stepped sideways before going deeper.

"You think you should leave?"

"I'm only here because she is." She looked down. "In a funny sort of way Di's the odd one out. Old Henry and me, we kind of live from day to day. Know what I mean. We couldn't be innocent if we tried. Di's the other way around."

The girl in the water plunged and began to swim away.

"And she doesn't realize?"

"Not really. She's stupid. The way clever girls are sometimes. Okay, she sees through old Henry. The person she can't see through is herself." The Freak was avoiding his eyes now; there was almost a shyness about her. "If you could try and get her to talk. Maybe this evening. We'll get Henry off to bed early. She needs someone from outside."

"Well of course . . . I'll try."

"Okay." She was silent a moment, then she pushed abruptly up and knelt back on her heels. A grin. "She likes you. She thinks your work's sensational. It was all an act. Yesterday afternoon."

"She told me."

She appraised him a moment, then stood; for a second guyed the modest Venus, one hand over her loins, the other over her breasts.

"We shan't look."

She went to the water. David stood and got out of his clothes. He came alongside the Freak when the peaty water was around his waist. She flashed a smile at him, then swanned forward with a little scream. A moment later he dived in himself and swam out after the distant head.

Five hours later the same head faced him across the dinner table, and he was beginning to find it difficult to think of anything else. She had appeared only briefly before dinner, she was busy in the kitchen with the Freak; and now she had changed into a black shirt and another long skirt, striped browns and a burnt orange; night and autumn; and done her hair up in a way that managed to seem both classically elegant and faintly disheveled. There was just a tiny air that she was out to kill; and she was succeeding. The more he learned her, the more he watched her, the more he liked her; as temperament, as system of tastes and feelings, as female object. He knew it, and concealed it . . . not only to her, partly also to himself; that is, he analyzed what he had so rapidly begun to find attractive about her — why that precise blend of the physical and the psychological, the reserved and the open, the controlled and the (for he had also begun to believe what the Freak had said) uncertain, called so strongly to something in his own nature. Strange, how these things hit you out of the blue, were somehow inside you almost before you could see them approaching. He felt a little bewitched, possessed; and decided it must be mainly the effect of being without Beth. They lived so close, one had forgotten what the old male freedom was like; and perhaps it was most of all a matter of having to have some personal outlet for his feelings about the whole day. He had enjoyed it enormously, when he looked back. It had been so densely woven and yet simple; so crowded with new experience and at the same time primitive, atavistic, time-escaped. Above all he felt accepted, almost one of the household now.

With the girls his credentials had been established by his swimming with them; he had realized afterward that that had been needed — to prove he was a sport, on the Freak's level; that he condoned a choice at the Mouse's more thinking one. He had caught up with her some hundred yards from the shore. They had chatted a little about the lake, the temperature, the niceness of it, as they trod water some ten feet apart. He saw the Freak go back on shore. Breasley seemed still asleep under the fir tree. They had swum slowly back together, toward the thin figure drying herself. He came out of the water beside the Mouse, and the Freak had handed him her damp towel. The sunlight, the trees, the intuition of watching eyes; what faint shadows of embarrassment he still felt had very little to do with the girls . . . or only with the whiteness of his skin beside theirs.

He had not dressed at once, but sat propped back on his arms beside his clothes, drying off a little more in the sun. The two girls lay on their backs, their heads toward him as before, feet to the water. The deep peace of the lake, the serene isolation; or not quite, at the end of the farthest vista there was a tiny movement, an angler, a line being cast, a speck of peasant blue. He said nothing. He felt a kind of mental — an abstract? — randiness; a sinuous wave of the primeval male longing for the licitly promiscuous, the polygamous, the caress of two bodies, sheikdom. That wickedly casual remark from the old man about what the two girls needed bred daydreams; time out of responsibility . . . such a shiftingness of perception, what one was, what one suppressed. Not much more than twelve hours ago he had very nearly dismissed and condemned them as beneath his notice; and now what had been lazily hypothetical during lunch had grown, even then, so much closer, more precise in its potentialities, more imaginable. It was like the days or weeks one might have spent on a painting, bringing it up, refining it, all compressed into a few hours. One knew why, of course. The hurtling pressure of time, prosaic reality — that long drive to Paris, he had to be there, or almost there, by this same hour the next day. Perhaps it constituted the old man's real stroke of genius, to take an old need to escape from the city, for a mysterious remoteness, and to see its ancient solution, the Celtic green source, was still viable; fortunate old man, to stay both percipient and profoundly amoral, to buy this last warm solitude and dry affection with his fame. David glanced back. Still he slept, as if dead. The way the two silent girls lay meant nothing prevented his long survey up and down the lines of their bodies; as perhaps they knew. Their tacitly sparing his modesty — more talk would have meant facing him — was also their secret advantage. He had a knowledge of a brutality totally alien to his nature: how men could rape. Something both tender and provocative in that defenselessness stirred him deeply.

He had stood up and put on his clothes. He would tell Beth, because sooner or later he told her everything; but not till they had made love again.

Then the slow walk home through the forest, a sudden mania in the girls — they had taken a slightly different route, to show him a picturesquely ruined farm in an overgrown clearing — for blackberries, a good old-fashioned English blackberry-and-apple pie. The old man claimed to despise "the damn' things," but played an amiably grumbling part, even pulling down some of the high sprays with the crook of his walking stick. For fifteen minutes or so they were all childishly absorbed in it. Another moment of prospective nostalgia for David — he would not be there to enjoy the eating; which was wrong, that was why they'd been in the kitchen. The Mouse had made the pastry, Anne done the fruit. Specially for him, they said, as if to atone for something emasculating in the situation, something unfair. He was touched.

For part of the way home after the blackberrying he had walked beside the Mouse, ahead of the other girl and the old man. Rather unexpectedly she had been a little shy, as if she knew that the Freak had said something — she both wanted to talk, he felt, and was on her guard against revealing too much. They had discussed the Royal College, why she had left it, but in a rather neutral, general sort of way. Apparently she had felt a kind of claustrophobia, too many elite talents cooped up in too small a space, she had become too self-conscious, too aware of what other people were doing; it had all been her fault. He glimpsed a different girl beneath the present one: rather highly strung, fiercely self-critical, over-conscientious — as the one piece of work of hers that he had seen suggested. She was also anxious not to make too much of it, her artistic future; or at any rate to bore him with it. They slid away to art education in general. He was warned she was a different person on her own, much more difficult to dissolve without the catalyst of the Freak. She had even stopped and turned, and waited to let the others catch up. He was fairly sure it hadn't been merely to give Henry no cause for jealousy. In a way the conversation was a failure. But it did not make her less attactive to him.

Perhaps nothing had better summed up his mood as they returned than the matter of the telegram from Beth that might or might not be waiting back at the house. It was no good pretending. He had unreservedly hoped, not of course that Sandy was seriously ill, but that something else delayed Beth's journey to Paris. They had even foreseen that, that she might have to put it off for a day or two more. That was all he wanted, just one day more. The wish had not been granted: there was no telegram.

As some compensation, he did have one last very useful tête-à-tête with Breasley. Most of his remaining questions of a biographical kind were answered — in the old man's fashion, but David sensed that he was not being seriously misled. At times there was even a convincing honesty. David had asked about the apparent paradox of the old man's pacifism in 1916 and his serving as medical orderly with the International Brigade during the Spanish Civil War.

"White feather, dear boy. Quite literal, you know. Had a collection of the damn' things. Didn't care, all a joke. Russell, he converted me. Hearing him talk, public lecture he gave. Best brain, best heart. Unique. Never met it again." They were up at the window table in his bedroom, with the two beds behind them. David had asked to be shown the Braque — and heard the story of the other Breasley once owned but had had to sell to pay for Coët and its conversion. The old man smiled at him. "Years go by. Keep thinking, don't you know. Whether it wasn't all just yellowbelly. Have to find out in the end. Get it out of your system. Know what I mean?"

"I can imagine."

The old man stared out of the window; the setting sun on the trees.

"Scared stiff. The whole time. Hated it. Had to draw. Only

way I got through." He smiled. "Not death. You prayed for death. Still hear the pain. Relive it. Wanted to pin it. Kill it. Couldn't draw it well enough."

"Perhaps not for yourself. You did for the rest of us."

The old man shook his head.

"Salt on the sparrow's tail. Mug's game."

David had led him into less traumatic areas of his life; and even risked, toward the end, giving the old man some of his own medicine. If he pretended ignorance of the parallels David had drawn in his article, how was it that the girls so admired his memory for paintings? Breasley cast him a wry look and pulled his nose.

"Little bitches gave the game away, did they?"

"I twisted their arms when you were asleep."

The old man looked down and smoothed the edge of the table.

"Never forgot a good picture in my life, David." He looked out over the garden again. "The names, yes. But what's a name. Bit of fiddle in a corner. That's all." He cocked a cryptic thumb back at the Braque and winked. The image survives; is all that matters.

"So I won't have to leave myself out of the bibliography?"

"Hanged man. Not the Verona thing. Fox. I think. Can't remember now."

He was talking about a detail in the background of the Pisanello *St. George and the Princess* and an echo in one of the most somber of the Coëtminais series, untitled, but *Desolation* would have done; a wood of hanged figures and of living ones who seemed as if they wished they were hanged.

"Fox escapes me."

"*Book of Martyrs*. Woodcuts. Old copy at home. Terrified me. Aged six, seven. Far worse than the real thing. Spain."

David risked a further step.

"Why are you so reluctant to reveal sources?"

The question visibly pleased the old man; as if David had fallen into a trap.

"My dear boy. Painted to paint. All my life. Not to give clever young buggers like you a chance to show off. Like shitting, yes? You ask why you do it. How you do it. You die of blocked arsehole. Don't care a fart in hell where my ideas come from. Never have. Let it happen. That's all. Couldn't even tell you how it starts. What half it means. Don't want to know." He nodded back at the Braque. "Old George had a phrase. *Trop de racine*. Yes? Too much root. Origin. Past. Not the flower. The now. Thing on the wall. *Faut couper la racine*. Cut the root off. He used to say that."

"Painters shouldn't be intellectuals?"

The old man smiled.

"Bastards. Never knew a good one who wasn't. Old Pickbum. Appalling fellow. Flashing his gnashers at you. Sooner trust a man-eating shark."

"But he was reasonably articulate about what he was doing?"

The old man puffed in violent disagreement. "Eyewash. My dear boy. *Fumisterie*. All the way." He added, "Very fast worker. Overproduced all his life. Had to cod people."

"*Guernica*?"

"Good gravestone. Lets all the scum who didn't care a damn at the time show off their fine feelings."

There was a flash of bitterness; a tiny red light suddenly; something still raw. David knew they were back with abstraction and realism and the old man's own record of Spain. The grudge against Picasso was explained. But Breasley himself drew back from that brink.

"*Si jeunesse savait* . . . know that?"

"Of course."

"That's all. Just paint. That's my advice. Leave the clever talk to the poor sods who can't."

David had smiled and looked down. Some time later he

had stood to go, but the old man stopped him before he could move away.

"Glad you've hit it off with the gels, David. Wanted to say. Gives 'em a break."

"They're a nice pair of kids."

"Seem happy, do they?"

"I've had no complaints."

"Not much to offer now. Bit of pocket money." He sought confirmation on something. "Never much good at wages. That sort of thing."

"I'm quite sure they're not here for that."

"Something regular. Might be better, don't you think?"

"Why don't you ask the Mouse?"

The old man was staring out of the window. "Very sensitive gel. Money."

"Would you like me to sound them out?"

Breasley raised a hand. "No, no, my dear fellow. Just your advice. Man to man, don't you know." Then he suddenly looked up at David. "Know why I call her the Mouse?"

"I did rather wonder."

"Not the animal."

The old man hesitated, then reached and took a sheet of notepaper from a drawer beside him. Standing at his shoulder, David watched him address himself to the paper as if to some formal document; but all he did was to print in pencil the letter M and then, after a space, the letters U, S, E. In the space between the M and the U the wrinkled hand drew, in five or six quick strokes, an O-shaped vulva. Then Breasley glanced dryly back up at David; a wink, the tip of his tongue slipped out like a lizard's. Almost before David had grasped the double meaning the piece of paper was crumpled up.

"Mustn't tell her."

"Of course not."

"Dread losing her. Try to hide it."

"I think she understands that."

The old man nodded, then gave a little shrug, as if age and fate must win in the end; and there was no more to be said.

All of which David had meditated on, as he lay in his bath soon afterward: how the relationship worked because of its distances, its incomprehensions, the reticences behind its façade of frankness . . . as a contemporary arrangement, a *ménage à trois* of beautiful young uninhibited people, it would very probably fail. There would be jealousies, preferences, rifts in the lute . . . and its being so locked away, islanded, out of David's own real and daily world, Blackheath and the rush-hour traffic, parties, friends, exhibitions, the kids, Saturday shopping, parents . . . London, getting and spending. How desperately one could long for . . . for this, suitably translated. Beth and he must definitely attempt it; perhaps Wales, or the West Country, which couldn't be all St. Ives, a cloud of postures around two or three serious names.

The poor sods who can't. Yes.

What he would finally remember about the old man was his wildness, in the natural history sense. The surface wildness, in language and behavior, was ultimately misleading — like the aggressive display of some animals, its deeper motive was really peace and space, territory, not a gratuitous show of virility. The grotesque faces the old fellow displayed were simply to allow his real self to run free. He did not really live at the *manoir*; but in the forest outside. All his life he must have had this craving for a place to hide; a profound shyness, a timidity; and forced himself to behave in an exactly contrary fashion. It would have driven him out of England in the beginning; but once in France he would have used his Englishness — for it was remarkable, when one thought, how much of a native persona he had retained through his long exile — to hide from whatever in French culture threatened to encroach. The fundamental Englishness of the Coëtminais series was already argued in a paragraph of the draft introduction, but David made a mental resolution to expand and strengthen it.

It began to seem almost the essential clue; the wild old outlaw, hiding behind the flamboyant screen of his outrageous behavior and his cosmopolitan influences, was perhaps as simply and inalienably native as Robin Hood.

The distance aspect of the relationship was in fact predominant during that dinner. Though he had had his whisky before, Henry drank only two glasses of wine with it, and even then cut heavily with water. He seemed tired, withdrawn, in a state of delayed hangover. Every year of his age showed, and David felt that the two girls and himself were in collusion, almost, to emphasize the abyss. The Freak was in a talkative mood, telling David about the agonies of her teacher training course in her own brand of slang and elliptic English. The old man watched her as if slightly puzzled by this sudden vivacity . . . and out of his depth. Half the time he was not very sure what she was getting at: micro-teaching, systems art, psychotherapy, they came from another planet. David could guess the enigma, to one who still lived the titanic battlefield of early twentieth-century art, of all this reduction of passionate theory and revolutionary practice to a technique of mass education, an "activity" you fitted in between English and maths. *Les Demoiselles d'Avignon*, and a billion tins of poster paint.

They had coffee, and the old man was now very nearly silent. The Mouse urged him to bed.

"Nonsense. Like to hear you young things talk."

She said gently, "Stop pretending. You're very tired."

He grumbled on a bit, sought male support from David, and received none. In the end the Mouse took him upstairs. As soon as they had disappeared, the Freak moved into the old man's chair at the head of the table. She poured David more coffee. She was less exotically dressed that evening — a black Kate Greenaway dress sprigged with little pink and green flowers. Its cottage simplicity somehow suited her better; or better what David had begun to like in her.

She said, "We'll go upstairs when Di comes back. You ought to seek her work."

"I'd like to."

"She's silly about it. Shy."

He stirred his coffee. "What happened to her boyfriend?"

"Tom?" She shrugged. "Oh, the usual. He couldn't take it, really. When she got accepted by the Royal College. He was the one who was supposed to get in."

"That happens."

"He was one of those boys who thinks he knows it all. Public school and all that. I couldn't stand him, personally. He was always so bloody sure of himself. Only Di could never see it."

"She took it badly?"

She nodded. "What I was saying. She's so innocent. In some ways." There was a little pause, then she stopped fiddling with her coffee spoon and surveyed him in the lamplight: her frankest eyes.

"Can I tell you a great secret, David?"

He smiled. "Of course."

"What I was trying to say this afternoon." She looked down the room to the stairs, then back to him, and lowered her voice. "He wants her to marry him."

"Oh God."

"It's so bloody daft, I . . ."

"You don't mean she's . . ."

She shook her head. "But you don't know her. So many ways she's much brighter than I am, but honestly she makes some daft decisions. I mean this whole scene." She grinned without humor. "Two smashing girls like us. We must be out of our tiny minds." She said, "We don't even joke about it anymore. Okay, with you this afternoon. But that's the first time in weeks."

"She's said no?"

"She says. But she's still here, isn't she? I mean, it's like she's got a father fixation or something." She sought his eyes again. "She's such a smashing girl, David. Honestly, you've no idea. My Mum and Dad, they're Jehovah's Witnesses. Absolutely barmy. I've had such fucking awful problems at home. I mean, I haven't *got* a home. I couldn't have survived without Di. Even this last year. Being able to write to her." She went on before he could speak. "And she's so inconsistent." She waved around the room. "She even turns all this into a reason for not marrying him. Crazy. Screw your whole life. Just as long as you don't get anything out of it."

"She's not going to meet anyone of her own age here."

"What I mean." She sprawled on an elbow, facing David across the table. They were still talking in low voices. "She won't even look at what there is. Frinstance last week we went into Rennes to do some shopping. A couple of French boys picked us up. In a café. Students. You know, it was all a gas. Fun. They were all right. So they chat us up. Di says we're staying on our *vacances* with a friend of her family's." She grimaced. "Then they want to drive out one day and see us." The fingers combed up through her hair. "Fantastic. You wouldn't believe it. Di's suddenly like a bloody security officer or something. The way she gave those boys the chop. Then straight back home and off with her clothes because old Henry's been lonely and wants a feel." She said, "And I mean *that*. You know, what . . . it's not the physical thing. He can hardly do it anymore, it's just . . . you know, David, sex, honest to God, I've seen it all. Much sicker scenes than this. But it's not the same with Di. She's just had that one twit at Leeds. For serious. That's why I'm so bad for her. She thinks it's either like it is with Henry or the way I used to go on. She just doesn't know what it's about. What it can be about."

"Have you —"

But he was not to learn whether she had thought of leaving

on her own. A door closed quietly upstairs. The Freak sat back in her chair, and David turned to see the subject of their conversation coming down the shadowed stairs. She waved toward them, the pool of light they sat in, then came down the room; slim and cool and composed, belying what had been said. She sat down again opposite David, with a little air of relief.

"He's been good today."

"As you predicted."

She raised crossed fingers. "And what have we been talking about?"

"You."

David added, "Whether you'd let me see your work."

She looked down. "There's so little to see."

"What there is."

"It's mostly drawing. I've done hardly any painting."

The Freak stood. "I'm going to show David. You can stay here if you like."

The two girls eyed each other a moment; a challenge and a reluctance, a ghost of some previous argument in private. But then the reluctant one smiled and stood.

David followed the girls upstairs, then down the corridor past his own room to a door at the east end of the house. It was another large room, there was a bed, but it had more the feel of a sitting-room; a student's room, if the art on the walls had not been original and distinguished, instead of homemade or in reproduction. The Freak went to a record player in one corner, began to sort through a pile of records. The girl beside him said, "Over here."

There was a long worktable, inks, watercolors, a tilted drawing board with a half-finished sketch pinned to it. The table was scrupulously neat, in contrast to the one in the old man's studio . . . very much the way David liked to have his own "bench" at home. The Mouse reached up a portfolio and put it on the table, but kept it closed in front of her for a moment.

"I'd gone completely nonrepresentational by the end of Leeds. I got into the RCA on that. So these are going backward really." She gave him a shy little smile. "What I began to feel I'd missed out."

Technically the drawing was impressive, if rather lacking in individuality. The coolness that was pleasant in her personality became a kind of coldness on paper, something too painstaking and *voulu*. There was rather surprisingly a complete absence of the quick freedom of the old man's line, its firmness and vigor — a comparison David did not have to make from memory, since the drawing that had been mentioned, his tossed-off little parody of the Freak in the Lautrec style, turned up in the portfolio. Its haste showed; and the instinctive mastery of living line. David was complimentary, of course; asked the standard questions, what she was trying to do, where she felt she was getting near it. The Freak now stood at his other side. He had expected pop music; but it was Chopin, turned low, mere background.

They came to a batch of drawings with additional watercolor washes, not representational, but color records that were something of the kind that David used himself. He liked them better, one or two tones, contrasts, the rather tentative workshop feel after the overmeticulous essays in pure draftsmanship. The Mouse went to a cupboard across the room and came back with four canvases.

"I have to keep them hidden from Henry. And I'm sorry if they look like bad David Williamses."

She looked for a place to hang them, then took a pencil drawing off the wall and handed it to David. Gwen John. He belatedly realized who the sitter was: Henry, he must have been about David's present age. Sitting bolt upright, in a wooden chair, a little stagy, self-important in spite of the informality of his clothes: a fierce young modernist of the late twenties. The Mouse tilted an angle lamp to light the place she had chosen. David put the ousted drawing down.

The canvases she showed bore no obvious similarity to his own work, beyond being delicately precise abstracts and on a smaller scale (like his own preferred working-size) than most such pictures in the manner. He very probably would not have noticed an influence if she hadn't mentioned it. But their quality, and this was a field where he was thoroughly at home — its problems, the viability of the solutions, was not something he had to pretend to see.

"Now I know why the College took you."

"One day they work. The next they don't."

"Normal. They work."

The Freak said, "Go on. Tell her they're bloody marvelous."

"I can't do that. I'm too envious."

"She's only asking five hundred each."

"Anne, stop being a fool."

David said, "Let's see that last one beside the sketch."

The sketch had been of a climbing rose against a wall; the painting was a trellis of pinks and grays and creams, a palette of dangers — which had been avoided. He would have been afraid of it himself, the inherent sentiment, the lack of accent. The ruling quarters of his own zodiac were more those of the colors of the clothes the Mouse wore: autumn and winter.

For twenty minutes or more they talked painting: his own work methods, media, a renewed interest he had in lithography, how he "grew" his ideas . . . all in a way he had done often enough when he taught, but had rather lost the habit of. Beth lived too near to him to need explanation, took all that for granted; and anyway, there had never been a similarity of stylistic purpose. He understood both critically and intuitively what this girl was trying to do. It did bear an analogy with his own development; in a more feminine, decorative kind of way — more concerned with textures and correspondences than form — she was abstracting from natural rather than artificial color ranges. She said Henry had influenced her in one way, by claiming that color could be drawn; she had learned a lot by forcing herself to prove that it couldn't.

They sat down, David in an armchair, the two girls opposite on a sofa. He discovered more about them, their home backgrounds, their friendship; Henry and the present were tacitly barred for a while. Again the Freak talked most, she was funny about her hair-raising bigoted parents, her variously rebellious brothers and a younger sister, the hell of a childhood and adolescence in the back streets of Acton. The Mouse was more reserved about her family. She was an only child, it seemed; her father owned and ran a small engineering works at Swindon. Her mother had "artistic" tastes, kept an antique shop as a kind of hobby in Hungerford. They had a smashing house there, the Freak put in. Georgian. Ever so posh. David had an impression of some wealth; of parents too intelligent to be stock provincial; and that she did not want to talk about them.

There came a little silence; and just as David was searching for some not too obvious way of getting them back to the present and future, the Freak was on her feet and standing over his chair.

"I'm going to bed, David. You mustn't. Di's a night bird."

She blew him a kiss, she was gone. She had done it too suddenly, too blatantly, and he was caught off balance. The girl he was left with would not look at him; she too knew it had been stage-managed.

He said, "Are you tired?"

"Not unless you are." There was an awkward moment. She murmured, "Henry gets nightmares. One of us always sleeps in his room."

He relaxed back in his chair.

"How on earth did he survive before you came?"

"His last lady friend left him two years ago. She was Swedish. She betrayed him in some way. Money. I don't know, he never talks about her. Mathilde says money."

"So he managed on his own for a bit?"

She took his point; and answered it with a faint smile.

"He didn't paint very much last year. He really does need help in the studio now."

"And I gather he's going to go on getting it?" It was more a statement than a question, and she looked down.

"Anne's been talking."

"A little. But if . . ."

"No, it's . . ."

She turned and put her bare feet up on the sofa, resting her back against one of its arms. She fiddled with a button on the black shirt. It was wild silk, faintly glossy; around each cuff, and the collar, a delicate edge of gold.

"How much did she say?"

"Just that she was worried."

She was silent a long moment; then spoke in a lower voice.

"About Henry wanting to marry me?"

"Yes."

"Did it shock you?"

He hesitated. "A bit."

"I haven't made up my mind." She shrugged. "I suppose it's just that when one's doing everything a wife would do . . ."

"Is the reverse true?"

"He needs me."

"I didn't quite mean that."

Again she was silent. He sensed that same struggle between wanting to talk and being afraid to that he had noticed after the blackberrying. But now she gave way.

"It's very difficult to explain, David. What's happened. Of course I can't love him physically. And I know perfectly well that at least half his love for me is sheer selfishness. Having his life run for him. But he really doesn't swallow his own myth anymore. The gay old dog thing is strictly for strangers. Deep down he's just a rather lonely and frightened old man. I don't think he'd paint anymore if I left. It would kill him. Perhaps even literally."

"Why are the alternatives marriage or leaving him?"

"They're not. It's just that I feel I can't walk out on him now. So what's it matter. If it makes him happier."

Still she fiddled with the button, her head slightly bent; a faint air of a guilty child. The sophisticated little crown of hair, the bare ankles and feet. She sat with her knees cocked up.

"Anne also said you were worried about seeming to be after his money."

"Not what people might say. What it might do to me." She said, "It's not as if he doesn't know what the collection's worth. The Braque's going to the Maeght when he dies. But even without that. I mean it's ludicrously out of scale. As a reward. But he does know that."

"What might it do to you?"

She smiled wryly. "I want to be a painter. Not a loaded widow." She said softly, "Get thee behind me, Coët."

"The garret theory is out of date."

"No struggle at all?"

"I'm not quite sure which side I'm supposed to be arguing for."

She smiled again, without looking at him.

"I'm only twenty-three years old. It seems rather early to be sure you'll never want to live anywhere else. In any other way."

"But you're tempted?"

She was slow to answer.

"The whole outside world. I don't even want to go into Rennes anymore. All those cars. People. Things happening. My parents, I've simply got to go home and see them. I keep putting it off. It's absurd. As if I'm under a spell. I even dreaded your coming. I really did love your show. Yet I made up my mind I wouldn't like you. Just because you come from out there and I thought you'd upset me and . . . you know."

She had left one of her own paintings on the wall behind

the sofa. He knew it was not out of vanity. What last remaining doubts he had had about Anne's judgment were gone; the cool self-confidence of that first evening had been a pose, like the indifference of their first encounter. But the painting hung there as a kind of reminder of an identity between them; which grew. The silences no longer mattered.

"Your parents know what's happening?"

"Not the whole . . . but they're not like Anne's. I could make them understand." She shrugged. "It's not that. Just the thought of leaving my little forest womb. Somehow here, everything remains possible. I'm just scared of making a decision. Either way." There was a tiny pattering sound, a moth banging against the lampshade behind the sofa. She glanced at it, then back at her lap. "And then I wonder whether there's any connection between becoming a decent painter and . . . being normal."

"You're not going to paint any better by forcing yourself to be abnormal."

"Doing what everyone expects."

"Surely what you ought to do is what you feel you need. And to hell with everyone."

"I don't know how to give up. That's my trouble. I always have to stick things out to the bitter end."

"You gave up the College."

"It was totally against my nature. You've no idea. Trying to prove I wasn't what I am. And anyway, it was only out of the frying pan. I'm even worse now than I was before."

She had subsided a little, her knees still up. The one light in the room was on the floor behind her. David's eyes hardly moved now from the shadowed profile of her face. There was a deep nocturnal silence, both inside the house and out; as if they were alone in it, and in the world. He felt he had traveled much farther than he expected, into the haunted and unpredicted; and yet in some strange way it seemed always immanent. It had had to come, it had had causes, too small, too manifold to have been detected in the past or to be analyzed now.

"This . . . affair you had ended badly?"

"Yes."

"His fault?"

"Not really. I expected too much. He was jealous about my getting into the College."

"Yes, Anne told me."

There was another little silence.

He said, "I'm not being very helpful."

"Yes you are."

"Platitudes."

"No."

And more silence, as if they were quite literally in the forest; the way hidden birds sing, spasmodically, secretly shifting position between utterances.

She said, "Anne's got this marvelous ability to give herself. To keep hoping. One day someone nice will realize what she is. Behind all the nonsense."

"What would happen if she left you here on your own?"

"That's something I try not to think about."

"Why?"

Again she was slow to answer.

"I feel she's my last hold on . . . the real world?" She added, "I know I'm using her. Her affection. A kind of messiness in her. The eternal student." She smoothed a hand along the back of the sofa. "Sometimes I wonder if I'm not bent or something."

She had touched on what had also touched David's mind once or twice during that day. He guessed that dubbing herself the freak of the two hid a truth. The physical side of her life with Henry must be deeply against the grain of her "innocent" self. She was in that sense much more perverse than Anne. Yet the real repression must be of a normal sexuality, a femaleness that cried out for . . .

He said gently, "Not a hope. If I'm a judge."

"I'm not serious. We've even discussed it. We . . ." but she didn't finish.

"It seems to me that this remarkable honesty you have about yourself is a kind of danger. You know. There's something to be said for instinct."

"I don't have much faith in my instincts."

"Why not?"

"Being an only child. Having no comparisons to go by. You can get your own age group so wrong. I had it with Anne in the beginning. We lived in the same house, but for months I didn't like her, I thought she was just a little tramp. Then one day I went to her room to borrow something. And she was crying — her sister, some upset at home. We began to talk. She told me all about herself. And we never looked back." She said nothing for a moment. "The same thing happened with Tom, in reverse. I started feeling sorry for him. He was terribly insecure underneath. So one moment you're turning up your nose at a heart of gold, the next you're giving body and soul to someone who's not worth it." She said, "I did try. After Tom. At the College. With another first-year boy. He was nice, but . . . it was just bed. Feeling lonely."

"Perhaps you expect too much."

"Someone who can see what I am?"

"That's rather difficult. If you're hidden away."

She shook her head. "Perhaps I don't want it to happen. I don't know anymore."

There was another silence. She stared at her skirt. He watched her present metaphorical nakedness, and thought of the previous literal one; and knew that words were swiftly becoming unnecessary; were becoming, however frank or sympathetic, not what the situation asked. The moth battered minutely again at the lampshade. There were others loosely constellated on the glass outside the window over her worktable, pale fawn specks of delicate, foolish organism yearning for the impossible. Psyches. The cruelty of glass: as transparent as air, as divisive as steel. She spoke again.

"I've got so frightened by strangers. It's ridiculous, the other day Anne and I were picked up by two law students in Rennes — did she tell you?"

She looked across at him then; and he shook his head.

"I was panic-stricken that they'd find out about Coët. Want to come here. As if I was a virgin or something. A nun. It's the effort of getting to know people. All the crossed wires. Or the ones I seem to produce."

He could have smiled then: the statement denied itself. Perhaps she sensed it.

She murmured, "Present company excepted."

He said softly, "Not that rare a species."

She nodded, once, but said nothing. She seemed almost frozen now on the sofa, hypnotized by her hands, by the need not to look at him.

"I wanted to meet you. Last November. After the show. To come and talk about my work."

He leaned forward. "Why on earth . . . it would have been so easy to fix." They had discovered that afternoon that David knew her tutor at the Royal College.

She gave a faint smile. "For the same reasons I wait till now to tell you?" She added, "And my one previous experience of inviting myself unwanted into a successful painter's life."

He had a sudden perception of the strange hazardousness of existence; of how little, a word from her, a raised 'phone, it would have taken for such a meeting to have been. Then what, he wondered; the same chemistry, in London? He didn't know; only that the now seemed more pregnant, more isolated, and somehow more inevitable. And he guessed, he began to know her so well, why the word had not been spoken: less a shyness than a kind of pride. There had been a photograph of him in the catalogue, a mention that he was married and had children. Perhaps that as well; already a flight from potential crossed wires. One way of not experiencing them was never to use the instrument.

"Do you wish you had?"

"It's too late for wishing."

Again neither of them spoke. Then she bent forward and touched her forehead against her knees. For a few moments he had both a fear and a wanting that she was about to cry. But with a sudden change of mood, or reaction to whatever she was thinking, she put her feet down off the couch and stood. He watched her walk to the worktable. She stared down at her portfolio a second, then looked up through the window at the night.

"I'm sorry. You didn't come here for all this."

"I wish desperately that I could help."

She began to tie up the portfolio. "You have. More than you know."

"It doesn't feel like it."

She said nothing for a moment or two.

"What do you think I should do?"

He hesitated, then smiled. "Find someone like me? Who isn't married? If that doesn't sound too impossibly vain."

She tied a final bow in the tags of black ribbon.

"And Henry?"

"Not even a Rembrandt has the right to ruin someone else's life."

"I'm not sure it isn't ruined already."

"That's self-pity. Not the real you."

"Cowardice."

"Also not the real you." He watched her staring out into the night again. "I know he dreads losing you. He told me. Before dinner. But he's lost women all his life. I think he's more inured to it than you imagine." He added, "And perhaps we could do something to make it easy. At least find him help in the studio."

He felt a traitor, then; but in a good cause. She lifted the portfolio and slipped it down beside the table, then shifted a wooden chair back to its center. But she remained with her hands on its back, turned away.

"It wouldn't be vain, David. But where do I find him?"

"You know the answer to that."

"I rather doubt if the College would take me back."

"I could very easily find out. When I return."

She moved and came behind the sofa, looking down across it at him.

"Can I get in touch? If I . . . ?"

"Henry has my address. Any time. Very seriously."

She dropped her eyes. He knew he ought to stand, the tying-up of the portfolio had been a hint that the evening was at an end, it was late, she hadn't sat down again. Yet he was aware that she did not want him to go and that he did not want to go himself; that more than ever now, behind all the honesty and the advice, tutor and student, a truth remained unsaid. A pretense, the undeclared knowledge of a shared imagination, hung in the air; in her half-hidden figure against the light on the floor behind, in the silence, the bed in the corner, the thousand ghosts of old rooms. One was stunned, perhaps; that knowledge could come so quickly . . . as if it was in the place, not oneself. How impatient it was of barriers and obstacles, how it melted truth and desire of all their conventional coats; one desired truth, one truthed desire, one read minds, jumped bridges, wanted so sharply, both physically and psychologically. And the closeness of tomorrow, the end of this, was intolerable. One had to cling to it, even though one felt embarrased, that some obscure loss of face was involved, the Dutch uncle being swiftly proved the emperor with no clothes.

He murmured, "It's time I went."

She smiled up at him; much more normally, as if he had been supposing things.

"I've taken to walking in the garden. Like Maud. Before I go to sleep."

"Is that an invitation?"

"I promise not to talk about myself anymore."

The secret tension broke. She went across the room to a painted tallboy and took out a cardigan, then returned, pulling on the sleeves, freeing a strand of hair from the back; smiling, almost brisk.

"Are your shoes all right? The dew's so heavy now."

"Not to worry."

They went silently downstairs and to the garden door. They couldn't go out the front, Macmillan made such a racket. He waited while she slipped on some wellingtons, then they left the house. There was a rising moon above the long roof, slightly gibbous in the haze, faint stars, one bright planet. One lighted window, the lamp in the corridor outside Henry's room. They strolled over the grass and then through the courtyard past the studio. A gate on its far side led to another small orchard. There was a kind of central walk between the trees, kept mown; in the background, the black wall of the forest. The dew was heavy and pearled. But it was warm, very still, a last summer night. The ghostly apple trees, drained of color; a cheeping of crickets. David glanced secretly at the girl beside him; the way she watched the ground as she walked, was so silent now, strict to her promise. But he had not imagined. It was here, now, the unsaid. He knew it in every nerve and premonitory fiber. His move: he drew back into speech.

"I feel as if I've been here for a month."

"Part of the spell."

"You think?"

"All those legends. I don't laugh at them anymore."

They spoke almost in whispers; like thieves; the ears of the invisible dog. He wanted to reach out and take her hand.

The last effort to distance. "He will turn up. The knight errant."

"For two days. Then leave."

It was said. And they walked on, as if it had not been said, for at least another five seconds.

"Diana, I daren't answer that."

"I didn't expect you to."

He had his hands in his coat pockets, forced forward.

"If one only had two existences."

She murmured, "Glimpses." Then, "It's just Coët."

"Where everything is not possible." He added, "Alas."

"I imagined so much about you. When I knew you were coming. Everything except not wanting you to leave."

"It's the same for me."

"If only you hadn't come alone."

"Yes."

Once more he had that uncanny sense of melted time and normal process; of an impulsion that was indeed spell-like and legendary. One kept finding oneself ahead of where one was; where one should have been.

And he thought of Beth, probably in bed by now in Blackheath, in another world, asleep; of his absolute certainty that there could not be another man beside her. His real fear was of losing that certainty. Childish: if he was unfaithful, then she could be. No logic. They didn't deny themselves the sole enjoyment of any other pleasure: a good meal, buying clothes, a visit to an exhibition. They were not even against sexual liberation in other people, in some of their friends; if they were against anything, it was having a general opinion on such matters, judging them morally. Fidelity was a matter of taste and theirs happened simply to conform to it; like certain habits over eating or shared views on curtain fabrics. What one happened to like to live on and with. So why make an exception of this? Why deny experience, his artistic soul's sake, why ignore the burden of the old man's entire life? Take what you can. And so little: a warmth, a clinging, a brief entry into another body. One small releasing act. And the terror of it, the enormity of destroying what one had so carefully built.

They stopped before another gate at the far end of the orchard. Beyond there was a dim ride through the forest.

She said, "It's my fault. I . . ."

"You?"

"Fairy tales. About sleeping princesses."

"They could live together. Afterward."

But he thought: would any decent prince have refused, just because they couldn't? When she waited, she said nothing — or everything. No strings now. If you want.

He had meant it to be very brief. But once he found her mouth and felt her body, her arms come around him, it had no hope of being brief. It very soon lost all hope of being anything but erotic. He was wanted physically, as well as emotionally; and he wanted desperately in both ways himself. They leaned back against the gate, her body was crushed against his. He felt the pressure of her hips, her tongue and all it offered in imitation, and did not resist. She was the one who brought it to an end, pulling her mouth abruptly away and turning her head against his neck. Their bodies stayed clung together. He kissed the top of her head. They stood there like that, in silence, for perhaps a minute. Once or twice he patted her back gently; and stared into the night and the trees; saw himself standing there, someone else, in another life. In the end she pulled gently away and turned against the gate, her back to him, with bowed head. He put an arm around her shoulders and moved her a little toward him, then kissed her hair again.

"I'm sorry."

"I wanted you to."

"Not just that. Everything."

She said, "It's all a lie, isn't it? It does exist."

"Yes."

There was a silence.

"All the time we were talking I was thinking, if he wants to go to bed with me I'll say yes and it'll solve everything. I'll know. It was all going to be so simple."

"If only it could be."

"So many if only's." He contracted his arm, held her a little closer. "It's so ironic. You read about Tristan and Yseult. Lying in the forest with a sword between them. Those dotty old medieval people. All that nonsense about chastity. And then . . ."

She pulled away and stood by the gatepost, four or five feet from him.

"Please don't cry."

"It's all right, David. Just let me be a second." She said, "And please don't say anything. I understand."

He searched for words, but found none; or none that explained him. Once again he felt hurtled forward — beyond the sex, the fancying, to where — her word — one glimpsed . . . and against that there rose a confrontation he had once analyzed, the focus of that same Pisanello masterpiece, not the greatest but perhaps the most haunting and mysterious in all European art, that had come casually up with the old man earlier that evening: the extraordinary averted and lost eyes of the patron saint of chivalry, the implacably resentful stare of the sacrificial and to-be-saved princess of Trebizond. She had Beth's face now. He read meanings he had never seen before.

The slight figure of the girl cast as dragon turned, a small smile on her face. She held out a hand.

"Shall we pretend this never happened?"

He took the hand and they began to walk back toward the house.

He murmured, "I could say so much."

"I know."

She pressed his hand: but please don't. After a step or two their fingers interlaced and squeezed; and did not relax, as if they were being pulled apart, must not be severed; and also as if hands knew what fools these mortals, or at least mortal intentions and mortal words, were. He saw her naked again, all the angles and curves of her body on the grass; he felt her mouth, the surrender in it. The trap of marriage, when the physical has turned to affection, familiar postures, familiar games, a safe mutual art and science; one had forgotten the desperate ignorance, the wild desire to know. To give. To be given to.

He had to let go of her hand to open and close the gate from the orchard into the courtyard. The catch made a little metallic sound, and Macmillan began to bark from somewhere in front of the house. He took her hand again. They silently passed the studio, he saw through the north window the long black shadow of the incomplete *Kermesse* canvas sleeping on its stand. The garden, the neurotically suspicious dog still barking. They came to the house, still without having said a word, and went in. She let go of his hand, bent and took off her wellingtons. A faint light reached back to them from the lamp in the corridor upstairs. She straightened and he sought her eyes in the shadows.

He said, "It can't solve anything. But please let me take you to bed."

She stared at him a long moment, then looked down and shook her head.

"Why not?"

"Knights errant mustn't lose their armor."

"With all its phony shine?"

"I didn't say that."

"As exorcism."

"I don't want it exorcised."

He had only made explicit what had seemed implicit outside, on the way back; that tense interlacing of the fingers, that silence. Bodies mean more than words; now, more than all tomorrows.

He said, "You know it's not just . . ."

"That's also why."

Still he sought for loopholes; reasons.

"Because I hung back?"

She shook her head, then looked into his eyes. "I shan't ever forget you. These two days."

She took a sudden step and caught his arms to prevent them reaching up toward her. He felt the quick press of her mouth against his, then she was walking toward the stairs. She turned to climb them, hesitated a fraction as she saw he was following, went on up. Past the door to Henry's room, then along the corridor. She did not look around, but she must have heard him close behind. She stopped with her back to him, outside his bedroom door.

"Just let me hold you for a little."

"It would only make it worse."

"But if an hour ago you . . ."

"That was with someone else. And I was someone else."

"Perhaps they were right."

She looked down the corridor at her own door.

"Where will you be this time tomorrow, David?"

"I still want to go to bed with you."

"Out of charity."

"Wanting you."

"Fuck and forget?"

He left a hurt silence. "Why the brutality?"

"Because we're not brutes."

"Then it wouldn't be like that."

"But worse. We wouldn't forget."

He moved behind her and put his hands on her shoulders.

"Look, the crossed wires are mainly words. I just want to undress you and . . ."

For one fleeting moment he thought he had found the answer. Something in her was still undecided. The maddening closeness, the silent complicity of everything around them —

a few steps, a frantic tearing-off of clothes in the darkness, a sinking, knowing, possessing, release.

Without turning she reached up and caught his right hand on her shoulder in the briefest convulsive grip. Then she was walking away. He whispered her name in a kind of incredulous despair. But she did not stop; and he felt frozen, fatally unable to move. He watched her go into her room, the door close; and he was left with all the agonized and agonizing deflation of a man who has come to a momentous decision, only to have it cursorily dismissed. He turned into his room and stood in its blackness in a rage of last chance; made out his faint shape there in the old gilt-framed mirror. A ghost, a no-man. The horror was that he was still being plunged forward, still melting, still realizing; as there are rare psychic phenomena read of, imagined, yet missed when they finally happen. To one part of him — already desperate to diminish, to devalue — it was merely a perverse refusal; and to another, an acute and overwhelming sense of loss, of being cleft, struck down, endlessly deprived . . . and deceived. He wanted with all his being — now it was too late; was seared unendurably by something that did not exist, racked by an emotion as extinct as the dodo. Even as he stood there he knew it was a far more than sexual experience, but a fragment of one that reversed all logic, process, that struck new suns, new evolutions, new universes out of nothingness. It was metaphysical: something far beyond the girl; an anguish, a being bereft of a freedom whose true nature he had only just seen.

For the first time in his life he knew more than the fact of being; but the passion to exist.

Meanwhile, in the here and now, he felt a violent desire to punish — himself, the girl so close, Beth far away in the London night. That word she had used . . . he saw her sitting on the sofa, her bowed head by the gate, her almost still-present face in the shadows downstairs . . . intolerable, intolerable, intolerable.

He went back out in the corridor and looked down toward Henry's room; then walked to the door at the other end. He did not knock. But neither did the door open. He tried the handle again, stood a few seconds. Then he did tap. There was no reply.

He was awakened by his own and unlocked door opening. It was a quarter past eight. The Freak came across to his bed with a glass of orange juice and handed it to him as he sat up. For a moment he had forgotten; and then he remembered.

"Your early call. Monsewer."

"Thanks."

He took a mouthful of the orange juice. She was wearing a polo-neck jumper, a knee-length skirt, which gave her an unwonted practical look. She stared down at him a moment, then without warning turned and sat on the end of his bed. She read from a sheet of message-pad paper in her hand.

" 'Tell Henry I've gone shopping. Back after lunch.' "

She looked up at the wall by the door, studiously avoiding David's eyes; and studiously waiting for his explanation.

"She's gone out?"

"Well it looks like it, doesn't it?" He said nothing; she waited. "So what happened?"

He hesitated. "We had a sort of misunderstanding."

"Okay. So what about?"

"I'd rather she told you."

She was apparently not to be put off by a mere curt tone of voice. She took a breath.

"You talked?" He said nothing. "I'd just like to know why she's gone off like this."

"Obviously. She doesn't want to see me."

"Well *why*, for Christ's sake?" She threw him a sharp little stare of accusation. "All yesterday. I'm not blind." She looked away. "Di doesn't talk with strangers. Has to be something fantastic to break that block."

"I haven't not realized that."

"But you just talked." She gave him another stab of a look. "Honest to God, I think you're so mean. You know it's not the sex. Just she needs a nice bloke. Just one. To tell her she's okay, she's normal, she turns men on."

"I think she knows that."

"Then why's she gone out?"

"Because there's nothing more to say."

"And you couldn't forget your bloody principles for just one night."

He spoke to the glass in his hand. "You've got it all rather wrong."

She stared at him, then struck her forehead. "Oh Christ. No. She didn't . . . ?"

He murmured, "Wouldn't."

She leaned forward, holding her mop of red hair.

"I give up."

"Well you mustn't. She needs you. More than ever at the moment."

After a second she leaned back and glanced at him with a wry grin, then touched his foot under the bedclothes.

"Sorry. I ought to have guessed."

She got off the bed and went to the window; opened the shutters, then remained there staring down at something outside. She spoke without turning.

"Old Henry?"

"Just the way we are." He felt embarrassed, in all senses undressed; and at the same time knew a need to be more naked still.

"I didn't imagine it, then?"

He was leaning on an elbow, staring down at the bedclothes.

"I didn't think things like this could happen."

"It's this place. You think, fantastic. When you first come. Then you realize it's the original bad trip."

There was a silence. She said, "Christ, it's such a bloody

mess, isn't it?" She looked up into the blue morning sky outside. "That sadistic old shit up there. You know, you sort of
seemed to fit. Really need each other." She gave him a fierce
little look back across the room. "You should have made it,
David. Just once. Just to spite the old bastard. Just for me."

"We lack your guts, Anne. That's all, really."

"Oh sure. My famous loose knickers."

He said gently, "Balls."

She returned beside the foot of the bed, watching him.

"Didn't like me when you came, did you?"

"That's just a fading memory now."

She examined the smile and his eyes for authenticity; then
abruptly bit her lips and twitched up a side of her jumper.
There was a flash of bare brown waist above the skirt.

"How about me instead? Time for a quickie?"

He grinned. "You're impossible."

She cocked a knee onto the end of the bed, crossed her arms
as if to tear off her jumper, leaned toward him; only the eyes
teased.

"I know all sorts of tricks."

He held out the empty glass.

"I'll try to imagine them. While I'm shaving."

She clasped her hands over her heart and threw her eyes up.
Then she moved and took the glass. She stood over him a
moment.

"I think old Di's crazy." She reached out a finger and dabbed
his nose. "You're almost dishy. For a born square."

And there was a second Parthian shot. Her head poked back
around the door.

"Oh, and I couldn't help noticing. Quite well hung, too."

Her kindness, frankness; God bless the poor in taste. But
that little touch of warmth and affection faded so fast, almost
before her footsteps died away. David lay back in his bed,
staring at the ceiling, trying to understand what had happened, where he had gone wrong, why she had condemned

him to this. He felt drowned in disillusion, intolerably depressed and shaken. The unendurable day ahead. Her body,
her face, her psyche, her calling: she was out there somewhere
in the trees, waiting for him. It was impossible, but he had
fallen in love; if not with her wholly, at least wholly with the
idea of love. If she had stood in the door that moment, begged
him not to leave, to take her away . . . he didn't know. Perhaps
if they had gone to bed together, if he had just had her naked
through the brief night, the sense of failure, of eternally missed
chance, would have been less brutal.

But he knew even that was an illusion. A final separation
then would have been impossible. Even if he had gone away to
Paris, as he must now; perhaps from anywhere else he could
have gone away for good, but here . . . they would have had to
meet again. Somehow, somewhere.

He had escaped that. But it felt like a sentence, not a pardon.

By midday, when he had driven a third or so of the two
hundred and fifty miles to Paris, he had still not recovered.
All but the automaton who drove down the endless miles of
route nationale remained at Coët. The old man had continued
at his most affable over breakfast, David really must come
again and bring his wife, must forgive him his faults, his age,
his "maundering on" . . . he was even wished well in his own
painting; but that did not compensate for the bitter knowledge
that the token acceptance of the invitation was a farce. He
was banned for life now, he could never bring Beth here.
They shook hands as he stood by the car. He kissed Anne on
both cheeks, and managed to whisper a last message.

"Tell her . . . what we said?" She nodded. "And kiss her
for me."

The ghost of a dry grimace. "Hey, we're not *that* desperate." But her brown eyes belied the flipness; and it was
the last time he had felt like smiling.

The journey had begun badly: not three hundred yards

after he had closed the gate on the private road to Coët, something orange-brown, a mouse, but too big for a mouse, and oddly sinuous, almost like a snake, but too small for a snake, ran across the road just in front of his car. It seemed to disappear under the wheels. David slowed and glanced back; and saw a minute blemish on the dark tarmac of the deserted forest lane. Something, a faint curiosity, a masochism, a not wanting to leave, any excuse, made him stop and walk back. It was a weasel. One of his wheels must have run straight over it. It was dead, crushed. Only the head had escaped. A tiny malevolent eye still stared up, and a trickle of blood, like a red flower, had spilt from the gaping mouth. He stared down at it for a moment, then turned and went back to the car. The key of the day had been set.

All along the road to Rennes he looked for a figure by a parked white Renault. He did not completely lose hope until he got on the *autoroute* that bypassed the city to the south. Then he knew the agony of never seeing her again. It seemed almost immediately like a punishment. Her disappearance that morning proved it: he had the blame. His crime had been realizing too late; at the orchard gate, when she had broken away; and he had let her, fatal indecision. Even back in the house, something in him, as she had known, had asked not to be taken at his word. He had failed both in the contemporary and the medieval sense; as someone who wanted sex, as someone who renounced it.

His mind slid away to imaginary scenarios. Beth's plane would crash. He had never married. He had, but Diana had been Beth. She married Henry, who promptly died. She appeared in London, she could not live without him, he left Beth. In all these fantasies they ended at Coët, in a total harmony of work and love and moonlit orchard.

Futile, they would have disgraced an adolescent; and they compounded his bleakness, for it was also a kind of shock, though the reality of those first few minutes after she had left him had already sunk into his unconsciousness, that this could happen to him, could disturb and upset him so deeply; and what it said of a past complacency. It defined so well what he lacked. His inadequacy was that he did not believe in sin. Henry knew sin was a challenge to life; not an unreason, but an act of courage and imagination. He sinned out of need and instinct; David did not, out of fear. What Anne had said: just to spite the old bastard. He was obsessed with means, not ends; with what people thought of him, not what he thought of himself. His terror of vanity, selfishness, the Id, which he had to conceal under qualities he called "honesty" and "fairmindedness" . . . that was why he secretly so enjoyed reviewing, the activity pandered to that side of him. The ultimate vanity (and folly, in an artist) was not to seem vain. That explained the high value he put in his own painting on understatement, technical decency, fitting the demands of his own critical-verbal vocabulary — the absurd way he always reviewed his own work in his imagination as he painted it. It all added up to the same thing: a fear of challenge.

And that was precisely what had happened to him: a challenge, and well beyond the moral and sexual. It had been like a trap, he saw this now as well. One sailed past that preposterously obvious reef represented by the first evening with the old man, and one's self-blindness, priggishness, so-called urbanity, love of being liked, did the rest. The real rock of truth had lain well past the blue lagoon.

The farther he drove, the less inclined he felt to excuse himself. There was a kind of superficial relief at being able to face Beth more or less openly — but even that seemed a consolation prize awarded the wrong man. He had finally stayed faithful by benefit of a turned key. And even that, the being technically innocent, that it should still mean something to him, betrayed his real crime: to dodge, escape, avert.

Coët had been a mirror, and the existence he was returning to sat mercilessly reflected and dissected in its surface . . . and how shabby it now looked, how insipid and anodyne, how safe. Riskless, that was the essence of it: was why, for instance, he was driving much faster than usual. Between the towns the roads were comparatively empty, he was making ample time, the wretched plane didn't land till after seven. One killed all risk, one refused all challenge, and so one became an artificial man. The old man's secret, not letting anything stand between self and expression; which wasn't a question of outward artistic aims, mere styles and techniques and themes. But how you did it; how wholly, how bravely you faced up to the constant recasting of yourself.

Slowly and inexorably it came to David that his failure that previous night was merely the symbol, not the crux of the matter. He remembered the old man's crude and outlandish pun on the word Mouse; if one wanted signs as to the real nature of the rejection. Bungling the adventure of the body was trivial, part of the sexual comedy. But he had never really had, or even attempted to give himself, the far greater existential chance. He had had doubts about his work before; but not about his own fundamental nature, or at any rate that there was not in it the potential wherewithal to lay the ghost that profoundly haunts every artist: his lastingness. He had a dreadful vision of being in a dead end, born into a period of art history future ages would dismiss as a desert; as Constable and Turner and the Norwich School had degenerated into the barren academicism of the midcentury and later. Art had always gone in waves. Who knew if the late twentieth century might not be one of its most cavernous troughs? He knew the old man's answer: it was. Or it was unless you fought bloody tooth and fucking nail against some of its most cherished values and supposed victories.

Perhaps abstraction, the very word, gave the game away. You did not want how you lived to be reflected in your painting; or because it was so compromised, so settled-for-the-safe, you could only try to camouflage its hollow reality under

craftsmanship and good taste. Geometry. Safety hid nothingness.

What the old man still had was an umbilical cord to the
past; a step back, he stood by Pisanello's side. In spirit, anyway. While David was encapsulated in book knowledge, art
as social institution, science, subject, matter for grants and
committee discussion. That was the real kernel of his wildness. David and his generation, and all those to come, could
only look back, through bars, like caged animals, born in
captivity, at the old green freedom. That described exactly the
experience of those last two days: the laboratory monkey
allowed a glimpse of his lost true self. One was misled by the
excess in vogue, the officially blessed indiscipline, the surface
liberties of contemporary art; which all sprang from a profound frustration, a buried but not yet quite extinguished
awareness of nonfreedom. It ran through the whole recent
history of art education in Britain. That notorious diploma
show where the fine arts students had shown nothing but
blank canvases — what truer comment on the stale hypocrisy
of the teaching and the helpless bankruptcy of the taught?
One could not live by one's art, therefore one taught a travesty of its basic principles; pretending that genius, making it,
is arrived at by overnight experiment, histrionics, instead of
endless years of solitary obstinacy; that the production of the
odd instant success, like a white rabbit out of a hat, excuses
the vicious misleading of thousands of innocents; that the
maw of the teaching cesspit, the endless compounding of the
whole charade, does not underpin the entire system. When
schools lie . . .

Perhaps it was happening in the other arts — in writing,
music. David did not know. All he felt was a distress, a nausea
at his own. Castration. The triumph of the eunuch. He saw,
how well he saw behind the clumsiness of the old man's
attack; that sneer at *Guernica*. Turning away from nature and
reality had atrociously distorted the relationship between

painter and audience; now one painted for intellects and theories. Not people; and worst of all, not for oneself. Of course it paid dividends, in economic and vogue terms, but what had really been set up by this jettisoning of the human body and its natural physical perceptions was a vicious spiral, a vortex, a drain to nothingness, to a painter and a critic agreed on only one thing: that only they exist and have value. A good gravestone; for all the scum who didn't care a damn.

One sheltered behind notions of staying "open" to contemporary currents; forgetting the enormously increased velocity of progress and acceptance, how quickly now the avant-garde became *art pompier;* the daring, platitudinous. It was not just his own brand of abstraction that was at fault, but the whole headlong postwar chain, abstract expressionism, neoprimitivism, Op Art and pop art, conceptualism, photorealism . . . *il faut couper la racine,* all right. But such rootlessness, orbiting in frozen outer space, cannot have been meant. They were like lemmings, at the mercy of a suicidal drive, seeking *Lebensraum* in an arctic sea; in a bottomless night, blind to everything but their own illusion.

The ebony tower.

As if to echo his inner gloom, the sky clouded over as he approached the Ile de France and the dull, stubbled plains around Chartres. Summer had died, autumn was. His life was of one year only; an end now to all green growth. Ridiculous, as he told himself at once. And yet the acute depression remained.

He came at last to the outskirts of Paris. The business of finding where he needed distracted him a little from all this soul-searching. Soon after five he booked into a likely looking hotel near Orly. They were giving Paris a miss, the destination in the Ardèche was a friend's cottage, another long day's driving. But they might stop somewhere. He dreaded the tomorrow, either way.

He had a shower and forced himself to reread his draft

introduction to *The Art of Henry Breasley*; while his impressions were still fresh, to see what needed changing, expansion, more emphasis. It was hopeless. Phrases and judgments that only a few days previously had pleased him . . . ashes, botch. The banality, the jargon, the pretense of authority. The reality of Coët rose again behind the tawdry words. He lay back on the hotel bed and closed his eyes. A little later he was on his feet and staring out of the window. For the first time in many years he had felt the sting of imminent tears. Absurd, absurd. He would die if he never saw her again. He searched for writing paper, but there wasn't any in the room, it wasn't that kind of hotel, an endless one-nighter. He took out his notepad; but could only sit and stare at it. Too much. Like messing on with a painting one knew was no good; that one could only walk away from, without looking back, to one's separate door in the night.

Underlying all this there stood the knowledge that he would not change; he would go on painting as before, he would forget this day, he would find reasons to interpret everything differently, as a transient losing his head, a self-indulgent folly. A scar would grow over it, then fall away, and the skin would be as if there had never been a wound. He was crippled by common sense, he had no ultimate belief in chance and its exploitation, the missed opportunity would become the finally sensible decision, the decent thing; the flame of deep fire that had singed him a dream, a moment's illusion; her reality just one more unpursued idea kept among old sketchbooks at the back of a studio cupboard.

But till then, he knew: he had refused (and even if he had never seen her again) a chance of a new existence, and the ultimate quality and enduringness of his work had rested on acceptance. He felt a delayed but bitter envy of the old man. In the end it all came down to what one was born with: one either had the temperament for excess and a ruthless egocentricity, for keeping thought and feeling in different compartments, or one didn't; and David didn't. The abominable and vindictive injustice was that art is fundamentally amoral. However hard one tried, one was hopelessly handicapped: all to the pigs, none to the deserving. Coët had remorselessly demonstrated what he was born, still was, and always would be: a decent man and eternal also-ran.

That last was the label that seemed to have been lurking for hours when it finally came to him. He was left staring at the petered rise, which he saw almost literally above the dreary sea of roofs, wet now in a drizzle, outside the hotel; the collapsed parallel of what he was beside the soaring line of all that he might have been.

He got to Orly to find the flight was delayed for half an hour. There was fog at Heathrow. David hated airports at the best of times, the impersonality, herding, sense of anonymous passage; the insecurity. He stood by the window of the visitors' lounge, staring out into the flat distances. Dusk. Coët was in another universe; one and an eternal day's drive away. He tried to imagine what they were doing. Diana laying the table, Anne having her French lesson. The silence, the forest, the old man's voice. Macmillan barking. He suffered the most intense pang of the most terrible of all human deprivations; which is not of possession, but of knowledge. What she said; what she felt; what she thought. It pierced deeper than all questionings about art, or his art, his personal destiny. For a few terrible moments he saw himself, and all mankind, quite clear. Something in him, a last hope of redemption, of free will, burnt every boat; turned; ran for salvation. But the boats proof to all flame, the ultimate old masters, kept the tall shadow of him where he was; static and onward, returning home, a young Englishman staring at a distant row of frozen runway lights.

The flight arrival was announced and he went down to where he could watch for Beth. He had brought her holiday luggage in the car, and she came out with the first passengers. A wave. He raised his hand: a new coat, surprise for him, a little flounce and jiggle to show it off. Gay Paree. Free woman. Look, no children.

She comes with the relentless face of the present tense; with a dry delight, small miracle that he is actually here. He composes his face into an equal certainty.

She stops a few feet short of him.

"Hi."

She bites her lips.

"I thought for one ghastly moment."

She pauses.

"You were my husband."

Rehearsed. He smiles.

He kisses her mouth.

They walk away together, talking about their children.

He has a sense of retarded waking, as if in a postoperational state of consciousness some hours returned but not till now fully credited; a numbed sense of something beginning to slip inexorably away. A shadow of a face, hair streaked with gold, a closing door. *I wanted you to.* One knows one dreamed, yet cannot remember. The drowning cry, jackbooted day.

She says, "And you, darling?"

He surrenders to what is left: to abstraction.

"I survived."

Eliduc

De un mut ancïen lai bretun
Le cunte e tute la reisun
Vus dirai . . .

A Personal Note

The working title of this collection of stories was *Variations*, by which I meant to suggest variations both on certain themes in previous books of mine and in methods of narrative presentation — though I should hate readers to feel themselves at a disadvantage because they are unfamiliar with my work or cannot swear hand on heart that they know the distinction between *récit* and *discours*. They may be reassured. One reason the working title was discarded was that the first professional readers, who do know my books, could see no justification for *Variations* whatever . . . beyond a very private mirage in the writer's mind. I have deferred to their judgment and, beyond this mention of it, kept the illusion to myself.

However, *The Ebony Tower* is also a variation of a more straightforward kind, and the source of its mood, as also partly of its theme and setting, is so remote and forgotten — though I believe seminal in the history of fiction — that I should like to resurrect a fragment of it. Besides, the unexplained mystery, as every agnostic and novelist knows, is black proof of an ultimate shirking of creative responsibility. I have a dead weasel on my conscience; and deeper still, a dead woman.

As a student of French at Oxford, I read omnivorously, though much more out of ignorance than intelligence. I had very little notion of my real tastes, having swallowed the then prevalent myth that only one's teachers had a right to personal preferences. This is not an approach I could attempt to sell to any student today, but it did have one advantage. Likes and dislikes were eventually formed on a strictly pragmatic basis; I learned to value what I couldn't, over the years, forget. One such obstinate survivor was Alain-Fournier's *Le Grand Meaulnes*. A number of young thesis writers have now told me they can see no significant parallels between *Le Grand Meaulnes* and my own novel *The Magus*. I must have severed the umbilical cord — the real connection requires such a metaphor — much more neatly than I supposed at the time; or perhaps modern academic criticism is blind to relationships that are far more emotional than structural.

I felt Henri Fournier's appeal from the beginning. That wasn't the case with another part of the student syllabus. Old French, with its latinities, its baffling orthographies, its wealth of dialect forms, may be fascinating to the linguist; but to someone who wants to read meaning and story, its difficulty is just plain irritating. Nevertheless, I was to discover later that one field of Old French literature refused to subside into the oblivion I wished on the whole period once I had taken Finals. This field — "forest" would be more appropriate — was that of the Celtic romance.

The extraordinary change in European culture that took place under the influence of the British (in the original Celtic sense of that word) imagination has never, I suspect, been fully traced or acknowledged. The mania for chivalry, courtly love, mystic and crusading Christianity, the Camelot syndrome, all these we are aware of — a good deal too aware, perhaps, in the case of some recent travesties of that last center of the lore. But I believe that we also owe — emotionally and imaginatively, at least — the very essence of what we have meant ever since by the fictional, the novel and all its children, to this strange northern invasion of the early medieval mind. One may smile condescendingly at the naïveties and primitive technique of stories such as *Eliduc;* but I do not think any writer of fiction can do so with decency — and for a very simple reason. He is watching his own birth.

Biographically, next to nothing is known of Marie de France. Even the name is only a deduction, made long after her death, from a line in one of her fables — *Marie ai nun, si suis de France.* My name is Marie and I come from . . . but it isn't even certain that she intended what we today think of as France. The region around Paris, the Ile de France, is more probable. There are faint linguistic and other grounds for supposing she may have come from the part of Normandy called the Vexin, which borders on the Paris basin.

At some time she went to England, perhaps in or with the court of Eleanor of Aquitaine. The king to whom she dedicates her *Lais,* or love stories, may have been Eleanor's husband, Henry II, Becket's cross; and there is even a plausible possibility that Marie was Henry's illegitimate sister. His father, Geoffrey Plantagenet, had a natural daughter of that name, who became the abbess of Shaftesbury Abbey about 1180. Not all medieval abbesses led solemn and devout lives; and in any case the romances were almost certainly composed in the previous decade. The fact that the other two works by Marie that have survived are religious and certainly date from after 1180 reinforces the identification. If "Marie de France" was indeed the Marie from the wrong side of the Angevin blanket who became abbess of Shaftesbury, she must have been born before 1150, and we know that the abbess survived until about 1216.

It is very difficult to imagine the *Lais* being written by other than a finely educated (therefore, in that age, finely born) young woman; that she was romantic and high-spirited is easily deduced; and that her work was a tremendous and rapid literary success a wealth of contemporary manuscripts and translations bear witness . . . and one might even proceed to see her as an early victim of male chauvinism, sent to Shaftesbury to mend her wicked ways. There is certainly evidence that her stories were not approved by the Church. Very soon after the *Lais* came into the world, a gentleman named Denis Piramus — a monk in fact, but evidently a born reviewer by nature — wrote a sourly sarcastic account of her popularity. He knew why the stories gave their aristocratic audiences such dubious pleasure: they were hearing what they wanted to happen to themselves.

Overtly Marie set out in the *Lais* to save some Celtic tales from oblivion: stories from the diffuse folk-corpus scholars call the *matière de Bretagne,* and of which the Arthurian cycle and the story of Tristan and Yseult are now the best remembered. Whether she first heard them from French or English sources is unknown, since her own description of their provenance, *bretun,* was then used racially of the Brythonic Celts and not geographically — it included the Welsh and the Cornish as well as the Bretons proper. There are records of how far the Celtic minstrels wandered long before Marie's time, and she could have heard their performances at any major court.

But far more important than this quasi-archaeological service was the transmutation that took place when Marie grafted her own knowledge of the world on the old material. Effectively she introduced a totally new element into European literature. It was composed not least of sexual honesty and a very feminine awareness of how people really behaved — and how behavior and moral problems can be expressed through things like dialogue and action. She did for her posterity something of what Jane Austen did for hers — that is, she set a new standard for accuracy over human emotions and their absurdities. One may bring the two even closer, since the common ground of all Marie's stories (what she herself would have termed *desmesure,* or passionate excess) is remarkably akin to the later novelist's view of sense and sensibility. Another similarity is much harder for us to detect today, and that is of humor. Because her stories are so distant from us, we tend to forget that much of their matter was equally distant from her own twelfth century; and we grossly underestimate both her and her contemporary audience's sophistication if we imagine them listening with totally straight faces and credulity. That was no more expected than that we should take our own thrillers, Wild Westerns and sci-fi epics without a pinch of salt.

Marie's irony is all the harder to detect now for another historical reason. Her *Lais* were not meant to be read in silence — or in prose. In the original they are in rhyming octosyllabic couplets, and they were to be performed, sung and mimed, probably to a loose melody, or to a variety of them, and perhaps in places spoken almost conversationally against chords and arpeggios. The instrument would have been the harp, no doubt in its Breton form, the *rote*. The Romantics turned minstrelsy into an irredeemably silly word; but what little evidence we have suggests a very great art, one we have now lost beyond recall. In the case of writers like Marie de France, to see only the printed text is rather like having to judge a film by the script alone. The long evolution of fiction has been very much bound up with finding means to express the writer's "voice" — his humors, his private opinions, his nature — by means of word manipulation and print alone; but before Gutenberg we are lost. I will cite one small instance in the story you are about to read. Twice Marie is very formal about the way her hero visits the wayward princess he is in love with; he does not crash into her rooms, he has himself properly announced. One may take it as a piece of padding, a conventional show of courtly etiquette. But I think it much more probable that it was a dry aside and directed at her first listeners — indeed, if what we know of Henry II is true, and Marie was related to him, I could hazard a guess at whom the little gibe was directed.

I have attempted to convey at least a trace of this living, oral quality in my translation, which is based on the British Museum H text (Harley 978), in Alfred Ewert's edition.* It only remains to remind readers of the three real-life systems against which the story is anachronistically told. The first is the feudal system, which laid a vital importance on promises sworn between vassal and lord. It was not only that the power structure depended on a man being as good as his word; all civilized life depended on it. Today we can go to law over a broken contract; in those days you could only take to arms. The second context is the Christian, which is responsible for the ending of *Eliduc*, but not much else. Marie is patently more interested in the human heart than the immortal soul. The third system was that of courtly love, where the same stress on keeping faith was applied to sexual relations. It is hardly a fashionable idea in the twentieth century; but *amour courtois* was a desperately needed attempt to bring more civilization (more female intelligence) into a brutal society, and all civilization is based on agreed codes and symbols of mutual trust. An age in which the *desmesure* of Watergate — in my view far more a cultural than a political tragedy — can happen should not find this too difficult to understand.

---

* I must thank Dr. Nicholas Mann, of Pembroke College, Oxford, for help over some particularly difficult lines.

I AM GOING TO GIVE YOU the full story of a very old Celtic tale, at least as I've been able to understand the truth of it.

In Brittany there was once a knight called Eliduc. He was a model of his type, one of the bravest men in the country, and he had a wife of excellent and influential family, as finely bred as she was faithful to him. They lived happily for several years, since it was a marriage of trust and love. But then a war broke out and he went away to join the fighting. There he fell in love with a girl, a ravishingly pretty princess called Guilliadun. The Celtic name of the wife who stayed at home was Guildelüec, and so the story is called *Guildelüec and Guilliadun* after their names. Its original title was *Eliduc*, but it was changed because it's really about the two women. Now I'll tell you exactly how it all happened.

Eliduc's overlord was the king of Brittany, who was very fond of the knight and looked after his interests. Eliduc served him faithfully — whenever the king had to go abroad, Eliduc was left in charge of his territories, and kept them safe by his military skills. He got many favors in return. He was allowed to hunt in the royal forests. No gamekeeper, even the most resolute, dared stand in his way or complain about him. But other people's envy of his good luck did its usual work. He was slandered and traduced, and brought into bad relations with the king. Finally he was dismissed from the court without any reason. Left in the dark, Eliduc repeatedly asked to be allowed to defend himself before the king — the slanders were lies, he had served the king well, and happily so. But no answer came from the court. Convinced he would never get a hearing, Eliduc decided to go into exile. So he went home and called together all his friends. He told them how things lay with the king, of the anger toward him. Eliduc had done the best he could and there was no justice in the royal resentment. When the plowman gets the rough edge of his master's tongue, the peasants have a proverb: *Never trust a great man's love*. If someone in Eliduc's position is sensible, he puts more trust in the love of his neighbors. So now he says* he's sick of Brittany, he'll cross the sea to England and amuse himself there for a while. He'll leave his wife at home; have his servants take care of her, along with his friends.

Once it was made, he kept to this decision. He fitted himself — and the ten horsemen he took with him — out handsomely for the journey. His friends were very sad to see him go, and as for his wife . . . she accompanied him for the first part of the journey, in tears that she was losing him. But he swore solemnly that he would stay true to her. Then he says good-bye and rides straight on to the sea. There he takes ship, crosses successfully and arrives at the port of Totnes.

There were several kings in that part of England, and they were at war. Toward Exeter in this country there lived a very powerful old man. He had no male heir, simply an unmarried daughter. This explained the present war: because he had refused her hand to an equal from another dynasty, the other king was putting all his land to the sack. He had trapped the old king in one of his fortified cities.† No one there had the courage to go out and join combat, general or single, with

---

* The shifts to the narrative present (like those into dialogue) are all in the original.
† The text says "in a castle," but it seems clear that Exeter, then a walled city, is meant. Marie would have known of its importance in West Saxon times and of William the Conqueror's siege of 1068. The Saxons took East Devon and Exeter from the Celts in the latter half of the seventh century, so Marie's original source for *Eliduc* must antedate that time. Totnes, incidentally, is a frequently mentioned port in the *matière de Bretagne*.

the invader. Eliduc heard about all this and decided that since there was war he would stay in those parts instead of going on. He wanted to help the besieged king, who was getting into worse and worse trouble and faced with ruin and disaster. He would hire himself out as a mercenary.*

He sent messengers to the king, explaining in a letter that he had left his own country and had come to help him; but he was at the king's disposal and if he didn't want Eliduc's services, then Eliduc asked only for safe-conduct through his lands, so that he could go and offer his fighting abilities somewhere else. When the king saw the messengers, he was delighted and welcomed them warmly. He summoned the castle commander and ordered that an escort be provided immediately for Eliduc and that he should be brought to him. Then the king had lodgings arranged. All that was necessary for a month's stay was also provided.

The escort were armed and horsed and sent to fetch Eliduc. He was received with great honor, having made the journey without trouble. His lodging was with a rich townsman, a decent and well-mannered man who gave up his tapestry-hung best room to the knight. Eliduc had a good meal prepared and invited to it all the other anxious knights who were quartered in the city. He forebade his own men, even the most grabbing, to accept any gift or wages for the first forty days.

On his third day at Exeter the cry ran through the city that the enemy had arrived and were all over the surrounding countryside — and already preparing an attack on the city gates. Eliduc heard the uproar from the panicking townspeople and immediately donned armor. His companions did the same. There were fourteen other knights capable of fighting in the town, the rest being wounded, or captured. Seeing Eliduc mount his horse, they go to their lodgings and put on

---

* . . . *en soudees remaneir.* The knight *soudoyer* has to be understood (at least in romance) in a far more honorable, and honor-driven, sense than in the contemporary or even the Renaissance use of "mercenary." Perhaps the Japanese samurai is the best equivalent.

their own armor as well. They won't wait to be called, they'll go out of the gates with him.

"We'll ride with you, sir," they now say. "And whatever you do, we'll do the same."

Eliduc answers. "My thanks. Is there anyone here who knows an ambush place? A defile? Somewhere where we might catch them hopping? If we wait here, we'll get a good fight. But we have no advantage. Has anyone a better plan?"

"There's a narrow cart road, sir. Beside that wood by the flax field over there. When they've got enough loot, they'll return by it. They ride back carelessly from such work, as a rule. Like that they're asking for a quick death."

It could be over in a flash; and much damage done.

"My friends," said Eliduc, "one thing for certain. Nothing venture, even when things look hopeless, then nothing gain — either in war or reputation. You're all the king's men, you owe him complete loyalty. So follow me. Wherever I go, and do as I do. I promise you there won't be setbacks if I can help it. We may not get any loot. But we'll never be forgotten if we beat the enemy today."

His confidence spread to the other knights and they led him to the wood. There they hid by the road and waited for the enemy to return from their raid. Eliduc had planned everything, showed them how they should charge at the gallop and what to cry. When the enemy reached the narrow place, Eliduc shouted the battle challenge, then cried to his friends to fight well. They struck hard, and gave no quarter. Taken by surprise, the enemy were soon broken and put to flight. The engagement was brief. They captured the officer in command and many other knights, whom they entrust to their squires. Eliduc's side had had twenty-five men, and they took thirty of the enemy. They also took a great deal of armor, and a quantity of other valuable things. Now they return triumphantly to the city, full of this splendid victory. The king was there on a tower, desperately anxious for his men. He complained bitterly, having convinced himself that Eliduc was a traitor and had lost him all his knights.

They come in a crowd, some laden, others bound — many more on the return than at the going out, which was why the king was misled and stayed in doubt and suspense. He orders the city gates closed and the people up on the walls, bows and other weapons at the ready. But they have no need of them. Eliduc's party had sent a squire galloping on ahead to explain what had happened. The man told the king about the Breton mercenary, how he had driven the enemy away, how well he had conducted himself. There was never a better handler of arms on horseback. He had personally captured the enemy commander and taken twenty-nine prisoners, besides wounding and killing many others.

When the king hears the good news, he's beside himself with joy. He came down from the tower and went to meet Eliduc; then thanked him for all he had done and gave him all the prisoners for ransoming. Eliduc shared out the armor among the other knights, keeping no more for his own men than three horses that had been allocated to them. He distributed everything else, even his own rightful part as well, among the prisoners and the other people.

After this exploit the king made Eliduc his favorite. He retained him and his companions for a whole year and Eliduc gave his oath of faithful service. He then became the protector of the king's lands.

The king's young daughter heard all about Eliduc and his splendid actions — how good-looking he was, such a proud knight, how civilized and openhanded. She sent one of her personal pages to request, to *beg* Eliduc to come and amuse her. They must talk, get to know each other, and she would be very hurt if he didn't come. Eliduc replies: of course he'll come, he looks forward very much to meeting her. He got on his horse; and taking a servant with him, he goes to chat with the girl. When he's at the door of her room, he sends the page ahead. He doesn't barge in, but waits a little, till the page comes back. Then with gentle expression, sincere face and perfect good manners he addressed the young lady formally and thanked her for having invited him to visit her. Guilliadun was very pretty, and she took him by the hand* and led him to a couch, where they sat and talked of this and that. She kept stealing looks at him . . . his face, his body, his every expression . . . and said to herself how attractive he was, how close to her ideal man. Love fires his arrow, she falls headlong in love. She goes pale, she sighs, but she can't declare herself, in case he despises her for it.

Eliduc stayed a long time, but in the end took his leave and went away. Guilliadun was very unwilling to let him go, but there it was. He returned to his lodgings, unsmiling and very thoughtful. The girl alarmed him, since she was the king's daughter and he the king's servant. She had seemed so shy, yet subtly accused him of something. He feels badly done by — to have been so long in the country, yet not to have seen her once till now. Yet when he said that to himself, he felt ashamed. He remembered his wife, and how he had promised to behave as a husband should.

Now she had met him, the girl wanted to make Eliduc her lover. She had never liked a man more — if only she can, if only he'll agree. All night she was awake thinking of him, and had neither rest nor sleep. The next morning she got up at

---

* As a mark of favor, allowed her by her higher rank. Normally medieval gentlemen took the lady's left hand, and by the fingers alone. Even men held delicate hands like this — going arm-in-arm was almost unknown before the Renaissance. This partly explains, or is explained by, the high erotic value accorded the female hand throughout the Middle Ages, and even as late as Holbein. I may mention here that the seductive use of see-through fabrics is well attested from other (shocked masculine) sources of the period. It helps to visualize Guilliadun — Guilli- means golden — to borrow a passage from another of Marie's stories (*Lanval*): "She was dressed like this: in a white linen shift, loosely laced at the sides so that one could see the bare skin from top to bottom. She had an attractive slim-waisted figure. Her neck was as white as snow on a branch; bright eyes in a pale face, a lovely mouth, a perfect nose, dark eyebrows; but her hair was wavy and corn-colored. In the sun it had a light finer than gold thread."

dawn and went to a window and called down to her page. Then she revealed everything to him.

"Dear God," she says, "I'm in such a state, I've fallen into such a trap. I love the new mercenary. Eliduc. Who's fought so brilliantly. I haven't slept a wink all night, my eyes just wouldn't shut. If he's really in love with me, if he'll only show he's serious, I'll do anything he likes. And there's so much to hope for — he could be king here one day. I'm mad about him. He's so intelligent, so easy-mannered. If he doesn't love me, I'll die of despair."

When he'd heard all she had to say, the young page gave her good advice: no need to give up hope so soon.

"My lady, if you're in love with him, then let him know it. Send him a belt or a ribbon — or a ring. To see if it pleases him. If he's happy to accept the gift, looks glad to hear from you, then you're in. He loves you. And show me an emperor who wouldn't dance for joy if he knew you fancied him."

The girl mulled over this advice.

"But how shall I know just by a gift whether he really wants me? You don't realize. A gentleman has to accept, whether he likes the sender or not. One has to take such things with good grace. I should loathe it if he made fun of me. But perhaps you could learn something from his expression. So get ready. Quickly. And go."

"I am ready."

"Take him this gold ring. And here, give him my belt. And be very warm when you greet him for me."

The page turned away, leaving her in such a state that she very nearly calls him back. Nevertheless she lets him go — and then begins to rave to herself.

"Oh God, I've fallen in love with a foreigner! I don't even know if he's of good family. Whether he won't suddenly disappear. I shall be left in despair. I'm insane to have made it all so obvious. I'd never even spoken with him before yesterday, and now I'm throwing myself at him. I think he'll just despise me. No he won't, if he's nice he'll like me for it. It's all in the lap of the gods now. If he doesn't care for me at all, I shall feel such a fool. I'll never be happy again, as long as I live."

Meanwhile, as she agonized on like that, the page rode fast on his way. He found Eliduc and gave him in private the kind of greetings the girl had asked. Then he handed him the little ring and the belt. The knight had thanked him, then put the ring on his finger and fastened the belt* around his waist. But he said nothing else to the page, asked him nothing — except that he offered him his own ring and belt in return. But the page didn't accept them and went away back to his young mistress. He found her in her room; then passed on Eliduc's return of greetings and his thanks.

"For pity's sake, don't hide the truth. Does he really love me?"

"I think so. He wouldn't deceive you. In my opinion he's playing polite and being shrewd — he knows how to hide his feelings. I said hallo to him for you and gave him the presents. He put the belt on himself, and was rather careful to get it right. Then the ring on his finger. I didn't say anything else to him. Or he to me."

"But did he realize what it meant? Because if he didn't, I'm lost!"

"I honestly don't know. But if you must have my solemn opinion, then, well, since he didn't turn up his nose at what you sent, he doesn't exactly . . . hate you?"

"Stop teasing me, you cheeky boy! I'm perfectly well aware he doesn't hate me. How could I ever hurt him? Except by loving him so much. But if he does, he deserves to die. Until I've spoken with him myself, I won't have anything to do with him. Either through you or anyone else. I'll show him

* The fashionable belt of the Middle Ages had links, with a hook at one end. It was fastened with a free end left hanging at the side. There is a superb fourteenth-century example in thornwood, made for a lady of Breton family, in the Victoria and Albert Museum.

[130]

myself how wanting him tears me apart. But if only I knew
how long he was staying here!"

"Lady, the king has him under contract for a year. That
ought to be time enough to show him how you feel?"

When she heard Eliduc wasn't going away, Guilliadun was
in ecstasy: how wonderful that he must stay! What she didn't
know was the torment Eliduc had been in from the moment he
set eyes on her. Fate had dealt him a cruel hand — that promise
to his wife when he left home, that he'd never look at another
woman. Now his heart was in a vise. He wanted to stay faithful. But nothing could hide the fact that he had hopelessly
fallen for Guilliadun and her prettiness. To see her again and
talk with her, kiss her and hold her in his arms . . . yet he
could never show her this longing, which would disgrace him
— on the one hand for breaking his promise to his wife, on
the other because of his relationship with the king. He was
torn in two; then mounted his horse, and havered no more. He
calls his friends to him, then goes to the castle to speak to the
king. If it can be managed, he will see the girl — and that is
why he hurries so.

The king has just risen from table and gone to his daughter's
rooms, and now he's begun to play chess with a knight from
overseas. On the other side of the chessboard, his daughter
had to show the moves. Eliduc came forward. The king greeted
him kindly and made Eliduc sit beside him. He spoke to his
daughter.

"My dear, you must get to know this gentleman. And pay
him every honor. There's no finer knight in the country."

The girl was delighted to hear this command from her
father. She stands up, invites Eliduc to sit with her well away
from the others. Both are struck dumb with love. She dared
not explain herself to him, and he was afraid to speak as well
. . . except to thank her for the presents she had sent him: he
had never liked a present so much. She tells him she is pleased
that he is pleased. Then suddenly why she sent him the ring,

and her belt as well — that her body was his, she couldn't resist, she loved him to madness, she gave herself to his every wish. If she couldn't have him, he knew, he must know it was true, no other man would ever have her.

Now it was Eliduc's turn.

"Princess, I'm so happy that you love me. All joy. That you should like me so much — how could I feel otherwise? I shan't ever forget it. You know I'm promised to your father for a year, under oath that I shan't leave till the war's ended. Then I shall go home. Provided you'll let me. I don't want to stay here."

"Eliduc, I'm so grateful for your frankness. You're so honest, you know such a lot. Long before you go you'll have decided what to do with me. I love you, I trust you more than anything else in the world."

They knew now that they were sure of each other; and on that occasion no more was said.

Eliduc goes back to his lodgings, enchanted at how well things have turned out. He can talk as often as he likes with Guilliadun, they're wildly in love.

He now occupied himself so well with the war that he captured the enemy king, and liberated the old king's country. His military reputation grew, as did that of his ingenuity and public generosity. On this side of his life everything went very well.

But during this same time the king of Brittany had sent three messengers over the sea to find Eliduc. Things at home were in a very bad way, and getting worse. All his strong points were under siege, his lands being put to the sword. With increasing bitterness, the king regretted having driven Eliduc away. His judgment had been distorted by the malicious advice he had listened to. Already he had thrown the treacherous clique who had blackened Eliduc and intrigued against him into permanent exile. Now, in his hour of great need, he commanded, he summoned, he begged Eliduc — in the name of the trust that had existed between them ever since the knight first paid homage to him — to come and save the situation. He was in the direst straits.

Eliduc read this news. It distressed him deeply. He thought of Guilliadun. He loved her now to the anguished depths of his being, and she felt the same for him. But there had been no madness between them — nothing improper, theirs was no casual affair. Caressing and talking, giving each other lovely presents — the passionate feeling between them hadn't gone beyond that. She kept it so on purpose, because of what she hoped. She thought he'd be entirely hers, and hers alone, if she played her cards right.

She did not know there was a wife.

"Alas," thinks Eliduc to himself, "I've gone astray. I've stayed too long here. It was cursed, the day I first set eyes on this country. I've fallen head over heels in love. And she with me. If I have to say farewell to her now, one of us will die. Perhaps both. And yet I must go, the king of Brittany's letter commands it, and there's my promise to him. To say nothing of the one I swore my wife. I must pull myself together. I can't stay any longer, I have no alternative. If I were to marry Guilliadun, the Church would never stand for it. In all ways it's a mess. And oh God, to think of never seeing her again! I must be open with her, whatever the cost. I'll do whatever she wants, whichever way she sees it. Her father has got a decent peace, no one wants war with him anymore. I'll plead the king of Brittany's need and ask for permission to leave before the day's out. It was what was agreed — I'd go to him as soon as we had peace here. I'll see Guilliadun and explain the whole business. Then she can tell me what she wants, and I'll do my best to make it come true."

Without further delay, Eliduc went to the king to seek leave. He explained the situation in Brittany and showed him the letter the king there had sent him — the cry for help. The old king reads the command and realizes he will lose Eliduc.

He is very upset and worried. He offered him a share of his possessions, a third of his heritage, his treasury — if he'll only stay, he'll do so much for him that Eliduc will be eternally grateful.

But Eliduc stayed firm.

"At this juncture, since my king's in danger and he's taken such trouble to find me, I must go to his assistance. Nothing would make me stop here. But if you ever need my services again, I'll willingly return — and bring plenty of other knights with me."

At that the king thanked him and gave him leave to go without further argument. He puts all his household possessions at Eliduc's disposal — gold and silver, hounds and horses and beautiful silks. Eliduc took no more than he needed. Then he politely told the king that he would like very much to speak with his daughter, if it were allowed.

"Consent is a pleasure," said the king.

Eliduc sends a young lady ahead to open the door of Guilliadun's room. Then he goes in to speak with her. When she saw him, she cried out his name and passionately clung to him. Then they discussed his problem, and he explained briefly the necessity for his journey. But when he had made it all clear, and yet pointedly still not asked for her permission to leave, for his freedom, she nearly fainted with the shock. Her face went white. When Eliduc sees the agony she is in, he begins to go mad. He keeps kissing her mouth and begins to cry in sympathy. At last he takes her in his arms and holds her until she recovers.

"You sweetest thing, oh God, listen — you're life and death to me, you're my whole existence. That's why I've come. So that we can talk about it, and trust each other. I must go home. I've got your father's permission. But I'll do whatever you want. Whatever may happen to me."

"Then take me with you, if you don't want to stay! If you

don't, I'll kill myself. Nothing good or happy will ever happen to me again."

Gently Eliduc tells her how much he loves her; how beautiful she is. "But I've solemnly sworn to obey your father. If I take you away with me I'll be breaking my oath to him before its term is over. I swear, I promise you with all my heart that if you'll let me leave you now for a while, but name a day on which I must come back, then nothing on earth will stop me doing so — as long as I'm alive and in good health. My life's entirely in your hands."

She loved him so much. So she gave him a final date, a day by which he must return and take her away. They parted in tears and misery, exchanging their gold rings and tenderly kissing each other.

Eliduc rode to the sea. The wind was good and the crossing quick. When he gets home, the king of Brittany is overjoyed, and so are Eliduc's relations and friends and everyone else — and especially his wife, who remained as attractive and worthy of him as ever. But all the time Eliduc stayed turned in on himself, because of the shock love affair in England. Nothing he saw gave him any pleasure, he wouldn't smile — he'll never be happy till he sees Guilliadun again. His wife was very depressed by his secretive behavior, since she had no idea what caused it. She felt sorry for herself; kept asking if he hadn't heard from someone that she'd misbehaved while he was abroad. She'll willingly defend herself before the world, whenever he wants.

"My lady, no one's accused you of anything bad. But I've solemnly sworn to the king in the country where I've been that I shall return to him. He has great need of me. I told him I'd be on my way within a week, as soon as the king of Brittany had peace. I've got a huge task ahead of me before I can return. I can't take pleasure in anything at all until I've got back there. I *will* not break promises."

And that was all he told his wife. He went to join the king

of Brittany and helped him greatly. The king adopted his strategy and saved his kingdom. But when the date approached that Guilliadun had named, Eliduc intervened to make peace. He agreed to all the terms the enemy wanted, then he got ready to travel and picked his companions — two nephews he was fond of and one of his pages, a boy who had known what was going on and had carried messages between Eliduc and Guilliadun. Besides them, only his squires; he didn't want anyone else. He made these companions swear to keep the secret.

He waits no longer, puts to sea and soon arrives in Totnes. At last he was back where he was so longed for. Eliduc was very cunning. He found an inn well away from the harbor, since he was very anxious not to be seen . . . traced and recognized. He got his page ready and sent him to Guilliadun to tell her he had returned and kept strictly to his promise. By night, when darkness had fallen, she must slip out of the city; the page would escort her and Eliduc come to meet her. The boy changed into a disguise and went all the way on foot straight to Exeter. He cleverly found a way to get into her private apartments; then greeted the princess and told her her lover had come back. He found her sad and hopeless, but when she hears the news she breaks down and begins to cry, then kisses and kisses the page. He told her she must leave with him that evening; and they spent the whole day planning their escape in every detail.

When night had come, they stole cautiously out of the city alone together. They were terrified someone might see them. She wore a silk dress delicately embroidered in gold and a short cloak.

About a bowshot from the city gate there was a copse enclosed in a fine garden. Eliduc, who had come to fetch her, waited under the hedge. The page led her to the place. Eliduc sprang down from his horse and kissed her: such joy to meet again. He helped her onto a horse, then mounted his own and took her bridle. They rode quickly away, back to the port of

Totnes, and boarded the ship at once: no other passengers but Eliduc's men and his beloved Guilliadun. They had favorable winds and settled weather, but when they came near the coast of Brittany they ran into a storm. A contrary wind drove them out away from the harbor. Then the mast split and broke, and they lost all the sails. They prayed in despair — to God, to St. Nicholas and St. Clement — to Our Lady, that she might invoke Christ's protection for them, save them from drowning and bring them to land. Backward and forward they were driven along the coast, the storm raging around them. One of the sailors began to shout.

"What are we doing? My lord, it's the girl you've brought aboard who's going to drown us all. We'll never reach land. You have a proper wife at home. But now you want another woman. It's against God and the law. Against all decency and religion. So let's throw her in the sea, and save our skins."

Eliduc hears what the man cries, and nearly goes berserk.

"You son of a whore, you fiend, you rat — shut your mouth! If she goes into the sea, I'll make you pay for it!"

He held Guilliadun in his arms, gave her what comfort he could. She was seasick, and riven by what she'd just heard: that her lover had a wife at home. She fainted and fell to the deck, deathly pale; and stayed like that, without breath or sign of consciousness. Eliduc knew she was only there because of him, and sincerely thought she was dead. He was in agony. He stood up and rushed at the sailor and struck him down with an oar. The man collapsed to the deck and Eliduc kicked the body over the side, where the waves took it away. As soon as he had done that, he went to the helm. There he steered and held the ship so well that they came to the harbor and land. When they were safely in, he cast anchor and had the gangway let down. Still Guilliadun lay unconscious, her only appearance that of death. Eliduc wept without stop — if he had had his way, he would have been dead with her. He asked his companions their advice, where he could carry her. He refused to leave her side until she was buried with every honor and full ritual, and laid to rest in holy ground. She was a king's daughter, it was her due. But his men were at a loss and could suggest nothing. Eliduc began to think for himself. His own house was not far from the sea, not a day's ride away. There was a forest around it, some thirty miles across. A saintly hermit had lived there for forty years and had a chapel. Eliduc had often spoken with him.

I'll take her there, Eliduc said to himself, I'll bury her in his chapel. Then bestow land and found an abbey or a monastery. Nuns or canons, who can pray for her every day, may God have mercy on her soul.

He had horses brought and ordered everyone to mount, then made them promise they would never betray him. He carried Guilliadun's body in front of him, on his own horse. They took the most direct road and soon entered the forest. At last they came to the chapel, and called and knocked. But no voice answered and the door stayed closed. Eliduc made one of his men climb in and open it. They found a fresh tomb: the pure and saintly hermit had died that previous week. They stood there sad and dismayed. The men wanted to prepare the grave in which Eliduc must leave Guilliadun forever, but he made them withdraw outside the chapel.

"This isn't right. I need advice first from the experts on how I can glorify this place with an abbey or a convent. For now we'll lay Guilliadun before the altar and leave her in God's care."

He had bedding brought and they quickly made a resting place for the girl; then laid her there, and left her for dead. But when Eliduc came to leave the chapel, he thought he would die of pain. He kissed her eyes, her face.

"Darling heart, may it please God I'll never bear arms again or live in the outer world. I damn the day you ever saw me. Dear gentle thing, why did you come with me? Not even a queen could have loved me more trustingly. More deeply. My heart breaks for you. On the day I bury you, I'll enter a monastery. Then come here every day and weep all my desolation out on your tomb."

Abruptly then he turned from the girl's body and closed the chapel door.

He had sent a messenger on ahead to tell his wife he was coming, but tired and worn. Full of happiness at the news, she dressed to meet him; and welcomed him back affectionately. But she had little joy of it. Eliduc gave her not a single smile or a kind word. No one dared to ask why. He stayed like that for a couple of days — each early morning, having heard mass, he took the road to the forest and the chapel where Guilliadun lay . . . still unconscious, without breathing, no sign of life. Yet something greatly puzzled him: she had hardly lost color, her skin stayed pink and white, only very faintly pale. In profound despair, Eliduc wept and prayed for her soul. Then having done that, he returned home.

The following day, when he came out of the church after mass, there was a spy — a young servant his wife had promised horses and arms to if he could follow at a distance and see which way his master went. The lad did as she ordered. He rides into the forest after Eliduc without being seen. He watched well, saw how Eliduc went into the chapel, and heard the state he was in. As soon as Eliduc came out, the servant went home and told his mistress everything — all the sounds of anguish her husband had made inside the chapel. From being resentful, she now felt touched.

"We'll go there as soon as possible and search the place. Your master must be off soon to court, to confer with the king. The hermit died some time ago. I know Eliduc was very fond of him, but that wouldn't make him behave like this. Not show such grief."

Thus for the time being she left the mystery.

That very same afternoon Eliduc set off to speak with the king of Brittany. His wife took the servant with her and he led her to the hermitage chapel. As soon as she went in she saw the bed and the girl lying on it, as fresh as a first rose. She pulled back the covering and revealed the slender body, the slim arms, the white hands with their long and delicately smooth-skinned fingers. She knew the truth at once — why Eliduc had his tragic face. She called the servant forward and showed him the miraculous corpse.

"Do you see this girl? She's as lovely as a jewel. She's my husband's mistress. That's why he's so miserable. Somehow it doesn't shock me. So pretty . . . to have died so young. I feel only pity for her. And I still love him. It's a tragedy for us all."

She began to cry, in sympathy for Guilliadun. But as she sat by the deathbed with tears in her eyes a weasel darts out from beneath the altar. The servant struck at it with a stick to stop it running over the corpse. He killed it, then threw the small body into the middle of the chancel floor. It had not been there long when its mate appeared and saw where it lay. The living animal ran around the dead one's head and touched it several times with a foot. But when this failed, it seemed distressed. Suddenly it ran out of the chapel into the forest grass. There it picked a deep red flower with its teeth, then carried it quickly back and placed it in the mouth of the weasel the servant had killed. Instantly the animal came back to life. The wife had watched all this, and now she cried out to the servant.

"Catch it! Throw, boy! Don't let it escape!"

He hurled his stick and hit the weasel. The blossom fell from between its teeth. Eliduc's wife went and picked it up, then returned and placed the exquisite red flower in Guilliadun's mouth. For a second or two nothing happened, but then the girl stirred, sighed, and opened her eyes.

"Good lord," she murmured, "how long I've slept!"

When the wife heard her speak, she thanked heaven. Then she asked Guilliadun who she was.

"My lady, I'm British born, the daughter of a king there. I fell hopelessly in love with a knight, a brave mercenary called

Eliduc. He eloped with me. But he was wicked, he deceived me. He had a wife all the time. He never told me, never gave me the least hint. When I heard the truth, I fainted with the agony of it. Now he's brutally left me helpless here in a foreign country. He tricked me, I don't know what will become of me. Women are mad to trust in men."

"My dear," said the lady, "he's been quite inconsolable. I can assure you of that. He thinks you're dead, he's been mad with grief. He's come here to look at you every day. But obviously you've always been unconscious. I'm his real wife, and I'm deeply sorry for him. He was so unhappy . . . I wanted to find out where he was disappearing to, so I had him followed, and that's how I found you. And now I'm glad you're alive after all. I'm going to take you away with me. And give you back to him. I'll tell the world he's not to blame for anything. Then I shall take the veil."

She spoke so comfortingly that Guilliadun went home with her. The wife made the servant get ready and sent him after Eliduc. He rode hard and soon came up with him. The lad greeted Eliduc respectfully, then tells him the whole story. Eliduc leaps on a horse, without waiting for his friends. That same night he was home, and found Guilliadun restored to life. He gently thanks his wife, he's in his seventh heaven, he's never known such happiness. He can't stop kissing Guilliadun; and she keeps kissing him shyly back. They can't hide their joy at being reunited. When Eliduc's wife saw how things stood, she told her husband her plans. She asked his formal permission for a separation, she wished to become a nun and serve God. He must give her some of his land and she would found an abbey on it. And then he must marry the girl he loved so much, since it was neither decent nor proper, besides being against the law, to live with two wives. Eliduc did not try to argue with her; he'll do exactly as she wants and give her the land.

In the same woodlands near the castle that held the hermitage chapel he had a church built, and all the other offices of a nunnery. Then he settled a great deal of property and other possessions on it. When everything was ready, his wife took the veil, along with thirty other nuns. Thus she established her order and her new way of life.

Eliduc married Guilliadun. The wedding was celebrated with great pomp and circumstance, and for a long time they lived happily together in a perfect harmony of love. They gave a great deal away and performed many good deeds, so much so that in the end they also turned religious. After great deliberation and forethought, Eliduc had a church built on the other side of his castle and endowed it with all his money and the greater part of his estate. He appointed servants and other religious people to look after the order and its buildings. When all was ready, he delays no more: he surrenders himself with his servants to omnipotent God. And Guilliadun, whom he loved so much, he sent to join his first wife. Guildelüec received her as if she were her own sister and did her great honor, teaching her how to serve God and live the religious life of the order. They prayed for the salvation of Eliduc's soul, and in his turn he prayed for both of them. He found out by messengers how they were, how they comforted each other. All three tried in their own ways to love God with true faith; and in the end, by the mercy of God in whom all truth reposes, each died a peaceful death.

The noble Celts composed this story long ago to enshrine the strange adventure of these three. May it never be forgotten!

Poor Koko

* — · — · · — · · — · · — · · — · · — · · — · · — · · — · · — · · — · · — · *

Byth dorn re ver dhe'n tavas re hyr,
Mes den hep tavas a-gollas y dyr.

CERTAIN MELODRAMATIC SITUATIONS derived from the detective story and the thriller have been so done to death by the cinema and television that I suspect a new and nonsensical law of inverse probability has been established — the more frequently one of these situations is shown on the screen, the less chance there is of its taking place in the viewer's real life. Ironically enough I had maintained an analogous argument with a bright young genius from the BBC only a month or two before the deeply distressing experience that is the subject of this narrative. He had been rather humorlessly upset by my cynical declaration that the more abhorrent a news item the more comforting it was to the recipient, since the fact that it had happened elsewhere proved that it had not happened here, was not happening here, and would therefore never happen here. I had to climb down, needless to say, and to admit that the latterday Pangloss in all of us who regard tragedy as a privilege of other people was a thoroughly wicked and antisocial creature.

Nonetheless, when I first woke, that night of my ordeal, I lay as much in a state of incredulity as of fear. I told myself I had been dreaming, that what had seemed to shatter must have done so in my nocturnal unconscious, not in external reality. Propped on one elbow, I surveyed the darkened room, then listened on with straining ears. Yet still reason told me that what I feared was a thousand times more probable in

London than where I actually found myself. Indeed I was on the point of sinking back and putting my somewhat childish reaction down to this first night alone in a comparatively strange house. I have never been a lover of silence, in people or in places, and I missed the familiar all-night sounds from outside my London flat.

But then there came from below a light chink, or clink, as if something metallic had accidentally touched an edge of glass or china. A mere creak, the thump of a door banging gently to, might have allowed of other possibilities. This was a sound that did not. From vaguely alarmed I very swiftly became exceedingly frightened.

A friend of mine once maintained that there is a class of experiences we should all have had before death if we wished to claim to have lived fully. Believing one was certain to be drowned was an example. Being caught in bed — all this took place at a not very serious dinner party — with someone else's wife was another; seeing a ghost was a third, and killing another human being a fourth. I recall that although I added one or two equally preposterous suggestions of my own I was a little peeved to have to admit in secret that not one of these experiences had ever in reality been mine. My life had had its problems, but murder has never appeared a viable solution to them — or only momentarily, in the case of one or two unforgivably unfair reviews of my books. My atrocious eyesight prevented me from any sort of active service in the Second World War. I had been in bed once with someone else's wife — during that same war — but the husband was safely in North Africa during the whole of our brief liaison. My inadequacy as a swimmer has kept me very secure from any danger of drowning, and ghosts, with an unaccountable lack of interest in their own cause, appear resolutely to shun skeptics like myself. But here I finally was, after a safe sixty-six years of existence, undergoing yet another of those "vital" experiences: knowing one was not alone in a house where one believed one was.

If books have not taught me to admire and desire truth in writing, I have wasted my entire life, and the last thing I wish to do in this account is to present myself as other than I am. I have never pretended to be a man of action, though I like to think a certain sense of self-humor, an irony, makes the word bookish a little unjust. I learned very early, at boarding school, that a small reputation for wit — or at least a certain skill at puncturing the pretentious — can offset in part the damning labels of "bookworm" and "swot" with all but the most crassly athletic. No doubt I have indulged the characteristic malice of the physically deprived, and I certainly won't pretend that I haven't always enjoyed — and I'm afraid, helped propagate on occasion — the kind of gossip that redounds to another writer's discredit. Nor was my most successful potboiler, *The Dwarf in Literature*, quite the model of objective and erudite analysis it pretended to be. Very regrettably I have always found my own faults more interesting than other people's virtues; nor can I deny that books — writing them, reading, reviewing, helping to get them into print — have been my life rather more than life itself. It seems fitting that I should have been where I was that night entirely because of one.

Of the two suitcases that had accompanied me in the taxi from the station at Sherborne the previous day, the larger had been full of paper — notes, drafts and essential texts. I was near the end of a lifetime's ambition — a definitive biography and critical account of Thomas Love Peacock. I must not exaggerate, I hadn't begun serious work until some four years previously; but the desire to have such a book to my credit had been with me since my twenties. There had always been good practical reasons why my other efforts should have had the priority they seemed to demand; but this was the closest to my heart. I had duly cleared decks for the assault on the final summit, only to find London, the abominable new London that seems determined to ape New York, had vetoed my small project. A long-threatened and much larger one was suddenly in course of execution across the street from my Maida Vale flat. It was not only the din and the dust of the initial demolition and the knowledge that the wretched pseudoskyscraper progress intended to erect on the rubble of what had been a quietly solid Italianate terrace would very soon deprive me of a treasured westward view. I came to see it as the apotheosis of all that Peacock had stood against; all that was not humane, intelligent and balanced. Resentment at this intrusion began to affect what work I did; certain draft passages merely used Peacock as an excuse for irrelevant diatribes against my own age. I have nothing against such diatribes in their proper place, but I knew that in giving way to them here I was betraying both my subject and my own better judgment.

I expatiated one evening on all this with some distress (and not without some benefice aforethought) to two old friends in their Hampstead home. I had over the years spent a number of agreeable weekends at Maurice and Jane's cottage in North Dorset, though I must confess my pleasure there was rather more in the company than the rural environment. I am not a country lover, having always much preferred nature in art to nature in actuality. However, I now thought of Holly Cottage and its isolated combe as nostalgically as one could wish — and as a perfect refuge in my hour of need. My demurs when the refuge was offered were very perfunctory. I smilingly submitted to Jane's teasing over my sudden yearning for a countryside whose presiding genius she adored and for whom I had, in her view, a disgracefully lukewarm regard . . . Thomas Hardy has never been my cup of tea. I was duly furnished with keys, an impromptu shopping guide from Jane and a rundown on the functional esoterica of the electric water pump and the central heating from Maurice. Thus armed and briefed I had, in the late afternoon that preceded this rude awakening in the night, taken possession of my humble temporary version of the Sabine farm with a very genuine sense of joy. A part of my shock — and incredulity — was undoubtedly caused by my having gone to sleep in that prospective certainty of fertile concentration I had so comprehensively lacked during the previous two weeks.

I was acutely aware, as I sat bolt upright in my bed, that the sound I was now listening for was not in the living room below, but on the stairs. My frozen position was absurd — and of course highly uncourageous. But it was not simply that I was alone. The cottage was alone. There was a farm four hundred yards down the lane, and beyond that, some half a mile or so on, the village, where no doubt the constable was fast asleep in his bed. The telephone was in the living room below, so he might as well have been on the other side of the world as regards present assistance. To be sure, I could have made loud noises, in the hope that the intruder would find discretion the better part of burglary. I had a notion that professional thieves eschew violence. But common sense told me that a remote Dorset upland was hardly the place where professional burglars would pursue their *métier*. My visitor was much more likely to be some nervous village amateur. A conversation I had once had with Maurice came wryly to mind: how the only reason the crime rate was so low in rural areas such as this was the close-knit social structure. When everyone knew everyone else, crime was either difficult or desperate.

Nor did some faint last hope that the clinking sound might have had a natural explanation survive long. There came a scrape, as of a chair being moved aside. I had to face the reality: Holly Cottage was being "done." It was only too easy to guess why — despite Maurice's statistics — it had been selected. Its isolation was obvious; and it must have been common knowledge locally that it was owned by London weekenders, whose more extended stays were confined to the summer. The day was a Wednesday — now a Thursday, since my watch told me it was after one — and the month November. I do not drive, there was no motorcar outside to warn of occupation; and I had gone to bed early in order to be fresh for a long first day's work.

So far as I knew, there was nothing of great value in the cottage — certainly not by a professional thief's standards. The place had been furnished with Jane's usual simplicity and good taste. I knew there were one or two pieces of nice china, some paintings of the nineteenth-century naïve-pastoral genre that (for reasons beyond my personal comprehension) fetch a price these days. I could recall no silver; and I supposed Jane would hardly have left anything very precious in the jewelry line there.

Yet another sound came — to my small relief, from below still. It seemed vaguely pneumatic, perhaps caused by the sticking of some cupboard door. I lacked the familiarity with the native sounds of houses one gains only from prolonged living in them. However, I did at last take some positive action — that is, I groped for my glasses in the darkness and put them on. Then I got my legs from under the bedclothes and sat on the edge of the bed. No doubt it was symptomatic that I did all this with the greatest caution, as if I were the burglar. But I simply did not see what I could do. I was certain to come off worse if it came to a struggle. I could not reach the telephone without a confrontation and the youth — I had determined it was some long-haired village lout, with fists like hams and a mind to match — would hardly let me use it without a fight. And then I was also listening for something else — for the sound of a low voice. I didn't feel at all sure that I had to deal with just one person. The cheapest form of Dutch courage is an accomplice.

I must confess too, in retrospect, to a purely selfish motive. It was not my property that was being stolen. The only things of overwhelming value to me personally were the papers and the rest to do with my Peacock. I had laid them out on a table in the other downstairs room, the one farthest from me, the sitting room. They would hardly be in any danger from the semi-illiterate who was rummaging down below. They might conceivably have warned a more intelligent person that the cottage was not after all empty, but as to more obvious signs of occupation . . . I had fallen a victim both to my laziness and my always incipient neatness — having cleared away and washed up after the light supper I had cooked for myself, and not having bothered, as Jane had recommended, to light a log fire in the hearth to "cheer the place up." The weather was muggy, mild after London, and I had also not bothered with the central heating — merely switched on an electric fire, which would now be quite cold. The refrigerator remained off, since I had not yet shopped for perishables. The red light of the water heater glowed in the cupboard beside my bed. Then I had reopened the curtains downstairs ready for the morning, and brought my other suitcase upstairs with me. Even consciously, I could not have erased signs of my presence more effectively.

The predicament grew intolerable. Further sounds came that showed the person below was quite confident that he had the house to himself. True, however much I strained to hear, I caught not the faintest murmur of another voice; but it was increasingly obvious that sooner or later the thief would try his luck upstairs. All my life I have had a hatred of violence, indeed of most kinds of physical contact. I had not been in a fight since early childhood. A master at my preparatory school had once, in the callous manner of his kind, referred to me as a shrimp, and the sobriquet was unanimously adopted by my then friends. It never seemed to me very accurate, since shrimps have at least a certain speed of movement and agility and I had never had even those small compensations for a puny stature and a total lack of "muscle." It was only comparatively recently in my life that I had outgrown the family belief that I was constitutionally condemned to an early death. I like to class myself — in no other but a physical sense, I hasten to add — with Pope, Kant and Voltaire. I am trying to explain why I did nothing. It was not so much fear of injury or death as the awareness of how futile any action that provoked them was certain to be.

And then there was that sense of fertile concentration I spoke of just now — it had been an assurance of a still vigorous intellectual life ahead. I felt so eager to kill off the final draft, to have my fascinating and still grossly underrated subject alive and on the polished page. I had seldom been so confident at the three-quarter stage of a book; and I felt an equal determination now, as I sat on that bed, to let nothing in this ridiculous present situation endanger my bringing it to its due completion.

But my dilemma in the quick remained painful. I expected at any moment to hear footsteps mount the stairs. Then there came a sound that made my heart jump with unexpected relief — a sound that I could place. The cottage front door was closed by a wooden latch. There was a bolt, which could be opened in silence. But the latch was a shade stiff and tended to clack as one forced it up. That was what I had heard. To my joy the next sound came from outside. I recognized the small squeak of the little wicket gate that led from the narrow front garden to the lane. It seemed that against all expectation my unwelcome visitor had decided that he had got enough. I do not know what impulse made me stand up at this point and feel my way carefully to the bedroom window. It had been very dark outside when I took a brief breath of fresh air — with that smug sense of illegal proprietorship people who have been lent houses have — at the front door before going up to bed. Even in broad daylight my shortsightedness would have made any kind of useful identification dubious. Yet something in me wished to catch a glimpse of a dark shape . . . I cannot say why. Perhaps it was merely to be quite sure I was now left in peace.

So I cautiously peered down from the small window that

overlooked the lane past the cottage. I expected to see very little; to my surprise, and consternation, I could see quite well — and for a very simple reason. The lights in the living room below were evidently still on. I made out the white slats of the gate. Of the man who had left, no sign. For a few seconds all was still. Then there was the sound of a car door being closed — lightly, with care, but not the absolute care someone who might have suspected my presence would have used. I risked opening the curtain wider, but the car, van, whatever it was, was hidden behind the overgrown clump of holly that gives the cottage its name. I had a brief puzzlement as to how it could have been driven up and parked there without my being awakened. But the lane is gently on the mount past the cottage. Very probably it had been coasted down with the engine switched off.

I did not know what to think. The closing car door suggested departure. But the lights left on — no thief, however inept, would make such a blunder if he were really leaving the scene of the crime. I was not kept in suspense long. There was suddenly a shape at the wicket gate. It passed through and toward the house, out of my sight, almost before I could start back. Events moved with a chilling rapidity. Quick footsteps mounted the stairs. I had an abrupt access of panic: I must do something, I must act. Yet I stood by the window in a kind of catatonia, quite unable to move. I think I was more frightened of my own terror than of its cause. What kept me frozen there was the saner knowledge that I must not act upon it.

The steps reached the small landing across which the doors to the cottage's two bedrooms face each other. What I should have done if the intruder had first turned to the right instead of the left . . . in some strange way it was a distinct mercy to hear the handle of my own door turn. All was darkness, I could see nothing and my state of paralysis endured, as if I still futilely hoped that this unknown presence would turn away. But a torch came on. It discovered at once the disturbed bed I had just left; and a fraction of a second later I was discovered myself by the window — in all my foolishness, barefooted, in pajamas. I recollect I raised an arm over my eyes to shade them from the dazzling beam, though the gesture must also have seemed one of helpless self-defense.

There was a silence, in which it was evident that the person holding the torch was not going to run. I made a feeble attempt to normalize the situation.

"Who are you? What are you doing here?"

The questions were respectively stupid and nugatory, of course, and received the answer, or lack of it, they deserved. I tried again.

"You have no right to be here."

I was spared the torch for a moment. I heard the door of the bedroom opposite open. But then almost at once I was dazzled by the glare of the mirrored bulb again.

There was another pause. Then, at last, a voice.

"Get back into bed."

The tone reassured me a little. I had expected a Dorset, at any rate an aggressively uneducated accent. This was flat and quiet.

"Go on. Into bed."

"There's no need for violence."

"Okay. So like I say."

I hesitated, then went back to the bed and sat nervously on its edge.

"Cover your legs."

Again I hesitated. But I had no alternative. At least I was being spared physical brutality. I put my legs beneath the bed-clothes, and remained sitting upright. The torch still blinded me. There was more silence, as if I were being deciphered and assessed.

"Now the goggles. Take 'em off."

I removed my glasses and put them on the table beside me. The torch left me for a moment, searching for the switch. The room was filled with light. I made out the blurred shape of a young man of medium height with the most bizarre yellow hands; then that he was in some kind of bluish blouse suit, I think of denim. He crossed the room to where I sat in bed. I detected a kind of loose athleticism, and judged him to be in his early twenties. A certain ectoplasmic quality about his face that I had first put down to my myopia now explained itself. It was covered to his eyes with a woman's nylon stocking. The hair was dark, beneath a red knitwear cap; the eyes brown. They now surveyed me for a long moment.

"Why you so shit scared, man?"

The question was so absurd that I did not attempt to answer it. He reached and picked up my glasses, then tried the lenses briefly. I realized the incongruous yellow of the hands was that of kitchen gloves — of course, to avoid fingerprints. Again the eyes above the mask, like those of some concealed and suspicious animal, stared down at me.

"Never happened to you before?"

"It most certainly has not."

"Nor me. We'll play it by ear. Right?"

I gave some kind of nod of assent. He turned and went to where I had been standing when he came in. There he opened the window, then casually tossed my glasses into the night — at least I saw the gesture of his arm that could only mean that. I did feel anger then; and the folly of expressing it. I watched him close the window, then relatch it and draw the curtains. Now he came back to the foot of the bed.

"Right?"

I said nothing.

"Relax."

"I do not find this a relaxing situation."

He folded his arms and contemplated me for a few seconds; then he pointed a finger, as if I had asked him the solution to some problem.

"I'll have to tie you up."

"Very well."

"Don't mind then?"

"I unfortunately have no choice."

Another silence: then he gave a snuffle of amusement.

"Jesus. The number of times I've imagined this. Thousands of ways. But never like this."

"I'm sorry to disappoint you."

Again there was a pause for assessment.

"Thought you only used the place weekends."

"I happen to be borrowing it from the owners."

He devoted more thought to that, then pointed a yellow finger down at me again.

"I get it."

"You get what?"

"Who wants to get bashed for just friends. Right?"

"My dear young man, I am half your size and three times your age."

"Sure. Only kidding."

He turned and looked around the room. But I seemed to intrigue him more than its professional opportunities. He leaned against a chest of drawers and addressed me again.

"Just what you read. How the old crumblers always have a go. Come tottering at you with their pokers and carving knives."

I drew a breath.

He said, "Property. What it does to people. Know what I mean?" He added, "Doesn't apply in your case. So."

I found myself staring at my feet beneath the blankets. Of all the fictional horrors connected with the situation that I had ever seen or read of, not one had included motivational analysis of the victim from its prime cause. He gestured with the torch.

"Should have made a noise, man. I'd've been out like a dose of salts. Wouldn't have known who you were."

"May I venture to suggest you get on with what you came to do?"

Again there was a snuffle. He remained staring at me. Then he shook his head.

"Fantastic."

I had imagined various forms of action, swift and purposeful, and distinguished only by their degrees of unpleasantness; not this obscene simulacrum of a quiet chat between chance-met strangers. Heaven knows I should have felt relieved; yet I would have preferred a devil I knew — or who at least conformed better to one's general notion of his kind. He must have perceived something of this in my face.

"I knock off empty houses, friend. Not tiny people."

"Then kindly stop gloating over it."

I had spoken sharply; and we went a further step in absurdity. There was almost a gentle reproach in his voice.

"Hey. I'm the one who's supposed to be jumpy. Not you." He opened the yellow hands. "Just had a terrible shock, man. You could have been up here loading a shotgun. Anything. Blown my guts out the moment I opened that door."

I gathered strength.

"Isn't it sufficient that you've broken into the house of two decent, law-abiding and not particularly well-off people and intend to rob them of things that have no great value, but which they happen to love and cherish . . ." I did not finish the sentence, perhaps because I didn't quite know how to say what it was that was superfluous in his manner. But my own had grown too belatedly indignant. The quietness of his voice was all the more galling for having been invited.

"Nice house in London as well, have they?"

I had realized by then that I was dealing with someone who belonged to that baffling (to my generation) new world of the classless British young. No one detests class snobbery more sincerely than I do and that the young of today have thrown out so many of the old shibboleths does not disturb me in the least. I wish merely that they did not reject so many other things — such as a respect for language and intellectual honesty — because they mistakenly believe them to be shamefully bourgeois. I was familiar with not dissimilar young men on the fringes of the literary world. They too generally had nothing to offer but their airs of emancipation, their supposed classlessness; and so clung to them with a frightening ferocity. In my experience their distinguishing trait was a needle-sharp sensitivity toward anything that smacked of condescension, a phrase that comprehended all that challenged their own new idols of confused thinking and cultural narrow-mindedness. I knew the particular commandment I had just transgressed: thou shalt not own more than a grubby back-street pad.

"I see. Crime as the good revolutionary's duty?"

"Not just the bread alone. Now you mention it."

Suddenly he picked up a wooden chair from beside the chest of drawers, reversed it and sat across it, his arms perched on the back. Again I was accused by the finger.

"Way I see it, my house has had burglars in since the day I was born. You with me? The system, right? You know what Marx said? The poor can't steal from the rich. The rich can only rob the poor."

I recalled then an oddly similar — in tone if not in content — conversation I had had only a week or two before with an electrician who had come to do some rewiring in my London flat. He had chosen to harangue me for twenty minutes on the iniquity of the trade unions. But he had had the same air of sublime irrefutability. Meanwhile, the present lecture continued.

"Tell you something else. I play fair. I don't take more than I need, right? Never the big stuff. Just places like this. I've had the real class. In my hands. And left it right where I found it. Dear old fuzz, they shake their heads, tell the bereaved owner he's lucky to have had such a ham job done.

Like only a clown could have missed the Paul de Lamerie salver. The first period Worcester teapot. The John Sell Cotman. Right? Except the real clowns are the ones who don't know class is ten to one red hot from the moment you touch it. So any time I'm tempted, I just think of the system, you with me? What's killing it. Greed. Me too. If I ever let it. So I'm never greedy. Never done time. Never will."

I have had a good many people try to justify bad behavior to me; but never in such ridiculous circumstances. Perhaps the greatest absurdity was that red woolen hat. It had to my poor vision a distinct resemblance to a cardinal's biretta. To say that I began to enjoy myself would be very far from the truth. But I did begin to feel that I had the makings of a story to dine out on for months to come.

"Another thing. What I do. Okay, it hurts people . . . what you said. Stuff they love. All that. But maybe it helps them see what a fucking fraud the whole business of property is." He slapped the back of the chair he was sitting across. "I mean, you ever thought? It's mad. This isn't my chair or your chair. Your mates' chair. Just a chair. Doesn't really belong to anyone. I often think that. You know, I take stuff home. Look at it. I don't feel it's mine. It's just whatever it is, right? Doesn't change. Just is." He leaned back. "Now tell me I'm wrong."

I knew any attempt at serious argument with this young buffoon would be like discussing the metaphysics of Duns Scotus with a music-hall comedian: one could only become his butt. His questions and baits were clumsy invitations to a pratfall; yet I had a growing sense that I must try to humor him.

"I agree that wealth is unfairly distributed."

"But not with my way of doing something about it."

"Society wouldn't survive very long if everyone shared your views."

Again he shifted; then shook his head, as if I had made

some bad move in a game of chess. Suddenly he stood up and replaced the chair, and began to open the drawers of the chest. His examination seemed very cursory. I had placed some loose coins and my keys on the top and I heard him finger them apart. But he pocketed nothing; meanwhile I prayed silently that he would overlook the absence of a wallet. It was in my coat, on a hanger behind the door, which opened, and was now opened, against the wall — and was therefore hidden. He turned to face me once more.

"That's like, if everyone did themselves in tomorrow, there wouldn't be a population problem."

"I'm afraid I don't see the parallel."

"You're just saying words, man." He moved nearer the window and stared at himself in a little Regency mirror. "If everyone did this, if everyone did that. But they don't, do they? Like if the system was different, I wouldn't be here. But I'm here. Right?"

As if to emphasize his hereness, he lifted the mirror off the wall; and I gave up playing Alice to this Wonderland of non sequiturs. *I am what I am* may be all very well in its most famous context, but it is not a basis for rational conversation. He seemed to accept that I was silenced by his refutation of the categorical imperative, and now moved to a pair of water-colors that hung on the back wall of the room. I saw him unhook and pore over each in turn, for all the world like some prospective bidder at a country auction. He eventually put them under his arm.

"Across the way — anything there?"

I took a breath. "Not so far as I know."

But he disappeared with his "goods" into the other room. He was careless of sound now. I heard more drawers being opened, a wardrobe. There was nothing I could do. A dash downstairs to the telephone, even with my vanished glasses on, would not have had the faintest chance of success.

I saw him come out and stay bent over a shape on the

landing, some bag or grip. There was a rustling of paper. At last he straightened and stood in the doorway of my own room again.

"Not much," he said. "Never mind. Just your money, and that's it. Sorry."

"My money?"

He nodded toward the chest of drawers.

"I'll leave you the change."

"Haven't you taken enough?"

"Sorry."

"I have very little with me."

"Then you won't miss it. Right?"

He made no threatening gesture, there was no obvious menace in his voice, he simply stood watching me. But further prevarication seemed useless.

"Behind the door."

He pointed his finger at me again, then turned and swung the door to. My sports jacket was revealed. It was absurd, but I felt embarrassed. Wanting to save the bother of finding a bank in Dorset, I had cashed a check for fifty pounds just before I left London. Of course he found the wallet and notes at once. I saw him take the latter and flip through them. Then, to my surprise, he came and dropped one on the end of the bed.

"Fiver for trying. Okay?"

He tucked the rest of the money away in a hip pocket, then fingered idly on through the wallet. At last he took out and scrutinized my banker's card.

"Hey-hey. It's just clicked. That's you on the table down there."

"On the table?"

"All that typing and stuff."

The first three chapters had been typed out, and he must have looked at the title page and remembered my name.

"I came here to finish a book."

"You write books?

"When I'm not being burgled."

He went on through the wallet.

"What kind of books?"

I made no reply.

"What's the one downstairs about then?"

"About someone you won't have heard of and please can we get this disgusting business over and done with?"

He closed the wallet and threw it down beside the five-pound note.

"Why you so sure I know nothing?"

"I did not mean to suggest that."

"You people always get people like me so wrong."

I tried to hide my mounting irritation. "The subject of my book is a long-dead novelist called Peacock. He is not greatly read these days. That is all I meant to say."

He watched me. I had transgressed another new commandment, and I knew I must be more guarded.

"Okay. So why you writing a book about him?"

"Because I admire his work."

"Why?"

"It has qualities I think our own age rather lacks."

"Such as?"

"Humanism. Good manners. A strong belief in common . . ." it was on the tip of my tongue to say "decency" . . . "sense."

"Me, I like Conrad. He's the greatest."

"Many people share your view."

"You not?"

"He's a very fine novelist."

"The greatest."

"Certainly one of the greatest."

"I have a thing about the sea. Know what I mean?" I nodded in what I hoped was a suitably approving manner, but his mind was evidently still on my snub over writers he would not have heard of. "I see books lying around sometimes. Novels. History. Art books. I take 'em home. Read 'em. Like I bet you I know more about antiques than most dealers. See, I go to museums. Just to look. I'd never do a museum. Way I see it, you don't just do a museum, you do every other poor sod who goes to look." He seemed to expect some answer. I gave another faint nod. My back was aching, I had sat so tensely through all this nonsense. It was not his manner, but the tempo he set: *andante* when all should have been *prestissimo*. "Museums is how it ought to be. No private ownership. Just museums. Where everyone can go."

"As in Russia?"

"Right."

Literary men are, of course, perennially susceptible to the eccentric. Endearing is hardly the adjective to apply to someone who has just parted you from forty-five pounds you can ill afford. But I have a small skill at mimicking accents — for telling anecdotes that rely on that rather cruel ability — and I was beginning, beneath fear and exasperation, to savor one or two of my tormentor's mental and linguistic quirks. I gave him a thin smile.

"In spite of what they do to thieves there?"

"Man, I wouldn't do this there. Simple as that. You have to hate, yes? Plenty to hate here. No problem. Okay, so they've screwed a lot of things up. But least they're trying. That's what people like me can't stand in this country. Nobody's trying. You know the only people who try in this country? The fucking Tories. I mean, there's a bunch of real pro's. Blokes like me, we're peanuts beside them."

"My friends who own this cottage are not Tories. In fact, very far from it. Nor am I, for that matter."

"Big deal."

But he said it lightly.

"We hardly qualify as a blow for the cause."

"Hey, you trying to make me feel guilty or something?"

"Just a shade more aware of the complexities of life."

He stood staring down at me for a long moment, and I thought I was in for another bout of his pseudo-Marcusian — if that is not a tautology — naïveties. But suddenly he pulled back the wrist of one of his yellow gloves and looked at a watch.

"Too bad. It's been fun. Right. Now. I have way-way-way to drive, so I make myself a cup of coffee. Okay? You, you get up, take your time, put on your clothes. Then you trot downstairs."

My briefly lulled fears sprang back to life.

"Why my clothes?"

"I have to tie you up, man. And we don't want you to get cold waiting. Do we?"

I nodded.

"That's a good boy." He went to the door, but turned. "And sir — coffee too?"

"No thank you."

"Cuppa? I'm easy."

I shook my head, and he went downstairs. I felt weak, more badly shaken than I had realized; and I knew what I had just experienced was the comparatively pleasant part of the process. I now had to endure hours of being tied up, and I didn't see how I was to be released. Wanting no disruption, I had done nothing about having my mail forwarded, therefore no postman was likely to call. Milk, as Jane had warned me, I had to go and fetch for myself at the farm. I could not imagine why anyone should come anywhere near the cottage.

I got up and started to dress — and to review what I had deduced of the new-style Raffles downstairs. His fondness for his own voice had at least allowed me to form some dim impression of his background. Wherever he originally came from, I felt fairly sure that his normal milieu was now London — a large city, at any rate. I could detect no clear regional accent. That might have argued a less working-class origin

than his grotesque language suggested; but on the whole I felt
he had climbed rather than fallen. He had very plainly wished
to impress on me that he had some pretentions to education.
Indeed I could believe that he had, say, passed his A-levels
and even perhaps had a year at some Redbrick university. I
saw in him many of the defense mechanisms, born of a sense
of frustration, that were familiar to me from some of my own
friends' children.

Maurice and Jane's own younger son had (to the intense
mortification of his parents, who in characteristic Hampstead-
liberal fashion were nothing if not tolerant to the youth revo-
lution) recently taken to showing many of the same airs and
ungraces. Having dropped out of Cambridge and the "total
futility" of studying the law — his father's being a solicitor
no doubt made that renunciation doubly agreeable — he had
announced that he was going to compose folk music. After a
few months of increasing petulance (or so I understood from
his parents) at not achieving instant success in that field, he
had retired — if that is the word — into a Maoist commune
run by some property millionaire's flyaway daughter in South
Kensington. I recite his career a little flippantly, but the very
genuine and understandable distress of Maurice and Jane at
the mess Richard was making of his young life was not a
laughing matter. I had had an account of a bitter evening
when he first walked out on Cambridge, in which he de-
nounced their way of life and everything to do with it. Their
two lifetimes of fighting for sane good causes, varying from
nuclear disarmament to the preservation of the plane trees in
Fitzjohn's Avenue, were suddenly thrown back in their faces
— their chief crime (according to Jane) being the fact that
they still lived in a house they had bought when they first
married in 1946 for a few thousand and which now happened
to be worth sixty or more. Their kind have become the stock-
in-trade of every satirist about, and no doubt there is a dissonance between the pleasant lives they lead in private and

the battle for the underprivileged they conduct in public. Perhaps a successful solicitor should not have a fondness for first nights, even though he gives his legal knowledge free to any action group that asks for it; perhaps a Labour councillor (as Jane was for many years) should not enjoy cooking dinners worthy of an Elizabeth David; but their real worst crime in Richard's eyes was to think that this balanced life was intelligently decent, instead of blindly hypocritical.

Though I sympathized with Maurice's outrage and his accusations of selfish irresponsibility, perhaps Jane was more accurate in her final diagnosis. She argued, I think correctly, that though *épater la famille* formed an element in the boy's downfall, the real cancer in him and his like was an intransigent idealism. He was so besotted — or bepotted — by visions of artistic glory and a nobly revolutionary way of life that the normal prospect before him was hopelessly rebarbative. As Jane had rather neatly put it, he wanted Everest in a day; if it took two, he lost interest.

My own specimen of youth in revolt had merely solved his problems a little more successfully — by a kind of perverted logic one could say more convincingly — than young Richard with his Little Red Book. At least he supported himself financially, in his fashion. The sub-sub-Marxism was a joke, of course; a mere trendy justification after the act, as Marx himself, dear old middle-class square that he was, would have been the first to demonstrate.

I need hardly say that I didn't at the time draw the kind of extended parallel with Richard I have just made. But I had thought of the boy as I stood putting my clothes on — and no sooner thought than implicated him. I had already wondered how the young man downstairs had known that Holly Cottage existed. The more I considered, the more improbable a place it seemed for the lightning to strike. Then he had apparently known the owners lived in London. He could have found that out at the farm or the local pub; but he seemed too fly to invite unnecessary risks of that sort. So why should he not have learned about Maurice and Jane and their cottage from the horse's — to be precise, the rebellious colt's — mouth? I had certainly never seen anything vicious or spiteful in Richard and I couldn't imagine that he would have deliberately urged anyone to "do" his parents' property — whatever he may have shouted at them in a moment of crisis. But he might have talked about it among his collection of would-be young world-changers . . . and I had evidence enough that my own young joker fancied himself as a political philosopher of the same ilk. He had also just revealed that he had a long drive ahead. That suggested London. The hypothesis shocked me, but it rang plausibly probable.

I was still trying to confirm it by some other chance thing he had let fall when I heard his voice from the foot of the stairs.

"Ready when you are, dad."

I had to go down. I sought desperately for some innocent question that might help clinch my guess. But none came to mind — and even if I were right, he must have seen the danger as soon as I revealed myself a friend of Richard's parents.

I found him sitting by the solid old farm table in the center of the living room. He had a mug of coffee in his hand, which he raised, no doubt sarcastically, toward me when I appeared. Beyond him I saw the lighted doorway through to the kitchen.

"Sure you don't want coffee?"

"No."

"Nip of brandy then? There's some in the cupboard."

His mixture of gall and solicitude once more made me take breath.

"No thank you."

I glanced around the room. I saw two or three paintings were missing and I suspected that there was less china on the dresser beside which I stood than when I had last seen it.

"Better go through there then." He nodded back at the kitchen, and for a moment I did not understand what he meant. "Calls of nature and all that."

Maurice and Jane had had a lavatory and bathroom added at the back of the cottage.

"How long do you . . ."

"Anyone due around in the morning?"

"No one at all."

"Okay."

He crossed to the corner of the room, and I saw him pick up the telephone directory there and leaf through it.

"Your phone's out, by the way. Sorry."

He leafed on, then tore a page from the book.

"Right? I'll call the local fuzz around ten. If I wake up." But he added quickly, "Just a joke, man. Relax. I promise." Then he said, "You going or not?"

I went into the kitchen — and saw the door out into the garden. There was a jagged black hole in its previously smooth expanse of glass; and I secretly cursed my absent hostess for her sacrifice of period accuracy to domestic amenity. My own very present guest came and stood in the doorway behind me.

"And don't lock yourself in by mistake. Please."

I went into the lavatory and closed the door; and found myself staring at the bolt. There was a narrow window that gave on the cottage's back garden. I could just have negotiated it, I suppose. But he would have heard me open it; and the garden had a thick banked hedge all around it — the only practicable exit was to come to the front of the house.

When I returned to the living room, I saw he had placed a Windsor chair in front of the open hearth, which he now offered to me. I stood by the doorway, trying to escape this last indignity.

"I am perfectly prepared to give you my word. I won't raise the alarm until you've had time for your . . . getaway, whatever it is."

"Sorry." He offered me the chair again, and held a ring of something up; then realized that I couldn't make it out. "Sticky tape. It won't hurt."

Something in me continued to bridle against this final humiliation. I did not move. He came toward me. His wretched nylon-masked face, in some way obscene, as if molten, made me take a step back. But he didn't touch me.

I pushed past him and sat down.

"Good boy. Now put your mitts along the rests, will you?" He held up two strips of colored paper he must have torn out of some magazine in readiness. "Over your wrists, right? Then you won't get your hairs tweaked when the tape comes off."

I watched him bend the paper around my left wrist. Then he began to tape it tightly to the chair arm. In spite of myself I could not stop my hands trembling. I could see his face, even — it was my impression — the shadow of a moustache under the nylon.

"I should like to ask one thing."

"Go on then."

"What made you pick on this house?"

"Thinking of taking it up, are you?" But he went on before I could answer. "Okay. Curtains. Color of paintwork. For a start."

"What does that mean?"

"Means I can smell weekend places a mile off. Nice classy piece of fabric hanging in a window. Twenty quid's worth of oil lamp on the sill. Dozens of things. How's that then? Not too bad?"

It seemed very tight, but I shook my head. "And why this part of the world?"

He started on the other wrist. "Anywhere there's daft gits who leave their houses empty."

"You come from London?"

"Where's that then?"

Very plainly I would extract nothing of significance from him. Yet I detected a faint unease beneath the facetiousness. It was confirmed when he rather hurriedly changed the subject from his life to mine.

"Written a lot of books, have you?"

"A dozen or so."

"How long's it take?"

"That depends on the book."

"What about the one you're doing now?"

"I've been researching it for several years. That takes more time than the actual writing."

He was silent for a few moments as he finished the taping of the other wrist. Then he bent down. I felt him push my left ankle back against the chair leg; then the constriction of the adhesive tape began there.

"I'd like to write books. Maybe I will one day." Then, "How many words is a book?"

"Sixty thousand is the normal minimum."

"Lot of words."

"I haven't found you short of them."

He glanced up briefly from his work.

"Not how you expected. Right?"

"I won't attempt to deny that."

"Yeah. Well . . ."

But again he fell silent, winding the tape. He had found a pair of scissors somewhere, and now he severed the end around my left ankle, and moved to the other foot.

"I'd tell it how it really is. Not just this. Everything. The whole scene."

"Then why don't you try?"

"You're joking."

"Not at all. Crime fascinates people."

"Sure. Lovely. Then look who comes knocking on my door."

"You'd have to disguise actual circumstances."

"Then it wouldn't be how it is. Right?"

"Do you think Conrad —"

"He was Conrad, wasn't he?"

I heard the snip of the scissors that showed my final limb was secured; then he pulled outward on my legs to ensure that the tape did not give.

"Anyway. Several years. Yes? That's a lot of time."

He stood and stared down at his work. I had the uncomfortable feeling that I had now become a parcel, a mere problem in safe packaging. Yet there was a relief, too. No violence could take place now.

He said, "Right."

He went into the kitchen, but came back almost at once with a length of washing line and a kitchen knife. He stood in front of me, measuring off a couple of arms' widths, and began to cut and saw at the cord with the knife.

"Maybe you? Write about me — how about that?"

"I'm afraid I couldn't write about something I don't begin to understand."

With a sharp tug he finally detached the end he wanted. He passed behind the chair, and I heard his voice from above my head.

"What don't you understand?"

"How someone who is apparently not by any means a fool can behave as you are."

He laced the washing line through the slats at the back of the chair. His arm came over my shoulder and led it around my chest and under my other arm.

"Back straight, will you?" I felt the line tighten. Then the free end was passed around again. "Thought I explained all that."

"I can understand young people who go in for left-wing violence — even when they disrupt public life. At least they are acting for a cause. You seem to be acting purely for your private profit."

In saying that I was, of course, hoping for some more substantial clue to confirm my hypothesis over Richard. But he
didn't rise to the bait. I felt him knotting the cord behind the
chair. Then once again he came in front of me and looked me
over.

"How's that?"

"Extremely uncomfortable."

He stood watching me a moment. Then there came another
of his pointed fingers.

"Man, your trouble is you don't listen hard enough."

I said nothing. He contemplated me a moment further.

"Now I load up. I'll be back to say tara."

He picked up a large grip from beneath the window on the
lane, and went to the front door, which I could partly see
through the living-room doorway. He propped it open with
the grip, then disappeared for a moment into the sitting room.
He came out of there with something pale and square under
his arm, I think a carton box; picked up the grip, then went
on out into the night. The front door swung gently to. There
was silence for nearly a minute. Then I heard the faint sound
of a car door being closed. The wicket gate squeaked, but he
did not come straight into the house. I saw why, when he did
reappear. He showed me my glasses, which he put on the
table.

"Your pebbles," he said. "Still in good nick. Sure you don't
want a brandy?"

"No thank you."

"Electric fire?"

"I'm not cold."

"Right. Just got to gag you then."

He picked up the tape and the scissors.

"There's no one within earshot. I could shout all night."

He seemed to hesitate a moment, then shook his head.
"Sorry, man. Must do."

I now watched him peel and cut four or five lengths from

the tape, which he laid in a row on the table beside us. When he reached forward with the first of them I instinctively jerked my head aside.

"This is totally unnecessary!"

He waited. "Come on. Let's end as we began."

I am sure I should have struggled if he had used force. But he was like some bored nurse with a recalcitrant patient. In the end I closed my eyes and turned my head to face him. I felt the plaster pressed obliquely against my grimly resentful mouth. Then it was smoothed down on my cheeks; then the other lengths. I felt near panic again, that I should not be able to breathe through my nose alone. Perhaps he had something of the same fear, for he watched me closely in silence for several moments. Then he picked up the knife and scissors and went into the kitchen. I heard them replaced in a drawer. The kitchen light was switched off.

I am going to state what followed as baldly as possible. I could not in any case find adequate words to describe what I suffered.

I had every reason to suppose that he was now going to leave me to my miserable vigil. He would walk out, and that would be the last of him. But when he came back from the kitchen he stooped by the dresser and opened one of its bottom doors. Then he stood up with an armful of the old newspapers Jane kept there for lighting the fire. I watched, still baffled by what he was doing — I had said I wasn't cold — as he knelt at the hearth of the old chimney that ran half the length of the wall beside me. He began to ball and crumple the newspaper on the central hearthstone. Through this, and all that followed, he did not once look at me. He behaved exactly as if I had not been there.

When he rose and disappeared through to the sitting room, I knew . . . and did not know — or could not believe. But I had to believe when he returned. I recognized only too well the red covers of the large ledger in which I had my master plan and longhand drafts of various key passages; and the small brown rectangular box that held my precious card index of references. I strained violently at my wrists and ankles, I attempted to cry out through the tape over my mouth. Some kind of noise must have emerged, but he took no notice.

Monstrously, I was obliged to watch as he crouched and set my four years of intermittent but irreplaceable work on the hearth beside him, then calmly leaned forward, lighter in hand, and set fire to two or three ends of the newspaper. When it began to blaze he quietly fed batches of typescript to the flames. There followed a thick folder of photostated documents — copies of manuscript letters, of contemporary reviews of Peacock's novels that I had laboriously traced down, and the like. I made no further sound, I was beyond it — what was the use? Nothing would stop him now from this bestial and totally gratuitous act of vandalism. It is absurd to speak of dignity when one is bound hand and foot, and I felt tears of helpless rage only too close at hand; but my last resort was to suppress them. I closed my eyes for a few moments, then opened them again at the sound of pages being torn from the ledger. With the same insufferably methodical calmness he fed them to the mounting holocaust, whose heat I now felt through my clothes and on my face, or what was left bare of it. He retreated a little and started tossing new fuel forward rather than dropping it on the pyre as hitherto. The reference cards were shaken out and fluttered down to be consumed. After a while he reached for a poker that lay beside the fireplace and pushed one or two merely charring sheets and cards to where they also caught flame. If only I had had that poker in a free hand! I would happily have smashed his skull in with it.

Still without looking at me, he went back to the sitting room. This time he returned with the ten volumes of my copiously annotated *Collected Works* and various previous biographies and critical books on Peacock that I had brought with me and piled on the table. They all had countless slips of paper jutting out; their importance had been only too conspicuously declared. They too were consigned one by one to the flames. He waited patiently, juggling the books open with the poker when they seemed slow to catch. He even noticed that my copy of Van Doren's *Life* was broken-spined and duly wrenched it apart to aid it on its way. I thought he would now wait till every page, every line of print was burnt to nothingness. But he straightened when he threw the last volume on the top of the rest. Perhaps he realized that books burn much less easily than loose paper; or relied on them to char and smolder away through the night; or did not care, now that the major damage had been done. He stared down for a long moment into the hearth. Then at last he turned to me. His hand moved; I thought he was going to strike me. But all I was presented with, a foot from my face, as if to make sure that even someone as "blind" as I was could not mistake the gesture, was the yellow hand clenched into a fist — and incomprehensibly, with the thumb cocked high. The sign of mercy, when there was no mercy.

He must have left his hand in that inexplicable position for at least five seconds. Then he turned away and went to the door. He cast a last look around the room, seemingly without anger, a mere neat workman's check that everything was left in order. I think I was not included in his glance.

The light went out. I heard the front door open, then close. The wicket gate squeaked, and then that too was shut. I sat distraught, with the flames and malevolently licking shadows; with the acrid smell, surely the most distressing of all after burnt human flesh, of cremated human knowledge. A car door was shut, an engine started — a maneuvering, a changing of gears as he turned in the lane, a flicker of headlights on the drawn curtains. Then I heard the car draw away up the hill from the village. In that direction the lane (I knew, since the taxi that had brought me the previous evening had taken it) eventually joined the main road to Sherborne; and passed nowhere in the process.

I was left to silence, catastrophe and the dying flames.

I shall not labor the agonies of those next nine or ten hours; of watching that fire die away, of increasing discomfort, of raging anger at the atrocious blow that had fallen. I refused all thought of building on the only too literal ashes before me. The world was insane, I no longer wished to have anything to do with it. I would devote the rest of my life to revenge, to tracking that sadistic young fiend down. I would comb every likely coffee bar in London, I would make Maurice and Jane give the most exact description of everything that had been stolen. I would ruthlessly pursue my suspicions over Richard. Once or twice I dropped off, only to awaken again a minute or two later, as though from a nightmare — only to learn that the nightmare was the reality. I moved arms and legs as much as I could to keep my circulation going. Repeated attempts to loosen either bonds or the gag failed completely; and so did my efforts to shift the chair. Again I cursed Jane, or the matting she had had laid over the stone floor. The legs refused to slide on it, and I could not get any sort of purchase. I knew numbness, and then great cold — made all the more bitter for my having refused his offer to prevent it.

An intolerably slow dawn crept through the curtains. Soon afterward an early car passed down toward the village. I made a vain attempt to shout through my gagged mouth. The car swept on and out of hearing. Once more I tried to edge the chair toward the window, but made barely a yard of distance after a quarter of an hour of effort. A last jerk of frustration nearly overbalanced the chair backward, and I gave up. A little later I heard a tractor coming up the lane, no doubt from the farm. Again I made every attempt to cry for help. But the machine dragged slowly past and up the hill. I began then to be seriously afraid. Whatever confidence I had invested in the young man had been completely lost in those final minutes. If he could do that, he could do anything. To break his promise about telling the police would be nothing to him.

It eventually occurred to me that in edging forward, toward the front of the cottage, I was making a mistake. There were knives in the kitchen behind; and indeed I found it easier to proceed backward, as I could exert a better pressure with the soles of my shoes. I started to inch my way back toward the kitchen. There was an edge of rush mat that proved hideously difficult to negotiate. But by eleven I had at last crept through into the kitchen — and felt very near weeping. Already I had had to pass water as I sat; and try as I would, I could not get my fingers up to any drawer where cutlery was kept. I was finally reduced to an inert despair.

Then at last, soon after midday, I heard another car approach — the seventh or eighth of the morning. But this one stopped outside the cottage. My heart leaped. A few moments later I heard a knock on the front door. I cursed myself for not having followed my original plan of movement. There was a further knock, then silence. I seethed at the stupidity of country policeman. But I did the man an injustice. Very soon afterward there was a concerned official face staring at me through the jagged hole in the glass of the kitchen door.

And that was that.

Nearly a year has passed now since that moment of rescue, and I will be brief over the factual aftermath.

The constable who released me proved kind and efficient — indeed I had nothing but kindness and efficiency from everyone else that day. As soon as he had cut me free, he insisted on providing the immemorial English answer to all the major crises of existence. Only when he had watched me down two cups of his dark brown tea did he return to his car and radio in a report. I had hardly changed into clean clothes before a doctor arrived, very soon followed by two plainclothesmen. The doctor declared me none the worse, and I then had a long questioning from the detective sergeant. The constable went off meanwhile to telephone Maurice and Jane from the farm.

At least I found that I was not mistaken in believing that I had a story to dine out on. "The cheeky devil!" and similar comments interrupted all my account. The burning of my book completely nonplussed the sergeant — had I, like, any enemies? I had to disillusion him as to the lengths to which the London literary *mafiosi* will go to gain their foul ends; but that the cottage had been "chosen" surprised him rather less. The kind of crime, and of criminal, was increasingly frequent. I even detected a certain grudging admiration. These "random loners" were smart customers, it seemed; never "did a job" near where they lived, but based themselves on some big city and exploited the new mania for the weekend cottage. The sergeant confessed it was difficult to know where to look. It could be London . . . or Bristol, Birmingham, anywhere. He blamed it all on the motorways and the new mobility they allowed the "villains."

Of Richard, on reflection I said nothing. I felt I owed it at least to Maurice and Jane to discuss the matter with them in private first — the constable had spoken to Jane in Hampstead, and she had sent her commiseration, with the assurance that they would come down at once. Then the farmer and his wife appeared, full of apologies for not having heard anything; then a telephone engineer . . . I was grateful for all the coming and going, which at least took my mind off the blow I had suffered.

Maurice and Jane arrived by car, soon after seven, and I had to go through my story all over again. Ignorant of my personal loss until they arrived, they were kind enough then to treat their own misfortune as nothing beside mine. I introduced my suspicion as regards Richard as obliquely as possible, but I did not spare them the details of the political philosophizing I had received. In the end I saw Jane look at Maurice, and knew that four had been reached. A few minutes later Maurice took the bull by the horns and was on the telephone to his son in London. He was diplomatic — naturally he didn't accuse him of conscious complicity — but as firmly probing as a good solicitor should be. He came away from the receiver to say that Richard swore he had never even mentioned the cottage — and that he (Maurice) believed him. But I could see he was troubled. When the sergeant appeared again a little later to take a full list of what had been stolen, I heard Maurice lay the matter before him. I understand the "commune" was subsequently raided, but nothing more incriminating was found than the inevitable cannabis. No young man there matched my description who had not a sound alibi; and nothing resulted from this line of investigation.

Nor indeed from any other in the weeks and months that followed; it has remained, in public terms, no more than an unsolved minor crime. I cannot even claim that it has irreparably affected my writing self. I spent a month of misery — I suppose in something very like a profound sulk — which no one who had known what the book meant to me was allowed to alleviate. But I hadn't taken everything to do with it to Dorset. A carbon of the first three typed-out chapters had remained in London; and I found that my memory was a good deal better than I had previously suspected. Some kind of challenge was involved. I decided one day that my friends were right and that the Peacock could be reconstituted; and already I am more than halfway on the road to doing just that.

This must seem a very flat end to my adventure. But I have not quite finished what I want to say. There is a sense in which what I have so far written is no more than a preamble.

Just as my reconstituted Peacock cannot be quite the same as the one that was torn, so to speak, from the womb, I cannot be sure that I have reproduced the events of that night with total accuracy. I have tried my best, but I may have exaggerated, especially in the attempts to transcribe my persecutor's dialogue. He did not perhaps employ the idiot argot of Black Power (or wherever it derives from) quite as repetitively as I have described; and I may have misread some of his apparent feelings.

But what concerns me far more than one or two minor misinterpretations or inaccuracies of memory is my continuing inability to make sense of what happened. I have written it down principally to try to come to some sort of positive conclusion. What haunts me most can be put as two questions. Why did it happen? Why did it happen to me? In essence: what was it in me that drove that young demon to behave as he did?

I cannot regard it merely as some offbeat incident in the war between the generations. I cannot even see myself as typical of my generation and (in spite of what I may have said in my first weeks of anger) I do not think he is typical of his — or to be more precise, I do not think that that last unforgivable action is typical of his. They may despise us; but young people in general seem to me much more averse to hating than we were at their age. Everyone knows their attitude to love, the horrors of the permissive society and all the rest of it; very few have noted that in devaluing love, they have also rather healthily devalued hate. The burning of my book was in some way linked to the need — presumably on both sides — for anathema. In that I believe he was very far from typical.

There comes next an enigma; the fact that this unforgivable act was preceded by a surprisingly mild, almost kind, course of behavior. When he said he did not want to hurt me physically, I believed him. It was not said ambiguously, as some kind of threat by paradox. He meant, I am virtually sure, exactly what he said. Yet that cannot square with the vicious cruelty (to a powerless older man) of what he finally did. I tended at first to read a cold calculation into his behavior: from the start he was kind only to deceive — or at least from the moment when he linked me with the book downstairs. But now I simply do not know. I would give a very great deal — I think even an

absolution, if that were a condition of putting the question —
to know when he truly decided to do it. My unfortunate moment of condescension in the bedroom annoyed him; and my
questioning of his motives, compared to that of genuine young
political revolutionaries, also no doubt stung. But neither
seemed, or seems still, to have merited quite such savage retri-
bution.

Then there is the other enigma — of that distinct air of reproach at my behavior he showed at the very beginning. I have
some guilty conscience here, because this is the first time I
have told the truth about it. I claimed to the police, and to
Maurice and Jane, that I was surprised asleep in bed. No one
blamed me for not trying to resist — in that, intruder and victim have been in a minority of two. I am still not sure that I
really blame myself. What regrets I have depend on my credit-
ing his own assertion: that if I had only made a noise, he would
have decamped. In any case it makes no sense that he burned
my book because I failed to attack him. Why should he punish
me for making things easy? And what in his actual behavior,
with its very apparent touchiness, suggested that standing up
to him would have helped prevent what happened? Supposing
I had been sarcastic and insulting, what you will . . . should I
have got off any better?

I have tried to list what he might have hated in me, both
reasonably and unreasonably: my age, my physical puniness,
my myopia, my accent, my education, my lack of guts, my
everything else. I must certainly have seemed precious, old-
fashioned, square, and all the rest of it, but surely all that
could not have added up to much more than the figure of a
vaguely contemptible elderly man. I can hardly have stood for
what he called Them, the "system": capitalism. I belonged to a
profession he seemed to have some respect for — he liked
books, he liked Conrad. So why could he not like — or rather,
why did he have to hate me? If he regarded my book on Peacock in the puritanical kind of way of the *New Left Review*,

as mere parasitism on a superseded bourgeois art form, he would surely have said so. And he was not even remotely like an intellectual Marxist.

To Maurice and Jane this quasi-political is the most convincing explanation. But I think they are a little biased by the trauma in their own family that Richard has caused. I regard it as no true analogy with my young man at all. He at no time linked me personally with "Them." He showed no interest in my political views. He attacked something quite plainly apolitical: my book.

There remains strongly with me the impression of a better mind than his language suggested, as if he half knew he was talking nonsense and was partly doing so to test me: if I gave him so much rope to play the clown, then I deserved to be made a fool of in my turn. But I suspect that this is being over-complicated. At heart, what he said and how I reacted to it had no importance. In hindsight I can imagine quite other courses our conversation might have taken, and yet ended with the same dire result.

I must mention one other theory of Maurice's: that the boy was some kind of schizophrenic and that the effort and stress of being restrained with me built up until the more violent side of his personality had to be displayed. But *after* he must have made the decision, he was still pressing brandy on me and offering to put on the fire for warmth. This seems altogether too conscious for schizophrenia. Besides, at no point did he offer me personal physical violence or suggest that the point of the exercise was to show me that he had such a side. I was bound and gagged. He could have punched me, slapped my face, done what he liked. But I am convinced that my body was always safe from him. What was under attack was something else.

Now there is, I believe, an important clue in that curious last gesture — the aggressive cocked thumb thrust in my face. Very plainly it was not meant to convey its classical significance: no mercy was being extended. Equally obviously it cannot have carried its most common modern meaning: "everything is all right." I noticed it used frequently by the demolition workmen opposite my flat when I returned to London — a spectacle that I found now carried a certain morbid fascination for me, since death and destruction were much on my mind; and I was struck by the variety of meanings they extracted from the cocked thumb. It said simply "yes," when noise made shouting difficult; or "I understand, I will do what you want"; it could also rather paradoxically convey both the instruction to carry on (if, for instance, held continuously raised to a backing lorry-driver) and that of "stop — perfect" (when suddenly raised in the same maneuver). But what was lacking in all these uses was aggression. It was not till some months later that I saw the light.

I have a small vice, I am rather fond of watching association football matches on television. Quite what I derive from this vacuous pursuit beyond the intellectual's sense of superiority at the sight of so much mindless energy devoted to the modern equivalent of the Roman circus, I am not sure. But what caught my attention one evening was a player running out of the "tunnel" onto the arena who showed just this aggressive thumb to a band of screaming supporters in the stands nearby; one or two even responded in kind. The significance (the game had not started) was clear: our courage is high, we are going to beat the enemy, we shall win. The echo was very sharp. I suddenly saw my thief's gesture as a warning: a grim match was about to start, and the opposing team he represented was determined to win. He was effectively saying, you are not going to get away with this so easily as you think. It may seem that such a message might with much more cause have been mine to him. But I think not. Burning my papers was simply a supporting proof of the cocked thumb; what underlay both was a fear, or certainly a detestation of the fact that in this particular match I entered the field with the odds on my

side. However improbably, in the actual physical circumstances, in some way I remained in his view the overdog.

All this leads me to a tentative conclusion. I have very little
evidence for it, and what I do I have already undermined by
confessing that I cannot swear to its complete accuracy. But
I think some of his linguistic usages (certainly recurrent, if not
quite so much as I have suggested) are very significant. One
was that use of "man." I know it is very common among
young people. But it seemed just a shade deliberate in its application to myself. Though partly insulting in intention, I think
it also disguised a somewhat pathetic attempt to level. It
wished to convey that there was nothing between us despite
the differences in age, education, background and all the rest;
but in reality it showed a kind of recognition, perhaps even a
kind of terror of all that did separate us. It may not be too
farfetched to say that what I failed to hear ("Man, your trouble
is you don't listen hard enough") was a tacit cry for help.

The other usage is that of "right" as a ubiquitous tag to all
manner of statements that do not require it. I know it is also
so commonplace among the young that it may be dangerous to
see more in it than a mere psittacism — a mindless parroting.
For all that, I suspect it is one of the most revealing catch-
phrases of our century. It may grammatically be more often an
ellipsis for "Is that right?" than for "Am I right?" — but I am
convinced the psychological significance is always of the latter
kind. It means in effect, *I am not at all sure that I am right*. It
can, of course, be said aggressively: "Don't you dare say I am
wrong!" But the thing it cannot mean is self-certainty. It is
fundamentally expressive of doubt and fear, of so to speak
hopeless *parole* in search of lost *langue*. The underlying mis-
trust is of language itself. It is not so much that such people
doubt what they think and believe, but they doubt profoundly
their ability to say it. The mannerism is a symptom of a cultural breakdown. It means "I cannot, or I probably cannot,

communicate with you." And that, not the social or economic, is the true underprivilege.

It is very important, or so I have read, when faced with primitive tribes, to know the significances they attach to facial expression. Many a worthy and smiling missionary died because he did not realize he was greeting men to whom the baring of the teeth is an unmistakable sign of hostility. I believe something of the same kind takes place when right-users face those who manage to get by without the wretched word. I won't be so absurd as to maintain that if I had interspersed my own remarks with a few reciprocal mans and rights the night would then have taken a different path. But I am convinced that the fatal clash between us was of one who trusts and reveres language and one who suspects and resents it. My sin was not primarily that I was middle-class, intellectual, that I may have appeared more comfortably off financially than I am in fact; but that I live by words.

I must very soon have appeared to the boy as one who deprived him of a secret — and one he secretly wanted to possess. That rather angry declaration of at least some respect for books; that distinctly wistful desire to write a book himself (to "tell it how it really is" — as if the poverty of that phrase did not *ab initio* castrate the wish it implied!); that striking word-deed paradox in the situation, the civil chat while he went around the room robbing; that surely not quite unconscious incoherence in his views; that refusal to hear, seemingly even to understand, my mildly raised objections; that jumping from one thing to another . . . all these made the burning of my book only too justly symbolic in his eyes. What was really burned was my generation's "refusal" to hand down a kind of magic.

My fate was most probably sealed from the moment I rejected his suggestion that I write about him myself. I took the wish at the time as a kind of dandyism, a narcissism, call it what you will — print as a mirror for the ego. But I think what he really invited — at any rate subconsciously — was the loan of some of this magic power . . . and perhaps because he could not really believe in its existence until he saw it applied to himself. In a sense he placed his own need in the scales against what I had called a long-dead novelist; and what he must have resented most was the application of this precious and denied gift of word-magic to no more than another obscure word-magician. I presented a closed shop, a select club, an introverted secret society; and that is what he felt he had to destroy.

I do not say this was all, but I am convinced it was the heart of it. The charge against all of us, old and young, who still value language and its powers, is unjustified to be sure. Most of us have willy-nilly done our best to see that the word, its secrets and its magics, it sciences and its arts, survive. The true villains of the piece are well beyond individual control: the triumph of the visual, of television, the establishment of universal miseducation, the social and political (can any ancient master of language be groaning louder in his grave than Pericles?) history of our unmanageable century and heaven knows how many other factors. Yet I do not want to portray myself as an innocent scapegoat. I believe my young demon was right in one thing.

I *was* guilty of a deafness.

I have quite deliberately given this account an obscure title and an incomprehensible epigraph. I did not elect for the first without trying it out on various guinea pigs. The general impression seemed to be that Koko must be some idiosyncratic spelling for the more usual Coco, and that the phrase therefore meant something to the effect of "poor clown." That will do for a first level of meaning, though I shouldn't like to see it attached to only one of the two participants — or for that matter to have the adjective taken in only one of its senses. Koko has in fact nothing whatever to do with Coco of the red proboscis and the ginger wig. It is a Japanese word and means correct filial behavior, the proper attitude of son to father.

My incomprehensible epigraph shall have the last word, and serve as judgment on both father and son. It comes with a sad prescience from an extinct language of these islands, Old Cornish.

> Too long a tongue, too short a hand;
> But tongueless man has lost his land.

The Enigma

---

*Who can be
muddy and yet,
settling, slowly
become limpid?*
— TAO TE CHING

THE COMMONEST KIND of missing person is the adolescent girl, closely followed by the teen-age boy. The majority in this category come from working-class homes, and almost invariably from those where there is serious parental disturbance. There is another minor peak in the third decade of life, less markedly working-class, and constituted by husbands and wives trying to run out on marriages or domestic situations they have got bored with. The figures dwindle sharply after the age of forty; older cases of genuine and lasting disappearance are extremely rare, and again are confined to the very poor — and even there to those, near vagabond, without close family.

When John Marcus Fielding disappeared, he therefore contravened all social and statistical probability. Fifty-seven years old, rich, happily married, with a son and two daughters; on the board of several City companies (and very much not merely to adorn the letterheadings); owner of one of the finest Elizabethan manor houses in East Anglia, with an active interest in the running of his adjoining eighteen-hundred-acre farm; a joint — if somewhat honorary — master of foxhounds, a keen shot . . . he was a man who, if there were an -arium of living human stereotypes, would have done very well as a model of his kind: the successful City man who is also a country landowner and (in all but name) village squire. It would have been very understandable if he had felt that one or the other side of his life had become too time-consuming . . . but the most profoundly anomalous aspect of his case was that he was also a Conservative Member of Parliament.

At two thirty on the afternoon of Friday, July 13, 1973, his elderly secretary, a Miss Parsons, watched him get into a taxi outside his London flat in Knightsbridge. He had a board meeting in the City; from there he was going to catch a train, the 5:22, to the market-town headquarters of his constituency. He would arrive soon after half past six, then give a "surgery" for two hours or so. His agent, who was invited to supper, would then drive him the twelve miles or so home to Tetbury Hall. A strong believer in the voting value of the personal contact, Fielding gave such surgeries twice a month. The agenda of that ominously appropriate day and date was perfectly normal.

It was discovered subsequently that he had never appeared at the board meeting. His flat had been telephoned, but Miss Parsons had asked for, and been granted, the rest of the afternoon off — she was weekending with relatives down in Hastings. The daily help had also gone home. Usually exemplary in attendance or at least in notifying unavoidable absence, Fielding was forgiven his lapse, and the board went to business without him. The first realization that something was wrong was therefore the lot of the constituency agent. His member was not on the train he had gone to meet. He went back to the party offices to ring Fielding's flat — and next, getting no answer there, his country home. At Tetbury Hall Mrs. Fielding was unable to help. She had last spoken to her husband on the Thursday morning; so far as she knew he should be where he wasn't. She thought it possible, however, that he might have decided to drive down with their son, a postgraduate student at the London School of Economics. This son, Peter, had talked earlier in the week of coming down to Tetbury with his girl friend. Perhaps he had spoken to his father in London more recently than she. The agent agreed to telephone Mrs. Fielding again in half an hour's time, if the member had still not arrived by then.

She, of course, also tried the London flat; then failing there, Miss Parsons at home. But the secretary was already in Hastings. Mrs. Fielding next attempted the flat in Islington that her son shared with two other LSE friends. The young man who answered had no idea where Peter was, but he "thought" he was staying in town that weekend. The wife made one last effort — she tried the number of Peter's girl friend, who lived in Hampstead. But here again there was no answer. The lady at this stage was not unduly perturbed. It seemed most likely that her husband had simply missed his train and was catching the next one — and for some reason had failed, or been unable, to let anyone know of this delay. She waited for the agent, Drummond, to call back.

He too had presumed a missed train or an overslept station, and had sent someone to await the arrival of next trains in either direction. Yet when he rang back, as promised, it was to say that his deputy had had no luck. Mrs. Fielding began to feel a definite puzzlement and some alarm; but Marcus always had work with him, plentiful means of identification, even if he had been taken ill or injured beyond speech. Besides, he was in good health, a fit man for his age — no heart trouble, nothing like that. What very tenuous fears Mrs. Fielding had at this point were rather more those of a woman no longer quite so attractive as she had been. She was precisely the sort of wife who had been most shaken by the Lambton-Jellicoe scandal of earlier that year. Yet even in this area she had no grounds for suspicion at all. Her husband's private disgust at the scandal had seemed perfectly genuine . . . and consonant with his general contempt for the wilder shores of the permissive society.

An hour later Fielding had still appeared neither at the party offices nor Tetbury Hall. The faithful had been sent away, with apologies, little knowing that in three days' time the cause of their disappointment was to be the subject of headlines. Drummond agreed to wait on at his desk; the supper, informal in any case, with no other guests invited, was forgotten. They would ring each other if and as soon as they had news; if not, then at nine. It was now that Mrs. Fielding felt panic. It centered on the flat. She had the exchange check the line. It was in order. She telephoned various London friends, on the forlorn chance that in some fit of absentmindedness — but he was not that sort of person — Marcus had accepted a dinner or theater engagement with them. These inquiries also drew a blank; in most cases, a polite explanation from staff that the persons wanted were abroad or themselves in the country. She made another attempt to reach her son; but now even the young man who had answered her previous call had disappeared. Peter's girl friend and Miss Parsons were similarly still not to be reached. Mrs. Fielding's anxiety and feeling of helplessness mounted, but she was essentially a practical and efficient woman. She rang back one of the closer London friends — close also in living only two or three minutes from the Knightsbridge flat — and asked him to go there and have the block porter open it up for him. She then called the porter to give her authority for this and to find out if perhaps the man had seen her husband. But he could tell her only that Mr. Fielding had not passed his desk since he came on duty at six.

Some ten minutes later the friend telephoned from the flat. There was no sign of Marcus, but everything seemed perfectly as it should be. He found and looked in the engagements diary on Miss Parson's desk, and read out the day's program. The morning had been barred out, it seemed; but there was nothing abnormal in that. It was the MP's habit to keep Friday morning free for answering his less pressing correspondence. Fortunately Mrs. Fielding knew a fellow director of the company whose board meeting was down for three o'clock. Her next move was to try him; and it was only then that she learned the mystery had started before the failure to catch the 5:22 train;

and that Miss Parsons had also (sinisterly as it seemed, since Mrs. Fielding knew nothing of the innocent trip to Hastings) disappeared from the flat by three o'clock that afternoon. She now realized, of course, that whatever had happened might date back to the previous day. Marcus had been at the flat at nine on the Thursday morning, when she had spoken to him herself; but everything since then was uncertain. Very clearly something had gone seriously wrong.

Drummond agreed to drive over to the Hall, so that some plan of action could be concerted. Meanwhile, Mrs. Fielding spoke to the local police. She explained that it was merely a precaution . . . but if they could check the London hospitals and the accident register. Soon after Drummond arrived, the message came that there had been no casualties or cases of stroke in the last twenty-four hours that had not been identified. The lady and Drummond began to discuss other possibilities: a political kidnapping or something of the sort. But Fielding had mildly pro-Arab rather than pro-Israeli views. With so many other more "deserving" cases in the House, he could hardly have been a target for the Black September movement or its like; nor could he — for all his belief in law and order and a strong policy in Ulster — have figured very high on any IRA list. Virtually all his infrequent Commons speeches were to do with finance or agriculture.

Drummond pointed out that in any case such kidnappers would hardly have kept silent so long. An apolitical kidnapping was no more plausible — there were far richer men about . . . and surely one of the two Fielding daughters, Caroline and Francesca, both abroad at the time, would have been more likely victims if mere ransom money was the aim. And again, they would have had a demand by now. The more they discussed the matter the more it seemed that some kind of temporary amnesia was the most likely explanation. Yet surely even amnesiacs were aware that they had forgotten who they were and where they lived? The local doctor was called from in front of his television set and gave an off-the-cuff opinion over the line. Had Mr. Fielding shown forgetfulness recently? Worry, tenseness? Bad temper, anxiety? All had to be answered in the negative. Then any sudden shock? No, nothing. Amnesia was declared unlikely. The doctor gently suggested what had already been done regarding hospital admissions.

By now Mrs. Fielding had started once more to suspect some purely private scandal was looming over the tranquil horizon of her life. Just as she had earlier imagined an unconscious body lying in the London flat, she now saw a dinner for two in Paris. She could not seriously see the prim Miss Parsons's as the female face in the candlelight; but she had that summer spent less time in London than usual. At any moment the telephone would ring and Marcus would be there, breaking some long-harbored truth about their marriage . . . though it had always seemed like the others one knew, indeed rather better than most in their circle. One had to suppose something very clandestine, right out of their class and normal world — some Cockney dolly-bird, heaven knows who. Somewhere inside herself and the privacies of her life, Mrs. Fielding decided that she did not want any more inquiries made that night. Like all good Conservatives, she distinguished very sharply between private immorality and public scandal. What one did was never quite so reprehensible as letting it be generally known.

As if to confirm her decision, the local police inspector now rang to ask if he could help in any other way. She tried to sound light and unworried, she was very probably making a mountain out of a molehill, she managed the man, she was desperately anxious not to have the press involved. She finally took the same tack with Drummond. There might be some natural explanation, a lost telegram, a call Miss Parsons had forgotten to make, they should at least wait till the morning. By then Peter could also have gone to the flat and searched more thoroughly.

The Filipino houseboy showed Drummond out just after

eleven. The agent had already drawn his own conclusions. He too suspected some scandal, and was secretly shocked — not only politically. Mrs. Fielding seemed to him still an attractive woman, besides being a first-class member's wife.

The errant Peter finally telephoned just after midnight. At first he could hardly believe his mother. It now emerged that his girl friend Isobel and he had had dinner with his father only the evening before, the Thursday. He had seemed absolutely normal then; had quite definitely not mentioned any change of weekend plan. Peter soon appreciated his mother's worry, however, and agreed to go around to the Knightsbridge flat at once and to sleep there. It had occurred to Mrs. Fielding that if her husband had been kidnapped, the kidnappers might know only that address; and might have spent their evening, like her, ringing the number in vain.

But when Peter telephoned again — it was by then a quarter to one — he could only confirm what the last visitor had said. Everything seemed normal. The in-tray on Miss Parsons's desk revealed nothing. There was no sign in his father's bedroom of a hurried packing for a journey, and the suitcases and valises had the complement his mother detailed. There was nothing on any memo pad about a call to the agent or to Mrs. Fielding. In the diary sat the usual list of appointments for the following week, starting with another board meeting and lunch for midday on the Monday. There remained the question of his passport. But that was normally kept in a filing cabinet in the office, which was locked — Fielding himself and Miss Parsons having the only keys.

Mother and son once more discussed the question of alerting the London police. It was finally decided to wait until morning, when perhaps the secondary enigma of Miss Parsons could be solved. Mrs. Fielding slept poorly. When she woke for the fifth or sixth time, just after six on the Saturday, she decided to drive to London. She arrived there before nine, and spent half an hour with Peter going once more through the flat for any clue. None of her husband's clothes seemed to be missing; there was no evidence at all of a sudden departure or journey. She tried Miss Parsons's home number in Putney one last time. Nobody answered. It was enough.

Mrs. Fielding then made two preliminary calls. Just before ten she was speaking to the Home Secretary in person at his private house. There were obviously more than mere criminal considerations at stake, and she felt publicity was highly undesirable until at least a first thorough investigation had been made by the police.

A few minutes later the hunt was at last placed firmly in professional hands.

By Saturday evening they had clarified the picture, even if it was still that of a mystery. Miss Parsons had soon been traced, with a neighbor's help, to her relatives in Hastings. She was profoundly shocked — she had been with the Fieldings for nearly twenty years — and completely at a loss. As he had gone out the day before, she remembered Mr. Fielding had asked if some papers he needed for the board meeting were in his briefcase. She was positive that he had meant to go straight to the address in Cheapside where the meeting was to be held.

The day porter told the police he hadn't heard the address given the taxi driver, but the gentleman had seemed quite normal — merely "in a bit of a hurry." Miss Parsons came straight back to London, and opened up the filing cabinet. The passport was where it should be. She knew of no threatening letters or telephone calls; of no recent withdrawals of large sums of money, no travel arrangements. There had been nothing the least unusual in his behavior all week. In private, out of Mrs. Fielding's hearing, she told the chief superintendent hastily moved in to handle the inquiry that the idea of another woman was "preposterous." Mr. Fielding was devoted to his wife and family. She had never heard or seen the slightest evidence of infidelity in her eighteen years as his confidential secretary.

Fortunately the day porter had had a few words with the cab driver before Fielding came down to take it. His description was good enough for the man to have been traced by midafternoon. He provided surprising proof that amnesia could hardly be the answer. He remembered the fare distinctly, and he was unshakable. He had taken him to the British Museum, not Cheapside. Fielding hadn't talked, he had read the whole way — either a newspaper or documents from the briefcase. The driver couldn't remember whether he had actually walked into the museum, since another immediate fare had distracted his attention as soon as Fielding paid him. But the museum itself very soon provided evidence on that. The chief cloakroom attendant produced the briefcase at once — it had already been noted that it had not been retrieved when the museum closed on the Friday. It was duly unlocked — and contained nothing but a copy of *The Times*, papers to do with the board meeting, and some correspondence connected with the constituency surgery later that day.

Mrs. Fielding said her husband had some interest in art, and even collected sporting prints and paintings in an occasional way; but she knew of absolutely no reason whatever why he should go to the British Museum . . . even if he had been free of other engagements. To the best of her knowledge he had never been there once during the whole of her life with him. The cloakroom porter who had checked in the briefcase seemed the only attendant in the museum — crowded with the usual July tourists — who had any recall at all of the MP. He had perhaps merely walked through to the north entrance and caught another taxi. It suggested a little the behavior of a man who knew he was being followed; and strongly that of one determined to give no clue as to his eventual destination.

The police now felt that the matter could not be kept secret beyond the Sunday; and that it was better to release the facts officially in time for the Monday morning papers rather than have accounts based on wild rumors. Some kind of mental breakdown did seem the best hypothesis, after all; and a photograph vastly increased chances of recognition. Of course they checked far more than Mrs. Fielding realized; the help of Security and the Special Branch was invoked. But Fielding had never held ministerial rank; there could be no question of official secrets, some espionage scandal. None of the companies with whom he was connected showed the least doubt as to his trustworthiness . . . a City scandal was also soon ruled out of court. There remained the possibility of something along the Lambton-Jellicoe lines: a man breaking under the threat of a blackmailing situation. But again there was nothing on him of that nature. His papers were thoroughly gone through; no mysterious addresses, no sinister letters appeared. He was given an equally clean bill by all those who had thought they knew him well privately. His bank accounts were examined — no unexplained withdrawals, even in several preceding months, let alone in the week before his disappearance. He had done a certain amount of share-dealing during the summer, but his stockbrokers could show that everything that had been sold had been simply to improve his portfolio. It had all been reinvested. Nor had he made any recent new dispositions regarding his family in his will; cast-iron provisions had been effected many years before.

On the Monday, July 16, he was front-page news in all the dailies. There were summaries of his career. The younger and only surviving son of a High Court judge, he had gone straight from a first in law at Oxford into the army in 1939; had fought the North African campaign as an infantry officer and gained the MC; contracted kala-azar and been invalided home, finishing the war as a lieutenant colonel at a desk at the War Office, concerned mainly with the provost-marshal department. There had followed after the war his success as a barrister specializing in company and taxation law, his giving up the Bar in 1959 for politics; then his directorships, his life in East Anglia, his position slightly right of center in the Tory party.

There were the obvious kinds of speculation, the police having said that they could not yet rule out the possibility of a politically motivated kidnapping, despite the apparently unforced decision not to attend the scheduled board meeting. But the Fieldings' solicitor, who had briefed the press, was adamant that there was categorically no question of unsavory conduct in any manner or form; and the police confirmed that to the best of their knowledge the MP was a completely law-abiding citizen. Mr. Fielding had not been under investigation or surveillance of any kind.

On the assumption that he might have traveled abroad with a false name and documents, a check was made at Heathrow and the main ports to the Continent. But no passport official, no airline desk-girl or stewardess who could be contacted could recall his face. He spoke a little French and German, but not nearly well enough to pass as a native — and in any case, the passport he had left behind argued strongly that he was still in Britain. The abundant newspaper and television coverage, with all the photographs of him, provoked the usual number of reports from the public. All were followed up, and none led anywhere. There was a good deal of foreign coverage as well; and Fielding most certainly did not remain unfindable for lack of publicity. He was clearly, if he was still alive, hidden or in hiding. The latter suggested an accomplice; but no accomplice among those who had formerly known the MP suggested himself or herself. A certain amount of discreet surveillance was done on the more likely candidates, of whom one was Miss Parsons. Her telephone at home, and the one at the flat, were tapped. But all this proved a dead end. A cloud of embarrassment, governmental, detective and private, gathered over the disappearance. It was totally baffling, and connoisseurs of the inexplicable likened the whole business to that of the *Marie Celeste.*

But no news story can survive an absence of fresh developments. On Fleet Street Fielding was tacitly declared "dead" some ten days after the story first broke.

Mrs. Fielding was not, however, the sort of person who was loath or lacked the means to prod officialdom. She ensured that her husband's case continued to get attention where it mattered; the police were not given the autonomy of Fleet Street. Unfortunately they had in their own view done all they could. The always very poor scent was growing cold; and nothing could be done until they had further information — and whether they got that was far more on the lap of the gods than a likely product of further inquiries. The web was out, as fine and far-flung as this particular spider could make it; but it was up to the fly to make a move now. Meanwhile, there was Mrs. Fielding to be placated. She required progress reports.

At a meeting at New Scotland Yard on July 30, it was decided (with, one must presume, higher consent) to stand down the team till then engaged full-time on the case and to leave it effectively in the hands of one of its junior members, a Special Branch sergeant hitherto assigned the mainly desk job of collating information on the "political" possibilities. Nominally, and certainly when it came to meeting Mrs. Fielding's demands for information, the inquiry would remain a much higher responsibility. The sergeant was fully aware of the situation: he was to make noises like a large squad. He was not really expected to discover anything, only to suggest that avenues were still being busily explored. As he put it to a colleague, he was simply insurance, in case the Home Secretary turned nasty.

He also knew it was a small test. One of the rare public-school entrants to the force, and quite obviously cut out for higher rank from the day he first put on a uniform, he had a kind of tightrope to walk. Police families exist, like Army and Navy ones, and he was the third generation of his to arm the law. He was personable and quick-minded, which might, with his middle-class manner and accent, have done him harm; but he was also a diplomat. He knew very well the prejudices his type could only too easily arouse in the petty-bourgeois mentality so characteristic of the middle echelons of the police. He might think this or that inspector a dimwit, he might secretly groan at some ponderous going-by-the-book when less orthodox methods were clearly called for, or at the tortured, queasy jargon some of his superiors resorted to in order to sound "educated." But he took very good care indeed not to show his feelings. If this sounds Machiavellian, it was; but it also made him a good detective. He was particularly useful for investigations in the higher social milieux. His profession did not stand out a mile in a Mayfair gaming house or a luxury restaurant. He could pass very well as a rich, trendy young man about town; and if this ability could cause envy inside the force, it could also confound many stock notions of professional deformation outside it. His impeccable family background (with his father still a respected county head of police) also helped greatly; in a way he was a good advertisement for the career — undoubtedly a main reason he was picked for an assignment that must bring him into contact with various kinds of influential people. His name was Michael Jennings.

He spent the day following the secret decision in going through the now bulky file on Fielding, and at the end of it he drew up for himself a kind of informal summary that he called *State of Play*. It listed the possibilities and their counter-arguments.

1. Suicide. No body. No predisposition, no present reason.
2. Murder. No body. No evidence of private enemies. Political ones would have claimed responsibility publicly.

3. Abduction. No follow-through by abductors. No reason why Fielding in particular.
4. Amnesia. He's just lost, not hiding. Doctors say no prior evidence, not the type.
5. Under threat to life. No evidence. Would have called in police at once, on past evidence.
6. Threat of blackmail. No evidence of fraud or tax dodging. No evidence of sexual misbehavior.
7. Fed up with present life. No evidence. No financial or family problems. Strong sense of social duties all through career. Legal mind, not a joker.
8. Timing. Advantage taken of Parsons's afternoon off (warning given ten days prior) suggests deliberate plan? But F. could have given himself longer by canceling board meeting and one with agent — or giving Parsons whole day off. Therefore four hours was enough, assuming police brought in at earliest likely point, the 6:35 failure to turn up for his surgery. Therefore long planned? Able to put into action at short notice?

The sergeant then wrote a second heading: *Wild Ones.*

9. Love. Some girl or woman unknown. Would have to be more than sex. For some reason socially disastrous (married, class, color)? Check other missing persons that period.
10. Homosexuality. No evidence at all.
11. Paranoia. Some imagined threat. No evidence in prior behavior.
12. Ghost from the past. Some scandal before his marriage, some enemy made during wartime or legal phases of career? No evidence, but check.

13. Finances. Most likely way he would have set up secret account abroad?

14. Fox-hunting kick. Some parallel, identification with fox. Leaving hounds lost? But why?

15. Bust marriage. Some kind of revenge on wife. Check she hasn't been having it off?

16. Religious crisis. Mild C of E for the show of it. Zero probability.

17. Something hush-hush abroad to do with his being an MP. But not a muckraker or cloak-and-dagger type. Strong sense of protocol, would have consulted the FO, at least warned his wife. Forget it.

18. Son. Doesn't fit. See him again.

19. Logistics. Total disappearance not one-man operation. Must have hideout, someone to buy food, watch for him, etc.

20. *Must* be some circumstantial clue somewhere. Something he said sometime to someone. Parsons more likely than wife? Try his Westminster and City friends.

After some time the sergeant scrawled a further two words, one of which was obscene, in capitals at the bottom of his analysis.

He began the following week with Miss Parsons. The daughters, Francesca and Caroline, had returned respectively from a villa near Málaga and a yacht in Greece and the whole family was now down at Tetbury Hall. Miss Parsons was left to hold the fort in London. The sergeant took her once more through the Friday morning of the disappearance. Mr. Fielding had dictated some fifteen routine letters, then done paperwork on his own while she typed them out. He had made a call to his stockbroker; and no others to her knowledge. He had spent most of the morning in the drawing room of the flat; not gone out at all. She had left the flat for less than half an hour, to buy some sandwiches at a delicatessen near Sloane Square. She had returned just after one, made coffee, and taken her employer in the sandwiches he had ordered. Such impromptu lunches were quite normal on a Friday. He seemed in no way changed from when she had gone out. They had talked of her weekend in Hastings. He had said he was looking forward to his own, for once with no guests, at Tetbury Hall. She had been with him so long that their relationship was very informal. All the family called her simply P. She had often stayed at the Hall. She supposed she was "half-nanny" as well as secretary.

The sergeant found he had to tread very lightly indeed when it came to delving into Fielding's past. P. proved to be fiercely protective of her boss's good name, both in his legal and his political phases. The sergeant cynically and secretly thought that there were more ways of breaking the law, especially in the City, than simply the letter of it; and Fielding had been formidably well equipped to buccaneer on the lee side. Yet she was adamant about foreign accounts. Mr. Fielding had no sympathy with tax-haven tricksters — his view of the Lonrho affair, the other Tory scandal of that year, had been identical to that of his prime minister's. Such goings-on were "the unacceptable face of capitalism" to him as well. But at least, insinuated the sergeant gently, if he *had* wanted to set up a secret account abroad, he had the know-how? But there he offended secretarial pride. She knew as much of Mr. Fielding's financial affairs and resources as he did himself. It was simply not possible.

With the sexual possibilities, the sergeant ran into an even more granitelike wall. She had categorically denied all knowledge before, she had nothing further to add. Mr. Fielding was the last man to indulge in a hole-in-the-corner liaison. He had far too much self-respect. Jennings changed his tack.

"Did he say anything that Friday morning about the dinner the previous evening with his son?"

"He mentioned it. He knows I'm very fond of the children."

"In happy terms?"

"Of course."

"But they don't see eye to eye politically?"

"My dear young man, they're father and son. Oh they've had arguments. Mr. Fielding used to joke about it. He knew it was simply a passing phase. He told me once he was rather the same at Peter's age. I know for a fact that he very nearly voted Labour in 1945."

"He gave no indication of any bitterness, quarrel, that Thursday evening?"

"Not in the least. He said Peter looked well. What a charming girl his new friend was." She added, "I think he was a tiny bit disappointed they weren't going down to the Hall for the weekend. But he expected his children to lead their own lives."

"So he wasn't disappointed by the way Peter had turned out?"

"Good heavens no. He's done quite brilliantly. Academically."

"But hardly following in his father's footsteps?"

"Everyone seems to think Mr. Fielding was some kind of Victorian tyrant. He's a most broad-minded man."

The sergeant smiled. "Who's everyone, Miss Parsons?"

"Your superior, anyway. He asked me all these same questions."

The sergeant tried soft soap: no one knew Mr. Fielding better, she really was their best lead.

"One's racked one's brains. Naturally. But I can still hardly believe what's happened. And as for trying to find a reason . . ."

"An inspired guess?" He smiled again.

She looked down at the hands clasped over her lap. "Well. He did drive himself very hard."

"And?"

"Perhaps something in him . . . I really shouldn't be saying this. It's the purest speculation."

"It may help."

"Well, if something broke. He ran away. I'm sure he'd have realized what he had done in a very few days. But then, he did set himself such very high standards, perhaps he would have read all the newspaper reports. I think . . ."

"Yes?"

"I'm only guessing, but I suppose he might have been . . . deeply shocked at his own behavior. And I'm not quite sure what . . ."

"Are you saying he might have killed himself?"

Evidently she was, though she shook her head. "I don't know, I simply don't know. I feel so certain it was something done without warning. Preparation. Mr. Fielding was a great believer in order. In proper channels. It was so very uncharacteristic of him. The method, I mean the way he did it. If he did do it."

"Except it worked? If he did mean it to?"

"He couldn't have done it of his own free will. In his normal mind. It's unthinkable."

Just for a moment the sergeant sensed a blandness, an impermeability in Miss Parsons, which was perhaps merely a realization that she would have done anything for Fielding — including the telling, at this juncture, of endless lies. There must have been something sexual in her regard for him, yet there was, quite besides her age, in her physical presence, in the rather dumpy body, the pursed mouth, the spectacles, the discreetly professional clothes of the lifelong spinster secretary, such a total absence of attractiveness (however far back one imagined her, and even if there had once been something between her and her employer, it would surely by now have bred malice rather than this fidelity) that made such suspicions die almost as soon as they came to mind. However, perhaps they did faintly color the sergeant's next question.

"How did he usually spend free evenings here? When Mrs. Fielding was down in the country?"

"The usual things. His club. He was rather keen on the theater. He dined out a lot with friends. An occasional game of bridge."

"He didn't gamble at all?"

"An occasional flutter. The Derby and the Grand National. Nothing more."

"Not gaming clubs?"

"I'm quite sure not."

The sergeant went on with the questioning, always probing toward some weak point, something shameful, however remote, and arrived nowhere. He went away only with that vague hint of an overworked man and the implausible notion that after a moment of weakness he had promptly committed hara-kiri. Jennings had a suspicion that Miss Parsons had told him what she wanted to have happened rather than what she secretly believed. The thought of a discreetly dead employer was more acceptable than the horror of one bewitched by a chit of a girl or tarred by some other shameful scandal.

While he was at the flat, he also saw the daily woman. She added nothing. She had never found evidence of some unknown person having slept there; no scraps of underclothes, no glasses smudged with lipstick, no unexplained pair of coffee cups on the kitchen table. Mr. Fielding was a gentleman, she said. Whether that meant gentlemen always remove the evidence, or never give occasion for it in the first place, the sergeant was not quite sure.

He still favored, perhaps because so many of the photographs suggested an intensity (strange how few of them showed Fielding with a smile) that gave also a hint of repressed sensuality, some kind of sexual-romantic solution. A slim, clean-shaven man of above average height, who evidently dressed with care even in his informal moments, Fielding could hardly have repelled women. For just a few minutes, one day, the sergeant thought he had struck oil in this barren desert. He had been checking the list of other persons reported missing over that first weekend. A detail concerning one case, a West Indian secretary who lived with her parents in Notting Hill, rang a sharp bell. Fielding had been on the board of the insurance company at whose London headquarters the girl had been working. The nineteen-year-old sounded reasonably well educated; her father was a social worker. Jennings saw the kind of coup every detective dreams of — Fielding, who had not been a Powellite, intercepted on his way to a board meeting, invited to some community center do by the girl on behalf of her father, falling for black cheek in both senses . . . castles in Spain. A single call revealed that the girl had been traced — or rather had herself stopped all search a few days after disappearing. She fancied herself as a singer, and had run away with a guitarist from a West Indian club in Bristol. It was strictly black to black.

With City friends and parliamentary colleagues — or what few had not departed for their holidays — Jennings did no better. The City men respected Fielding's acumen and legal knowledge. The politicians gave the impression, rather like Miss Parsons, that he was a better man than any of them — a top-class rural constituency member, sound party man, always well-briefed when he spoke, very pleasant fellow, very reliable . . . they were uniformly at sea over what had happened. Not one could recall any prior hint of a breakdown. The vital psychological clue remained as elusive as ever.

Only one MP was a little more forthcoming — a Labour maverick, who had by chance cosponsored a nonparty bill with Fielding a year previously. He had struck up some kind of working friendship, at least in the precincts of the House. He disclaimed all knowledge of Fielding's life outside, or of his reasons for "doing a bunk"; but then he added that "it figured, in a way."

The sergeant asked why.

"Strictly off the record."

"Of course, sir."

"You know. Kept himself on too tight a rein. Still waters and all that. Something had to give."

"I'm not quite with you, sir."

"Oh come on, laddie. Your job must have taught you no one's perfect. Or not the way our friend tried to be." He expanded. "Some Tories are prigs, some are selfish bastards. He wanted to be both. A rich man on the grab and a pillar of the community. In this day and age. Of course it doesn't wash. He wasn't all that much of a fool." The MP dryly quizzed the sergeant. "Ever wondered why he didn't get on here?"

"I didn't realize he didn't, sir."

"Safe seat. Well-run. Never in bad odor with his whips. But that's not what it's all about, my son. He didn't fool 'em where it matters. The Commons is like an animal. You either learn to handle it. Or you don't. Our friend hadn't a clue. He knew it. He admitted it to me once."

"Why was that, sir?"

The Labour MP opened his hands. "The old common touch? He couldn't unbend. Too like the swindler's best friend he used to be." He sniffed. "Alias distinguished tax counsel."

"You're suggesting he cracked in some way?"

"Maybe he just cracked in the other sense. Decided to tell the first good joke of his life."

Jennings smiled; and played naïve.

"Let me get this right, sir. You think he was disillusioned with Tory politics?"

The Labour MP gave a little grunt of amusement.

"Now you're asking for human feeling. I don't think he had much. I'd say just bored. With the whole bloody shoot. The House, the City, playing Lord Bountiful to the yokels.

He just wanted out. Me, I wish him good luck. May his example be copied."

"With respect, sir, none of his family or close friends seem to have noticed this."

The MP smiled. "Surprise, surprise."

"They were part of it?"

The MP put his tongue in his cheek. Then he winked.

"Not a bad-looking bloke, either."

"*Cherchez la femme?*"

"We've got a little book going. My money's on Eve. Pure guess, mind."

And it really was a guess. He had no evidence at all. The MP concerned was a far more widely known figure than Fielding — a pugnacious showman as well as professional Tory-hater — and hardly a reliable observer. Yet he had suggested one thwarted ambition; and enemies do sometimes see further than friends.

Jennings next saw the person he had marked down as theoretically a key witness — not least since he also sounded an enemy, though where friend was to be expected. That was the son, Peter. The sergeant had had access to a file that does not officially exist. It had very little to say about Peter; little more indeed than to mention who he was the son of. He was noted as "vaguely NL [New Left]"; "more emotional than intellectual interest, long way from hardcore." The "Temporary pink?" with which the brief note on him ended had, in the odd manner of those so dedicated to the antisocialist cause that they are prepared to spy for it (that is, outwardly adopt the cause they hate), a distinct air of genuine Marxist contempt.

The sergeant met Peter one day at the Knightsbridge flat. He had something of his father's tall good looks, and the same apparent difficulty in smiling. He was rather ostentatiously contemptuous of the plush surroundings of the flat; and clearly impatient at having to waste time going over the same old story.

Jennings himself was virtually apolitical. He shared the general (and his father's) view that the police got a better deal under a Conservative government, and he despised Wilson. But he didn't like Heath much better. Much more than he hated either party he hated the general charade of politics, the lying and covering-up that went on, the petty point-scoring. On the other hand he was not quite the fascist pig he very soon sensed that Peter took him for. He had a notion of due process, of justice, even if it had never been really put to the test; and he positively disliked the physical side of police work, the cases of outright brutality he had heard gossip about and once or twice witnessed. Essentially he saw life as a game, which one played principally for oneself and only incidentally out of some sense of duty. Being on the law's side was a part of the rules, not a moral imperative. So he disliked Peter from the start less for political reasons than for all kinds of vague social and games-playing ones . . . as one hates an opponent paradoxically both for unfairly taken and inefficiently exploited advantages. Jennings himself would have used the simple word "phony." He did not distinguish between an acquired left-wing contempt for the police and a hereditary class one. He just saw a contempt; and knew much better than the young man opposite him how to hide such a feeling.

The Thursday evening "supper" had arisen quite casually. Peter had telephoned his father about six to say that he wouldn't be coming home that weekend after all. His father had suggested they have a meal together that evening, to bring Isobel along. Fielding wanted an early night, it was only for a couple of hours. They had taken him to a new kebab-house in Charlotte Street. He liked "slumming" with them occasionally; eating out like that was nothing new. He had seemed perfectly normal — his "usual urbane man-of-the-world act." They had given up arguing the toss about politics "years ago." They had talked family things. About Watergate. His father had taken *The Times* line on Nixon (that he was being unfairly impeached by proxy), but didn't try seriously to defend the White House administration. Isobel had talked about her sister, who had married a would-be and meanwhile impoverished French film director and was shortly expecting a baby. The horrors of a cross-channel confinement had amused Fielding. They hadn't talked about anything seriously, there had been absolutely no hint of what was to happen the next day. They had all left together about ten. His father had found a taxi (and had returned straight home, as the night porter had earlier borne witness) and they had gone on to a late film in Oxford Street. There had been no suggestion of a final farewell when they said good night to him.

"Do you think you ever convinced your father at all? In the days when you did argue with him?"

"No."

"He never seemed shaken in his beliefs? Fed up in any way with the political life?"

"Extraordinary though it may seem, also no."

"But he knew you despised it?"

"I'm just his son."

"His only son."

"I gave up. No point. One just makes one more taboo."

"What other taboos did he have?"

"The usual fifty thousand." Peter flicked his eyes around the room. "Anything to keep reality at bay."

"Won't it all be yours one day?"

"That remains to be seen." He added, "Whether I want it."

"Was there a taboo about the permissive society?"

"Which aspect of it?"

"Did he know the nature of your relationship with Miss Dodgson?"

"Oh for God's sake."

"I'm sorry, sir. What I'm trying to get at is whether you think he might have envied it."

"We never discussed it."

"And you formed no impression?"

"He liked her. Even though she's not quite out of the right drawer, and all that. And I didn't mean by taboos expecting his son —"

The sergeant raised his hand. "Sorry. You're not with me. Whether he could have fancied girls her age."

Peter stared at him, then down at his sprawled feet.

"He hadn't that kind of courage. Or imagination."

"Or need? Your parents' marriage was very happy, I believe."

"Meaning you don't?"

"No, sir. I'm just asking you."

Peter stared at him again a long moment, then stood up and went to the window.

"Look. All right. Maybe you don't know the kind of world I was brought up in. But its leading principle is never, never, never show what you really feel. I *think* my mother and father were happy together. But I don't really know. It's quite possible they've been screaming at each other for years behind the scenes. It's possible he's been having it off with any number of women. I don't think so, but I honestly don't know. Because that's the world they live in and I have to live in when I'm with them. You pretend, right? You don't actually show the truth till the world splits in half under your feet." He turned from the window. "It's no good asking me about my father. You could tell me anything about him and I couldn't say categorically, that's not true. I *think* he was everything he outwardly pretended to be. But because of what he is and . . . I just do not know."

The sergeant left a silence.

"In retrospect — do you think he was deceiving you all through that previous evening?"

"It wasn't a police interrogation, for Christ's sake. One wasn't looking for it."

"Your mother has asked in very high places that we pursue our inquiries. We haven't very much to go on."

Peter Fielding took a deep breath. "Okay."

"This idea of a life of pretense — did you ever see any awareness of that in your father?"

"I suppose socially. Sometimes. All the dreadful bores he had to put up with. The small-talk. But even that far less often than he seemed to be enjoying it."

"He never suggested he wanted a life without that?"

"Without people you can use? You're joking."

"Did he ever seem disappointed his political career hadn't gone higher?"

"Also taboo."

"He suggested something like it to someone in the House of Commons."

"I didn't say it wasn't likely. He used to put out a line about the back benches being the backbone of parliament. I never really swallowed that." He came and sat down again opposite the sergeant. "You can't understand. I've had this all my life. The faces you put on. For an election meeting. For influential people you want something out of. For your old cronies. For the family. It's like asking me about an actor I've only seen onstage. I don't know."

"And you've no theory on this last face?"

"Only three cheers. If he really did walk out on it all."

"But you don't think he did?"

"The statistical probability is the sum of the British Establishment to one. I wouldn't bet on that. If I were you."

"I take it this isn't your mother's view?"

"My mother doesn't have views. Merely appearances to keep up."

"May I ask if your two sisters share your politics at all?"

"Just one red sheep in the family."

The sergeant gave him a thin smile. He questioned on; and received the same answers, half angry, half indifferent — as if it were more important that the answerer's personal attitude was clear than the mystery be solved. Jennings was astute enough to guess that something was being hidden, and that it could very probably be some kind of distress, a buried love; that perhaps Peter was split, half of him wanting what would suit his supposedly independent self best — a spectacular breakdown of the life of pretense — and half wishing that everything had gone on as before. If he was, as seemed likely, really just a temporary pink, his father's possible plunge into what was the social, if not the political, equivalent of permanent red must be oddly mortifying; as if the old man had said, If you're really going to spit in your world's face, then this is the way to do it.

When the sergeant stood to go, he mentioned that he would like to see the girl friend, Isobel Dodgson, when she returned to London. She had been in France, in Paris, since some ten days after the disappearance. It had seemed innocent enough. Her sister had just had the expected baby and the visit had apparently been long agreed. Even so — someone else's vision of a brilliant coup — Miss Dodgson and the comings and goings of her somewhat motley collection of French in-laws had been watched for a few days — and proved themselves monotonously innocent. Peter Fielding seemed rather vague about when exactly she would return. He thought it might not be for another week, when she was due back at her job at a publisher's.

"And she can't tell you anything you haven't heard ten times already."

"I'd just like to see her briefly, sir."

Jennings went on his way then, with once more next to nothing, beyond the contemplation of an unresolved Oedipus complex, for his pains.

He descended next, by appointment, on Tetbury Hall itself;

though before he gave himself the pleasure of seeing its beamed and moated glory, he called on a selected handful of the neighbors. There he got a slightly different view of his subject, and an odd consensus that something thoroughly nasty (if unspecified) had happened. Again, there was praise without reservation for the victim, as if *De mortuis* was engraved on every county heart. Fielding was such a good master of hounds, or would have been if he hadn't been so often unavoidably absent; so "good for the village"; so generally popular (unlike the previous member). The sergeant tried to explain that a political murder without any evidence for it, let alone a corpse, is neither a murder nor political, but he had the impression that to his listeners he was merely betraying a sad ignorance of contemporary urban reality. He found no one who could seriously believe for a moment that Fielding might have walked deliberately out of a world shortly about to enter the hunting and shooting season.

Only one person provided a less conventional view of Fielding, and that was the tweed-suited young man who ran his farm for him. It was not a world Jennings knew anything about, but he took to the laconic briskness of the thirty-year-old manager. He sensed a certain reflection of his own feelings about Fielding — a mixture of irritation and respect. The irritation came very clearly, on the manager's side, from feeling he was not sufficiently his own boss. Fielding liked to be "consulted over everything"; and everything had to be decided "on accountancy grounds" — he sometimes wondered why they hadn't installed a computer. But he confessed he'd learned a lot, been kept on his toes. Pressed by Jennings, he came up with the word "compartmentalized"; a feeling that Fielding was two different people. One was ruthless in running the farm for maximum profit; another was "very pleasant socially, very understanding, nothing snobbish about him." Only a fortnight before the "vanishing trick" happened, he had had a major planning get-together with Fielding. There had not been the faintest sign then that the owner knew he would never see the things they discussed come to fruition. Jennings asked finally, and discreetly, about Mrs. Fielding — the possibility that she might have made her husband jealous.

"Not a chance. Not down here, anyway. Be around the village in ten minutes."

Mrs. Fielding herself did not deny the unlikelihood. Though he had mistrusted Peter, the sergeant had to concede some justice to the jibe about keeping up appearances. It had been tactfully explained to her that Jennings, despite his present rank, was "one of our best men" and had been working full-time on the case since the beginning — a very promising detective. He put on his public-school manner, made it clear that he was not out of his social depth, that he was glad of the opportunity to meet her in person.

After telling her something of what he had been doing on the case, he began, without giving their origins, by advancing the theories of Miss Parsons and the Labour MP. The notion that her husband might have realized what he had done and then committed suicide or, from shame, remained in hiding, Mrs. Fielding found incredible. His one concern would have been for the anxiety and the trouble he was causing, and to end it as soon as possible. She conceded that the inevitable publicity might irreparably have damaged his political career — but then he had "so much else to live for."

She refused equally to accept that he was politically disappointed. He was not at all a romantic dreamer, he had long ago accepted that he lacked the single-minded drive and special talents of ministerial material. He was not good at the cut-and-thrust side of parliamentary debate; and he spent rather too much time on the other sides of his life to expect to be a candidate for any Downing Street list. She revealed that Marcus was so little ambitious, or foolishly optimistic, that he had seriously considered giving up his seat at the next election. But she insisted that that was not out of disillusion-ment — simply from a feeling that he had done his stint. The sergeant did not argue the matter. He asked Mrs. Fielding if she had formed any favorite theory herself during that last fortnight.

"One hardly seems to have talked of anything else, but . . ." she made an elegant and seemingly rather well-practiced ges-ture of hopelessness.

"At least you feel he's still alive?" He added quickly, "As you should, of course."

"Sergeant, I'm in a vacuum. One hour I expect to see him walk through that door, the next . . ." again she gestured.

"If he is in hiding, could he look after himself? Can he cook, for instance?"

She smiled thinly. "One hardly lives that sort of life, as you must realize. But the war. No doubt he could look after himself. As one does if one has to."

"No new name has occurred to you — perhaps someone from the distant past? — who might have been talked into hiding him?"

"No." She said, "And let me spare you the embarrassment of the other woman theory. It was totally foreign to his nature to conceal anything from me. Obviously, let's face it, he could have fallen in love with someone else. But he'd never have hidden it from me — if he did feel . . ."

Jennings nodded. "We do accept that, Mrs. Fielding. I actu-ally wasn't going to bring it up. But thanks anyway." He said, "No friends — perhaps with a villa or something abroad?"

"Well of course one has friends with places abroad. You must have all their names by now. But I simply refuse to believe that they'd do this to me and the children. It's un-imaginable."

"Your daughters can't help in any way?"

"I'm afraid not. They're here. If you want to ask them anything."

"Perhaps later?" He tried to thaw her with a smile. "There's another rather delicate matter. I'm terribly sorry about all this."

The lady opened her hands in an acquiescent way — a gracious martyrdom; since one's duty obliged.

"It's to do with trying to build up a psychological picture? I've already asked your son about this in London. Whether his political views weren't a great disappointment to his father?"

"What did he answer?"

"I'd be most grateful to have your opinion first."

She shrugged, as if the whole matter were faintly absurd, not "delicate" at all.

"If only he'd understand that one would far rather he thought for himself than . . . you know what I mean."

"But there was some disappointment?"

"My husband was naturally a little upset at the beginning. We both were. But . . . one had agreed to disagree? And he knows perfectly well we're very proud of him in every other way."

"So a picture of someone having worked very hard to build a very pleasant world, only to find his son and heir doesn't want it, would be misleading?"

She puffed.

"But Peter does want it. He adores this house. Our life here. Whatever he says." She smiled with a distinct edge of coldness. "I do think this is the most terrible red herring, sergeant. What worst there was long over. And one does have two daughters as well. One mustn't forget that." She said, "Apart from Peter's little flirtation with Karl Marx, we really have been a quite disgustingly happy family."

The sergeant began to have something of the same impression he had received from Miss Parsons: that the lady had settled for ignorance rather than revelation. He might be there because she had insisted that investigation went on; but he suspected that that was a good deal more for show than out of any desperate need to have the truth uncovered. He questioned on; and got no help whatever. It was almost as if she actually knew where her husband was, and was protecting him. The sergeant had a sudden freakish intuition that he ought really to be searching Tetbury Hall, warrant in hand, instead of chatting politely away in the drawing room. But to suppose Mrs. Fielding capable of such a crime required her to be something other than she so obviously was . . . a woman welded to her role in life and her social status, eminently poised and eminently unimaginative. The sergeant also smelled a deeply wounded vanity. She had to bear some of the odium; and in some inner place she resented it deeply. He would have liked it much better if she had openly done so.

He did see the two daughters briefly. They presented the same united front. Daddy had looked tired sometimes, he worked so *fantastically* hard; but he was a super daddy. The younger of the two, Caroline, who had been sailing in Greece when the event took place, added one tiny new — and conflicting — angle. She felt that people, "not even Mummy," realized how much the country side of his life meant to him — the farm, it drove Tony (the farm manager) mad the way Daddy was always poking around. But it was only because Daddy loved it, it seemed. He didn't really want to interfere, he "just sort of wanted to be Tony, actually." Then why hadn't he given up his London life? Caroline didn't know. She supposed he was more complicated "than we all ever realized." She even provided the wildest possibility yet.

"You know about Mount Athos? In Greece?" The sergeant shook his head. "Actually we sailed past it when I was out there. It's sort of reserved for monasteries. There are only monks. It's all male. They don't even allow hens or cows. I mean, I know it sounds ridiculous, but sort of somewhere like that. Where he could be alone for a bit, I suppose."

But when it came to evidence of this yearning for a solitary retreat, the two girls were as much at a loss as everyone else. What their brother found hypocritical, they had apparently found all rather dutiful and self-sacrificing.

A few minutes later, Mrs. Fielding thanked the sergeant for his labors and, although it was half past twelve, did not offer him lunch. He went back to London feeling, quite correctly, that he might just as well have stayed there in the first place.

Indeed he felt near the end of his tether over the whole bloody case. There were still people he had down to see, but he hardly expected them to add anything to the general — and generally blank — picture. He knew he was fast moving from being challenged to feeling defeated; and that it would soon be a matter of avoiding unnecessary work, not seeking it. One such possible lead he had every reason to cross off his list was Isobel Dodgson, Peter's girl friend. She had been questioned in detail by someone else during the preliminary inquiry, and had contributed nothing of significance. But he retained one piece of casual gossip about her at the Yard; and a pretty girl makes a change, even if she knows nothing. Caroline and Francesca had turned out much prettier in the name than in the meeting.

She came back from Paris on August 15, in the middle of one of the hottest weeks for many years. The sergeant had sent a brief letter asking her to get in touch as soon as she returned, and she telephoned the next morning, an unbearably sultry and humid Thursday. He arranged to go up to Hampstead and see her that afternoon. She sounded precise and indifferent: she knew nothing, she didn't really see the point. However, he insisted, though he presumed she had already spoken with Peter, and was taking his line.

He fell for her at once, in the door of the house in Willow Road. She looked a little puzzled, as if he must be for someone else, though he had rung the bell of her flat and was punctual to the minute. Perhaps she had expected someone in uniform, older; as he had expected someone more assured.

"Sergeant Mike Jennings. The fuzz."

"Oh. Sorry."

A small girl, a piquant oval face, dark brown eyes, black hair; a simple white dress with a blue stripe in it; down to the ankles, sandals over bare feet . . . but it wasn't only that. He had an immediate impression of someone alive, where everyone else had been dead, or playing dead; of someone who lived in the present, not the past; who was, surprisingly, not like Peter at all. She smiled and nodded past him.

"I suppose we couldn't go on the Heath? This heat's killing me. My room doesn't seem to get any air."

"Fine."

"I'll just get my key."

He went and waited on the pavement. There was no sun; an opaque heat-mist, a bath of stale air. He took off his dark blue blazer and folded it over his arm. She joined him, carrying a small purse; another exchange of cautious smiles.

"You're the first cool-looking person I've seen all day."

"Yes? Sheer illusion."

They walked over the little climb to East Heath Road; then across that, and over the grass down toward the ponds. She didn't return to work until the next Monday; she was just a general dogsbody at the publisher's. He knew more about her than she realized, from the checking that had been done when she was temporarily under suspicion. She was twenty-four years old, a graduate in English, she had even published a book of stories for children. Her parents were divorced, her mother now lived in Ireland, married to some painter. Her father was a professor at York University.

"I don't know what on earth I can tell you."

"Have you seen Peter Fielding since you got back?"

She shook her head. "Just over the 'phone. He's down in the country."

"It's only routine. Just a chat, really."

"You're still . . . ?"

"Where we started. More or less." He shifted his blazer to the other arm. One couldn't move without sweating. "I'm not quite sure how long you've known the Fieldings."

They walked very slowly. His compliment had been true, though meant as a way of saying he liked her dress. In spite of the heat she seemed cool beneath the white cotton; very small-bodied, delicate, like sixteen; but experienced somewhere, unlike sixteen, certain of herself despite those first moments of apparent timidity. A sexy young woman wearing a dark French scent, who tended to avoid his eyes, answering to the ground or to the Heath ahead.

"Only this summer. Four months. Peter, that is."

"And his father?"

"We've been down two or three times to the grand baronial home. There was a party in London at the flat. Occasional meals out. Like that last one. I was really just his son's bit of bird. I honestly didn't know him very well."

"Did you like him?"

She smiled, and for a brief moment said nothing.

"Not much."

"Why not?"

"Tories. Not the way I was brought up."

"Fair enough. Nothing else?"

She looked at the grass, amused. "I didn't realize you were going to ask questions like this."

"Nor did I. I'm playing it by ear." She flashed him a surprised look, as if she hadn't expected such frankness; then smiled away again. He said, "We've got all the facts. We're down to how people felt about him."

"It wasn't him in particular. Just the way they live."

"What your friend described as the life of pretense?"

"Except they're not pretending. They just are, aren't they?"

"Do you mind if I take my tie off?"

"Please. Of course."

"I've spent all day dreaming of water."

"Me too."

"At least you've got it here." They were passing the ladies' pond, with its wall of trees and shrubbery. He gave her a dry little grin, rolling his tie up. "At a price."

"The lezzies? How do you know about them?"

"I did some of my uniformed time up the road. Haverstock Hill?"

She nodded; and he thought, how simple it is, or can be . . . when they don't beat about the bush, say what they actually think and know, actually live today instead of fifty years ago; and actually state things he had felt but somehow not managed to say to himself. He had grown not to like Fielding much, either; or that way of life. Just that one became brainwashed, lazy, one swallowed the Sunday color-supplement view of values, the assumptions of one's seniors, one's profession, one forgot there are people with fresh minds and independence who see through all that and are not afraid. . . .

Suddenly she spoke.

"Is it true they beat up the dirty old men there?"

He was brought sharply to earth; and was shocked more than he showed, like someone angling for a pawn who finds himself placed in check by one simple move.

"Probably." She had her eyes on the grass. After a second or two he said, "I used to give them a cup of tea. Personally." But the pause had registered.

"I'm sorry. I shouldn't have asked that." She gave him an oblique glance. "You're not very police-y."

"We're used to it."

"Something I heard once. I'm sorry, I . . ." She shook her head.

"It's okay. We live with it. Overreact."

"And I interrupted."

He hitched his coat over his back, and unbuttoned his shirt. "What we're trying to discover is whether he could have got disillusioned with that way of life. Your friend told me his father hadn't the courage — either the courage or the imagination to walk out on it. Would you go with that?"

"Peter said that?"

"His words."

She didn't answer for a moment.

"He was one of those men who sometimes seem to be somewhere else. You know? As if they're just going through the motions."

"And what else?"

Again that pause. "Dangerous isn't the word — but someone . . . very self-controlled. A tiny bit obsessional? I mean someone who wouldn't be easily stopped if he'd argued himself into something." She hit her head gently in self-remonstrance. "I'm not putting this very well. I'm just surprised that Peter —"

"Don't stop."

"There was something sort of fixed, rigid underneath. I think that could have produced courage. And this abstracted thing he showed sometimes. As if he were somewhere else. And that suggests a kind of imagination?" She grimaced. "The detective's dream."

"No, this is helpful. How about that last evening? Did you get that somewhere-else feeling then?"

She shook her head. "Oddly enough he was much jollier than usual. Well . . . I say jolly. He wasn't that kind of person, but . . ."

"Enjoying himself?"

"It didn't seem only politeness."

"Someone who's made up his mind? Feels good about it?"

She thought about that, staring down. They walked very

slowly, as if at any moment they would turn back. She shook her head.

"I honestly don't know. There certainly wasn't any buried emotion. Nothing of the farewell about it."

"Not even when he said goodbye?"

"He kissed me on the cheek, I think he touched Peter on the shoulder. I couldn't swear about the actual movements. But I'd have noticed if there'd been anything unusual. I mean, his mood was slightly unusual. I remember Peter saying something about his getting mellow in his old age. There was that feeling. That he'd put himself out to be nice to us."

"He wasn't always?"

"I didn't mean that. Just . . . not simply going through the motions. Perhaps it was London. He always seemed more somewhere-else down in the country. To me, anyway."

"That's where everyone else seems to think he was happier."

Again she thought, and chose her words. "Yes, he did enjoy showing it all off. Perhaps it was the family situation. Being *en famille.*"

He said, "I've got to ask you something very crude now."

"No. He didn't."

The answer came back so fast that he laughed.

"You're my star witness."

"I was waiting for it."

"Not even a look, a . . . ?"

"I divide the looks men give me into two kinds. Natural and unnatural. He never gave me the second sort. That I saw."

"I didn't mean to suggest he'd have made a pass at you, but whether you felt any kind of general . . ."

"Nothing I could describe."

"Then there was something?"

"No. Honestly not. I think it was just me. Psychic nonsense. It's not evidence."

"Do I get on my knees?"

Her mouth curved, but she said nothing. They moved up, on a side path, toward Ken Wood.

He said, "Bad vibes?"

She hesitated still, then shook her head. The black hair curled a little, negligently and deliciously, at its ends, where it touched the skin of her bare neck.

"I didn't like being alone with him. It only happened once or twice. It may have just been the political thing. Sympathetic magic. The way he always used to produce a kind of chemical change in Peter."

"Like how?"

"Oh, a kind of nervousness. A defensiveness. It's not that they used to argue the way they once apparently did. All very civilized, really. You please mustn't say saything about this. It's mostly me. Not facts."

"The marriage seemed okay to you?"

"Yes."

"You hesitated."

She was watching the ground again as they mounted the grassy hill. "My own parents' marriage broke up when I was fifteen. I sort of felt something . . . just the tiniest whiff. When the couple know and the children don't. I think in real relationships people are rude to each other. They know it's safe, they're not walking on ice. But Peter said they'd always been like that. He told me once, he'd never once heard them have a row. Always that façade. Front. Perhaps I just came in late on something that had always been there."

"You never had chat with Mrs. Fielding?"

"Nothing else." She pulled a little face. "Inch-deep."

"This not wanting to be alone with him —"

"It was such a tiny thing."

"You've already proved you're telepathic." She smiled again, her lips pressed tight. "Were these bad vibes sexual ones?"

"Just that something was suppressed. Something . . ."

"Let it come out. However wild."

"Something he might suddenly tell me. That he might break down. Not that he ever would. I can't explain."

"But an unhappiness in him?"

"Not even that. Just someone else, behind it all. It's nothing, but I'm not quite making it up after the facts." She shrugged. "When it all happened, something seemed to fit. It wasn't quite the shock it ought to have been."

"You think the someone else was very different from the man everyone knew?" She gave her slow, reluctant nod. "Nicer or nastier?"

"More honest?"

"You never heard him say anything that suggested he was changing his politics? Moving leftward?"

"Absolutely not."

"Did he seem to approve of you as a future daughter-in-law?"

She seemed faintly embarrassed at that.

"I'm not interested in getting married yet. It's not been that sort of relationship."

"Which they understood?"

"They knew we were sleeping together. There wasn't any separate room nonsense when we stayed down there."

"But he liked you in some way you didn't like? Or is that oversimplifying?"

Suddenly she gave him a strange look: a kind of lightning assessment of who he was. Then she looked away.

"Could we go and sit down a moment? Under that tree?" She went on before he could say anything. "I'm holding out on you. There's something I should have told you before. The police. It's very minor. But it may help explain what I'm trying to say."

Again that quickness: a little smile, that stopped him before he could speak.

"Please. Let's sit down first."

She sat cross-legged, like a child. He took a cigarette packet out of his blazer pocket, but she shook her head and he put it away. He sat, then lay on an elbow opposite her. The tired grass. It was totally airless. Just the white dress with the small blue stripes, very simple, a curve off her shoulders down above her breasts, the skin rather pale, faintly olive; those eyes, the line of her black hair. She broke off a stalk of dry grass and fiddled with it in her lap.

"That last meal we had." She smiled up. "The last supper? Actually I was alone with him for a few minutes before Peter arrived. He'd been at some meeting at the LSE, he was a tiny bit late. Mr. Fielding never was. So. He asked me what I'd been doing all week. We're doing a reprint of some minor Late Victorian novels — you know, those campy illustrated ones, it's just cashing in on a trend — and I explained I'd been reading some." She was trying to split the grass-stalk with a nail. "It's just this. I did mention I had to go to the British Museum reading room the next day to track one down." She looked up at the sergeant. "Actually in the end I didn't. But that's what I told him."

He looked down from her eyes. "Why didn't you tell us?"

"I suppose 'no one asked me' isn't good enough?"

"Not from someone of your intelligence."

She went back to the grass-stalk. "Then sheer cowardice? Plus the knowledge that I'm totally innocent."

"He didn't make a thing of it?"

"Not at all. It was just said in passing. I spent most of the time telling him about the book I'd been reading that day. That was all. Then Peter came."

"And you never went to the museum?"

"There was a panic over some proofs. I spent the whole of Friday in the office reading them." She looked him in the eyes again. "You could check. They'd remember the panic."

"We already have."

"Thank God for that."

"Where everybody was that afternoon." He sat up and stared away across the grass to Highgate Hill. "If you're innocent, why keep quiet about it?"

"Purely personal reasons."

"Am I allowed to hear them?"

"Just Peter. It's actually been rather more off than on for some time now. Since before. The real reason we didn't go down to Tetbury that weekend was that I refused to." She glanced up at the sergeant, as if to see whether she had said enough; then down again into her lap. "I felt the only reason he tried to get me down there was to put me in what you just said — the future daughter-in-law situation? Using something he pretends to hate to try and get me. I didn't like it. That's all."

"But you still wanted to protect him?"

"He's so desperately confused about his father. And I thought, you know . . . whatever I said, it would seem fishy. And Mrs. Fielding. I mean, I *know* I'm innocent. But I wasn't sure anyone else would. And I couldn't see, I still can't, that it proves anything."

"If he did go to see you, what could he have wanted?"

She uncrossed her legs, and sat sideways to him, hands clasped around the knees. "I thought at first something to do with me being in publishing. But I'm just a nobody. He knew that."

"You mean some kind of book? Confession?"

She shook her head. "It doesn't make sense."

"You should have told us."

"The other man didn't explain what he wanted. You have."

"Thanks. And you've still been wicked."

"Duly contrite."

The head was bowed. He pressed a smile out of his mouth.

"This feeling he wanted to tell you something — is that based on this, or something previous?"

"There was one other tiny thing. Down at Tetbury in June.

He took me off one day to see some new loose-boxes they'd just had put up. It was really an excuse. To give me a sort of pat on the back. You know. He said something about being glad Peter had hit it off with me. Then that he needed someone with a sense of humor. And then he said: *Like all us political animals*." She spoke the words slowly, as if she were listing them. "I'm sure of that. Those words exactly. Then something about, one sometimes forgets there are other ways of seeing life. That was all, but he was sort of trying to let me know he knew he wasn't perfect. That he knew Tetbury wasn't my scene. That he didn't despise my scene as much as I might think." She added, "I'm talking about tiny, very faint impressions. And retrospective ones. They may not mean anything."

"Peter obviously didn't know about the museum thing?"

"It didn't come up. Fortunately. Something in him always liked to pretend I didn't earn my own living."

He noted that past tense.

"And he wouldn't have believed you — if he had known?"

"Do you?"

"You wouldn't be here now, otherwise. Or telling me."

"No, I suppose I wouldn't."

He leaned back again, on an elbow; and tried to calculate how far he could go with personal curiosity under the cover of official duty.

"He sounds very mixed-up. Peter."

"The opposite really. Unmixed. Like oil and water. Two people."

"And his father could have been the same?"

"Except it's naked with Peter. He can't hide it." She was talking with her head bent, rocking a little, hands still clasped around her knees. "You know, some people — that kind of pretentious life, houseboys waiting at table and all the rest of it. Okay, one loathes it, but at least it's natural. Peter's mother." She shrugged. "She really believes in the formal hostesss bit. Leaving the gentlemen to the port and cigars." She glanced sideways at him again. "But his father. He so obviously wasn't a fool. Whatever his political views."

"He saw through it?"

"But something in him was also too clever to show it. I mean, he never sent it up. Apologized for it, the way some people do. Except for that one thing he said to me. It's just some kind of discrepancy. I can't explain." She smiled at him. "It's all so tenuous. I don't even know why I'm bothering to tell you."

"Probably because you know I'm torn between arresting you for conspiracy to suppress evidence and offering you a cup of tea at Ken Wood."

She smiled and looked down at her knees, let three or four seconds pass.

"Have you always been a policeman?"

He told her who his father was.

"And you enjoy it?"

"Being a leper to most of your own generation?"

"Seriously."

He shrugged. "Not this case. No one wants it solved now. Sleeping dogs and all that. Between ourselves."

"That must be foul."

He smiled. "Not until this afternoon, anyway." He said quickly, "That's not a pass. You're just about the first person I've seen who makes some kind of sense on it all."

"And you're really nowhere nearer . . . ?"

"Further. But you may have something. There was someone else. Saying more or less what you've said. Only not so well."

She left another pause.

"I'm sorry I said that thing just now. About police brutality."

"Forget it. It does happen. Coppers also have small daughters."

"Do you really feel a leper?"

"Sometimes."

"Are all your friends in the police?"

"It's not that. Just the work. Having to come on like authority. Officialdom? Obeying people you don't always respect. Never quite being your own man."

"That worries you?"

"When I meet people I like. Who can be themselves."

She stared into the distance.

"Would it ever make you give it up?"

"Would what?"

"Not being your own man?"

"Why do you ask?"

"Just . . ." she shrugged. "That you should use that phrase."

"Why?"

She said nothing for a moment, then she looked down at her knees. "I do have a private theory. About what happened. It's very wild." She grinned at him. "Very literary. If you want to hear it, it will cost you one cup of tea." She raised the purse. "I didn't bring any money."

He stood and held out a hand. "You're on."

They walked toward the trees of Ken Wood House. She kept obstinately to her bargain. Her "theory" must wait till they had their tea. So they talked more like the perfect strangers, hazard-met, that they were; about their respective jobs, which required a disillusioning on both sides as to very much of the supposed glamor and excitement attached to them. She admitted, when he revealed that he knew about the children's stories, to a general literary ambition — that is, a more adult one. She was trying to write a novel, it was so slow, you had to destroy so much and start again; so hard to discover whether one was really a writer or just a victim of a literary home environment. He felt a little bit the same about his own work; and *its* frustrations and endless weeks of getting nowhere. They rather surprisingly found, behind the different cultural backgrounds, a certain kind of unspoken identity of situation. He queued up behind his witness at the tea counter, observing the back of her head, that tender skin above the curve of the dress, the starchy blue stripes in its mealy whiteness; and he knew he had to see her again, off-duty. He had no problems with girls. It was not a physical thing, a lack of confidence sexually; not even a class or a cultural thing; but a psychological thing, a knowledge that he was — despite the gaffe, but even the gaffe had been a kind of honesty — dealing with a quicker and more fastidious mind in the field of emotions and personal relationships . . . that, and the traditional ineligibility of his kind for her kind, with the added new political bar, if the intelligence was also progressive, that he had referred to as a leprosy. Something about her possessed something that he lacked: a potential that lay like unsown ground, waiting for just this unlikely corn-goddess; a direction he could follow, if she would only show it. An honesty, in one word. He had not wanted a girl so fast and so intensely for a long time. Nevertheless, he made a wise decision.

They found a table to themselves in a corner. This time she accepted a cigarette.

"So let's have it."

"Nothing is real. All is fiction."

She bit her lips, lips without makeup, waiting for his reaction.

"That solves the case?"

"Lateral thinking. Let's pretend everything to do with the Fieldings, even you and me sitting here now, is in a novel. A detective story. Yes? Somewhere there's someone writing us, we're not real. He or she decides who we are, what we do, all about us." She played with her teaspoon; the amused dark eyes glanced up at him. "Are you with me?"

"By the skin of my teeth."

"A story has to have an ending. You can't have a mystery without a solution. If you're the writer you have to think of something."

"I've spent most of this last month —"

"Yes, but only in reality. It's the difference between I haven't many facts, so I can't decide anything — and I haven't many facts, but I've simply got to decide something."

He felt a little redressment of the imbalance — after all a fault in this girl, a cerebral silliness. It would have irritated him in someone less attractive in other ways; now it simply relieved him. He smiled.

"We play that game too. But never mind."

She bit her lips again. "I propose to dismiss the *deus ex machina* possibility. It's not good art. An awful cheat, really."

"You'd better . . ."

She grinned. "The god out of the machine. Greek tragedy. When you couldn't work out a logical end from the human premises, you dragged in something external. You had the villain struck down by lightning. A chimney pot fell on his head. You know?"

"I'm back on my feet."

"Of course the British Museum thing may have been pure coincidence. On the other hand the vanished man might have been really determined to see that girl. So I think the writer would make him — when he found she wasn't in the reading room afte: all — telephone the publishers where she works. There's a blank in her day. Between just after half past five, when she left work, until about eight, when she met Peter Fielding to go to a rather ghastly party."

And suddenly he felt more seriously out of his depth. He was being teased — which meant she liked him? Or he was being officially mocked — which meant she didn't?

"They met then?"

She raised a finger.

"The writer *could* have made them meet. He'd have to make it a kind of spur-of-the-moment thing. Obviously it could have been much better planned, if the missing man had had it in mind for some time. He'd have to say something like . . . I've just broken under all the hidden pressures of my life, I don't know who to turn to, you seem quite a sympathetic and level-headed girl, you —"

"This level-headed girl would be telling me all this?"

"Only if she was quite sure it couldn't be proved. Which she might. Given that at this late date the police have apparently never even suspected such a meeting."

"Correction. Found evidence of."

"Same thing."

"All right."

"So he might just have made her pity him? This seeming hollow man pouring out all his despair. A hopelessness. Terribly difficult to write, but it could be done. Because it so happens the girl is rather proud of her independence. And her ability to judge people. And don't forget she really hasn't any time at all for the world he's running away from." The real girl played with her plastic teaspoon, looked up at him unsmiling now; trying him out. "And there's no sex angle. She'd be doing it out of the kindness of her heart. And not very much. Just fixing up somewhere for him to hide for a few days, until he can make his own arrangements. And being the kind of person she is, once she'd decided it was the right thing to do, nothing, not even rather dishy young policemen who buy her cups of tea, would ever get the facts out of her."

He stared at his own cup and saucer. "You're not by any chance . . . ?"

"Just one way the writer might have played it."

"Hiding people isn't all that easy."

"Ah."

"Especially when they've acted on the spur of the moment and made no financial arrangements that one can discover. And when they're not spur-of-the-moment people."

"Very true."

"Besides, it's not how I read her character."

"More conventional?"

"More imaginative."

She leaned away on an elbow, smiling.

"So our writer would have to tear this ending up?"

"If he's got a better."

"He has. And may I have another cigarette?"

He lighted it for her. She perched her chin on her hands, leaned forward.

"What do you think would strike the writer about his story to date — if he reread it?"

"He ought never to have started it in the first place."

"Why?"

"Forgot to plant any decent leads."

"Doesn't that suggest something about the central character? You know, in books, they do have a sort of life of their own."

"He didn't mean evidence to be found?"

"I think the writer would have to face up to that. His main character has walked out on him. So all he's left with is the character's determination to have it that way. High and dry. Without a decent ending."

The sergeant smiled down. "Except writers can write it any way they like."

"You mean detective stories have to end with everything explained? Part of the rules?"

"The unreality."

"Then if our story disobeys the unreal literary rules, that might mean it's actually truer to life?" She bit her lips again. "Leaving aside the fact that it *has* all happened. So it must be true, anyway."

"I'd almost forgotten that."

She set out her saucer as an ashtray.

"So all our writer could really do is find a convincing reason why this main character had forced him to commit the terrible literary crime of not sticking to the rules?" She said, "Poor man."

The sergeant felt the abyss between them; people who live by ideas, people who have to live by facts. He felt obscurely humiliated, to have to sit here and listen to all this; and at the same time saw her naked, deliciously naked on his bed. Her bed. Any bed or no bed. The nipples showed through the thin fabric; the hands were so small, the eyes so alive.

"And you happen to have it?"

"There was an author in his life. In a way. Not a man. A system, a view of things? Something that had written him. Had really made him just a character in a book."

"So?"

"Someone who never put a foot wrong. Always said the right thing, wore the right clothes, had the right image. Right with a big *r*, too. All the roles he had to play. In the City. The country. The dull and dutiful member of parliament. So in the end there's no freedom left. Nothing he can choose. Only what the system says."

"But that goes for —"

"Then one has to look for something very unusual in him. Since he's done something very unusual?" The sergeant nodded. She was avoiding his eyes now. "All this dawns on him. Probably not suddenly. Slowly. Little by little. He's like something written by someone else, a character in fiction. Everything is planned. Mapped out. He's like a fossil — while he's still alive. One doesn't have to suppose changes of view. Being persuaded by Peter politically. Seeing the City for the nasty little rich man's casino it really is. He'd have blamed everything equally. How it had used him. Limited him. Prevented him." She tapped ash from her cigarette.

"Did you ever see his scrapbooks?"

"His what?"

"They're in the library down at Tetbury. All bound in blue morocco. Gilt-tooled. His initials. Dates. All his press cuttings. Right back to the legal days. *Times* law reports, things like that. Tiniest things. Even little local rag clippings about opening bazaars and whatnot."

"Is that so unusual?"

"It just seems more typical of an actor. Or some writers are like that. A kind of obsessive need to know . . . that they've been known?"

"Okay."

"It's a kind of terror, really. That they've failed, they haven't registered. Except that writers and actors are in far less predictable professions. They can have a sort of eternal optimism about themselves. Most of them. The next book will be fabulous. The next part will be a rave." She looked up at him, both persuading and estimating. "And on the other hand they live in cynical open worlds. Bitchy ones. Where no one really believes anyone else's reputation — especially if they're successful. Which is all rather healthy, in a way. But he isn't like that. Tories take success so seriously. They define it so exactly. So there's no escape. It has to be position. Status. Title. Money. And the outlets at the top are so restricted. You have to be prime minister. Or a great lawyer. A multimillionaire. It's that or failure." She said, "Think of Evelyn Waugh. A terrible Tory snob. But also very shrewd, very funny. If you can imagine someone like that, a lot more imagination than anyone ever gave him credit for, but completely without all the safety valves Waugh had. No brilliant books, no Catholicism, no wit. No drinking, no impossible behavior in private."

"Which makes him like thousands of others?"

"But we have a fact about him. He did something thousands of others don't. So it must have hurt a lot more. Feeling failed and trapped. And forced — because everything was so standard, so conforming in his world — to pretend he was happy as he was. No creative powers. Peter's told me. He wasn't even very good in court, as a barrister. Just specialized legal knowledge." She said, "And then his cultural tastes. He told me once he was very fond of historical biography. Lives of great men. And the theater, he was genuinely quite keen on that. I know all this, because there was so little else we could talk about.

And he adored Winston Churchill. The biggest old ham of them all."

A memory jogged the sergeant's distracted mind: Miss Parsons, how Fielding had "nearly" voted Labour in 1945. But that might fit.

He said, "Go on."

"He feels more and more like this minor character in a bad book. Even his own son despises him. So he's a zombie, just a high-class cog in a phony machine. From being very privileged and very successful, he feels himself very absurd and very failed." Now she was tracing invisible patterns on the top of the table with a fingertip: a square, a circle with a dot in it. The sergeant wondered if she was wearing anything at all beneath the dress. He saw her sitting astride his knees, her arms enlacing his neck, tormenting him; and brutality. You fall in love by suddenly knowing what past love hadn't. "Then one day he sees what might stop both the rot and the pain. What will get him immortality of a kind."

"Walking out."

"The one thing people never forget is the unsolved. Nothing lasts like a mystery." She raised the pattern-making finger. "On condition that it stays that way. If he's traced, found, then it all crumbles again. He's back in a story, being written. A nervous breakdown. A nut case. Whatever."

Now something had shifted, little bits of past evidence began to coagulate, and listening to her became the same as being with her. The background clatter, the other voices, the clinging heat, all that started to recede. Just one thing nagged, but he let it ride.

"So it has to be for good?"

She smiled at him. "God's trick."

"Come again."

"Theologians talk about the *Deus absconditus* — the God who went missing? Without explaining why. That's why we've never forgotten him."

He thought of Miss Parsons again. "You mean he killed himself?"

"I bet you every penny I possess."

He looked down from her eyes.

"This writer of yours — has he come up with a scenario for that?"

"That's just a detail. I'm trying to sell you the motive."

He was silent a moment, then sought her eyes. "Unfortunately it's the details I have to worry about."

His own eyes were dryly held. "Then your turn. Your department."

"We have thought about it. Throwing himself off a night ferry across the Channel. But we checked. The boats were crowded, a lot of people on deck. The odds are dead against."

"You mustn't underrate him. He'd have known that was too risky."

"No private boats missing. We checked that as well."

She gave him a glance under her eyebrows; a touch of conspiracy, a little bathing in collusion; then looked demurely down.

"I could tell you a suitable piece of water. And very private."

"Where?"

"In the woods behind Tetbury Hall. They call it the lake. It's just a big pond. But they say it's very deep."

"How does he get there without being seen?"

"He knows the country around Tetbury very well. He owns a lot of it. Hunting. Once he's within walking distance from London, he's safe."

"And that part of it?"

"Some kind of disguise? He couldn't have hired a car. Or risked the train. By bus?"

"Hell of a lot of changing."

"He wasn't in a hurry. He wouldn't have wanted to be anywhere near home before nightfall. Some stop several miles away? Then cross-country? He liked walking."

"He still has to sink himself. Drowned bodies need a lot of weight to stay down."

"Something inflatable? An air mattress? Car tire? Then deflate it when he's floated far enough out?"

"You're beginning to give me nightmares."

She smiled and leaned back and folded her hands in her lap; then she grinned up and threw it all away.

"I also fancy myself as an Agatha Christie."

He watched her; and she looked down, mock-penitent.

"How serious are you being about all this?"

"I thought about it a lot in Paris. Mainly because of the British Museum thing. I couldn't work out why he'd have wanted to see me. I mean if he didn't, it was a kind of risk. He might have bumped into me. And you can't walk into the reading room just like that. You have to show a pass. I don't know if that was checked."

"Every attendant there."

"So what I think now is that it was some kind of message. He never meant to see me, but for some reason he wanted me to know that I was involved in his decision. Perhaps because of Peter. Something for some reason he felt I stood for."

"A way out he couldn't take?"

"Perhaps. It's not that I'm someone special. In the ordinary world. I was probably just very rare in his. I think it was simply a way of saying that he'd have liked to talk to me. Enter my world. But couldn't."

"And why Tetbury Hall?"

"It does fit. In an Agatha Christie sort of way. The one place no one would think of looking. And its neatness. He was very tidy, he hated mess. On his own land, no trespassing involved. Just a variation on blowing your brains out in the gunroom, really."

He looked her in the eyes. "One thing bothers me. Those two hours after work of yours that day."

"I was only joking."

"But you weren't at home. Mrs. Fielding tried to telephone you then."

She smiled.

"Now it's my turn to ask how serious you're being."

"Just tying ends up."

"And if I don't answer?"

"I don't think that writer of yours would allow that."

"Oh but he would. That's his whole point. Nice people have instincts as well as duties."

It was bantering, yet he knew he was being put to the test; that this was precisely what was to be learned. And in some strange way the case had died during that last half hour; it was not so much that he accepted her theory, but that like everyone else, though for a different reason, he now saw it didn't really matter. The act was done; taking it to bits, discovering how it had been done in detail, was not the point. The point was a living face with brown eyes, half challenging and half teasing; not committing a crime against that. He thought of a ploy, some line about this necessitating further questioning; and rejected it. In the end, he smiled and looked down.

She said gently, "I must go now. Unless you're going to arrest me for second sight."

They came to the pavement outside the house in Willow Road, and stood facing each other.

"Well."

"Thank you for the cup of tea."

He glanced at the ground, reluctantly official.

"You have my number. If anything else ... ."

"Apart from bird-brained fantasy."

"I didn't mean that. It was fun."

There was a little silence.

"You should have worn a uniform. Then I'd have remembered who you were."

He hesitated, then held out his hand. "Take care. And I'll buy that novel when it comes out."

She took his hand briefly, then folded her arms.

"Which one?"

"The one you were talking about."

"There's another. A murder story." She looked past his shoulder down the street. "Just the germ of an idea. When I can find someone to help me over the technical details."

"Like police procedure?"

"Things like that. Police psychology, really."

"That shouldn't be too difficult."

"You think someone . . . ?"

"I know someone."

She cocked her left sandal a little forward; contemplated it against the pavement, her arms still folded.

"I don't suppose he could manage tomorrow evening?"

"How do you like to eat?"

"Actually I rather enjoy cooking myself." She looked up. "When I'm not at work."

"Dry white? About eight?"

She nodded and bit her lips with a touch of wryness, perhaps a tinge of doubt.

"All this telepathy."

"I wanted to. But . . ."

"Noted. And approved."

She held his eyes a moment more, then raised her hand and turned toward the front door; the dark hair, the slim walk, the white dress. At the door, after feeling in her purse and putting the key in the lock, she turned a moment and again raised her hand briefly. Then she disappeared inside.

The sergeant made, the next morning, an informal and unsuccessful application to have the pond at Tetbury Hall dragged. He then tried, with equal unsuccess, to have himself taken off the case, indeed to have it tacitly closed. His highly circumstantial new theory as to what might have happened received no credence. He was told to go away and get on with the job of digging up some hard evidence instead of wasting his time on half-baked psychology; and heavily reminded that it was just possible the House of Commons might want to hear why one of their number was still untraced when they returned to Westminster. Though the sergeant did not then know it, historical relief lay close at hand — the London letter-bomb epidemic of later that August was to succeed where his own request for new work had failed.

However he was not, by the time that first tomorrow had closed, the meal been eaten, the Sauvignon drunk, the kissing come, the barefooted cook finally and gently persuaded to stand and be deprived of a different but equally pleasing long dress (and proven, as suspected, quite defenseless underneath, though hardly an innocent victim in what followed), inclined to blame John Marcus Fielding for anything at all.

The tender pragmatisms of flesh have poetries no enigma, human or divine, can diminish or demean — indeed, it can only cause them, and then walk out.

The Cloud

O, you must wear your rue with a difference.

A LREADY A NOBLE DAY, young summer soaring, vivid with promise, drenched blue and green, had divided them, on the terrace beside the mill, into sun and shadow. Sally and Catherine lay stretched, as if biered, on flattened wooden beach chairs with orange mattresses, of the kind one sees at Cannes; in dark glasses and bikinis, silent, outside the scope of other activity. Peter sat at the breakfast table in shorts, barefooted and barechested, opposite Paul and Annabel Rogers in the parasol shade. The three children were down on the lawn beneath the terrace, trying to catch whirligigs at the water's edge; knelt snatching at the surface, little cries, murmurs among themselves. Inky-blue dragonflies fluttered past; then a butterfly of a pale sulphur-yellow. From across the river, one saw a quietly opulent bourgeois glade of light, bright figures, red and aquamarine parasol blazoned on top (amusing *trouvaille* at some local sale) with the word *Martini*; the white cast-iron furniture, sun on stone, the jade-green river, the dense and towering lighter green walls of willows and poplars. Downstream, the dim rush of the weir, and a hidden warbler; a rich, erratic, un-English song.

The scene possessed a strange sense of enclosure, almost that of a painting, a Courbet perhaps — or would have if the modern clothes of the eight personages and their colors had not clashed, in a way a totally urban and synthetic age cannot be expected to notice, with the setting. It was so leafy, so liquid — and at that very moment a hidden oriole called from the trees behind the mill and gave this particular combination of heat, water and foliage a voice, defined exactly its foreignness, its faint subtropicality — so leafy, so liquid, so richly of its place and season, Central France and late May. And the Anglo-Saxon voices. So many things clashed, or were not what one might have expected. If one had been there, of course.

"Decisions, decisions," murmured Paul amicably.

Whereat Apostle Peter smiled, putting his hands behind his neck, arching his hairy chest — guess what, beneath my shorts — to the sun.

"Your fault. That dinner. One needs twenty-four hours to recover."

"We did actually promise the children," said Annabel.

"Honestly, Tom won't care. He'll be happy messing down there all day."

Annabel looked down there. "Ours will. I'm afraid."

Paul suggests that Peter and Sally need not come.

"No, no, of course we will." Peter descends his arms, grins sideways at them across the table. "Just the rat race. Set us dumb helots free, we collapse into total inertia." Then: "You need training for this." Then: "You've forgotten how us poor working sods live."

Annabel smiles: she hears rumors.

"Go on. Rub it in." He waves a pink-and-white arm at the river, the all of it. "Honestly. Some people."

"You'd be bored to death."

"Oh yeah. Just try me. I mean, seriously, what would you take now, Paul?"

"Forty? If I was pushed."

"Christ."

But suddenly Peter clicks his fingers, straightens, sits to face them. He is small, moustached, gray-eyed; assured, one knows; and suspects, dynamic. He knows he is known as dynamic. Smart little rhesus, his cage is time. He grins, finger out.

"To hell with the bloody program. Much better idea. I get Granny to buy the place as a rest home for exhausted producers. Yes?"

"You can have it for ten bob if you swing that one."

Peter extends a flattened hand, reads an imaginary letter.

"Dear Mr. Hamilton, We await your explanation of an item on your last expense account, to wit one superbly converted and altogether divine French water mill for which you have charged the inexplicably high sum of fifty new pence. As you know, for your grade the disbursement ceiling under this heading is forty-nine pence per annum and in no circumstances —"

Screams. Mercifully.

"Daddy! Daddy! There's a snake!"

The two men stand, the sunbathing girls look up. Annabel calls quietly, "Keep away from it."

Sally, cocked kerchiefed head, says, "Aren't they dangerous?"

Annabel smiles in the parasol shadow.

"They're only grass snakes."

Sally stands and joins Peter and Paul at the corner of the terrace, by the parapet with the spaced pots of geraniums and agaves over the water. Catherine sinks back, her head turned away.

"There it is! There!"

"Tom, keep back!" shouts Peter.

The elder little girl, Candida, pulls him officiously away. They see the snake swimming sinuously along beside the stone bank, its head making a ripple. It is small, not two feet long.

"My God, it really is a snake."

"They're quite harmless."

The girl Sally clasps her elbows and turns away. "I don't like them."

"And we all know what *that* means."

She looks around and puts out her tongue at Peter. "And I still don't like them."

Peter smiles and kisses the air between; then leans back beside Paul and stares down.

"Oh well. Proves it's paradise, I suppose."

The snake disappears among some yellow iris in the shallow water at the foot of the terrace wall. With Peter everything is always about to disappear. Now he turns and sits on the edge of the parapet.

"When we going to have our session, Paul?"

"This evening?"

"Fine."

The three children come trailing up the steps to the terrace. Candida looks reproachfully across at Annabel.

"Mummy, you said you wouldn't just sit around all morning."

Annabel stands, holds out her hand. "Then come and help me pack up."

Sally, kneeling to lie on her beach chair, says, "Annabel, can I . . . ?"

"No, please. It's just getting things out of the fridge."

Catherine lies silent behind her dark glasses, like a lizard; sun-ridden, storing, self-absorbed; much more like the day than its people.

They straggle across a meadow on the far bank of the river, the bearded Paul ahead, carrying the drinks basket, with his daughters and the little boy; Annabel and her sister Catherine a little way behind, carrying the other two baskets; and thirty yards again behind them, the television producer Peter and his girl friend Sally. Knee-deep in the May grass, the long-stemmed buttercups and the marguerites; beyond, above, the approaching steep stone hills, rock faces in the scrub, the different world they make for. Swifts scream, high in the azure sky. There is no wind. Paul and the children enter a wood, disappear in the leaves and shadow, then Annabel and her sister follow. The last pair idle in the flowery sunlight. Peter has his arm around the girl's shoulders, she is speaking.

"I can't work her out. It's almost like she's a mute."

"They did warn me."

She throws him a little look. "Fancy?"

"Oh come on."

"You kept looking at her last night."

"Just to show nice. And you can't be jealous about last night."

"I'm not. Just curious."

He pulls her closer. "Thanks all the same."

"I thought men liked still waters."

"You're joking. She's hamming it up."

She looks at him under her eyebrows. He shrugs; then his bitten smile, like a sniff. She looks away. "I'd be the same. If it had been you." He kisses the side of her head. "Pig."

"Such a goddam thing of it."

"You mean *you* wouldn't. If it was me."

"Sweetie, one doesn't have to —"

"You'd be in bed with some new bird."

"Wearing black pajamas."

She pushes him away, but she smiles. She wears a dark brown sleeveless top over cotton trousers striped pale mauve, white and black; bell-bottomed and pert-arsed. She has long blond hair, which she tosses too often. Her face has a vaguely babyish defenselessness and softness. She invites regiments and rape; Laclos immortalized her. Even Paul, one has eyes too, eyes her; much cast as the trendy girl friend, a plaything in plastic playlets. P is her letter of the alphabet. Peter takes her hand. She stares ahead.

She says, "Tom's loving it, anyway." Then: "I wish he still

wouldn't look at me as if he doesn't know who I am." He squeezes her hand. "I feel Annabel's done better with him in a few hours than I've done in three days."

"She's had training, that's all. Tom's age, they're all selfish little bastards. You know. We're all just substitute boys. That's how he marks people."

"I have tried, Peter."

He kisses the side of her hair again; then runs a hand down her back and caresses her bottom.

"Do we really have to wait till tonight?"

"Cheeky bugger."

But she flirts the pert bottom and smiles.

Ahead, Annabel breaks a silence with Catherine, who has put on a pair of white Levi's, a pink shirt; a striped red woolen bag, Greek, over one shoulder.

"You didn't have to come, Kate."

"It's all right."

"Well try and talk a little more. Please?"

"I've got nothing to say. I can't think of anything."

Annabel shifts the basket she is carrying to the other hand; a surreptitious glance at her sister.

"I can't help it about them."

"I know."

"You needn't make it quite so obvious."

"I'm sorry."

"Paul being —"

"Bel, I realize."

"And at least she tries."

"I can't shut off behind a smiling face. The way you do."

They walk a few steps in silence.

Catherine says, "It's not just . . ." Then, "Other people's happiness. Feeling you're the odd woman out. For the rest of time."

"It will pass." She adds, "If you try."

"Now you sound like Mama."

Annabel smiles. "That's what Paul's always saying."

"Clever Paul."

"Mean."

"Invited."

"That's not fair."

Catherine answers the quick look with a smile.

"Stupid old Bel? With her horrid husband and her horrid house and her horrid children? Who could possibly envy her?"

Annabel stops; one of her little performances.

"Kate, I don't sound like that!"

"Yes you do. And I'd much rather have to envy you than not." She says back over her shoulder, "At least you're real."

Annabel walks behind her. "Anyway, Candy *is* horrid. I simply must do something about her." Then, "It's his lordship's fault. He keeps saying 'passing phase.' I.e., don't for God's sake bother me with my own children."

Catherine smiles. Annabel says, "It's not funny." Then, "And I don't know why you've taken against them so much."

"Because they devalue everything."

"Not half as much as you undervalue."

That sets Catherine silent a moment.

"Ten-a-penny human beings."

"You don't even know them." Bel adds, "I think she's rather sweet."

"Like saccharine?"

"Kate."

"I can't stand actresses. Especially bad ones."

"She tried very hard last night." Catherine gives a little shrug. "Paul thinks he's terribly clever."

"Usable."

"You really are the most frightful intellectual snob."

"I'm not blaming Paul."

"But they are friends of ours. Peter is."

Catherine turns toward Bel, lowers her glasses, for a moment looks her in the eyes: you know perfectly well what

I mean. Another silence, the sound of the children's voices through the trees ahead. Annabel lets Catherine lead the way again where the path narrows, speaks at her back.

"You read such horrors into people. It's not necessary."

"Not people. What makes them what they are."

"Except you blame them. You seem to blame them."

Catherine makes no answer.

"Well you do."

From behind, she sees Catherine give a little nod, and knows it to be sarcastic, not agreeing. The path widens and Bel comes beside her again. She reaches out a hand and touches the sleeve of Catherine's pink shirt.

"I like that color. I'm glad you bought it."

"Now you're being transparent."

Ridiculous, terrible: one cannot hide the smile.

" 'Catherine! I will not have you speaking to your mother like that!' "

Wicked Bel, mimicking to pierce, to remind; when one wept with rage, and there was only one sane and understanding being in the world. Toward whom one now reaches a hand, and feels it pressed . . . and then, how typical, that wicked oblique egocentricity, how cheaply feminine, oh how one hated her sometimes (what had he once said, the obsidian beneath the milk), having one so near bared, and glancing off, as if it was all a joke, just pretending . . .

"Oh Kate, look! There are my butterfly orchids."

And Annabel leads the way up a little sunlit clearing in the trees beside the path, to where five or six slender white columns of the delicate flower stand from the grass — and kneels, oblivious to all but them. By the two tallest. Catherine stands beside her.

"Why are they yours?"

"Because I found them last year. Aren't they beautiful?"

Bel is thirty-one, four years older than her sister, a prettier woman, plumper and rounder-faced, pale face and fox-red hair, more Irish, dry gray-green Irish eyes, though the blood is only from a grandmother's side and they have never lived there, lack the accent. In her old straw hat and her loose-sleeved cream dress she looks a little of the matron, the eccentric, the latterday lady of letters; always in shadow; her freckled skin is allergic to the sun. That calculated insouciance in her clothes, yet always a sort of haphazard elegance, a difference that every woman who comes to know her well ends by envying . . . even loathing; not fair, to be so often more rememberable than the fashion-conscious. And now, from across the river, a nightingale suddenly bursts into song. Annabel stares at her orchids, touches one, bends to sniff the flowers. Catherine stares down at her kneeling sister. They both turn at Peter's voice.

"They're wild orchids," says Annabel. "Butterfly orchids."

The man and the slightly taller long-haired girl come beside Catherine, who moves aside. They seem disappointed, a little at a loss when they see how small and insignificant the plants are.

"Where's the cellophane and pink ribbon?"

Sally laughs, Annabel waves a reproachful hand back at him; Catherine stares a moment at his face, then looks down.

"I say, do let me take your basket," says Peter.

"It doesn't matter."

But he takes it. "Male liberation."

She smiles faintly.

Annabel stands up. They hear Candida's voice calling them on through the trees; the lush French trees; the young and peremptory, high-pitched English voice.

A lovely lizard; all green.

They came together, the five adults and the three children, and strolled on together through the shadow and sunlight, the three women and the children now a little in the lead, the two men talking behind; through sunlight and shadow, always the water to their left; shadows of conversation, sun-lights of silence. Voices are the enemy of thought; not thought; thinking. One (blessed sanctuary) could see Catherine trying to make an effort, smiling at Sally across her sister, even asking one or two questions, like someone playing ping-pong against her will . . . foolish game, but if you insist, if Bel insists, if the day insists. All three women half tried to hear through their own voices what the two men were saying behind them. The "session" had informally begun, it seemed. That would be Peter, always eager to set things going, to bring things together, to get organized; before the main chance disappeared, like a snake into a clump of yellow iris. As a secret miser gets tense when he sees his money being spent; smiles and suffers; then breaks.

The key thing, he was saying, was an angle, a hook to hang the program on. An explanation, really — why so many came to buy houses in the area, was it just economic, for example? Some kind of escape? Merely a trend, the snowball effect? He fired out ideas, hardly listening to Paul's answers; already one sensed the futility of the exercise, the unnecessary fuss of it all, the endless planning and discussing of what would have been just as good with no planning, without all the talk; as a news story has to be done, fast and by luck and improvised. A kind of essay, he was saying; in depth; not just fancy photography, how-lucky-some-people-are. All that jazz.

Candida screamed as a kingfisher, a flash of azure, skimmed away ahead of them.

"I saw it first! Didn't I, Mummy?"

Like unnecessary italics, always underlining the obvious.

"I absolutely don't want fifty minutes of pretty pictures," said Peter, as if pretty pictures might seriously harm his career.

What one lost, afterward, was what one had never had strongly at the best of times: a sense of continuity. Such as, I must do this, B, even though it has no apparent purpose, beauty or meaning, because it comes between A and C. So now everything became little islands, without communication, without farther islands to which this that one was on was a stepping-stone, a point with point, a necessary stage. Little islands set in their own limitless sea, one crossed them in a minute, in five at most, then it was a different island but the same: the same voices, the same masks, the same emptiness behind the words. Only the moods and settings changed a little; but nothing else. And the fear was both of being left behind and of going on: of the islands past and the islands ahead. One is given to theories of language, of fiction, of illusion; and also to silly fancies. Like dreaming one is a book without its last chapters, suddenly: one is left forever on that last incomplete page, a loved face kneeling over wild orchids, a voice breaking the silence, a stupid crack — transfixed, for ever and ever, like a bad photograph. And the only one who understood . . . Bel is a subtle cow, and Paul, impervious oxlike Paul — one really doesn't know why one's here.

But nor one why one should be anywhere else, unless to discover a wish that one was here after all. Perhaps continuity is simply having wishes, little safe bright chains of streetlights ahead. The most frightening is not wanting love from anyone, or ever again. Even if he returned . . . each is the condition. To forgive nothing and give nothing and want nothing was what it all really meant; to settle for being taken like a parcel from one little island to the next, observing and judging and hating — or was it challenging? Surprise me, prove I'm wrong, string the islands together again?

One must hide the impression of that. It would never do to have one's misery taken advantage of.

They stop where the hillsides come steep to the river, announcing the gorge ahead; the river faster, rocks and runnels; the land unfarmable, even by French peasants. Just upstream of where they stop lumbers and sprawls a picturesque agglomeration of huge gray boulders, like a herd of stone elephants come to water at the river's edge. Bel selects a place, a little plateau above the water under a beech tree, where there is shade and sun; kneels and begins, helped by Sally and Catherine, to unpack the baskets. Paul picks up the two bottles of wine and the Coca-Cola tins and takes them down to the river to cool. The two little girls go with him, then slip out of their shoes, dip cautious feet where a tributary runs shallowly over the stones; scream; while Peter wanders on a little way with his son, free it seems to play father for a minute or two now that he has had his say, his business, his morning's justification for existing.

Paul takes off his shoes and stockings, rolls up his trousers, methodical and comical, like an elderly tripper at the seaside; Paul with his prematurely aging hair and beard streaked black and white, almost cropped, obscurely nautical rather than literary, a dense shade too would-be intellectual and *distingué*; now paddling and poking after Candida and Emma, turning over stones for crayfish. The three women under the beech tree stand. Sally unzips the side of her pants, peels and stands out of them, takes off her brown top. She still wears the bikini she had on at the mill; indigo and white flowers, a brass ring at each hip, another joining the straps of the upper part behind; svelte little pods, lissom legs. The skin does not match the fabric of the bikini, which requires a deep tan. One notes again. She swans off toward Peter and the boy, standing on a boulder some fifty yards away. Bel and Catherine walk down into the sun toward Paul and the little girls. The sparkling water, the splashing feet; the dragonflies and butterflies; the buttercups and oxeyes and little blue flowers like splashes of sky. The voices, movements; kaleidoscope, one shake and all will disappear. Bel's freckled-milky skin as she smiles, her vacant Juno smile, beneath the wide brim of her rush hat; it has fenestrations, an open lattice around the crown. Nuclei, electrons. Seurat, the atom is all. The first truly acceptable island of the day. *En famille;* where children reign. For bonny sweet Robin is all my joy. Which time she chanted snatches of old tunes.

"It's lovely," bawls Candida back at them, with her usual ineffably judicious authority. "Come on. We don't want to eat yet."

"I wish I believed in hitting children," murmurs Bel.

Catherine smiles and kicks off her espadrilles.

The next island, five, or is it ten, minutes later. Paul has caught a crayfish, a very small one; the lovely incoherence, the brief construct, disintegrates. They all circle him as he lifts each stone. Candy and Emma in anticipation as each stone rises, crayfish or not; they scream for Peter and Sally and Tom to come back. Hunting, serious. Paul snatches, a larger little lobster shape between his fingers, just in time to show his guests. Good God. Fantastic. Candida rushes back with a hastily emptied plastic box from the picnic place beneath the beech. Peter wades in beside Paul. Lovely. Competition. A game. Sally takes Tom's hand and leads him to the plastic box to show what Daddy is looking for. The little boy stares, then flinches back when one of the crayfish tries to jump out. Sally kneels, her bare arm around the child's shoulders. Like a transfer scene on a Regency teacup; posed Faith, Hope and Charity; for those to whom tea is not enough.

A figure appears, from the trees, from the way they came: a fisherman, a peasant come fishing, in rubber boots and faded blues, ruddy-skinned, an old straw hat with a black band; a man of fifty or so, solid, indifferent to them. He carries a long bamboo rod parallel with the ground over one shoulder; a canvas haversack, a bleached pale green, over the other. They stop looking for crayfish a second; stand, the men looking rather foolish, boyishly guilty, trespassing in the water; the children too, as if sensing that this intruder brings some obscure danger. But he walks quietly on out past the picnic place into the sunlight and down over the grass toward them, heading upstream. They see he has a squint. As he comes to them and passes, he tips a finger toward the brim of his hat.

" 'Sieurs — 'dames."

"Bon jour," says Paul. Then, "Bonne pêche."

"Merci."

And he goes stolidly on toward the boulders and the choked trees of the gorge beyond; disappears; yet leaves a wake, some reminder that this is a foreign land with its own life and customs. One hears what? *Ça ira.* The murmur of mobs, nocturnal feet. The scythe blade set straight to the handle. Perhaps simply because he is a serious fisherman, he has a function in the day. The frivolous ones turn back to their pursuit. Only Catherine watches the blue back till it finally disappears.

Ah, ça ira, ça ira. Les aristocrats, on les pendra.

And leaves the water, as if he draws her after him. She slips her wet feet into her espadrilles, and begins to wander away, pretending to look at flowers, her back to the voices, the shouts and damns and buggers. Oh, that's a beauty. Bags him tonight. Hurry up please it's time. Goonight Bill. Goonight Lou. Goonight. Goonight. There is a little path around the back of the first huge boulder that lies barring, half in the water, half on the bank, the way. At the top Catherine looks back at the others. The two men work in tandem now, Peter lifting the stones, Paul pouncing. Bel turns idly away out of the water and wanders back toward the picnic tree. She takes off her hat and smoothes her hair, as if exhausted, as she comes to the shade.

Catherine goes on, down beyond the boulder, out of sight. The path goes on winding through the stone herd, evens out a little, then climbs steeply up into the trees again, above the river. It becomes noisy, tumultuous. The locals call this place the Premier Saut, the first leap; almost a fall, a rush of narrowed water, a famous place for trout. Catherine clambers down to the long pool that lies above it: the cool, the depths, the moss and ferns. A wagtail, a squirt of canary yellow, flies in little bounces to the far end of the pool. The girl sits on a stone at the water's edge, beneath the steep bank; stares at the placid dark green water upstream, the dapples and flecks of sunlight, the dancing fly-motes, the bird with its neurotic tail. She picks up a twig and tosses it into the pool, watches it drift, then gather speed and be sucked down out of sight over the choked tumble of the Saut. He is gone, he is gone.

Now she sits slightly shrugged forward, as if she is cold, her elbows clasped, staring at the water. She begins to weep. It seems without emotion. Tears well slowly from her eyes and creep down her cheeks beneath the sunglasses. She makes no attempt to brush them away.

Bel calls from under the tree, beside the pink check cloth and its spread-out array of *charcuterie*, long loaves, cheeses, knives, the picnic tumblers; the apples and oranges, the three little pots of chocolate mousse for the children.

Candida calls back. "Oh Mummy! We're not *ready* yet!"

But Paul murmurs to her, Sally turns, whitebodies her willowy way back toward Bel; a w-girl now; then Emma, the younger daughter, running, passes her, and little Tom starts running too, as if the food will all be gone. Then the two men and Candida bearing the plastic box with the seven crayfish now caught, the latter complaining that one more and there would be one each for supper, they must catch more after lunch. Yes, yes, of course they will. But everyone's hungry. Paul remembers the wine, goes to where it has been cooling; the bottle of Muscadet *sur lie*; the other of Gros-Plant can wait.

"Hands up for Cokes!"

They sit and sprawl, the adults and children, around the cloth. Only Paul stands, busy with the corkscrew. Peter smacks Sally's bottom as she kneels forward to pour the Cokes for the children.

"This is the life!"

"Do you mind!"

He kisses the bare side of her back and winks across it at Tom.

Annabel calls. "Kate? Eating!"

Then Candida and Emma. "Kate! Kate!"

"That's enough. She'll come when she wants."

Emma says, "It might all be gone."

"Because you're a pig."

"I'm not!"

"Yes you are!"

"Candy!"

"Well she is." And she pounces, as her sister's hand moves. "Guests first."

Bel says, "Darling, hold the wineglasses for Daddy."

Sally smiles across the cloth at Emma; a prettier child, shyer and quieter; or perhaps it is just by contrast with her little pseudo-adult of a sister. If only Tom . . . she spreads *pâté* on bread for him, and he watches suspiciously.

"Mm. This looks heavenly."

Emma asks if the crayfish can have some. Peter laughs, and she looks hurt. Candida tells her she is silly. Bel makes Emma move and sit by her. Now Candida looks hurt. Paul glances out from the shade upstream toward the boulders, then looks down at Bel. She gives a little nod.

"Daddy, where are you going?"

"Just to look for Auntie Kate. She may have fallen asleep."

Candida throws a little glance at her mother. "I bet she's crying again."

"Darling, eat your lunch. Please."

"She's always crying."

"Yes. Peter and Sally understand. We all understand. And

we're not going to talk about it." She makes a little *moue* toward Sally, who smiles. Peter pours the wine.

"Mummy, can I have some?"

"Only if you stop talking so much."

Paul stands on the first boulder, watching up into the gorge. Then he disappears. They eat.

Peter: "I say, this stuff's marvelous. What is it?"

"The *rillettes?*"

Candida says, "Haven't you ever eaten it before?"

"Them," says Bel.

"We eat them every day. Almost."

Peter smacks his head.

"Caught out again. Just about to close his greatest deal. Then they found out he'd never eaten *rillettes.*" He puts his sandwich down, turns away, covers his face in his hands. A sob. "I'm sorry, Mrs. Rogers. I'm not fit to be seen at your table. I ought never to have presumed."

They hear Paul calling for Kate up the gorge. Peter gives another stage sob.

Bel says, "Now see what you've done."

"He's being silly."

"Peter's very, very sensitive."

Sally winks across at Candida. "Like a rhinoceros."

"Can I have some more?" asks little Tom.

"More, *please.*"

"Please."

Peter peers back around through his fingers at Candida. Suddenly she is a child again, and giggles; then chokes. Emma watches bright-eyed, then begins to giggle too. Little Tom watches gravely.

Paul saw the pink of her shirt some time before he reached the point on the path from which she had clambered down to the pool. He did not speak until he was standing there above her.

"Do you want to eat, Kate?"

She shook her head without turning, then reached for her dark glasses, on a stone beside her, and put them on. He hesitated, then climbed down beside her. After a moment, he reached out and touched the pink shoulder.

"If only we knew what to do."

She stared up the pool.

"It's so stupid. Something suddenly seems to take over."

"We do understand."

"I wish I did."

He sat on the stone beside her, half turned away.

"Have you got a cigarette, Paul?"

"Only Gauloises."

She accepted a cigarette from the packet he took out of his shirt pocket; bent to the match, inhaled smoke, then breathed out.

"Nothing has happened yet. Now is still before it happened. I know it will happen as it did happen. And I can't do anything about it."

He leaned forward with his elbows on his knees; a nod, as if such fantasies were quite rational, he shared them himself. Such a nice man; and trying, precisely because he was always trying. Be like me, be mild, be male, settle for what you have: sales if not name. Even after all these years the close beard, the fine mouth, made one expect asceticism, subtlety, stringent intelligence; not just decency, mediocrity, muddling through.

"Kate, you're not the kind of person one can inflict clichés on. Which leaves us poor mortals rather tongue-tied." She bowed her head a moment. "Why do you smile?"

She stared down at her hands. "You and Bel are the gods. I'm the poor mortal."

"Because we believe in clichés?"

She smiled faintly again; was silent, then spoke to humor him.

"Bel upset me. It wasn't her fault. I'm being such an arrogant bitch with those two."

"What did she say?"

"That."

"You're in great pain. We understand how difficult it is."
She breathed out smoke again.

"I've lost all sense of the past. Everything is present." But she shakes her head, as if putting it like that is so vague that it is pointless. "The past helps you make allowances. It's when you can't escape the . . ."

"Shouldn't the future help as well?"

"It's not attainable. You're chained to now. To what you are."

He picked up a pebble and tossed it a few feet out into the water. The trap, the rack; when you read people like books and know their signs better than they do themselves.

"Isn't the best way to break chains like that to force yourself to behave . . ." he doesn't finish the sentence.

"Normally?"

"At least the motions."

"Like Mr. Micawber? Something will turn up?"

"My dear, bread is also a cliché."

"And needs a hunger."

He smiles. "Well there is a kind of hunger, isn't there? At least for frustrating all of us who want to help you."

"Paul, I swear that every morning I . . ." she breaks off. They sit side by side, staring at the water.

He says gently, "It's not us, Kate. But the children. One gets too protective. But they really don't understand."

"I do try. Especially with them."

"I know."

"It's this having totally lost the power of volition. Feeling at the mercy of the tiniest remark. Happening. Everything being in question again. Trying to find out why. Why him. Why me. Why it. Why anything."

"I wish you'd try and write it all down."

"I can't. You can't write what you're living." She throws her cigarette-end into the water; then asks abruptly: "Are you and Bel frightened I shall try to kill myself as well?"

He says nothing, then, "Should we be?"

"No. But have you thought what it means that I haven't?"

For once he gives a question thought.

"We've hoped what it means."

"I think what it must really mean is that I like what I am. What I've become." She glances at him, the Roman head staring into the water; wise senator; wishing he hadn't come to find her. "I need hitting, really. Blowing up. Not sweet talk."

He leaves a pause. "I wish we weren't such very different people."

"I don't despise you, Paul."

"Just my books."

"You have thousands and thousands of happy readers to put against that." She says, "And I wouldn't envy Bel so much if I despised you."

He looks down. "Well . . ."

"That's false modesty. You know you work."

"In our fashion."

"I know what a despot Bel is. Underneath."

"Sometimes."

"We're not really sisters. Just two styles of intransigence."

He grins. "Of torture. Keeping a hungry man from his food."

And just as one couldn't help smiling at Bel's deliberate naïveté, pretty pink shirts indeed, one smiles now to hide the same offence: at the same glancing off, leaving one stranded, the impatience. One talks transubstantiation; and all the man thinks of is bread and wine.

She stands, and he stands as well, searching her eyes behind the dark glasses.

"We'll talk it all out, Kate. When they've gone."

Without warning she embraces him; and feels him flinch at the suddenness of it, this clutching at him. Her head is buried a moment against his shoulder, his arms come gingerly around her. He pats her back, then touches the top of her head with his mouth. Embarrassed, poor man. And she is already thinking: bitch, actress, calculatrix — why have I done this? And fool: what bishop carries gelignite — or would hand it over in his cathedral?

Dear ox. The brute part, to kill so capital a calf.

She leans away and grins up at his baffled eyes; then speaks like a green girl.

"Lucky Moslems."

Annabel sits with her back to the beech trunk; presiding mother-goddess, hatless and shoeless and slightly blowsy. Candida, who has drunk more than a glass of wine, lies sprawled asleep with her head in her lap. Every so often Bel touches her hair. Sally has moved away, to be in the sun; back to the grass, a bottle of Ambre Solaire by her side. Intimations of its scent wander to where the two men are, Peter on his elbow facing Paul, who still sits up. The two younger children are down by the water, building a pebble dam. Catherine sits propped on one arm, between Peter and Annabel, watching a small brown ant struggle through the grass stems with a crumb of bread. They have the wineglasses full of thermos coffee now.

Paul is adumbrating an angle for the program, the curious middle-classishness of English relations with France, how ever since the days of the *milord* and the grand tour the typical English visitor here has always been educated and reasonably well-off and of course conservative and how the resultant reported image has been of fastidious good living, food and wine snobbism and all the rest, a good place to forget all the disadvantages of living in a deeply puritanical country, though *ça va de soi* the puritanical side also allows one to despise their

politics and their ridiculous Napoleonic centralized bureau-
cracy profoundly at the same time from a different part of
oneself, so no wonder we had a reputation for perfidiousness,
we don't realize the arch-centralist nation of Europe is England, he means who else kowtows to London notions of life
as the British do, catch your Frog doing that, who else con-
forms so absurdly in the manner we behave and speak and
dress, take the way the French only care about the quality of
the food and the cooking, whereas all we care about is whether
the other diners are dressed properly and the bloody table-set-
ting looks nice and clean, we confuse terribly . . .

"Listen," says Bel. "There's an oriole."

And for a moment, Paul stops. They hear the liquid whistle
from across the river.

Bel says, "You never see them."

"Go on," says Peter. He reaches for a cigarette, belatedly
offers one to Catherine, who shakes her head. "This sounds
interesting."

Paul means we confuse quite ludicrously a notion, a myth of
a centralized France, ever since Versailles, and the actual contempt of the Frenchman for anything that stands in the way
of his individual pleasure. When we at home with our belief
that we're terribly free and democratic and politically independent are actually the most god-awful nation of conformers
when it comes to personal pleasure. That's why (rising to the
improvised paradox) every French government is inherently
fascist and the actual French nation inherently incapable of
accepting fascism for long; while *our* love of conforming is so
all-pervasive, so ideal a culture for a fascist takeover, that
we've had to evolve the whole constitutional gallimaufry (one
of his odd words) and God knows how many other public safe-
guards against our real natures.

"I'd love to tie this in somehow," says Peter.

Another thing, says Paul, pouring himself the last of the
Gros-Plant in Candy's glass, Peter having waved his hand at

it, another result of France not being a country where work-ing-class people from home ever come, no package tours, and one couldn't say anymore it was a proletarian hatred of dirty foreign food and filthy Latin sex, take the way (ah, the ways one takes) they flocked nowadays to Majorca and the Costa Brava and Italy and Yugoslavia and God knows where else, but much more a hatred of a country you had to be educated and sophisticated to enjoy, something you left to the bloody snobs and middle-class hedonists, or at least that was the ridiculous image of the place that had got about and as he was going to say before he got sidetracked, he's drunk too much, it also explained the corollary French illusion about England as a nation of fanatical stiff-upper-lipped and bowler-hatted mon-archomaniacs who lived for horses and dogs and *le sport* and the famous cold-blood and all the fucking rest of it. Take a château they knew only a few miles away and could Peter guess what had pride of place in the bloody drawing room? A framed letter from the Duke of Edinburgh's secretary thank-ing the count for his condolences on the death of His Royal Highness's father-in-law. You know, says Paul. One gives up.

"Does he speak English? Maybe we could use it."

Bel says, "Working-class people don't come to France be-cause it's too expensive. It's as simple as that."

Peter grins. "You're joking. You don't realize what some of them earn these days."

"Exactly," says Paul. "It's a cultural thing. Here they as-sume the customer wants the best. We assume they want the cheapest."

"We did a program on package tours a couple of years ago. Unbelievable, some of the reasons they gave. I remember one dear old bird in Majorca saying what she liked best was know-ing they all got the same food and the same sort of room."

He slaps his head; as if his incredulity proves the old bird's stupidity.

"My point. Damn the country where people are allowed to choose how they spend their money."

"If they have it," reiterates Bel.

"Nothing to do with money, for God's sake. I'm talking about being brainwashed." He turns to Peter again. "A French peasant, even a factory worker, cares just as much about his food and his wine as someone much higher up the economic ladder. As regards pleasure, they're totally egalitarian. I mean, take the way they'll lash out for a wedding. Just your peasant farmer, your postman. Magnificent food, Peter, you can't imagine. And all the concern about it, the care, the going to the butcher and discussing the meat, and the *patisserie* and the *charcuterie* and all the rest."

Praise God for economical additives.

Peter nods, then looks up with a glance that comprehends both Paul and Annabel.

"Lucky people, then? One can't dodge that?"

"One has a sense of privilege. Inevitably."

"But you seem to be arguing it should be scrapped. Do you really want the Manchester and Birmingham hordes here?"

Bel grins. "Good question. Ask Comrade Rogers."

He flaps a hand at his wife. "Only because the package tour is precisely what France has not got to offer. It's where you still have to discover things for yourself."

"Which requires an educated mind?"

"Just an open one. Not straitjacketed in the puritan ethic."

"I quite like this angle, too." He smiles at Annabel. "But how typical is he, Annabel?"

"Oh, I think a fairly standard expatriate reactionary. Don't you, Kate?"

Catherine gives a little smile, and says nothing.

"Come on, sister-in-law. Defend me from stabs in the back."

"If one's happy, obviously one doesn't want things to change."

"But one can want to share it a little?"

Bel answers for her. "Darling, why not face it? You're the biggest armchair socialist there ever was."

"Thank you."

"A bottle of Jolly, and you'll out-Mao everyone else in sight."

Peter sniggers. "I say, what a lovely word, Annabel. Out-Mao. I must remember that."

Paul wags a finger at Annabel; the awful Russian monk in him.

"My sweet, the aim of socialism, as I understand it, is to raise humanity. Not to pull everyone down to the lowest common denominator dear to every capitalist heart."

And they go on, and they go on; one hates Paul like this, the holding forth, the endless expounder of grand cultural rhubarb. When all one sees, somehow, is a tired rush of evening people, work-drained automata to whom one can be only profoundly lucky, above, chosen, helpless. To motivate, to explain them is the ultimate vulgarity and the ultimate lie . . . a kind of cannibalism. Eat butchered pork for lunch; then butchered other lives, chopped-up reality, for afters. The harvest is in. All that's left are the gleanings and leasings: fragments, allusions, fantasies, egos. Only the husks of talk, the meaningless aftermath.

And dense enough without all these circling, buzzing words; unreal enough, oh, quite unreal enough without the added unreality of all these hopping, seething, transilient male ideas and the knowledge that they were germs, they would breed, one winter evening mindless millions would watch their progeny and be diseased in their turn. One understood Bel's lazy irritation so well: not so much the pontificating, but to see him give way to it for so small a cause, such a worthless, shallow little *prick*; who saw nothing in trees but wood to build his shabby hutches of ephemeral nonsense from. To whom the real, the living, the unexplained is the outlaw; only safe when in the can.

One knew: Paul could have said that he wanted to extermi-
nate the French, what you will, the exact opposite of what he
had said, and the wretched little coffin-man would have nodded
and pronounced his incredibles and fantastics and looked for
an angle.

And one knew it was one's own fault: one should not have
called Bel a despot. It was all to disprove that; so proved it.

This: and the real trees, the two children by the water, the
silent girl in the sun, turned on her stomach now, primped
little white-and-indigo buttocks. The trees and scrub and sur-
facing boulders, the silent cliffs above, scorched lifeless planet,
windless sun, the day going stale like the ends of the loaves
from the lunch, no longer translucent and soaring, but somehow opaque and static; all the fault of the men's voices, the
endless futile and unhygienic scratching-at-sores of *soi-disant*
serious men's voices. Only women knew now. Even the vapid
girl knew only the sun on her back, the grass and earth below
her. Bel knew only herself and her sleeping child's head and
her other child's small movements below by the river; what
she gave to the conversation, even her little needling of Paul,
was indulgence, from her role as the quiet hub; to keep the
spokes turning a little. One had once seen Bel, a summer evening at home, just the four of them, needle Paul far more outrageously. He got up abruptly and walked out into the garden.
An embarrassed little silence. Then Bel as abruptly getting up
and leaving the room, going straight out, it was dusk, they had
seen it all through the window, go straight to where Paul stood
at the far end of the lawn. She made him turn and flung her
arms impulsively around him. It had seemed almost like a
lesson. They had watched from indoors, and he had smiled.
They had never discussed it or mentioned it afterward. One
stored it with old beads and brooches; to weep over, that
fashion and one's sense of presentable self had changed so
much.

If one were Bel; one's own, beyond all pride.

Now Emma came slowly back up to where the four adults were, and stood beside her mother.

"I want to lie like Candy."

"Darling, let her sleep. There's not room for you as well."

Emma sidles a look at her aunt, who reaches out a hand. The little girl kneels, then sinks and flops forward across her lap. Catherine strokes her fair hair, moves silky strands of it from her cheek.

Paul leans on an elbow, and yawns. "Now there's the most sensible one here."

Peter smiles sideways, up at Catherine. "Sorry. Monstrous to be talking shop on a heavenly day like this."

"I enjoyed listening."

She touches the collar of the child's yellow blouse, avoiding his eyes.

Paul grunts. "And not agreeing with one word of it."

Catherine makes a little shrug and looks across the picnic cloth at him. "Just thinking of what Barthes said."

Peter asks who Barthes is; as if, one feels, he thinks it is spelled Bart, and a Christian name. Paul explains. Peter clicks his fingers.

"Someone was talking to me about him only the other day." He sits up and turns toward Catherine. "What does he say?"

She speaks as if to Emma. "He analyzed tourist guides. In a book of essays. How they sell the notion that all utilitarian and all modern things are monotonous. The only interesting things are ancient monuments and the picturesque. How the picturesque has come to be associated almost uniquely with mountains and beaches in the sun." She adds, "That's all."

And beat that for incoherence.

Paul says, "The mountain bit started with the Romantics, surely."

She runs a finger down Emma's hair. It began with Petrarch; but one must not know too much.

"I think he was trying to point out that lack of imagination in traveling comes mainly from the middle classes. The middle-class notion of what is beautiful. How guides will devote three paragraphs to some church in a town, and then dismiss the real living town itself in two lines."

Paul sinks back, on the other side of the picnic cloth, and puts his hands behind his head. "For eminently good reasons, generally."

"If you think that thirteenth-century architecture matters more than twentieth-century reality."

"Why not? If one's on holiday."

She gives Paul's prone form a little look.

"Then why do you hate the false images of the British and the French? They're exactly the same form of selected reality."

"Don't see why."

Inane. Provoke her a little, she's almost human. He is smiling.

"You approve of bourgeois stereotypes of what's worth seeing on holiday. What's the difference between them and the bourgeois stereotypes of national character you dislike so much?"

He has closed his eyes. "If I can just have a brief nap, I shall think of a really crushing answer to that."

Bel says, "How are the mighty fallen."

"Boo." He crosses his hands over his stomach.

Peter lies back on an elbow, facing her. "Isn't this chap fantastically difficult to understand? I've been told."

"The general message is fairly plain."

Bel murmurs, "Kate edited one of his books in English."

"Good God. Did you really?"

"Not edited. Just proofread it."

"She practically rewrote the translation."

"If that's how you describe one or two small suggestions."

She warns Bel, or tries to warn her. Her look is not met. One doesn't catch Bel like that.

"So what is the general message?"

She hesitates, then plunges.

"That there are all kinds of category of sign by which we communicate. And that one of the most suspect is language — principally for Barthes because it's been very badly corrupted and distorted by the capitalist power structure. But the same goes for many other nonverbal sign-systems we communicate by."

Peter chews on a grass-stalk.

"You mean advertising — things like that?"

"That's a particularly flagrant field of manipulation. A lot of private communication is also advertising. Misuse — or just clumsy use, of signs." Too late to stop now, one is trapped. "A sentence is what the speaker means it to mean. What he secretly means it to mean. Which may be quite the opposite. What he doesn't mean it to mean. What it means as evidence of his real nature. His history. His intelligence. His honesty. And so on."

Paul speaks from apparent sleep. "Until everything about meaning matters except meaning. 'Pass me the salt' becomes a pregnant sign-structure. And the poor bloody salt never gets passed."

Catherine smiles. "Sometimes."

"Kraut," grunts Paul. "Not French."

Bel says, "Shut up. Go to sleep."

Peter is making signals: I'm a serious fellow. He even speaks slowly.

"This chap who was talking about him . . . isn't there something about the religion of the middle classes being the platitude?"

"I think he said the ethos."

"Because originality is disruptive — right?"

"It depends on the context."

Bel stares at her sister's bowed head, speculating.

"How?"

"There are middle-class contexts where one is expected to

sound original. Amusing. Even revolutionary. But the context is a kind of countermanding sign. It trumps."

Bel says, "For example, how quickly you go to sleep after lunch when you have finished cursing the society that allows you to go to sleep after lunch."

Paul murmurs, "I heard that."

Peter will not be distracted. "So real originality has to be actively revolutionary? Right? That's what this chap was getting at."

"I think people like Barthes are more interested in making people aware of how they communicate and try to control one another. The relation between the overt signs, whether they're verbal or not, and the real meaning of what is happening."

"But you have to change society first, don't you?"

"One hopes that's what more awareness does."

"But I mean, you know . . . if it's just picking up people's platitudes, it's just word-watching. Like bird-watching. No?"

"I presume even ornithology has its uses."

"Hardly central though, is it?"

"It would be if the bird was the basis of human society. As communication happens to be."

She sees out of the corner of her eyes, for through all this she has been looking down at Emma, that he nods. As if she has made a point. She realizes, it is very simple, she hates him; although he is fortuitous, ignorable as such, he begins to earn his right to be an emblem, a hideous sign. For he is not testing — or teasing — Barthes and semiotics, but her. He means childish little male things like: why don't you smile at me, what have I done, please show respect when I watch my language because I know you don't like my language.

Emma suddenly sits up, then goes to her mother and whispers in her ear. Bel holds her, kisses her cheek, she must wait.

"Do you think this could be got across on telly?"

"Could what . . . ?"

"This chap Barthes. What you've just been telling me."

"I should have thought it was essentially to be read."

"It wouldn't interest you? Sketch out a few ideas — I mean, if these sign things aren't all verbal, it might be fun to illustrate."

She casts him a quick look. He is prodding some insect in the grass with his stalk, head bent; long sandy hair. She looks back at Bel, who smiles gently, lethally, her arm around Emma.

"I'm not an expert on him. At all. There are hundreds —"

He grins up. "Experts write lousy scripts. One uses them to check. To interview, maybe. I'd much rather have someone who knows the essentials. Who's had to work things out for herself."

Bel says, "You're being offered a job."

Peter says, "Just an idea. Off the top of my head."

Catherine in a panic.

"But I . . ."

Peter says, "Seriously. If you'd like to come in and talk it over. Next time you're in town." He feels in a back pocket. "And do tell me the name of that book of essays."

"*Mythologies.*" She says it again, with the English pronunciation.

He writes it down in a little notebook. Catherine glances again at Bel, who has a dry air of amusement, approval, one cannot tell; then down again at Peter beside her.

"I really couldn't do it. I've never written a script in my life."

"Scriptwriters are ten a penny. No problem."

"What a horrid way to speak of the poor things," says Bel; then idly, "Of anyone, really."

Bitch.

"I'm sorry. But I . . ."

He puts the notebook back and shrugs.

"If you change your mind."

"I honestly shan't."

He opens his hands; and she looks at Bel, to let her know

she at least partly inspired the refusal. But Bel is armored bland. She urges Emma forward.

"Go on. Now."

Emma goes diffidently beside Catherine, then leans forward and whispers in her ear.

"Now?"

The little girl nods.

"Emma, I don't know if I can think of one."

"You can if you try." She adds, "Like last summer."

"I'm out of practice."

Bel says, "She's found a secret place. You won't be overheard."

"It's lovely. It's all secret."

"Just you and me?"

The little girl nods, very emphatically. Then she whispers, "Before Candy wakes up."

Catherine smiles. "All right."

"Come on. You must be quick."

She reaches for her Greek shoulder bag, then stands and takes Emma's hand. The child leads her away behind the tree to the path they came by, then along it. Peter watches them disappear, a little glance at Bel, then down to the ground in front of him.

"Not exactly making a hit there, I'm afraid."

"Oh good heavens, don't worry. She's a mass of defensive prickles at the moment. It was terribly kind of you to suggest it."

"She'll go back to . . . ?"

"I think so. When she's accepted what's happened."

"Bloody awful," says Peter.

"I suppose it is rather soon yet."

"Yes of course."

Paul begins to snore gently.

Bel murmurs, "Drunken old sod."

Peter grins, leaves a little silence. "I hear there's quite a lot of stuff still to come. Paul said."

"Yes. They hope enough for a final book."

"Terrible." He shakes his head. "Someone like that. And *like* that."

"They're always the most vulnerable, aren't they?"

He nods; then after a moment he shakes his head again. But now he glances around at the recumbent Sally, then down toward his son.

"Oh well. My celebrated intermittent father act."

He pushes up on his knees, then stands, blows a little kiss down at Bel — super lunch — and goes down to where Tom is building his dam.

"I *say*, Tom, my God, that's absolutely splendid."

Paul snorts in his sleep. Bel shuts her eyes, and dreams of a man she once knew, and wanted, but somehow never went to bed with.

The "secret" place is not very far, a little way up the slope from the path to where a stray boulder has lodged apart from the rest of the herd. There is a dell in the scrub beyond it; a stony dip out of sight that catches the sun, with daisies and the bright blue spires of clary, some clover, a single red poppy.

"Emma, that's lovely."

"Do you think they'll find us?"

"Not if we're quiet. Let's go and sit over there. Under the little tree." She sits, the child kneels beside her, expectant. "I tell you what. You pick some flowers. And I'll think of a story."

Emma scrambles up. "Any flowers?"

Catherine nods. She feels in her red bag for cigarettes; lights one. The child goes down into the sun on the floor of the little hollow, but looks back.

"About a princess?"

"Of course."

Nothing comes; no ghost of even the simplest narrative; only the ghost of that last shattered island. A kindness, what else? Even if as much to Bel to her. And nothing, nothing, but flight. To childhood, the little feminine thing in her yellow shirt and white briefs, bare-legged, gravely tugging at the recalcitrant flowers, being very good, silent, not looking, as if they are playing hide-and-seek; a game, not an art. One's little fair-haired niece, one's favorite, one's belief in innocence, soft skin, pursed mouth and candid eyes; whom one should love so much more than one did. That strange divide between young children and non-mothers; Sally, that gauche attempt to be unsexy, solicitous, nurselike. Why one really envied Bel. Evolution. One must not cry, one must concentrate.

If only. If only. If only.

"Are you ready?"

"Nearly."

"I'm hot."

"Come on then."

And the child climbs the few feet to where Catherine sits in the shade beneath the thorn tree, and kneels again with her flowers.

"They're nice."

"The blue ones are horrid. They won't break."

"Never mind."

Emma picks at one of the unopened oxeye daisies, then looks up at Catherine; then down again.

"I don't like it when you're unhappy."

"I don't like it either, Emma. But sometimes you can't help it."

The child stares at her draggle of flowers.

"I don't mind if you can't think of a story." She adds, "Not very much."

"Just a little much?"

Emma nods, pleased with this gradation. A waiting silence. Catherine inhales smoke, breathes it out.

"Once upon a time there was a princess."

And Emma moves, with the strange insistence of children that appropriate rituals should be observed; puts down the flowers, then crawls a foot forward and turns to sit beside Catherine, who puts her arm around her, draws her close.

"Was she pretty?"

"Of course. Very pretty."

"Did she win beauty contepitions?"

"Princesses are too grand for beauty competitions."

"Why?"

"Because they're for stupid girls. And she was a very clever girl."

"Was she more cleverer than you?"

"Much cleverer than me."

"Where did she live?"

"Just over the hill there. A long time ago."

"Is it a true story?"

"Sort of true."

"I don't mind if it isn't."

Catherine throws the cigarette away; grasps at the only straw in sight.

"She was also very sad. Do you know why?" Emma shakes her head. "Because she had no mummy and daddy. No brothers and sisters. Nobody."

"Will it end happily?"

"We'll have to see."

"I 'spect it will, don't you?"

This strange third world, beyond our powers. Catherine pats the little girl's side.

"One day she went on a picnic with all her brothers and sisters. And her mother and father, who were king and queen. They came here. Just where we are?" Emma nodded. "But she was naughty, she thought she'd play a trick. She'd hide and make them all look for her. So she came where we're sitting now, and she sat down, but then it was so hot, so she lay down, and then she felt very sleepy."

"She went to sleep."

"And she slept and she slept and she slept. And when she woke up it was dark. All she could see were the stars. She called and called. But no one answered. She was very frightened. She called again, again. But it was too late, they'd all gone home. All she could hear was the river. Laplaplaplaplap. Too late, too late, too late."

"Didn't they look for her?"

"It all happened such a long time ago that people didn't know how to count. Can you imagine that? Even the king could only count to twenty. And they had twenty-three children. So they used to count to twenty and make a guess."

"They missed her out."

"So she was all alone." And from nowhere, storied; granted a future, peripeteia. "She tried to walk home. But she kept falling, she didn't know where she was in the dark. She wandered farther and farther away. The brambles tore her dress, she lost a shoe. She began to cry. She didn't know what to do at all."

"Was she very frightened?"

Catherine pulls her niece a little closer. "You can't imagine how frightened. And it wasn't any better when dawn came. Because then she found she was in a huge forest. Nothing but trees, endless trees."

"Her mummy and daddy didn't know she was lost."

"They did realize. That next morning. And they came looking for her. But she'd wandered so far away in the night. And all they found was the shoe she'd lost."

"I 'spect they thought she was eaten by a wolf."

"You are clever. That's exactly it. So they went away home, very sad. And there she was, miles away in the forest and all alone. Very hungry. But then suddenly she heard a voice. It was a squirrel — you know? He showed her where there were nuts to eat. Then there came a bear, but not a fierce bear, a nice cuddly bear, and he showed her how to make a little house and a bed of ferns. And then all sorts of other birds and animals came and helped her and showed her how to live in the forest."

The little girl reached for Catherine's free hand, as if it were a toy. Her small fingers touched the silver wedding ring, tried to turn it.

"Then what happened?"

"They made a kind of pet out of her. They brought her food and flowers and pretty things for her house. And taught her about the forest. And how there was only one bad thing in it. Do you know what that was?" Emma shakes her head. "Men."

"Why?"

"Because cruel men came in the forest and hunted the poor animals. They were the only kind of men they knew, you see. So they thought all men were cruel. And they told her she must run away and hide if she ever saw them. And she believed them. So she became very shy and timid as well."

"Like a mouse."

"Just like a mouse." She runs fingers up Emma's yellow chest; who shivers and shrinks against Catherine's body. "And that's how she lived. For years and years. Until she was a big girl."

"How old was she?"

"How old do you want her to be?"

"Seventeen."

Catherine smiles at the blond head. "Why seventeen?"

Emma thinks a moment, then shakes her head: she doesn't know.

"Never mind. That's exactly what she was. Then something extraordinary happened. She came to this very same place again, just where we're sitting, and it was another very hot day, just like today. And once again she went to sleep. Under this very tree." Emma looks up, as if to remind herself it is there. "But when she woke this time, it wasn't night. It was still day. But even more terrible than before. Because all around her stood huge hunting dogs. Just like wolves. All growling and barking. There and there. And over there." She gives a shiver against Emma's side; who doesn't respond. This is going too far. "It was like a bad dream. She couldn't even scream out. But then something even worse appeared. Guess what?"

"A dragon?"

"Worse than that."

"A tiger."

"A man!"

"A hunting man."

"That's what she thought. Because he was dressed like one. But really he was very sweet and gentle. And he wasn't old. He was her age exactly. Seventeen. But you remember she believed the animals. So even though she could see he was very gentle, she was very frightened. She thought he must kill her. Even when he called the dogs away. Even when he picked some flowers and brought them up here where she was lying and knelt and told her she was the most beautiful girl in the whole world."

"She thought he was pretending."

"She just didn't know. She wanted to believe him. But then she kept thinking of what her animal friends had said. So she just lay very still and said nothing."

Now Emma moves, turns and twists and sinks back across her aunt's lap, staring up at her face.

"What happened next?"

"He kissed her. And suddenly she didn't feel frightened anymore. She sat up, and took his hands, and began to tell him everything. How she didn't know who she was, she'd forgotten her name. Everything. Because she'd been so long in the forest with the animals. And then he told her who he was. He was a prince."

"I knew."

"That's because you're clever."

"Is it the end?"

"Do you want it to be?"

Emma shakes her head firmly. She watches her aunt's face almost as if the prince and princess as well as phonemes might come from her mouth. One does not have to believe stories; only that they can be told.

"The prince said he loved her, he wanted to marry her. But there was a problem. Because he was a prince, he could only marry a princess."

"But she was a princess."

"She'd forgotten. She didn't have pretty clothes. Or a crown. Or anything." Catherine smiles down. "She hadn't any clothes at all."

"None!"

Catherine shakes her head.

Emma is shocked. "Not even . . . ?" Catherine shakes her head again. Emma bites her mouth in. "That's rude."

"She looked very pretty. She had lovely long dark brown hair. Lovely brown skin. She was just like a little wild animal."

"Didn't she get cold?"

"This was summer."

Emma nods, a little puzzled by this anomalous departure, but intrigued.

"So. In the end the prince had to go away, feeling very sad that he couldn't marry this beautiful little girl with no clothes. And she was in tears because she couldn't marry him. So here she was, crying and crying. Then suddenly there was a hoot. Toowhitawoo. From just up there. In the tree."

Emma cranes her head, then stares back at Catherine.

"What was it?"

"You know what it was."

"I've forgotten."

"An owl. An old brown owl."

"I knew really."

"Owls are very clever. And this was the oldest, cleverest owl of them all. He was really a magician."

"What did he say?"

"Toowhitawoo, toowhitawoo, do-on't . . . you-ou . . . cry."

Emma grins. "Say it again. Like that."

Catherine says it again. "Then he flew down beside her and told her what he could do. By magic. To be a princess you also have to live in a palace? Well. He could give her pretty clothes. Or he could give her a palace. But he couldn't give her both things at the same time."

"Why couldn't he?"

"Because magic is very difficult. And you can only do one piece of magic at a time." Emma nods. "All she thought about was seeing the prince again. So she begged the owl to give her the pretty clothes. One second she had nothing. The next she had a beautiful white dress and a crown of pearls and diamonds. And trunks and trunks of other clothes and hats and shoes and jewelry. Horses to carry them. Servants and maids. Just like a real princess. She was so happy that she forgot about the palace. She jumped on her horse and galloped away to the castle where the prince lived. And at first everything went marvelously. The prince took her to meet the king and queen, who thought she was very beautiful and must be very rich. With such lovely clothes and everything else. They said at once that the prince could marry her. Just as soon as they had visited her palace. She didn't know what to do. But of course she had to pretend she had a palace. So she invited them for the next day. Then they all dressed up and went out to see her palace. She told them exactly where to go. But when they got there . . . it was mad."

"There wasn't any palace."

"Just a rotten old bare field. All muddy and damp. And there she stood in the middle of it, in all her lovely clothes."

"They thought she was silly."

"The prince's father was very, very angry. He thought it must be some stupid joke. Especially when she curtsied and said, Welcome to my palace, your majesty. The princess was so frightened, she didn't know what to do. But the owl had told her the magic word that would turn her clothes into a palace."

"Tell me."

"It was his call backwards. Woo-a-whit-too. Can you say it?"

The little girl grins and shakes her head.

"She could. So she said it. And there in a flash was a beautiful palace. Orchards and gardens. But now she hadn't any clothes. Not a stitch. And you ought to have seen the faces of the king and queen. They were so shocked. Like you just now. How most terribly *rude*, said the queen. What a shameless girl, said the king. And the princess was in despair. She tried to hide, but she couldn't. The servants started laughing, and the king got madder and madder, and said he'd never been so insulted. The poor girl lost her head. She wished back all her clothes again. But then the palace disappeared, and they were back in the wretched old field. The king and queen had had enough. They told the prince she was a wicked witch, and he must never, never see her again. And then they all rode away, leaving her in tears."

"Then what happened?"

The oriole whistles down in the trees by the river.

"I haven't told you the prince's name. It was Florio."

"That's a funny name."

"It's very old."

"What was her name?"

"Emma."

Emma wrinkles her nose. "That's silly."

"Why?"

"I'm Emma."

"Why do you think Mummy and Daddy called you Emma?"

The little girl thinks, then gives a shrug: strange aunt, strange question.

"I think it was because of a girl in a story they read."

"The princess?"

"Someone a little like her."

"Was she nice?"

"When you got to know her." She prods Emma's tummy. "And when she didn't keep asking questions."

Emma wriggles. "I like questions."

"Then I'll never finish."

Emma covers her mouth with a grubby hand. Catherine kisses a finger and sets it between the watching eyes on her lap. The oriole whistles, closer, their side of the river now.

"The princess thought of all those years in the forest, when she'd been so happy. And how unhappy she was now. So in the end she came back here, to this tree, to ask the wise old owl what she should do. There he was up there, sitting on that branch, with one eye shut and the other open. She told him what had happened. How she had lost Prince Florio forever. Then the owl told her something very wise. That if the prince really loved her, he wouldn't care whether she was a princess or not. He wouldn't mind that she hadn't any clothes or jewels, or a palace. He would just love her for herself. And until he did that, she would never be happy. He said she mustn't go looking for him anymore. She must wait till he came to find her again. And then he told her that if she was very good, and very patient, and would do what he said, then he could do one last piece of magic. Neither the prince nor she would ever grow older. They would stay seventeen forever, until they met again."

"Was it very long?"

Catherine smiles down. "It's still. All these years and years.

They're both still seventeen. And they've never met." The oriole calls again, going away downstream. "Listen."

The little girl twists her head, then looks back up at her aunt. Once more, the strange trisyllabic flute. Catherine smiles.

"Flo-ri-o."

"It's a bird."

Catherine shakes her head. "The princess. She's calling his name."

A shaded doubt; a tiny literary critic — Reason, the worst ogre of them all — stirs.

"Mummy says it's a bird."

"Have you ever seen it?"

Emma thinks, then shakes her head.

"She's very clever. You never see her. Because she's shy about not having any clothes. Perhaps she's been in this tree all the time. Listening to us."

Emma casts a suspicious glance up into the thorn tree.

"It doesn't end happily ever after."

"You know when I went away before lunch? I met the princess. I was talking with her."

"What did she say?"

"That she's just heard the prince is coming. That's why she's calling his name so often."

"When will he come?"

"Any day now. Very soon."

"Will they be happy then?"

"Of course."

"And have babies?"

"Lots of babies."

"It is happy really, isn't it?"

Catherine nods. The innocent eyes search the adult ones, then the little girl slowly smiles; and the body moves like a smile, she rises, a sudden affectionate little tomboy, twists and straddles across Catherine's outstretched legs, slides and clings, forces her aunt down on her back, kissing her mouth, little pressed lips — then giggles wildly as Catherine rolls her away and tickles. She squeaks, squirms; then lies still, eyes brimming with suspense and mischief, the story already forgotten, or so it seems; a new small pint of energy to spend.

"Fou-ound you!" chants Candida at the top of her voice, standing beside the boulder that has masked them from the path below.

"Go away," says Emma, clinging possessively to Catherine as she sits up. "We hate you. Go away."

Three o'clock. Paul has awakened; he leans on his elbow beside Bel, who is now on her back, and reads *The Scholar Gipsy* aloud. Bel stares up into the leaves and branches of the beech tree. Paul's voice just reaches Sally, in the sun. Peter lies beside her, in his shorts. The three children are down by the river again, their occasional voices counterpointing the quiet drone of Paul's reading. Catherine is nowhere to be seen. It has become a strange day, in which the heat and stillness seem prolonged beyond their proper zenith. In the distance, somewhere down the valley, there is the sound of a tractor, but it is hardly audible above the faint rush from the Premier Saut, the hum of insects. The beech leaves are motionless, as if cast in translucent green wax and set under a huge bell-glass. Staring up into them, Bel has the delicious illusion that she is staring down. She thinks about Kate, or thinks she is thinking about her, as Paul reads; only occasional lines, small heightenings and shifts in his voice, impinge. It is a kind of easy guilt; to be made surer of one's own contentment. Bel believes in nature, in peace, drift, illogically in both the inevitable and a beneficent order of things; not in anything so masculine and specific as a god, but much more in some dim equivalent of herself watching gently and idiosyncratically behind all the science and the philosophy and the cleverness. Simple, poised, flowing like the river; the pool, not the leap . . . ruffled or ruffling on occasion only to prove that life is not, or need not be . . . and how nice a fabric would be of those leaves, green petals of Victorian words, how little changed, only the uses of words and even then only as the years changed the beech leaves, not at all really.

" 'Maidens who from the distant hamlets come To dance around the Fyfield elm in May . . .' "

How all coheres.

She began to listen to the great poem, one she knew almost by heart; past readings of it, sometimes she read, its private history in her life with Paul, its ramifications, memories; how one could live in it, if only Catherine, maidens in May . . . if only it hadn't to be all *Hamlet*, that wretched intellectual sob story, all walls and winds and winter puns. Willful flights from all simplicity. Absurd, to cast oneself as Hamlet; Ophelia perhaps, that one couldn't help at times. But the other needed such a perverse will, a deliberate choice. When Bel was at Somerville there had been an attempt at it: a female Hamlet. Absurd. One kept on thinking of pantomime principal boys, instead of Sarah Bernhardt as one was meant. Plots, drama, farfetched action: when there are lovely green poems to live by, men one suffers to read them and shall tonight perhaps, if one still feels like it, be mounted by. Absurd. If only one had cut out that thing in the *Observer* about how to dry leaves, glycerine was it, and keep their color. And how to calm Candy down, that dreadful stridency.

" 'Still nursing the unconquerable hope, Still clutching the inviolable shade, With a free onward impulse brushing through, By night, the silver'd branches of the glade — Far on the forest skirts, where none pursue . . .' "

She sleeps.

A stanza or two later Peter rises, looks down at Sally, at her back, she has undone the top part of her bikini, one can see the side of a white breast. He picks up his short-sleeved shirt, his sandals, walks down barefooted to where the children are. He finds the poetry-reading distinctly pretentious, vaguely embarrassing; and is bored, the way people slump around, the way Sally lies there drugged in the sun; the slowness. A ball to chuck around, anything, any outlet for normal energy. The children also bore him. He stands and watches.

Sally best, the rest of her bikini stripped off, behind a bush: a good quick ram. But she's a conventional girl, and shyer than she looks . . . just moldable, as all his girls since his departed wife have been; and with the price — not very clever, not very unexpected, not dry and percipient at all; when one came down to it, hopelessly out of her depth with Bel and her bloody sister. One should not have brought her. Just easy to have around. To lay, and be seen with. Like certain programs. One deserved, one wanted more.

At least Tom seems happy to be bossed about by the cocksure elder daughter, poor little bastard; she does for a stand-in for his mother. Peter pulls on the shirt and looks back beneath the beech. Paul's blue back, the procumbent Bel, collapsed cream dress, two pink-soled feet . . . let's face it, one fancied her, one didn't know why, but always had. Peter turns away upstream. He leans against the first boulder for a moment to fasten his sandals, then goes on, up into the trees, the choked ravine, above the Premier Saut, where Catherine wandered earlier. He even climbs down to where she sat and stares at the pool; thinks about swimming. Maybe a little too fast. He throws a twig into midpool. Definitely too fast. He unzips his shorts and urinates in the water.

He climbs back to the path, then up off it through the steep belt of trees toward the cliffs above. He comes out in the open. The land tilts up, patches of thorny scrub and broom, divided by long runs of stony scree. He begins to scramble up the nearest, fifty, then a hundred yards, to where he can look back over the trees and the boulders down to the clearing and the river: the small shapes of the children by the water, Sally lying as he left her, Paul and Annabel under the beech, cream and blue, doing their highly civilized thing. He feels for a cigarette, then remembers he has left them behind on the picnic cloth; wonders why he bothered. The heat. He turns and stares up at the cliff that towers above, gray and a reddish ochre, one or two overhangs already casting shadow in the westering sun. Angles. Death. He scrambles on, another hundred yards, to where the land becomes vertical, a wall of stone.

Now he works back along the foot of the cliff, above the scrub and talus below. There is some kind of goat track, ancient droppings. The cliff wears around, away from the river; the heat seems greater. He stares down at the children, wondering whether to call to them; some war whoop, something to break it all up. One didn't really care what people thought, cutting through other people's crap was what one was about; getting things done, flanneling here, riding roughshod there; have the game played by one's own quick rules. The great thing about producing, the pressure, one never stayed long, one moved around; one sucked the juice, then attacked the next. Still, one was a guest. One liked old Paul, for all his going on. One envied old Paul; very nicely, as what in essence one would like one day for oneself, did Bel. Those eyes that toyed, teased, smiled; and never quite gave. She was so unobvious. The dryness, the mock simplicity that took no one in; fifty Sallys in her little finger; and a smashing pair of tits, that dress last night.

A trim-bodied man of below average height, he turned and gazed up at the cliff over his head, and wondered comfortably if he was safe from falling rock.

The erotic sun. Male sun. Apollo, and one is death. His poem once. One lies in one's underclothes, behind dark glasses and fast-closed lids, aware of process, wretched moons; hidden and waiting. It must be close. One thought of it even with Emma, since he is there, also waiting, every moment now. That is why one can't stand other people, they obscure him, they don't understand how beautiful he is, now he has taken on the mask; so far from skeleton. But smiling, alive, almost fleshed; just as intelligent, beckoning. The other side. Peace, black peace. If one didn't see Emma's eyes, if one hadn't, when she said we hate, breathed yes yes yes. We hate. Barren. Had clutched at anything but this: the cowardice, waiting, wanting-not-daring.

Death. One had lied to the ox, it wasn't at all being unable to escape the present; but being all the futures, all the pasts, being yesterday and tomorrow; which left today like a fragile grain between two implacable and immense millstones. Nothing. All was past before it happened; was words, shards, lies, oblivion.

Why?

Childish. One must cling to structures, sure events. The interpretation of signs. One's own was alpha, one is precious (oh yes), rare, one sees. With all one's precious faults, one sees. One has committed a terrible crime, which proves one sees, since no one else admits its existence. One sawed the branch one was sitting on. One fouled one's own nest. One transgressed proverbs. *Ergo*, one must prove one sees. One saw, that is.

Tenses.

Pollution, energy, population. All the Peters and all the Pauls. Won't fly away. The dying cultures, dying lands.

Europe ends.

The death of fiction; and high time too.

Yet still one lies, as in a novel by an author one no longer admires, in an art that has become obsolete, feeling erotic and self-defiled; as if one had done it before one had, knowing it planned, proven, inevitable. As he took one once, in a churchyard; and wrote *Having among graves*. One did not like: the poem, not the having.

Il faut philosopher pour vivre. That is, one must not love. Tears of self-pity, hand hidden in the furtive hair. The transfer of epithets. Burn dry and extirpate; ban; annul; annihilate. I will not return. Not as I am.

And Catherine lies, composing and decomposed, writing and written, here and tomorrow, in the deep grass of the other hidden place she has found. Young dark-haired corpse with a bitter mouth; her hands by her sides, she does by thinking of doing; in her unmatched underclothes, black-shuttered eyes.

Where all is reversed; once entered, where nothing leaves. The black hole, the black hole.

To feel so static, without will; inviolable shade; and yet so potent and so poised.

There was still not the merest breath of wind, as Peter, now as bored with his half-hour sojourn in the wilderness as he had been when driven to seek it, made his way back down toward the others. They and the river dropped out of sight as he descended a slope of loose stones toward the herd of elephantine boulders, which reached back some way toward the cliffs. One didn't realize how large they were until one was down among them. Here and there the spaces between were choked with scrub. One had to go back, find easier passages. It was like a natural maze, though the cliffs behind meant one knew roughly what direction to take. He had misjudged the distance, the goat path must have angled farther away from the river than he realized. Then he nearly trod on a snake.

It was gone almost before he saw it. But some sort of pattern on its back? He was almost sure. It must have been an adder. It would certainly be an adder when he got back to tell them. He managed to tear a sideshoot off a straggling shrub and went more cautiously, rustling the green besom ahead of him as if geigering for mines. Then suddenly his little five-minute ordeal was at an end. He came on a path that led downhill toward the river; it was faint and sinuous, but it had purpose. He saw the top of Annabel's beech some two or three hundred yards below. The path flattened, wound through the massive boulders, which glittered faintly, they held mica, in the sun. Then, through a shadowed space between two of the megaliths, downhill, some forty feet away, he saw Catherine.

She lay on her back, beside another huge boulder. Her body was almost hidden in the long early summer grass; so nearly hidden he might have missed her. What had caught his eye were her red espadrilles, perched up on a stone behind her head.

"Kate?"

Her head turns and rises very quickly over the grass, to see him standing between the two boulders and smiling down. Accusing, craned, like some startled bird. He raises a pacifying hand.

"Sorry. Thought I'd better warn you. I've just seen an adder." He nods. "Just back there."

Still the dark glasses stare, then she sits up on one arm, looks briefly around, then looks back at him with a little shrug. None here. He sees she is not in the bikini of that morning, but her underclothes, which do not match: a white bra, dark maroon lower down; not as she would wish to be seen. The dark glasses say it is his fault that there are adders. He is eternally an intruder; a subtractor.

"Suppose you haven't got a cigarette on you?"

She hesitates, then reluctantly reaches sideways and raises a packet of Kents from the grass. He throws away the branch of broom and comes down to where she is. She stays propped on one arm, her legs curled away. He sees the folded Levi's and pink shirt she has been using as a pillow. She offers the packet up, then reaches again toward the red Greek shoulder bag and hands up a lighter; both, small white box and orange polythene cylinder, without looking at him.

"Thanks. You?"

She shakes her head. He lights the cigarette.

"Sorry if I was tactless after lunch. I honestly didn't mean it to sound like charity."

She shakes her head again, looking at his feet. It doesn't matter; please go away now.

"I can imagine how . . ." but imagination apparently fails him in midsentence. He passes back the lighter and the cigarettes. She takes them silently. And he gives up, a little helpless gesture of the hands.

"Didn't mean to disturb you. Just the adder."

He is already turning away when she moves; her arm, almost with the rapidity of the snake. The fingers catch him just above the bare ankle, the briefest clutch, but enough to stop him. Then the hand reaches beside the pile of clothes and picks up a tube of sun cream. She holds it up toward him, then tips it toward her back. It is a change of attitude so sudden, so unexpected, so banal, so implicitly friendly despite the expressionlessness of her face, that he grins.

"Of course. My forte."

She turns on her stomach and lies on her elbows. He sits beside her, well well well, and unscrews the cap from the tube; a little protruding tongue of café-au-lait. She shakes her dark hair forward, then raises a hand to make sure it is free of her shoulders; lies there, staring down at her pile of clothes, waiting. He eyes her averted face and smiles to himself. Then he squeezes a small worm of the cream onto his left palm.

"How much per square foot?"

But her only answer is a minute shrug. He reaches across and begins to rub the cream on her left shoulder, then down toward the blade. There are faint impressions of grass, from when she was lying on her back. The skin is warm, drinks the cream. He takes away his hand and levels the palm for another worm. As if she has been waiting for this momentary loss of contact, she sinks forward, flat, then twists back her hands and unfastens the bra. He sits arrested, halfway through the squeeze; as if he has come to an unexpected fork in a road; as someone arguing will suddenly see a concealed refutation of his own case in his previous statement. He squeezes. Silence. She leans up on her elbows again, her chin propped on her hands, staring away.

He murmurs, "You've got very smooth skin."

But now he understands, he knows she won't answer. He begins to massage cream into the shoulder nearest him, more this time, then down to where the skin has been puckered, slightly wealed, by the straps of the bra. She shows not the least response to his circling palm, though he rubs more firmly, more slowly, down each side, down the center to the small of the back. When he stops to press out more cream, a sweet scent, faintly of roses, patchouli, she sinks forward and flat again, her face turned away, cushioned on her hands, elbows out. He rubs backward and forward above the dark purple band that divides her body.

"Good?"

She says nothing; not the slightest sign. The heat, the supine body. He hesitates, swallows, then speaks in an even lower voice.

"Legs?"

She lies absolutely still.

Below, out of sight, a child's scream, like a stab, of mixed rage and complaint; it sounds like Emma. A fainter wail, imminent tears. Then a screamed "I *hate* you!"

It is Emma.

There is a calming voice. Then silence.

Peter's hand has stopped in the hollow of Catherine's back; now it continues, touching slowly up and down, the fingers creeping farther and farther down the sides, in some pretense of indifferent thoroughness; when all is erect, cocked, wild, in all senses wild; the bloody nerve, the savage tamed; the knowing one will; and somehow outrageously funny as well as erotic. He lets his fingers caress along her hidden left side and smooth on the brink of the armpit. She moves the left arm from under her face, reaches a hand back to her hip and pushes down on the side of the briefs. Then replaces her hand beneath her cheek. Peter hesitates, then throws his cigarette away; reaches and takes the fabric where she touched it. She pivots her body to one side, then to the other, so that he can bare her. He presses more cream out and begins to smoothe it over the cheeks, over the curve of the waist, then up and back. He leans and kisses her right shoulder, bites it gently; sweet-scented grease. She makes no response at all. He leans on his elbow alongside her and his left hand caresses, caresses, a little lower, the soft skin at the top of the thighs, the cheeks, the line of the crack.

He strips off his shirt. Then he kneels up, a quick look around. He bends over her and pulls at the twisted strand of purple. When it comes to her knees, she raises the bottom of her legs for it to be freed. But that is all. She lies naked, head averted, waiting. He kneels up and looks around again; then sits, balances back and pushes off his shorts. He comes on all fours across her back, his hands by her armpits. She moves her head so that it is pressed straight down on the backs of her hands and to the ground. He pulls gently on the left shoulder, to make her turn. She lies inert. He pulls with more strength, she gives a little, her body half turns, though her face stays twisted, hidden, down to the ground. He forces her around, more roughly, on her back. Now the exposed face twists away to the left. Profile. The bare throat, the mouth. He reaches and takes the dark glasses away. The eyes are closed. He moves a strand of dark hair from the cheek. Then he crawls and crouches back, kisses the pubic hair, then the navel, then each breast. She is excited, whatever she pretends. He lowers himself on her, searching for the averted mouth. But as if the weight of him is a trigger, she twists her face farther away. He insists, and she jerks the head wildly to the other side; a sudden willfulness, her nails in his shoulders, frantic pushing him away, writhing, struggling, shaking her head violently from left to right. He kneels up again, on all fours. Her hands drop. She lies still, head twisted away.

"Ka-ate! Pee-ter!"

The children's, Paul's, perhaps Sally's and Bel's as well; voices in chorus, concerted, as if conducted. There is a faint echo from the cliff. Then inevitably, Candida's alone.

"We're go-ing!"

Going.

Catherine turns her head and opens her eyes and stares up into Peter's face. It is strange, as if she can't really see him, as if she is looking through his knowing, faintly mocking smile. He has, will always have, the idea that it was something beyond him; not Peter. It is a pose, of course; just the sick game of a screwed-up little neurotic in heat. Very sick; and very sexy. To have it like this, just once; to have those pale and splintered eyes.

"Ka-ate! Pee-ter!"

She stares up at him for three or four seconds more, then she twists around quietly and submissively, as if it is his will, between his straddled legs and arms; on her stomach again, face buried in the ground, and waits.

Sally had dressed and Bel was standing and talking to her about children's clothes by the three repacked picnic baskets under the beech. Paul and the three children were still in the water, trying to find more crayfish while they waited. It was Bel, who happened to be facing that way, who first saw Peter, his wave, as he reappeared along the path from downstream. She raised an indolent hand in reply, and Sally turned. He came smiling.

"Sorry. Rough country in them thar hills."

"We've been shouting our heads off."

"It's stiff with adders. I was scared the kids would try and meet me."

Sally flinches. "Adders!"

"Damn near put my foot on one."

"Oh Peter!"

Bel says, "I should have warned you. There are a few."

"It's okay. It beat a swift retreat."

"Ugh." Sally turns away.

Bel smiles. "You didn't see Kate by any chance?"

He looks past her, searching. "No. Isn't she . . . ?"

"Never mind. She may have started home." She turns and calls down to the others. "Come on. Peter's back."

"Oh Mummy! We haven't got nearly enough yet."

Bel walks down toward the water. Sally eyes Peter.

"Where did you go?"

"Just up there." He waves vaguely toward the cliffs.

"I wish you wouldn't go off like that. I was frightened."

He looks around at the grass. "I got bored. Old Paul and his reading. How's Tom been?"

"All right."

"Seen my ciggies?"

She bends over one of the baskets, rummages, hands them to him. Candida comes up, accusing.

"We shouted and shouted!"

He tells her about the adders. They are safely plural now. Down by the water, Bel stands facing Paul, staring past him up toward the gorge.

"It really is too bad. I just don't know what to do about her."

"She may have gone on."

"Then at least she could have told us." She speaks to Emma, still dabbling with little Tom around the dam they have built. "Darling, we're going now. Take Tom and put your clothes on." Emma takes no notice. Bel looks at Paul. "I decided this afternoon. We worry too much. It plays into her hands."

"Do you want me to look?"

"No." She speaks more sharply. "Emma!"

Then to Paul: "I thought you wanted to work with Peter, anyway."

"That was the general idea."

"I don't know what she's trying to prove."

"I doubt if she does herself." He turns toward Emma. "Emma, you're quite sure Aunt Kate didn't say she was going home when you left her?"

"Is she lost again?"

Bel holds her hand out. "No, darling. It doesn't matter. Do come on. And Tom."

Paul says, "I don't mind."

Bel gives him a sideways look. "No."

She takes Emma's hand, then little Tom's, and starts back to the beech tree. Sally comes to meet them, and relieves her of Tom. Paul follows, rubbing his beard.

Under the tree, Candida says they can't go home without Kate. Bel says she's probably gone home to make tea. Peter asks which way she went. Sally kneels, drying Tom's legs and feet on a dark green towel. Candida suggests Kate has been bitten by an adder. Bel smiles.

"They don't kill you, darling. We'd have heard her. She's probably just wandered on."

Playing Hamlet to an asp.

Sally passes the towel to Bel.

"It's all wet," complains Emma, squirming away.

"Baby," says Candida.

Paul turns away, smiles wryly at Peter.

"What the good picnic really needs is an old-fashioned regimental sergeant major."

Peter grins. "Super day. Smashing place. Be nice to use it somehow."

"Sorry about Kate. She's being very difficult."

"Hope it isn't us."

"Good God no. Just . . . Bel worries."

Bel's firm voice. "Emma, if you don't shut up, I shall smack you."

The two men turn, Emma stands with tight-pressed lips, on the brink, as her mother briskly rubs her legs. Candida does a cartwheel, to show that she isn't tired at all, and quite grown-up. Bel pulls up Emma's brick-pink trousers, then hooks them and kisses her head.

"Well," says Paul. "Onward, Christian soldiers?"

He leads the way, with Candida beside him, back along the path. Peter follows, holding his son's hand.

"Smashing day, Tom, wasn't it?"

Then Bel and Sally with Emma between them, asking about the crayfish.

A minute, the voices fade, the picnic place is empty; the old beech, the grass, the lengthening shadows, the boulders, the murmuring water. A hoopoe, cinnamon, black and white, swoops down across the water and lands on one of the lower boughs of the beech. After a pause, it flits down onto the grass where they sat; stands, flicks up the fan of its crest. Then it darts down with its curved bill, and an ant dies.

One of Emma's sandals has become undone, and Bel kneels. Sally walks on to catch up with Peter and Tom. Behind, as they move on again, Emma begins to tell her mother, if she swears she won't tell Candy, not forgiven for treading on a lovely twig house beside the dam, Princess Emma's forest-house that the animals helped her build, Aunt Kate's fairy story; or her already revised version of it, which will end without ambiguity. Ahead, Sally comes beside Peter, who still holds his son's hand. He reaches an absentminded arm around her back. She sniffs at his shoulder.

"Whose suntan have you been using?"

He sniffs as well. "God knows. It was just lying around." He winks and grimaces. "Tom wants to live here now."

She cranes forward. "Do you, Tom? Do you like it?"

The little boy nods. They have to walk in single file where the path narrows between the lush growth of the underwood. Peter pushes Tom ahead. Sally comes last, staring at Peter's back. The path broadens out again. Tom asks if they will have another picnic tomorrow.

"Probably, old man. I don't know. We'll have fun, anyway."

Sally walks a little behind Peter's shoulder, untouching, watching the side of his face.

"Are you sure you didn't see her?"

He gives her a sharp look. She stares at the path.

She says, "You smell like she did this morning."

He is amused and incredulous. "Darling. For God's sake." Then: "Don't be a twit. It was probably hers. I just picked it up after lunch."

Still she stares at the path. "I didn't notice it when we packed up."

"Then she must have taken it when she went off. And for God's sake stop being such a . . ."

He looks away.

"Thanks very much."

"Well you are."

"At least I know I'm a bore."

He jerks on his son's arm.

"Come on, Tom. Let's have a race. To that tree. Ready? Go!"

He races ahead for a few steps, but lets the four-year-old catch up and pass him.

"You won!" He takes his son's hand again and they face Sally as she walks slowly on to where they are. "Tom won."

She gives the child a thin, token smile. Peter reaches and takes the basket she is carrying, pulls her briefly to him with his other arm, whispers in her ear. "Actually I fancy her like mad. But I'm saving necrophilia for my old age."

She pulls away, only partly mollified.

"You make me feel insecure."

"Come on, Tom. Take Sally's hand."

They walk on, the little boy between them. He murmurs across the child's head.

"You'll have to find a better reason than that."

"You've just said one."

"Match drawn."

"You don't make any allowances."

"Look who's talking."

"You'd just like to leave me with your pajamas. During the day. Forget I exist."

He takes a breath; and is saved from answering. Ahead, where the trees give way to the first meadow, they see Paul and Candida standing in the open, turned, looking back into the sky. Candida sees them coming, and points excitedly. The foliage prevents them from realizing what she means. But once they are themselves out in the meadow, they see.

A cloud, but a mysterious cloud, the kind of cloud one will always remember because it is so anomalous, so uncorresponding with the weather knowledge that even the most unobservant acquire. It comes from the south, from behind the cliffs where Peter climbed, and whose closeness, at the picnic place, must have hidden what on a plain would have been obvious long before; so that it seems to have crept up; feral and ominous, a great white-edged gray billow beginning to tower over the rocky wall, unmistakable bearer of heavy storm. Always predicated by the day's stillness and heat . . . yet still it shocks. And the still peaceful and windless afternoon sunshine about them seems suddenly eerie, false, sardonic, the claws of a brilliantly disguised trap.

Peter says, "Christ. Where did that come from?"

Paul stands with folded arms, watching the cloud. "Happens sometimes. Too much heat too suddenly. Then cold air off the Pyrenees."

Candy looks at Sally. "It'll thunder-and-lightning all night." Then, "We're worried about Kate."

Paul smiles and ruffles her head.

"She'll see it. Anyway, she may be home already. Worrying about us."

"I bet she isn't." Candy, not to be condescended to, looks up at her father. "I bet you two francs, Daddy."

He ignores her and picks up his basket, then moves back beside Pete and Sally. "Look, why don't you go on. I'll just wait for Bel." He feels in his pocket. "Here's the key, Peter." He turns; "Candy, you take them home, will you, and —"

Candida points. "There they are. Dawdling as usual."

They all turn. Bel and Emma come slowly through the trees, Emma talking, in front, walking backward, so that she can watch her mother's face. But when she sees the face look up beyond her, she turns, then runs on to join the group in the meadow. Paul walks back toward Bel.

Avoiding Peter's eyes, Sally says, "Hadn't you better go and look for her too?"

He pulls a face. "I think they'd rather deal with it themselves." He looks down at his son. "Want a piggyback, Tom?"

Sally stares at him as he hoists the child up astride his neck, then runs a little circle in the grass, jolting the small and nervous face up and down. Tom clutches fast, too frightened to speak.

"I'd better come with you," says Candida to Sally. "You'll probably get lost if I don't."

Emma reaches them.

"Peter, can I have a piggyback? Please!"

Candida holds out an authoritarian arm to bar her way. "No you can't. We're going home."

"I want a piggyback."

Peter begins trotting on across the meadow, bouncing Tom up and down. Sally looks back to where Paul and Bel are now standing and talking; Paul with his hands on his hips, facing upstream.

Candida stares at her sister. "Just you try."

Then suddenly she makes a dash and catches Emma as she turns to run back toward her parents. Emma screams. Paul turns and bellows.

"Candy! Stop that!"

"Emma's being naughty!"

"I'm not!"

"Leave her alone. Go on home with Peter and Sally."

Sally says, "Come on, Candy."

Candida hesitates, then pinches her sister's arm; but lets go immediately and walks away. Another scream.

"You *beast!*"

Candida looks up at Sally, a shrug. "She's such a baby."

Emma dashes behind her, thumps her wildly on the back as she passes, then races on toward where Peter and Tom are jogging away across the meadow. Candida chases after her. Emma starts screaming. Then she falls. Her sister pounces on her. The screams are continuous, but not of real pain. Don't, don't, don't. Sally looks back to the wood. They seem to have given up with the children, now both backs are turned, as if they are waiting for Kate to appear on the path beyond them. Sally picks up the basket Peter has left on the grass and begins to walk to where Candida kneels over Emma, who is quieter, it seems after all it is a game now, more tickling than pinching. I promise, says Emma. I promise. Beyond them Peter and Tom disappear into the poplars on the far side of the meadow. Sally looks around at the cloud.

These people she did not know till yesterday; this strange country and countryside; this role she has to play, this no one female close she can turn to, this being vaguely exploited, despised, suspicious, unwanted, tired, sunburned, so far from home; pre-period, but it can't be; this wanting to cry, but not daring to. She walks on past the two children, ignoring them, though they look up, triumphant and mischievous, to be looked at. She begins to riffle, as she walks, through the children's spare clothes and the picnic cloth and scatter of things in the bottom of the basket she is carrying; as if she has lost something.

It happened? It happens?

It happened. She stopped searching when Candida ran up and started to walk beside her. The child said nothing, but kept glancing back. In the end Sally did the same: Emma in midfield, sprawled on her back, only her pink knees visible, shamming dead.

"She's only pretending," said Candida dismissively.

It happens.

After a few steps she says, "Why aren't you married to Peter?"

From across the river, if one had been a watching bird in the leaves, one would have seen them disappear; then Paul and Bel appear on the other side of the meadow, walking more quickly, toward where Emma now sits up, waiting for them. Paul points back toward the cloud and Bel glances around, no more, as she walks. They come to the little girl, who holds up her arms. They take one each and hoist her to her feet. Then on: after a little while she begins to skip and jump, supporting herself momentarily in midair between them, lifted by their hands. Each time she jumps her long fair hair tosses and flows back a second with the movement. They make little whoo-ing cries as she rides between them, in which she joins. But then they stop a moment. Paul picks his daughter up and she sets a small arm around his neck. The three walk on, less quickly, yet not idly; as if there is something to be caught up or, perhaps, to escape from.

They disappear among the poplars. The meadow is empty. The river, the meadow, the cliff and cloud.

The princess calls, but there is no one, now, to hear her.